Fateful Decisions

Trevor D'Silva

BLACK ROSE
writing™

The final approval for this literary material is granted by the author.

Second printing

This is a work of fiction. Names, characters, businesses, places, events and incidents are either the products of the author's imagination or used in a fictitious manner. Any resemblance to actual persons, living or dead, or actual events is purely coincidental.

ISBN: 978-1-61296-983-1
PUBLISHED BY BLACK ROSE WRITING
www.blackrosewriting.com

Printed in the United States of America
Suggested Retail Price (SRP) $20.95

Fateful Decisions is printed in Plantagenet Cherokee

I take the opportunity to thank Reagan Rothe of Black Rose Writing, for making it possible for me to have this book published. I thank Chris Jeffries, for bringing my idea for the book cover to life through his artistic talent. I also thank Maria Logan Montgomery, for helping me reedit the novel, especially the crucial sections, thereby making this book better than it was before.

Lastly, I would like to thank my parents, Christopher and Margaret, for encouraging me to persevere in my endeavor, through the years of my study and other preoccupations.

I dedicate this book to my parents, Christopher and Margaret,
for their unstinting support.

Fateful Decisions

Chapter 1

January 3, 1946

Rachel Johnson jumped out of the car and ran towards the pier. The cold January wind from the sea cut through her coat and chilled her to the bone. Voices were calling for her to slow down, but she paid no attention to them. People were running past her in the same direction, and she tried to keep up with them. For them, it was a happy occasion. However, Rachel was not sure what lay in store for her. She had been dreading this moment ever since she received two telegrams the previous month. She had not revealed the contents of one of the telegrams to anyone. Was it a mean trick? She would soon find out.

Rachel saw her friend, Martha, and she ran to stand next to her. There were cheers from the crowd, as the shape of a ship became visible on the horizon. People around her had waited four years for their loved ones to come back from war torn Europe. The person she was waiting for was coming back after twenty-three years.

Rachel felt two hands on her shoulders. She did not flinch, as she knew they belonged to her son whom she loved very much. She had almost lost him three times. Rachel wondered what his reaction would be since he had never met this person.

It was on a ship like the one approaching that her story began. A shy girl from Hartford, Vermont, had met two men who would change her life forever. From a timid, naïve girl, she was now the owner of a hotel empire. Thirty years had passed since that fateful transatlantic journey which originated from the same harbor.

Oblivious to the noise around her, her mind went back to the events that occurred thirty years ago.

New York, May 1, 1915

Lusitania blew her horn and began moving away from the pier. Two dark haired women, one nineteen and the other seventeen, ran out of their cabin onto the deck. They wanted to say goodbye to the crowd that had gathered on the pier to see the ship off. One of the women bumped into a man. She apologized and ran away to join her friend.

The man saw the bracelet dropped by the woman. He picked it up and tried to find her. When he could not, he put it into his pocket and together with his friend walked into the crowd gathered on the ship's deck.

Lusitania left New York Harbor and headed towards the Atlantic. The passengers dispersed leaving Fred and Rudy at the railing staring at the disappearing American coast. Fred at twenty-four, was dark haired and a year older than Rudy who was blond. Both were around six feet tall and had blue eyes.

"Well," said Rudy, "looking forward to England. A bit apprehensive though, as I have a German last name. Ever since I was fired from my last job, I have been conscious about it."

"You are an American citizen now. Do not express any sympathies for Germany on this ship or in England, and there will be no trouble. You know what the papers say about the atrocities committed by German soldiers in Europe," replied Fred, patting Rudy's back.

"The papers lie," shot back Rudy in anger. He then smiled and said, "I guess you are right. Let us go to the first class lounge and mingle."

"Great idea! However, remember our agreement not to mention our real reason for going to England."

Rudy smiled and replied, "Oh, your secret is safe with me. Your competitors and the newspapers will not get wind of it. If anyone asks, I will say that we are on a holiday."

"Now, that's a good friend and employee."

They both laughed as they walked towards the first class lounge.

May 4, 1915

Rachel Williams left her second class cabin, came onto the deck, and stood at the railing. She needed to clear her mind. She heard two men arguing behind her. She looked at them for a moment and then looked out to sea.

"Rudy, you cannot let what those men say about Germany upset you," said Fred.

"You have no idea what it is like when people talk bad about your birth country..."

Rudy noticed Rachel looking at them. He realized that she was the woman who bumped into him on the deck. He pointed her out to Fred and told him that he would like to return the bracelet to her. They walked towards her and stood behind her. Rachel was unaware of the two men behind her.

Rudy took a deep breath as if to muster up some courage and said, "Miss."

The woman did not turn back.

Again, he said, "Miss," with his voice slightly raised. The woman seemed to break away from her reverie. She turned around in surprise and said, "Yes, what do you want?"

Rudy held up the bracelet and said, "Does this belong to you?"

Her eyes lit up and she said, "Yes, thank you so much. I thought I had lost it."

"You dropped it when you bumped into Rudy," replied Fred.

"I am so sorry about that. I didn't want to miss the ship leaving the harbor."

"It's okay. I thought you had a traveling companion," Rudy added.

"Yes, Martha, but she is seasick. She is resting, and I have just come out to take a stroll and get some fresh air."

"I hope she feels better. By the way, my name is Rudolph

Holzmann, and this is my friend, Fredrick Johnson. You can call me Rudy; that is what everyone calls me."

"And you can call me, Fred. We are from Long Island."

The woman smiled and said, "My name is Rachel Williams from Hartford, Vermont."

She held out her hand and the men shook it.

The bell rang announcing that it was lunchtime. Rudy invited Rachel to have lunch with them, but she politely declined the invitation saying that she had to help Martha with her lunch, as she was weak and had to be spoon-fed. Fred then invited her for dinner; she smiled and readily agreed. They decided to meet at seven p.m. outside the first class dining hall. She thanked them, waved, and walked away happily.

"Well, that was someone interesting," said Fred, as the two men watched her walk away.

"Yes, a lot different and charming from the women in first class. If not for her losing the bracelet, we would never have met her," said Rudy, and they both entered the dining hall.

"Rachel," said Martha, "you know that you should be careful about meeting and trusting total strangers, especially young, unmarried men. Please don't go."

Martha Manning was a plain, slightly hefty woman, with a tanned complexion inherited from her Italian mother. She looked older than her age of nineteen. She was wise beyond her years and always looked out for Rachel who, on the other hand, was pretty and naïve, but her charm won over many men.

"Oh, Martha, why do you always fuss? I am almost eighteen. I can take care of myself. Besides, those two men were very kind to invite me for dinner after returning my bracelet. It is my chance to eat in the first class dining hall," said Rachel.

"I promised your guardian that I would look after you. You will be careful, won't you?" said Martha.

"Don't worry, I will." Rachel left closing the door behind her.

* * * * *

"Where is she?" asked Rudy. "It is almost five minutes past seven."

"I hope we didn't scare her. Perhaps we were too hasty in inviting her," said Fred.

They heard a voice behind them. "Well gentlemen, I'm sorry for the delay. Not used to being in the first class area."

They turned around and were stunned at her beauty. "You... You... look beautiful," was all Fred managed to say.

"Thank you," replied Rachel. "Aren't you two going to escort me in? Come on, don't be shy," she said, teasingly.

Fred pulled out a chair for Rachel, and she sat down. The two men sat on either side of her. Over dishes of filet mignon, salad, bread and wine, Rachel told them that her guardian was sending her to England to study art and literature. When she looked at them inquiringly, Fred glanced at Rudy and Rudy said, "We are going there on a holiday." Fred smiled at him approvingly.

The conversation between them went well, until Rachel mentioned an incident that happened at the beginning of the voyage. "I heard that three German stowaways were caught with a camera, and they are being detained below in the ship's cell. The camera was confiscated by Captain Turner," said Rachel.

"They should have been made to work for their passage. Treating them like criminals is awful just because they are Germans."

"Why, Rudy? There is a war going on with Germany and we need to be careful."

"Because I was fired from my job recently as I was German."

"Were you born in Germany, Rudy? I thought you were from Long Island," said Rachel, embarrassed.

"Yes, I was born in Berlin. Mother was from Hamburg, studying chemistry in Berlin, and she met my father who was a baker. I was nine when we immigrated in 1902. My father got a job working in a delicatessen. We stayed Holzmann because Father was always proud of his German heritage and did not want to Americanize his last name. He died two years ago of a stroke."

Fred could see that Rudy was a bit upset. The band began playing, and a few couples started dancing. Fred asked Rachel if she would like to dance and she accepted. They excused themselves and headed to the dance floor.

"He seemed upset with what I said," said Rachel, as they danced.

"He gets upset when people mention the war because he lost his job being a German."

"That is awful. How long have you two known each other?"

"We met in 1904 in Central Park when both of us were playing there. We stayed friends and went to Columbia University together. Our friendship has always been about competing. We competed in studies, sports, women…"

Suddenly, Rachel asked for the time. Fred put his hand into his breast pocket, looked at the watch, and said, "9:15."

"I have to go, Fred. Martha will be worried about me. I promised her that I would be back at 9:00."

"Can't you stay a little longer? I'm sure she would want you to enjoy your evening."

"No, I must go. She is very protective of me and has always been that way even when we were kids. I cannot let her be worried."

"All right, let us go back to the table." He sounded disappointed.

"What happened?" asked Rudy. "It seemed like you two were having a great time."

"I must leave. Martha will be worried. Thank you both for a wonderful time. I hope to see you two, maybe tomorrow."

Rachel took her bag and walked out. Fred looked disappointed as Rachel walked away.

"Maybe I should have had a go at her," said Rudy and laughed at Fred.

"Shut up, Rudy!" said Fred, very annoyed.

Rachel ran along the deck and opened the door to the cabin. She found Martha reading a book.

"Good, you're back. I was beginning to get worried about you. I thought they may have thrown you overboard."

"Don't be silly, Martha. You worry too much," she said, now out of breath.

"How was your evening?"

"Oh, it was wonderful. Let me tell you all about it," said Rachel and sat on the chair next to Martha's bed.

Rachel told Martha about her evening. After she had finished, Martha said, "I hope you do not fall sick after eating that food. I am concerned, since their friendship is about competing, they may be vying for your affection. I have a feeling that your life will be in turmoil if you get involved with these men."

"Martha, you're always pessimistic. This trip has just begun to get interesting. It would be fascinating to be pursued by two men at the same time. After we dock in England, we will go our separate ways, and I will never see them again. Let me enjoy the attention until then."

Martha sighed and continued reading her book.

May 7, 1915

At eleven a.m., the Lusitania came through the fog into the hazy sunshine. She was twenty-five miles off the coast of Ireland. Captain Turner was expecting to meet his naval escort, HMS Juno. When the escort did not arrive, a message arrived from the admiralty to alter the ship's course and head towards Ireland.

Kapitan, Leutnant Walter Schweiger saw that the fog had cleared and gave the order to surface. The U-20 blew her tanks and surfaced. Schweiger went up on the conning tower to join the lookouts. All of a sudden, one of the lookouts drew their attention to smoke.

Schweiger looked through the binoculars and saw that the smoke came from a ship. He gave orders for the U-20 to submerge and simultaneously change course to intercept the ship.

At about this time, Fred and Rudy had finished their lunch and were walking on the deck when they spotted Rachel.

Rachel was standing with her hands on the railing staring at the sea. She heard footsteps behind her and turned.

"Oh!" she said, her face lighting up with joy, "it's nice to see you two."

"It's nice to see you too," said Fred. "Where have you been?"

"I've been sick with fever and an upset stomach. Martha was right; all that food did make me sick. I can't wait to be on land."

Meanwhile, on the orders of Captain Turner, the ship turned to starboard side and headed towards Queenstown.

"Look, we seem to be heading towards land," said Rudy, pointing his finger. Fred and Rachel looked in the direction Rudy pointed.

"I think that's Ireland. Wonder why we're heading there," said Fred.

A few miles away, after Kapitan Schwieger got confirmation from his pilot that it was the Lusitania, the U-20 prepared for action. Schwieger looked into the attack periscope and saw the ship was heading toward land. Schwieger gave the order to fire. The G-type torpedo shot out of the forward tube and heading toward the ship.

Blissfully unaware of the approaching danger, the passengers were dining in their respective dining halls, and some were walking along the deck. Fred, Rudy, and Rachel were standing on the starboard side when they saw a woman point to an object approaching the ship. The other passengers on deck went to see this strange object coming towards them.

One of the men standing around yelled, "No, it can't be. It's a torpedo! Run to the other side."

Panic stricken, the passengers ran to the other side just as the torpedo struck the ship. The impact made the ship shudder. Dread set in among the passengers as they started to grasp the severity of the situation.

Rachel cried, "I must get Martha out onto the deck," and she ran towards the cabin.

Rudy and Fred ran after her, and Rudy managed to hold her hand, when the terrified passengers rushed out pushing Fred away from them. He shouted, "Go find Martha. I'll meet you near the life boats."

Rachel and Rudy ran along the deck towards Martha's cabin when there was a second explosion, which rocked the ship, causing some passengers to fall into the sea.

Rudy and Rachel managed to steady themselves, went towards Martha's cabin, and entered it. No one was there, and all their belongings were scattered on the floor. Rachel froze at the sight but then composed herself. She opened her desk and found that her documents and money were missing. She hoped that Martha had taken them with her. The life preservers were also missing.

"Rachel, we must leave," Rudy shouted.

Rudy grabbed her hand, and they ran out of the cabin together.

Captain Turner commanded the ship to go full speed towards the Irish coast, but the drop in pressure made the turbines unresponsive. The ship came to a sudden halt and began to list.

Fred felt the ship had come to a stop. He ran towards the portside to wait for Rudy and Rachel at the lifeboats. He saw that lifeboat No.2 was filled with passengers and was dangling precariously. A woman with a bag, holding the hand of a stewardess, stood in front of the lifeboat. Without any warning, the boat, filled with passengers, swung inboard towards the waiting passengers. The woman screamed as the lifeboat headed towards her. Fred caught her hand and pulled the woman and the stewardess aside. The boat missed them by a few inches but crushed the other passengers.

Fred saw a boat that was about to be lowered. He yelled at the crew lowering the boat to wait, and he told the two women to sit in the boat. The three of them got in. As the boat was being lowered, a woman came with her baby.

"Sorry, the boat is being lowered," said the crewman lowering the boat.

"Give me the baby," yelled Fred. The woman hesitated and shook her head.

"Give it to me. I will catch it, I swear." The woman held out the baby, and Fred stretched out his arms and caught it. He gave the baby to the stewardess and said to the woman,

"Jump, I will catch you."

The woman leaned forward and jumped. Fred caught her hand, but she slipped. The people in the boat watched with horror on their faces. Fred held onto her right hand with both his hands. One of the men next to him stretched forward and caught the woman's other hand. Together, they pulled her onto the boat. The boat now touched the water.

The ship's lights went out; Rachel and Rudy were running in the dark towards the lifeboats. As they tried to get outside, they heard cries for help. They looked, and through the little daylight that was coming from outside, they could see passengers trapped in an elevator.

"We have to help them," Rachel said. They went towards the elevator and tried to pry the doors open. The doors would not open. The ship's list got worse.

"We have got to go," shouted Rudy.

"We cannot leave them," Rachel shouted back.

"We have to, or we will drown." Rudy grabbed her hand and dragged her. She tried not to look at the faces of the terrified passengers trapped in the elevator. They were now out in the open. Meanwhile, the stern began to settle back. A wave swept them off the ship. Rudy managed to hold onto the railing, but Rachel was thrown into the sea, screaming. She tried to stay afloat. The water was cold and she had no life preserver. Rudy realized that she could not swim. He jumped into the sea, swam up to her, and caught her just as she was about to go under water. She was exhausted and weak from the fever and running. Rachel settled onto Rudy's body while he caught hold of a deck chair that was floating next to them.

The Lusitania was sinking. Her stern stood out from the water, and the propellers were visible. Without warning, she lunged forward into the water and disappeared, taking people still trapped inside her.

Rachel opened her eyes and saw the ship disappear. She saw passengers drown and some trying to save others as well as themselves. She closed her eyes, unable to bear the horror unfolding before her.

The survivors on Fred's lifeboat witnessed the sinking of the ship, and were shocked into silence.

"She is gone forever. It took just 18 minutes to sink after the torpedo struck her," one of the men said calmly looking at his watch.

One of the women looked at the fishing boats coming from the coast and shouted, "Hurry; people are dying." She started crying and held her face in both her hands.

Rudy held onto Rachel with one hand and a chair with the other.

The water was cold, and she could feel her body beginning to numb. She kept holding onto Rudy, as she felt herself losing consciousness.

Rachel's mind went back to April 1912. She was at her convent school in Connecticut when she heard the terrible news as one of her classmates held the newspaper for all to see.

"Impossible, my parents are on board the Titanic. They are returning from Europe."

Two days later, the headmistress called Rachel aside. She had received a telegram from Rachel's great aunt confirming the death of her parents. She ran to her room crying, and she buried her head in the pillow. She began to feel a deep hatred for her parents. Could they not have tried to stay alive for her sake? There were many survivors, and why did they have to die and leave her all alone?

After what seemed like an eternity, Rachel felt herself being pulled from the cold ocean. She rested her head on Rudy's shoulder while they were sitting in the lifeboat, too exhausted and cold to say anything.

Rudy began arguing with the men on the lifeboat when one of them accused the Germans of attacking the ship. The argument got heated when another passenger insisted that the second explosion was due to a second torpedo. Rudy insisted that he saw only one torpedo.

"Don't argue with them, they might throw you overboard," Rachel whispered in Rudy's ear.

Rudy realized that it was pointless arguing and kept quiet. The lifeboat made its way towards the Irish coast.

The survivors were taken to Queenstown. There, Rachel and Rudy were reunited with Fred. Rachel searched for Martha and found her standing next to a stewardess. Rachel, with tears of joy, went and hugged Martha.

Martha told Rachel that, when the stewardess was feeding her, they felt the ship shudder. As a precautionary measure, the stewardess helped Martha with the life preserver, and the stewardess wore the other. Martha took the bag containing the documents and money before leaving the cabin.

"I know. I went with Rudy to get you and you were gone. Rudy saved my life. Let me take you to meet them."

Martha thanked the stewardess and left with Rachel. "I did not get his name, but this wonderful man saved me and the stewardess. He also saved the life of a woman and her child," said Martha.

"I hope I get to meet him and thank him for saving you." They went towards Fred and Rudy who were talking.

"Oh, there he is. He's the one who saved me," said Martha, pointing at Fred.

"It's nice to see you again. I did not get your name," said Fred to Martha when he saw her approaching them.

"Fred, Rudy, this is Martha. Fred, thank you for saving Martha," Rachel said in gratitude.

"Finally, we get to meet you, Martha. Rachel has told us so much about you," said Rudy.

"Likewise. Nice to meet you both. Rudy, thank you for saving Rachel."

Martha turned to Rachel and said, "So, these are the men you were telling me about. I am glad that I was wrong. From now on, I will have more trust in your choice of men."

Martha and Rachel left for England on the first ship they could get passage on. Fred and Rudy came to see them off. As the ship left the harbor, Martha said, "Rachel, I have a feeling that I have seen Fred before, and we will meet them again."

Chapter 2

New York, July 1917

Two men got down from the car and stood in line with the other well-dressed people.

"I do not know, Fred, I am contributing money for America to go to war with my country of birth. I voted for President Wilson in 1916, because he promised that America wouldn't be involved with the war in Europe," Rudy whispered to Fred.

Fred patted him on the back and said, "America is now your country and your loyalty should lie here. Donating money to the American war effort will show that you are a patriotic American."

When their turn came, they produced their invitations and were allowed to enter. As they entered, they saw people dancing and talking to each other. Harold Joseph Hardy walked towards them with a slight limp. He was a tall man in his forties with red hair that was beginning to gray at the temples. Harold and Fred, being part of New York's elite society, would socialize in the same circles. They got along well, even though Harold was twenty years older. He shook Fred's hand and welcomed him.

"Harry, meet my friend, Rudolph Holzmann. We grew up together, and he is now working for me as my accountant."

Harold shook Rudy's hand and said, "It's nice of you two to come. The money collected today will support the American war effort in Europe and the war affected families."

"You have our contribution to the war effort," said Fred.

"Thank you. You can go to the table and deposit your checks. Enjoy yourselves. I must see to the other guests arriving."

Fred and Rudy deposited their checks and headed to the bar to get a glass of whiskey. As they were waiting, Fred drew Rudy's attention to a woman in a blue dress. Rudy turned and looked in the direction Fred was pointing, and his eyes widened when he recognized the woman.

"It is Rachel. Wonder what she is doing here."

"She looks beautiful; even better than the first time we saw her on the ship."

"Well," said Rudy, "the years have certainly made her more beautiful. Come, let us go talk to her."

Rachel saw Fred and Rudy walking towards her. She excused herself from the group of women she was talking to and went towards them. "Fred, Rudy, it's so nice to see you. When did you two come to Manhattan?"

Fred replied, "We arrived yesterday. When did you come back to America?"

"I finished my studies and came back in May," Rachel answered.

"I see you are married with a child," Fred continued.

Rachel chuckled and said, "Oh no, he's Martha and Harry's son. I came back for their wedding last summer. I was the maid of honor, and I'm now the godmother of their son, Sidney."

Martha came up to them and said, "Rachel, there you are. I was looking for you."

"Martha, remember Fred and Rudy? They saved us when the Lusitania sank."

Martha's face lit up when she recognized them. "Yes, I remember you both. You're Fred Johnson, the heir to the Johnson Hotels. No wonder I found you very familiar."

Fred laughed. "Guilty as charged. Rudy and I decided to keep our identities and our reason for our trip secret when we sailed because we were heading to London to buy a hotel. Due to the war, we decided not to. Martha, I received your wedding invite last year, but I was unable to attend the wedding because Father had just died. I never realized you were the Martha whom Harry was marrying."

"I understand. I met Harry in England, and we were on the same ship coming back to America. Before I knew it, he proposed and I accepted, a few hours before the ship docked at New York Harbor. I am glad that you could come to this Charity Ball. Harry is very patriotic and fought in the Spanish American War. He would have enlisted, but he cannot. He suffers from asthma, and his old war wound makes him limp."

Martha turned to Rachel and said, "Rachel, let me take Sidney. It's time for his nap."

Rachel handed Sidney to Martha. After Martha left, Rachel led them to an older woman in her early seventies sitting in a chair. A woman in a red dress stood next to her. She introduced the older woman as her great aunt and guardian, Victoria Harlow, and the young woman was her granddaughter Lucy.

"Rachel told me about you two. Thank you for saving Rachel and Martha," said Aunt Victoria.

The music stopped. Harold Hardy came onto the platform where the musicians were seated and gave a short speech, thanking the people for their donations.

After the National Anthem, Fred asked Victoria Harlow if they would like to spend a few days at his home in Long Island. Aunt Victoria looked at Rachel, and Rachel said, "Oh Fred, I have never been to Long Island and would love to go there."

"Then it is settled," said Aunt Victoria.

Fred said, "We can all travel by train. The scenery is beautiful, and I will send the car ahead to pick us up in Long Island."

Two days later, the five of them were on the train. On the way, Aunt Victoria told Fred and Rudy the circumstances of how she got to raise Lucy and Rachel. Victoria Harlow was the sister of Rachel's paternal grandfather. Lucy, orphaned during the San Francisco earthquake, came to live with her grandmother in Vermont. Rachel joined them after her parents died in the Titanic tragedy. Although Lucy was a year older than Rachel, the tragedy of losing their parents so young made them close like sisters.

The train reached the station and they alighted. Alfred, the chauffeur, escorted them to the car. The car navigated through the suburbs and reached two huge wrought iron gates. It then drove through the gates and stopped in front of a colonial style manor. The occupants got out.

Fred said, "Ladies, welcome to the Johnson Manor."

The butler, Robert, whose brown hair was graying, and the maids helped to unload the bags.

"You have a beautiful house and a lovely garden," said Rachel.

"Thank you. My grandfather built this place after buying this plot of land when he immigrated to America in the 1850s. He made his fortune in the Golconda Diamond Mines in India. He started a hotel in Manhattan and gradually built the rest of the Johnson Hotel Empire."

The women were amazed at the antiques in the house. Chinese vases and vases made from Benares brass, Persian carpets on the floor, and tapestries hung on the walls. There were fern plants and palm trees at certain corners, and glass chandeliers hanging from the ceiling.

The servants showed the guests their rooms, and they were told to be ready for dinner at eight p.m. Rudy wished them goodbye, and Alfred drove him home.

At quarter to eight., Fred was in the drawing room smoking his cigar. He got up and poured himself a glass of brandy. Rachel walked in wearing a green dress, and her brown hair was pinned on top of her head. She wore an emerald necklace to match her green dress. Fred could not take his eyes off her.

"Well, welcome," he managed to say.

"Thank you," she said.

She looked up at a painting of a very beautiful woman sitting in a chair over the fireplace. She looked at the next portrait and saw a debonair man with a moustach, dressed in a suit.

"Your parents, I presume," said Rachel.

"Yes, my mother died when I was five, and my father died last year of heart failure. My mother was a descendant of one of the Mayflower passengers."

"Aunt Victoria is the daughter of General Andrew Logan who fought for the Union Army in the Civil War. My mother was from Charleston, South Carolina and a supporter of the Confederacy. Aunt Victoria gives me grief all the time."

Fred chuckled. He pointed to a painting of a man dressed in a suit, which was the style of the mid nineteenth century. She noticed that Fred and his father resembled the man in the portrait. "That's my grandfather. He built this house in 1859."

"It must have been an adventurous life in India with the elephants, wild animals, the Maharajas, and the exotic ambiance of the Orient."

"Yes," said Fred. "From what I have read from his diary, he had a lot of exciting exploits in that country."

"Is Rudy coming for dinner?"

"Yes, he is. I told him to bring his mother along."

Just then, Victoria Harlow and Lucy entered the room. Fred greeted them and they began talking. As the clock struck eight, Robert came in and said, "Mr. Holzmann and his mother are here."

"Thank you, Robert. Show them in," said Fred.

After a minute, Rudy and his mother entered. Rudy was dressed in a suit and bow tie and his mother in a simple yellow dress. Mary Holzmann looked frail and a lot older than her forty-six years.

Rudy introduced his mother to the Harlows and Rachel. Mary Holzmann greeted them with a recognizable German accent. Robert came in and announced that dinner was served. The six of them followed Robert, and they sat at the dining table. Robert poured the wine while the maids brought the soup. Before eating, Fred raised his glass and said, "A toast to our country! May she be victorious in this war, and may our boys come back home safely."

The rest said, "Here, here," and clinked their glasses together.

After dinner, all of them went to the study for coffee or brandy. Robert poured the coffee, and Marcy, the senior maid, with graying hair, served them. They sat talking until the clock struck ten p.m. Mary Holzmann declared that she was tired and would like to go home. After wishing them goodbye, the Harlows too said that they would like to retire. Rachel said that she would follow later.

After the Harlows left, Rachel asked Fred, "When did Rudy become your accountant?"

"Rudy was fired from his job and couldn't get another because of his German last name, though he was good at his work. I hired him before we set sail on the Lusitania. He saved my business. I avoided a lot of trouble with the Bureau of Internal Revenue and with my creditors."

"Why didn't you two enlist?"

"I, being the sole owner, have to remain here managing the hotels, but I do contribute to the war effort. Rudy does not want to fight Germany, and he cannot join because his eyes give him trouble."

Rachel yawned and said, "Well, it has been a long day, and I better retire. She stood up and Fred stood up too.

"Good night, and thank you for a wonderful dinner," said Rachel.

She smiled at Fred and went towards the stairs.

Fred watched her as she ascended the stairs, and he wondered if he should put forth the question he wanted to ask her. He put that thought aside and went to his bedroom.

At the same time, Rudy was lying on his bed thinking about the same question Fred wanted to ask Rachel. He turned off the light and went to sleep.

The next day, the three women spent the day at the beach and shopping. They had dinner with Fred that evening. After dinner, the Harlows retired and, once again, Rachel and Fred were alone. Rachel looked outside and said, "It looks like a beautiful night with a full moon. Can we go outside for a stroll?"

"Sure," said Fred. He opened the glass door and they went out.

"Lovely moonlit night, isn't it?"

"Yes, it is," said Fred. "The moon looks beautiful; I have never seen so many stars in the sky."

"Yes, it is almost as if this night is made for lovers."

Fred grinned. "It may be so. You look beautiful in the moonlight."

Rachel looked at him, and Fred backed away with embarrassment.

"What did you say?"

Fred looked at her and said, "Rachel, will you marry me?"

She looked at him and was speechless.

"Rachel, will you marry me? I fell in love with you on the ship, and ever since I met you again, I realized that you are the one for me."

"But, we hardly know each other."

"That's not true. We know all there is to know about each other."

"Well, I am not ready to take that step..." and her voice trailed off.

Fred reached forward, held her, and kissed her on the lips. She broke away and sat down on the bench. "I am sorry if I was too hasty," he said, ashamed of himself.

"No, no, it's all right. Good night, Fred." Rachel got up and ran back into the house, leaving Fred staring at her. He stared until Rachel disappeared. He sat down with one hand on his head saying, 'stupid, stupid, stupid...' He then got up and went back into the house.

Rachel informed Lucy that she had a headache and would not come for breakfast. Fred had Marcy take Rachel a breakfast tray to her room. At nine a.m., the Harlows and Fred left the house for a tour of the vineyard and winery.

Rachel lay in bed replaying the events of the previous night in her mind repeatedly. The marriage proposal shocked her completely. She thought of Fred only as a good friend.

There was a knock on the door and Marcy stuck her head in. She said that Rudy was at the door, and he wanted to see her. Rachel told her to let him in, and she would be down in a few minutes.

She got up, washed her face, changed her clothes, and went downstairs. Rudy told her that he had come to talk to Fred and was surprised that he had left so early. Rachel told him that Fred was showing the Harlows the vineyard and the winery. She did not go due to the headache.

Rudy insisted that she come to his house and that the morning air would do her good. Rachel politely refused but relented as Rudy kept persisting.

She put on a hat and got into a horse drawn carriage, which Rudy had hired, and rode away.

The carriage went into a street with dilapidated houses. There were children running with filthy clothes on, and Rachel could see women washing clothes and hanging them on the clotheslines. She was shocked at the filth and squalor.

The carriage stopped at house No. 27. They got out and Rudy paid the coachman. Rudy went to the front door and knocked. They heard footsteps, and Mary Holzmann opened the door.

Mrs. Holzmann greeted Rachel and was pleased to see her.

"Good morning, Frau Holzmann."

"You speak German? I never thought any American girl would know to address me as Frau. We do not speak German anymore since we have to keep a low profile due to the war."

"Sister Ingmar at my convent school was German, and I also had some German friends in London."

They entered the house. It seemed a modest house, just enough for two people. Mrs. Holzmann asked Rachel to sit down and went into the kitchen to get refreshments. Rachel looked at the fireplace and saw three pictures on the mantelpiece. She went towards the pictures and looked at them. Rudy said, "Those are the pictures of my parents. My picture was taken when I was 8 years old.

Rachel said, "Your father was a very handsome man. You look just like him. You have his blond hair and square jaw." She turned and smiled at Rudy. Rudy was better looking than Fred and had boyish good looks. She felt attracted to Rudy for the first time.

Mrs. Holzmann came out with a tray, and set it on a table. She poured three cups, added sugar, and handed them out. Rachel sipped the tea and felt her headache disappear. She felt much better and, for the first time that day, she was able to think clearly.

Mrs. Holzmann told Rachel about their life in Berlin and their decision to immigrate to America. She taught chemistry at the local high school. She was proud of Rudy for going to college and getting a good job. Mrs. Holzmann cut a cake and gave Rachel and Rudy a slice each. She got up and took the tray into the kitchen.

Rachel looked at Rudy and he smiled at her. She smiled back, and

Rudy took her hand into his and said,

"Rachel, I have something to ask you."

"What is it?" she mumbled.

"I want…"

Rachel tried to pull her hand away.

"Rachel, will you marry me?"

Rachel could not believe it. In less than twenty-four hours, she had received two marriage proposals from two good friends. She felt her headache come back with a vengeance. She got up. "Rachel, I have wanted to ask…"

"Sorry, I really must be getting back."

She started towards the door, when Mrs. Holzmann came out from the kitchen and asked her to stay for lunch. Rachel did not accept the invitation. She thanked Mrs. Holzmann for her hospitality and left the place.

Mrs. Holzmann turned to Rudy and said. "Strange girl! I wonder why she ran away."

Rudy did not answer. He saw Rachel run and get into a carriage. 'You blew it, you fool,' he said softly to himself. Rachel ran down the street, hailed a passing carriage, and got into it. She told the coachman where she wanted to go; the coachman looked surprised. Without a word, he turned and yelled at the horse to go. She closed her eyes, and they remained closed until the carriage reached Johnson Manor.

When she opened her eyes, she saw the front door of the manor and the coachman opening the door of the carriage for her. She paid the coachman, ran towards the front door, opened it, and ran to her bedroom. She lay on the bed and began thinking. She was not yet twenty and she had received two marriage proposals. Marriage was far from her mind. She wanted to become a nurse and help the war effort. She was glad that she was going back to Hartford the next day. She got up from the bed and went into the washroom. After freshening up, she went downstairs for lunch. All through lunch, she did not speak much, except when it was necessary while Aunt Victoria and Lucy told her about their outing. She was thinking about how she would face Fred when he came back in the evening, until she left the next day.

When Fred came home for dinner, she hardly looked at him, saying that her silence was due to her headache. After dinner, she went to her bedroom to pack and sleep. She felt better in the morning. She was relieved that she was leaving the events of the previous two days behind her for good.

After breakfast, Fred accompanied them to the station. Aunt Victoria and Lucy thanked Fred for his hospitality. Rachel remained silent. "Rachel," said Aunt Victoria, with a firm voice, "why haven't you thanked Fred? He has been very kind to us."

"Thank you," said Rachel, looking away with embarrassment.

Just then, the conductor blew the whistle, and the engine let out a gust of steam. Victoria Harlow thanked Fred again and they got in. The train let out one more gust of steam and pulled away from the station.

The next day, the three of them were back in Hartford. They collected their luggage, hired a horse drawn carriage, and were on their way home. As the carriage picked up speed, Rachel stuck her head out of the window and looked at the cornfields and meadows with the cattle grazing. It felt good to be home.

The carriage reached their residence and they got out. The house was not large but sufficient for a small family. There was a vegetable garden in front with a few rose and other flowering plants.

After settling down, they opened a tin of ham, made sandwiches, and had lunch. After lunch, Lucy declared that she would plant her rose cuttings, which Fred had given her, before they withered. Aunt Victoria took her feather duster and started dusting. Rachel said that she would work in the vegetable garden. She found her gardening gloves and began pulling out weeds. After half an hour, she entered the house tired and exhausted from working in the blazing sun. She washed her hands and sat on a chair.

Aunt Victoria came by her and said, "Rachel, what's the matter? I have noticed for the past two days that you have been very sad and acting strangely. You hardly smile and you look stressed."

"It's nothing, Aunt Victoria."

"Rachel, if something is bothering you, it is better you tell me. I, being older, can advise you what to do."

Rachel sat up and asked Aunt Victoria to keep what she told her confidential. Aunt Victoria assured her that she would. Rachel began telling her what happened. At the end, Rachel was emotional and told Aunt Victoria that she did not know what to do.

Aunt Victoria sat next to Rachel and said, "My dear, do not grieve. You have to think carefully and see who would be able to support you and give you a good life."

"Rudy saved my life and has always been kind to me and is good looking. On the other hand, Fred is financially stable, has been very kind to us and looked after us, but he is not as good looking as Rudy. I realized that I was attracted to Rudy's good looks and charm when I went to his house. I was never attracted to Fred but thought of him only as a good friend."

"My dear, just because a person has saved your life, does not mean that you are bound to him for life by marrying him. Don't go for looks. Fred saved Martha's life, but did she marry him? I am sure she is grateful, but neither she nor Fred thought about marrying each other. You must choose a man who can support you and the children and keep you secure for the rest of your life. From what you told me about Rudy's place, it looks like he will not be able to provide for you. Many factors go into a marriage than looks and gratitude. Please think about it and tell me what you decide."

Rachel got up to leave and Aunt Victoria said, "My child, remember that the man you want to marry is your own decision, and that decision has consequences."

"What do you mean?"

"I mean, about your life, the children you will have, and how everything will impact the world."

Rachel smiled and went to her room. She knew that Aunt Victoria's last piece of advice came from her wisdom, and she had to think carefully before making the right decision. She had no idea that many years later, she would think a lot about this piece of advice.

In the morning, Rachel came down for breakfast and found Aunt Victoria alone. She went to her and said, "Good morning, Aunt Victoria. I have thought about what you said, and I have made up my mind."

"Well, what is it?"

"I can see that Fred, in addition to being a wonderful man, can support me and provide for a family. He is a gentleman and is always very cheerful. He does love me a lot and is a genuine person. I will accept Fred's proposal."

"You must telegraph Fred that you accept his marriage proposal. Do not delay because there will not be another opportunity like this. Before you do that, I must be sure that you know you have picked the right person. I have met both of them, and they both seem like very fine gentlemen."

"Yes, I am sure, Aunt Victoria. Fred even told me that he loved me ever since he saw me on the Lusitania."

"All right, Rachel, since you are sure, I will respect your decision. Off you go."

Rachel went to the telegraph office and telegraphed Fred and Rudy. Rachel returned in the afternoon slightly exhausted. She had not eaten anything since dinner, and she could hear her stomach growling. She went into the kitchen and saw Aunt Victoria preparing lunch.

"Aunt Victoria, it is done. I telegraphed both of them."

"I have confidence in your decision, my dear. You have always been good at knowing what you wanted in life, and I am sure Fred is the right man for you. I feel it in my bones; old as they may be, I can still feel."

Rachel laughed and hugged Aunt Victoria.

* * * * *

Back in Long Island, Fred returned home, and after pouring himself a glass of brandy, he sat down in the drawing room, and began to read the latest bestseller. Just as he began reading, Robert came in with a telegram, and handed it to Fred, whose face lit up with a smile as he read it.

When Rudy arrived home that evening, Mary Holzmann pointed to the mantel, and told him of the telegram that had arrived earlier. Taking it to his room for privacy, Rudy began sobbing as he read the disappointing news from Rachel.

A few days later, Rachel looked out of the window and saw the postman coming. Rachel opened the door and the postman handed her the stack of envelopes. Rachel thanked him and went inside. She looked through the stack and found one from Fred, which she opened and read. Fred had written that he was delighted she accepted his marriage proposal, and he promised to be true to her and take care of her. He asked her to inform him when she could come to Long Island so that he could announce their engagement and plan for the wedding.

Rachel ran into the kitchen and showed the letter to Victoria Harlow. She hugged Rachel and said, "I am so happy for you. You are finally going to be married!"

Ten days later, the Harlows and Rachel were on their way to Long Island. Rachel felt sad because she knew that it would be a while before she would be back in Hartford.

At the station in Long Island, Fred and Alfred helped the women alight from the train, took their bags, and escorted them to the car.

Aunt Victoria whispered to Fred, "I'm glad that Rachel accepted your proposal. I'm sure that the two of you will be very happy together."

"Thank you, Mrs. Harlow. By the way, I have already arranged for the engagement party to be held four days from now, and the wedding will be two weeks after the engagement."

"That is too soon. I don't have my wedding dress yet," interjected Rachel.

"Don't worry, we can go to Macy's in Manhattan and get you a dress."

"I want to stitch my own dress."

"Then, we will get the material, and you can stitch it." Rachel smiled back at Fred and felt that she had made the right choice.

* * * * *

Rachel got down from the car, looked at the manor, and realized that in a few days she would be the mistress of this manor. The thought of her new life before her filled her with apprehension and at the same time excited her. After lunch, Fred called Rachel into the drawing room and closed the door. He asked her to sit down and close her eyes. He removed a box from his pocket, opened it, and asked Rachel to open her eyes. When she did, she saw the most magnificent diamond ring she had ever seen.

"It's beautiful," was all she could say.

Fred took her hand and placed the ring on her finger. "Now, I can show you off to the world."

The engagement party was held four days later. The guests eagerly assembled around the staircase. Rachel walked down the stairs wearing a blue dress and a diamond necklace, which was given to Rachel by Aunt Victoria as a wedding gift. Fred took Rachel's hand and said, "Ladies and gentlemen, this is Rachel Williams, my future wife."

Everyone clapped and cheered. Rachel was glad that they approved of her. She was nervous about meeting Fred's friends since they came from affluent families. As he took her around to meet their guests, people told her she was just as Fred had described her. Two men even told her that they were envious of Fred for marrying such a beautiful woman.

When the music began to play, Fred led her by the hand to the dance floor. As the first dance ended, she saw a familiar face standing next to a pillar.

"Rudy!" she exclaimed. She had forgotten all about him.

"What was that, dear?"

"I see Rudy standing at that pillar. Let me go speak to him."

"He must have just arrived. Let's meet him together."

No, no, let me talk to him. In a few days, I will be the mistress of this house, and it will be my duty to welcome guests. I better get attuned to it now." She squeezed Fred's hand before letting him go and headed in Rudy's direction.

Fred stared at Rachel as she walked towards Rudy. He was confused, wondering why she insisted on meeting Rudy herself. He shrugged his shoulders and walked towards the bar to get a drink.

"Good evening, Rudy. I am glad you came."

Rudy turned around in surprise and said, "Good evening, Rachel." He then lowered his voice and mumbled, "Congratulations."

Rachel saw the sadness in his handsome face. She went closer and whispered to Rudy to meet her outside on the other side of the balcony near the rose bushes in five minutes.

She walked away before he could respond. Five minutes later, she saw him come into the garden. She motioned him to go towards a row of tall bushes where they could talk without being seen or heard.

"Rudy, please tell me what is wrong."

"It is nothing, Rachel."

"I can see you're upset with me marrying Fred, and not you, aren't you?"

Rudy nodded his head. "I think, telling you face to face, would have been the right thing to do instead of sending a telegram. Both of you were in love with me, and both of you proposed to me within twenty-four hours of each other. I could choose only one of you. I chose Fred because he is a good man besides other reasons. Please be happy for us. I am sure you will find someone else in the future."

She held Rudy's hand in both hers. He looked into her blue eyes and saw the pain in them. He smiled and said, "I am sorry that I did not ask you sooner, but I am sure I will find someone at some point. Since you two are my friends, it would be very selfish of me not to be happy for both of you."

"Thank you, thank you," said Rachel and squeezed his hand in gratitude. A cool wind blew and the tall bushes began to sway. Rudy suggested that they go in.

"Let me go in first and then you follow later. People may think it odd if we walk in together," Rachel suggested. Rachel went in and tried to find Fred. A few seconds later, she saw Rudy entering.

"Ah, there you are! I have been looking for you." Fred took her by the hand and led her to the dance floor, and they began dancing. She looked around and saw Rudy talking to people. She was relieved.

That night, when Rachel went to bed, she had a good feeling about her decision. Her happiness was complete except that Martha and Harry would not be able to attend the wedding as they were in Florida. Rachel wanted Harry to give her away.

* * * * *

The big day arrived! Rachel could not believe that she was going to be married. She looked out of the window and saw the decorations and tents set up for the wedding. In a few hours, she would be a married woman.

Aunt Victoria and Lucy came in to help Rachel get ready. After she was fully attired, Rachel looked in the mirror. She was pleased with what she saw. She thanked Aunt Victoria and Lucy for helping her stitch her wedding dress.

Aunt Victoria looked at the clock and reminded them that it was time to go. Rachel took one final look in the mirror and adjusted the pearl necklace, which her mother had given her before she departed for Europe, never to return. She turned away from the mirror, and the three women walked out together.

They arrived at St. Mark's Church that was the local house of worship. "Thank you, Alfred. You did bring us to the church on time after getting Mr. Johnson here earlier."

Alfred smiled as he opened the door for her. "The next time I drive you home, you will be Mrs. Johnson." The three women went into the Brides Room. It was almost eleven a.m., and in a few minutes, she would enter the church as a bride. She looked at herself in the mirror and adjusted the flowers in her hair.

"I feel nervous, Aunt Victoria."

"Then you feel like a bride," came the terse reply.

Lucy came in and said, "I took a peek. Fred looks handsome, and Rudy is beside him as his best man."

She then smiled and said, "Rachel, you have a surprise guest."

"Who is it?"

The door opened and Rachel heard a familiar voice. "Hello, Rachel. You don't plan on getting married without me, do you?"

Rachel could not believe it. It was Martha. She went and hugged her.

"I thought you couldn't make it."

"I thought so too, but then I realized that you came for my wedding and it meant so much to me. I decided to do the same, and Harry agreed. Harry is waiting outside to walk you down the aisle."

They heard the organist begin to play.

"Time for us to go in," said Lucy.

Rachel smiled. She pulled the veil over her face and walked behind Lucy.

* * * * *

Harry Hardy took Rachel's arm, and they walked down the aisle together. The first people she saw were the staff from Johnson Manor and Alfred, sitting at the back of the church. She did not know the rest of the people, as they were all Fred's friends, though she had met some of them at her engagement party. She then saw a few relatives and friends from Hartford and finally, she saw Martha and Aunt Victoria sitting together. Both of them were wiping their eyes and smiling at her.

She saw Fred standing next to Rudy. Fred smiled at her, but Rudy was forcing himself to be cheerful. She understood his plight. Both the men were in love with her, and she had to disappoint one of them with her decision.

She stood next to Fred and handed her bouquet to Lucy. The priest began the nuptial ceremony with the sign of the cross. When it was time for the exchange of vows, Rachel felt her heart beating faster. This was it; no turning back. She saw Fred smiling as he repeated his vows after the priest, and she did the same. They were pronounced man and wife. Fred lifted her veil, and she saw the happiness on his face. He kissed her on the lips. This time, she responded, unlike the last time he kissed her in the garden when he proposed.

She got a glimpse of Rudy. He smiled, but his eyes betrayed his bravado. The rest of the ceremony continued, and Rachel tried to think of her life ahead.

After the ceremony, Fred and Rachel walked out of the church. Lucy came to her and said, "Congratulations, Mrs. Johnson. I wanted to be the first to call you that." Rachel laughed and hugged her.

Fred and Rachel went back to the manor as man and wife. She could not believe that she was now Mrs. Frederick Johnson. She was glad that Fred had asked Rudy to be his best man, and he agreed. She knew she had unnecessarily worried that she would break up their friendship. She was hopeful that Rudy would get over his disappointment, and she looked forward to the wedding reception and her new life.

The guests cheered as the bridal couple entered the garden for their reception. Rachel was amazed at how beautiful the garden and hall looked. Fresh flowers were brought in for the reception and placed everywhere. People complimented on how beautiful she looked and how her mother's pearl necklace looked elegant on her.

Rudy got up to toast the newly married couple. He made a few jokes and spoke about how important Fred's friendship was to him. He said that they made a very handsome couple and wished them a long and prosperous life together.

Rachel was pleased with the toast. Rudy seemed to be getting over his disappointment.

Fred got up to respond to the toast. He thanked the guests for coming, and the last part of his speech made everyone gasp. "Ladies and gentlemen, Rachel has made me very happy. She has filled the void that was in me ever since my parents died. As my wedding gift to her, I am making her the co-owner of my properties, which means, that she will own half of what I have: the hotels in New York, and also this manor."

They could hear the gasps from everyone in the audience. Fred smiled and sat down. It was a gift that was unheard of. Rachel tried to recover from the news of her newly found wealth. She could imagine the comments from the guests, accusing her of being a gold digger or saying that Fred was drunk.

After the reception, they headed to the Catskill Mountains for their honeymoon. Fred owned a farm that bred horses. Rachel loved horses and, therefore, Fred decided that they would spend their honeymoon there.

Chapter 3

November 1917

It had been almost three months since Rachel and Fred were married. One fall morning, Rachel woke up feeling sick. She felt nauseous and went to the washroom. After relieving herself, she dressed and went down for breakfast.

Fred looked at her and saw that she was not well. He told her to eat her breakfast. She looked at the scrambled eggs and bacon kept in front of her and pushed the plate away.

Fred told her to go to bed, and he telephoned Dr. Henry Thompson. Without a word, Rachel went upstairs and went to bed. She was too tired to change.

Fred waited anxiously outside the door, and it opened with a creak. Dr. Thompson came out smiling. "What is it, Doctor? How is she?"

"Go in, Rachel has some news for you. She insisted on telling you herself."

Fred went into the room and said, "What is it Rachel?"

Rachel smiled and said, "Fred, we're having a baby. Dr. Thompson says that the due date will probably be late July 1918."

"Is this true?" He looked at her in disbelief.

"Yes, it is. That's why I was feeling sick this morning."

He kissed her and said, "This is the happiest news I have had in all my life. Thank you, Rachel." He then hugged her. "I must send Aunt Victoria and Lucy a telegram telling them the good news. I will be back soon." Fred went out of the room and asked Robert to tell

Alfred to get the car ready.

Rudy walked in just as Fred was leaving the house. "Rudy, I have great news for you. Rachel is pregnant, and we're going to be parents in July." After saying this, Fred walked out of the house.

"That is great news..." Rudy managed to say. This was hard news to take. After the wedding, Rudy had not come to the manor, but had come this day on his way to work to discuss urgent matters with Fred. He had become a recluse, as he was still secretly upset over Rachel rejecting his marriage proposal, which he was getting over slowly. He went only to work and back home. Rudy was about to leave, when he heard someone call his name.

Rachel had not even thought about Rudy. She had been busy after her honeymoon learning about the business and traveling to New York City for meetings. She had ancestors that fought in the Union Army and the American Revolution, and was actively involved with the Daughters of Union Veterans of the Civil War and Daughters of the American Revolution. After Fred left the room, Rachel decided that she would take a walk in the garden. She was walking down the stairs, when she saw Rudy about to leave, and she called out to him.

Rudy turned and saw Rachel coming down the stairs. "Congratulations, Rachel. Fred just gave me the good news," Rudy said, forcing a smile.

"Thank you, Rudy. Fred is very excited, and he has rushed off to telegraph Aunt Victoria and Lucy the good news. I have never seen him this way."

"Yes, I see he is overjoyed. Anyway, I have to be going to the office. I think Fred will not be in today. Congratulations, once again. I am very happy for both of you."

"Thank you, Rudy, and please tell your mother the good news."

"I will," said Rudy and went out of the door.

Early March 1918

Christmas came and went. Rachel was sick from the day she found out that she was pregnant. She had morning sickness every day, and she hated it. She couldn't retain even her Christmas lunch. She felt better towards the end of January. Now she could get up without the fear of being sick.

One morning, Rachel received a call from Martha telling her that she would bring Sidney and spend the day with her. This delighted Rachel, and she looked forward to it.

However, on the day Martha was due to arrive, Martha called her and told her that she would not be able to meet her. Harry had returned from Kansas and was not feeling well. Martha expressed concern that Harry may have caught the flu that had started in the army barracks in Kansas or that Harry was exhausted from the journey. As a precaution, she sent Sidney, who was just a year old, to the house of Harry's sister.

After the call, Rachel picked up the newspaper. She read that the flu was spreading all over the country, especially in highly populated areas, claiming many casualties.

A few days later, she got the news that Harry was very ill. He was getting worse by the hour, and the doctors could not cure him. The following week, she heard that people in Queens, New York, had contracted the flu, and it seemed to be moving all over the city. She decided that in order to save herself, she must leave the city. That night, at dinner, she told Fred about her concerns.

"Fred, the flu seems to be spreading all over the city, and I am afraid that it may come this way. I think we better go to the Catskills and stay there for a while."

"The flu is all over the country, Rachel. It is impossible to escape this."

"I think we'd better leave, Fred. I do not want to get sick and endanger our unborn child."

"No arguments, Rachel. That is final. I know what's best. I'm sure you will be safe here."

She could not believe it. This was their first argument, and she knew that she was right. Whenever she felt something would go wrong, it usually did. A few days later, Martha called Rachel and told her that Sidney had contracted the flu. There was no change in Harry's condition, and she was very fearful for him.

She called Dr. Thompson and asked him to speak to Fred. He agreed with Rachel about staying in the Catskills until the epidemic had passed and said that he would speak to Fred about it.

The next day, Fred told Rachel that Dr. Thompson telephoned, advising him to take Rachel away to escape the flu. Fred agreed with Rachel about going to the Catskills for a while. He would be taking Rudy along to discuss business matters with him. Rachel secretly smiled that her plan had worked and quickly packed her suitcase. That same afternoon, the three of them were in the car headed to the Catskills. Throughout the journey, Rachel noticed that Rudy was very talkative and in good spirits. She was relieved that there were no hard feelings and that Fred and Rudy were friends. They reached the horse farm, and Rachel was glad to be in the mountains again. She looked forward to riding horses and walking in the woods. There was also a farm owned by Farmer Joe close by, where they could get fresh milk and eggs every day. The smell of the fresh cold mountain air made her feel better. She wished that Martha and her family were with her.

Rachel felt tired and announced that she would be going straight to bed. She got up in the morning refreshed and found there were already fresh eggs and milk delivered by Farmer Joe. She went into the kitchen and prepared breakfast. After breakfast, they decided to spend the day relaxing by the lake. Rachel made corned beef sandwiches and brought a bottle of wine from the cellar. On the way to the lake, they went to the stables. They had bought a new Arabian horse, which Rachel had seen on her honeymoon but could not ride it because he was a bit wild and needed to be trained. She had even named him Emir, which meant 'Prince' in Arabic.

She went to the stable and spotted Emir standing in his stall. With his beautiful flowing white mane, and his regal look, he was handsome. He had become more docile and did not seem very agitated like the last time she saw him. She went towards his stall and patted him.

"He remembers you, Miss," said a voice from behind her.

She turned around and said, "Well, hello, Simon, how nice to see you again!"

"Nice to see you too, Mrs. Johnson," said Simon, the groom.

"How has Emir been doing?"

"He's a lot better since you last saw him. He does get very upset and difficult to control when he hears loud noises, especially during thunderstorms. I'm sure he will get better as the days go by."

"He will," said Rudy. "He just needs time to adjust, and he will be just as good as the other horses."

"Come on, let's go to the lake before the sun goes down and it gets chilly," said Fred.

Rudy and Rachel followed him, and they went to the lake beside the barn.

For March, the weather seemed great; the sun was shining and it was not too cold. Fred suggested that they ride the horses the next day. "Oh, that is a great idea! Can I come too?"

"No, Rachel, it is dangerous in your condition. No riding horses until you have had the baby."

"Just for a little while. The horse need not gallop."

"No, Rachel, I am afraid that will have to wait," said Fred, firmly. Rachel looked at Fred in anger and irritation and then looked away, as she finished her sandwich. She hated being pregnant. She had been sick and could not go horseback riding. She loved being outdoors and having a good time. She did not want to anger Fred again. Maybe, when the opportunity arose, she would go horseback riding without his knowledge.

The next day, Rudy and Fred went horseback riding and Rachel was left alone in the house. There was nothing else to do but read. She would go to the stable now and again, as she got bored, and look at Emir. She looked forward to the day when she could ride the horse. She felt a connection with Emir, and the very fact that Simon mentioned that Emir remembered her meant that they would get along well together.

When Rudy and Fred came back, they told Rachel about their excursion into the woods. She listened patiently but was still annoyed that she was not allowed to go. They had hunted a few rabbits and left them with Farmer Joe's wife to clean and cook for dinner that evening.

A few days later, Fred received a telegram that he must return to Manhattan to take care of some urgent business. He said he would be back in two days and left Rudy in charge.

This was the opportunity Rachel was waiting for! As soon as the car was out of sight, she went to the stable and ordered Simon to prepare Emir for riding. She went into the house and put on her riding clothes. As she was going out of the house, she almost bumped into Rudy. When Rudy cautioned her about Fred's concern about her riding while pregnant, she replied saying, "Fred worries too much. I cannot put my life on hold just because I'm carrying his child. See you later."

Simon helped Rachel get onto the horse. Emir walked to the other end of the farm and into the trail that led into the woods. It was almost dark when she got back, and Rudy was waiting at the door. "It's almost dark. I was worried about you."

"That was unnecessary. Emir and I got along just fine. We went to the stream flowing through the clearing in the woods two miles from here and had a nice time relaxing. Fred and I would go there every day when we were on our honeymoon, as I liked that place. I plan on going to the stream again tomorrow. The weather has been too nice to spend it sitting indoors."

"I know the spot you're talking about, but Rachel, I insist that you stay here."

"Rudy, you are not my father or my husband. I can take care of myself. Emir knows his way around, and we get along well. I will be fine."

After breakfast, Rachel went to the stables. Simon kept Emir ready and helped Rachel mount the horse. She was contended to spend another day with Emir. Rachel reached the stream and got down from the horse. She unpacked her lunch and ate the sandwich. She sat relaxing by the river with the warm sun on her face, when she suddenly heard a loud clap of thunder. She looked up and saw there were no clouds in the sky. She heard it again and at once looked at Emir. She saw him get very agitated. Emir started jumping and standing on his hind legs, neighing very loudly. She got up and tried to catch the reins to calm him down, but his foreleg hit her on the head, and she fell to the ground.

"No Emir, no, calm down, calm down."

The horse, still very agitated, moved towards her; one leg hit her on the abdomen, and the other grazed her forehead. The last thing she remembered before she lost consciousness was Emir running into the woods, and she felt a sharp pain engulf her.

Rachel felt a few rain drops fall on her face and woke up. The sun was setting in the horizon. She felt her dress was wet. She looked at her dress and saw a big red stain. She tried to get up but felt pain rush through her body. She touched her abdomen and wondered if the baby was alright. She got up and tried to walk.

'That's it Rachel, one step at a time,' she said to herself. She looked around and saw no signs of Emir. The raindrops had now become a slight drizzle, and she felt the temperature falling. She saw her bag, which had thankfully fallen down when Emir bolted into the woods. She opened it, pulled out a sweater and a hat, and put them on. 'I must get back before it rains.' Rachel moved her legs one step at a time and felt the pain shoot through her body. She walked away from the stream into the woods. It was pitch dark, and she could not see anything. She felt the rain come down harder as it soaked her. She knew that she was on the trail and held onto the branches of trees and bushes for support as she went ahead deeper into the woods. Finally, she could go no longer and collapsed. Her last thought was seeing Fred getting upset with her for not listening to him.

Rachel woke up in pain in a hospital room. Fred and a doctor were standing next to her. "Fred," was all she could say as she reached out and touched his hand. He held her hand and squeezed it.

"Where am I?"

"I am Dr. Spaulding, and you are in St. Steven's Hospital, Mrs. Johnson. You had a nasty accident."

"Will I be okay?"

"Yes, you are going to be fine. You were suffering from hypothermia when they found you in the woods."

"Oh my God, the baby! Is the baby okay? Fred, is the baby all right?" She started to panic.

"Yes, the baby is fine, Mrs. Johnson. You are, indeed, fortunate. You lost some blood; the breeches you wore under your skirt must have helped stem the bleeding and that probably is what saved you," said Dr. Spaulding.

"Thank you, Doctor. Fred, I'm so sorry for not listening to you and for endangering our baby."

Fred sat on a chair beside the bed and kissed Rachel's hand. "There, there, Rachel, I'm sure you didn't mean to do that. I'm just relieved that both of you survived."

"I will leave you two alone now," said the doctor and left the room.

"How did they find me?"

"When it was evening, Simon alerted Rudy that Emir had come back without you. He got the people at the stable to go in search of you. It was raining, and they went to the spot you said you would be. They didn't find you. They searched the woods close by and found that you had wandered off the trail and passed out. They carried you to the house and asked Farmer Joe to take you to the hospital in his car. That's how you got here."

"How long have I been unconscious?"

"For four days."

"Fred, it was strange that I heard two claps of thunder, and there was not a single cloud in the sky. I also had a strange feeling of being watched. When I was lying on the ground, just before I passed out, I thought I heard footsteps and someone looking at me."

"No, Rachel. It might have been just Emir watching you. The two claps of thunder you heard may have been shots from a hunter's gun. I don't care; I'm just glad that you're safe."

She saw the pain on his face and felt guilty about how she foolishly almost got herself and their baby killed. Fred asked the neighboring farmers if there were any hunters in that area around the time of Rachel's accident. They all said that there were none they were aware of.

Two days later, Rachel left the hospital. She was in tears as she came back home. She thought she would never see the manor again and was glad to be back.

Later in the day, as she rested, Fred gave her the terrible news. Harry Hardy had passed away, although he did put up a fight and wanted to live. The doctors said that probably his age and exhaustion from the Kansas trip might have hastened his death. However, Sidney was recovering.

"Poor Martha," said Rachel and began to cry. Fred sat on the bed and held her in his arms.

The funeral of Harry Hardy was held a few days later at St. Patrick's Cathedral. Rachel did not attend, but Fred did. After the funeral, Fred suggested that Martha come and stay with them for a few days. Martha declined politely because she had to see to the Hardy Estate. Her task now was to take the seat made vacant by her husband's death, and keep the estate and the family's steel business going for her son.

Rachel gradually got over her accident and the death of Harry Hardy. She was counting the days until her delivery and looked forward to being a mother. The tragedy of almost losing the baby stirred her maternal instincts. She was taking her pregnancy seriously for the first time.

At the end of July, Rachel developed pains and was rushed to St. Leo's Hospital. It was clear from the very beginning to Dr. Thompson that it would be a difficult labor. The baby was born later in the afternoon. Rachel heard the baby crying and one of the nurses telling her that she had given birth to a girl. She lost a lot of blood and was unconscious for three days. She had to have surgery, and she then developed a fever. She was allowed to see her daughter after she recovered.

The nurse brought the baby and helped Rachel to nurse her before leaving the room. When she had finished, Fred walked in. Rachel smiled at him and said,

"Isn't she a beauty?"

"Yes," said Fred. "What shall we name her?"

"We shall name her Barbara Rachel Johnson. Barbara, after my grandmother."

"Fine with me," said Fred.

"Look at the birth mark on her right shoulder. It almost looks like a horseshoe. It is big enough to cover the shoulder."

The nurse came in and said, "Mrs. Johnson, we will have to take the baby back to the nursery."

"Please, let me have her for a few more moments," she pleaded. Before the nurse answered, Dr. Thompson came in and said, "I am afraid I have to give you some bad news."

"What is it?" asked Rachel. "Is anything wrong with my daughter?"

"No, your daughter will be fine. It is you, I am afraid of. Please give the baby to the nurse. It's better that you do that first."

The seriousness and the authority in his voice, made Rachel obey him. After the nurse left, the doctor continued, "It is your uterus; it is damaged due to the difficult labor. The shock it received when the horse kicked you and also when you fell, must have caused it. We managed to stop the bleeding, but it is advisable not to conceive again. If you do, you will not live through the child-bearing process."

Dr. Thompson's words struck her very hard. She held Fred's hand and started crying. Dr. Thompson left the room.

"I am sorry that I was foolish and went riding on that horse. I was hoping that we would have a son the next time.

Fred tried not to look disappointed. He consoled her and said, "We cannot go back and change anything. Barbara is healthy. I love you both."

That comforted her and she stopped crying. Five days later, Barbara Johnson was taken to the Johnson Manor.

Chapter 4

November 11, 1918

At about five a.m., nine men waited in a railway carriage in a forest, thirty-seven miles North of Paris. The last signature was in place by five-twenty., and eleven a.m. was made the official time for the war to end. By five-forty., the news that the war would end had reached the capital cities of Europe and celebrations began immediately.

A few days earlier, Rachel decided to take Barbara along and spend a few days with Martha and Sidney. On the morning of November 11, Fred, who had received a phone call from his friend in the War Department, brought the news that the war was ending, and they were in a jubilant mood. The whole city was outside on the street celebrating.

Martha and Rachel rushed onto the streets of Manhattan and joined the celebrations. Martha was still in mourning, and Rachel was still recovering from her surgical ordeal, but this was a great cause for celebration.

A few days later, the Daughters of the Union Veterans of the Civil War had a banquet honoring women who had served in the Great War. Rachel and Martha, who were members, thought it was their duty to honor these women, so they helped to arrange the banquet. It was held on December 11, at the Waldrof Astoria Hotel.

It was at this banquet that Rachel's life changed. While waiting for the banquet to start, Martha introduced Rachel to Mary Connelly who served as a nurse during the war and was being honored that day.

"It is nice to meet you, Mary. What was it like being in France where the battles were raging?" asked Rachel excitedly.

"I can tell you one thing; war is not pretty but brutal. However, it is amazing how much women can do and just as well as men. Sadly, we never get the same respect."

"Why do you say that?"

"We took care of the wounded men, braving gunfire and exploding bombs, and helped with the war effort but still do not have the right to vote. I think we should be able to vote for our elected representatives and also for our president."

"I totally agree. Women need to get the right to vote and get the recognition they deserve. I take it that you are a suffragette?" said Rachel.

"Yes, I am, and you two are welcome to come for our weekly meetings. One of Alice Paul's close associates is coming to speak. The war put a damper on the movement, and since the war is over, we need to get back to pushing the government to obtain our rights."

"Well, I'll be glad to join, and I'm sure Martha will, too." Martha nodded in agreement just as the bell rang for the event to begin.

A few days later, Rachel and Martha went for their first suffragette meeting. They met other suffragettes and bonded with them.

Fiona Ellis, Alice Paul's associate, spoke at the meeting. One thing that struck Rachel was when she said, "During the war, women helped the government and the war effort by working in industries, factories, hospitals, and at the front by bravely dodging bullets, bombs, and gas attacks. Now that the war is over, we are being told to give our jobs to the men returning from Europe. We do not have to stand for this injustice. We want another inequity to be rectified. That is, the right for us to vote. We are equally capable of voting to elect our president and our representatives, and even President Woodrow Wilson thinks so. We are even capable of running a business like men, and women whose husbands run a business should learn everything about it and be ready to take over the reins when the men are no longer able to do so." Rachel, along with the other women in the room, rose and applauded. She was whole-heartedly in the movement.

Rachel helped the movement with her time and donations. As a result, she neglected Barbara, which Fred constantly disapproved of. Rachel observed that Barbara was getting more attached to Fred than she was to her. She was grateful for that, since she could now devote herself to her new passion. She decided to follow the words of Fiona Ellis and study the workings of the Johnson Hotel business. To make things easier for her, she hired a nanny.

Rachel hired Helen Macdonald in the early months of 1919. She was the first person to be interviewed and came with excellent references. Barbara took to Helen at once, and Helen proved to be an excellent nanny. She was a young war widow with three children. The youngest was just a baby. She left her children with her mother in Connecticut and came to work at the Johnson Manor.

Fred was not pleased with the new arrangement; however, when he saw that Barbara liked Helen and would not leave her, he decided not to intervene.

Rachel was very involved in the suffragette movement. She would go for the suffragette meetings in the city. She felt that motherhood tied her down at a time when she could contribute to society. Her biggest moment came when she met Alice Paul personally. Alice praised Rachel for her dedication and efforts, and for championing the cause for women to vote.

Rachel got closer to Rudy. He taught her everything he knew. She loved learning about the business and would discuss various aspects of the business with Fred over dinner. In many cases, he would exclaim, "Now, who would have thought that I married a smart woman who would advise me on business matters!"

When the amendment was passed, granting women the right to vote, Rachel was excited to vote for the first time in her life. It made her feel powerful. She was annoyed that Harding won and felt that her first vote was wasted. Fred wanted a change from the Wilson government and voted for Harding, whereas Rachel and her fellow suffragettes wanted a president who would follow Wilson's example and support women's rights. Nonetheless, she immersed herself in learning about the business and that made her annoyance dissipate.

In August 1920, Rachel received the news that Lucy was getting married. Lucy was marrying Paul Hatfield who worked for the State Department in his hometown Philadelphia. They had to hurry and get married since he was being posted to France. In September, Rachel, Fred, and Barbara attended the wedding. It was nice to see Aunt Victoria and Lucy again. Aunt Victoria was living in the same house in Hartford, because her daughter was living close by. Two days later, Lucy and her husband sailed for France.

It was after Lucy's wedding that Rachel started receiving letters that questioned Fred's fidelity. The letters suggested that Fred was having an affair with Helen, the nanny, who was hired to take care of Barbara. Rachel first thought it was a joke until the second letter came a month later. She did not show the two letters to Fred but kept them locked in her private desk.

In September 1921, it was Fred's thirtieth birthday. For the birthday, Rachel wanted to go to New Jersey, along with Barbara. When she told Fred about her plans for the birthday, he was thrilled. He insisted that they take Rudy along so that he could take them to the speakeasies there.

"Rudy knows all the best places to drink, and I trust his judgment and knowledge of those places," he said to Rachel with a laugh.

Rachel wanted Fred to be happy, so she went along with it. They left for the weekend to Atlantic City, New Jersey, in Fred's car. Helen was taken along. They reached Atlantic City and checked into a hotel. They could see signs that there was no alcohol being served in compliance with the Volstead Act.

That night, Rudy decided to take them to the speakeasy he frequented. 'Moscow Palace' was in an alley that looked more like a slum. Rachel was horrified at the filth and poverty. She saw prostitutes and men cavorting in public, and that disgusted her. She had never seen or been exposed to such debauchery in her life. They went into the building and could hear music being played. She looked around and saw a gramophone playing ragtime music and some people eating their dinner quietly.

Rudy opened the door hidden behind a shelf. They looked inside and saw people drinking. There were well-dressed persons along with ordinary people. This speakeasy welcomed everyone. They went inside and ordered whisky.

Rachel looked around and saw the band playing music. "What is that music?"

"It is called Jazz. It is becoming popular," replied Rudy. "People now listen to it on the radio."

"I've heard it at home once, but it sounds different on the radio," said Rachel.

"The main attraction here is a singer who dances, and she is amazingly beautiful."

"I can see that you are very well acquainted with her," said Fred.

"Yes, very well," said Rudy, with a grin on his face.

The lights dimmed. A man came on the stage and spoke with a foreign accent. "Ladies and Gentlemen, welcome to 'Moscow Palace'. Tonight, we have our usual singer, 'The Star of Russia', who will perform for you."

There were cheers from the audience. Many men were whistling and shouting words that Rachel could not understand but was thankful, for she knew that they were unacceptable.

The band started playing again, and the curtain rose. A beautiful woman with blond hair and wearing semi-transparent clothes came onto the stage and started singing. She was a good dancer. Rachel could see from her face that she did not enjoy dancing in front of people.

"Why is she called 'The Star of Russia'?" asked Rachel. The men did not answer.

She repeated the question a bit louder.

Rudy turned his head and replied, "Just between us, she is believed to belong to a Russian aristocratic family. She escaped from Russia during the revolution and came to America. Joshua Frankel, who owns this place and who introduced her, discovered her. She was given the name 'The Star of Russia'. She has been quite a sensation for some time."

"I am sure she is," said Rachel, with some annoyance in her voice.

The dance ended and people began clapping. Fred was clapping wildly. This annoyed Rachel. "How did you like her Fred?" Rudy asked.

"She was amazing. She has the voice of an angel and dances like one too."

"I knew you would like her; that is why I brought you here. This is my birthday gift for you," said Rudy.

"I wish you didn't," Rachel said under her breath. She hailed a passing waiter, "Waiter, another bottle of whisky, please."

"Rachel, you never drink that much. What's gotten into you?" asked Fred.

"Maybe 'The Star of Russia' has influenced me to have another drink," said Rachel, sarcastically.

"That is a good idea. Let's order some more," said Rudy.

Half an hour later, the three of them were drunk. Rudy, the least drunk of the lot, helped them out of the speakeasy.

At the hotel, with the help of Alfred, Rudy took Rachel and Fred to their room and placed them on the bed.

"Good night, you two. I wish you could see yourselves." Rudy laughed and closed the door.

Fred got up in the morning and looked for Rachel. She was not in the room. He found that their clothes were on the floor and realized that he had nothing on. 'What happened last night?' he wondered.

He got up, went to the washroom, washed his face, and put on fresh clothes. He went downstairs and found Rachel eating breakfast alone.

Rachel had a headache and had no recollection of what happened the previous night. She thought that they made love when Fred asked about waking up without any clothes on.

Just then, Rudy walked in. "Good morning, you two. Guess who will be joining us in a few minutes?"

"Who?" asked Rachel.

"The Star of Russia," replied Rudy.

"How did you manage to ask her to join us for breakfast?" asked Fred, with a smile on his face.

"I know her very well. Here she is now."

'The Star of Russia' walked in. Rudy got up and pulled out a chair for her. She thanked him and sat down. She held out a cigarette, and Rudy lit it for her. "Good morning. I am Anna Kolovsky from Russia." She had a very thick Russian accent.

"Good morning. I am Fred Johnson, and this is my wife, Rachel."

The waiter brought them coffee.

"Good morning, Mr. and Mrs. Johnson. I hear that you are the owners of the Johnson Hotels and Winery."

"Yes, we are co-owners. We saw your act last night. It was wonderful," said Fred.

"Thank you, Mr. Johnson. I am very glad that you liked it." She blew out some smoke from her mouth.

"Is it true that you belong to a Russian aristocratic family?" asked Rachel.

"Yes, I saw my parents and brothers being killed in the revolution. I managed to escape dressed up as a peasant." She began to cry. Rudy gave her his handkerchief. She took it and wiped away her tears.

"I am very sorry about your family," said Fred.

"Thank you. I'd better be going. I have to practice for my show. Will you all be coming to see me tonight?"

"Yes, we will not disappoint you," said Fred, enthusiastically.

She drank the last sip from the cup and got up to leave. "I will see you all tonight."

The men stood up and watched her leave.

"That woman smokes like a chimney," said Rachel, as she waved her hand to get rid of the smoke.

That evening, as Fred was getting ready to leave, he noticed that Rachel had not yet changed. "Aren't you going tonight?"

"No, I have a headache, and Helen has the night off. She has some relatives living close-by that she would like to visit. I will take care of Barbara tonight."

"All right, but I think you are missing out on a special night."

"I'm sure," she said, sarcastically.

Fred noticed the sarcasm and said, "Now, what's all that about? There is no need to be sarcastic."

"Fred Johnson, shame on you. I saw how you looked at her yesterday."

"At whom?"

"At Anna, the so called, 'Star of Russia'."

"Oh, Rachel! She is good looking, and men sometimes do get enamored by beautiful women." He laughed. "I am sure you look at other men."

"No, I don't," she replied sharply.

"Yes, you do. I've seen you look at Rudy. You don't fool me even for a moment. I know that he too proposed to you."

"How did you know?" she asked in surprise.

"I overheard you two talking near the bushes on our engagement night."

"What?" She was stunned.

"Yes, Rachel. I saw you two walk out together, so I followed you and hid in the bushes. I know why you chose those bushes. You didn't want people to see you talking to Rudy. It works both ways. You could not see me, but I heard everything."

"Then, why did you go ahead with the wedding?"

"Because I knew that you were concerned about my relationship with Rudy and that showed that you have a caring heart. Rachel, I have eyes only for you. You will never be replaced. I promise you that."

Just then, there was a knock on the door. Fred opened it and let Rudy in. "Are you two coming tonight?"

"Yes, I am. I am also trying to help Rachel make up her mind."

"It is too late now. Helen has gone off and Barbara is asleep. Besides, I do not like that 'Star of Russia'."

"The hotel maid can take care of Barbara."

"That is a good idea, Rudy. We can pay her to look after Barbara," said Fred and turned to Rachel. "Rachel, are you now going to come?"

"Yes. Please give me a few minutes."

Half an hour later, Joshua welcomed the three of them. They had a round of drinks and when the band stopped playing, the act began. Anna came out wearing the same outfit from the previous night and began singing. Rachel noticed that Fred could not keep his eyes off Anna. Rachel began to think about the argument they had earlier. The waiter kept bringing drinks to the table, and she could see that Fred was getting drunk. He cheered with the other men and this upset her even more.

"Fred, please stop."

Fred seemed absorbed with the singer and ignored Rachel. Rachel could not control herself and ran out of the speakeasy, crying. Lecherous men tried to accost her, but she escaped from them.

She walked for a while and saw a bench. She sat on it and began thinking about the past few days. She thought about the argument Fred and she had earlier and reflected on what he said about her having feelings for Rudy. Was it true? Did he see something she was not aware of? Fred did confess his love for her and maybe, that was good enough. He knew that she was a good and caring person.

Meanwhile, back at the nightclub, the dance had ended and Fred discovered that Rachel was missing

"Where is Rachel?" asked Fred. He got up but could not walk and could barely see anything ahead of him. He sat down.

"Fred, you stay here, and I will go find her," said Rudy. He went away and came back five minutes later.

"The man at the door said that he saw Rachel running down the street a while ago. I will go and get her."

"No… no, she is my wife, I need to go and get herrrrr."

"Fred, no, you're too drunk. You need to go to your room. You're in no condition to go and get her."

"Will you get heerrr for me… Rudy?"

"Yes, I will. Now, go to your room and wait there. I will take the car and look for Rachel. I will ask one of the men at the door to take you to your hotel."

He placed a few notes on the table and helped Fred get up. "Yeeeeeeeeeeees Rudy, you take the car, and I will go back to my room."

Rudy held onto Fred as he paid the doorman of the speakeasy to take Fred to the hotel, while he, Rudy, went to get the car.

Fred walked slowly, staggering, clinging onto the burly man. He could see people pass by making fun of him and laughing.

When they entered the hotel, the man left Fred at the bottom of the staircase and left without saying a word. 'I... I have got to go to the room; damn this alcohol.' He walked up the stairs holding the banister and came to his room. He tried the key but found the door was unlocked. He opened the door and saw the figure of a person in the dim light. "Who is it?"

"It's me, Rachel."

"Rachel, I thought you left me at the speakeasy."

"No, darling, I am here. I have been waiting for you all this time. Come to bed."

Fred could see a figure sitting on the bed. He smiled, went towards the bed, and fell into the arms of the woman. They started kissing. He started unbuttoning her clothes and began kissing her naked flesh.

* * * * *

Rudy searched for Rachel and saw her sitting on the bench on the boardwalk. He asked Alfred to stop the car and went towards her. "Rachel, Fred is worried about you."

"Rudy, what are you doing here?"

"We discovered that you were missing and that's why I've come looking for you. Fred is at the hotel waiting."

"How could he cheer on that dancer in front of me?"

"Well, he was a bit drunk. It makes men go wild."

"That is no reason for him to behave that way."

"Rachel, he loves you. He was worried about you. That's why he sent me to find you. Come, let me take you back to your hotel room."

"I will never enter another speakeasy if that's the way people behave. I will forgive Fred this time but will not stand for this sort of behavior again," she said, sobbing.

Rudy helped her get up. They got into the car, and Alfred drove them back to the hotel.

They climbed the stairs and Rachel said, "I must take Barbara to my room. Helen will be back tomorrow morning."

Rudy nodded and headed to his room.

She went into the room reserved for Helen and saw the hotel maid on a chair.

"Good evening, Mrs. Johnson. Barbara is sleeping soundly. She was no trouble at all," she said with an Irish accent.

"Thank you for looking after her, Bridget. I think my husband has paid you."

"Yes, he has, Mrs. Johnson."

Rachel picked up Barbara and went out of the room. Rudy was standing near the door. Rachel said 'good night' to Rudy and walked to her room. As she inserted the key, she noticed that the door was unlocked. She opened the door, turned on the light, and let out a scream.

She saw Fred in bed with Anna and was utterly shocked. She choked up at once and ran out of the room.

Fred got up and saw who he was in bed with.

Hearing Rachel scream, Rudy and Bridget came to the door. She handed the sleeping Barbara to Bridget and entered the room.

She got on the bed and started hitting Fred. She could smell the alcohol in his breath.

"You dirty pig, you swine."

Anna covered herself and left the room.

"Stop it, stop it," Rudy said, grabbing Rachel's arm.

"He cheated on me. He's a swine."

"No, Rachel, please listen, I thought she was you."

"Do not lie to me. You knew that I ran away. I am leaving you."

"No, you can't."

"Yes, I can, and I will. I have many friends in the suffragette movement who will support me. I also have many witnesses."

"Please think about Barbara. Do you want her to grow up in a broken home?"

"She is better off growing up without an adulterer for a father.

Now, get out all of you. Fred, you can sleep in the hallway or on the street. I don't care. As far as I'm concerned, you can go to hell."

Fred saw that there was no point in talking to her. He got up from the bed, took his clothes, and left the room, followed by Rudy and Bridget. Barbara woke up due to the noise and started crying. She would not go to Rachel, so Bridget took her and went out of the room. Rachel slammed the door after them.

"Fred, come on, Bridget will take care of Barbara. You can sleep in my room. Rachel will be fine in the morning. She's just upset," said Rudy. Fred said nothing and followed Rudy into his room.

One month later:

"Now, I have the house and the two hotels in New York City," Rachel said to Rudy.

"I don't blame you, but it would be nice if Fred and you were not going through a divorce."

"It is none of your business, Rudy. You are partly to blame. You're the one who introduced us to that awful woman. I knew when I first saw her that she was a woman of easy virtue."

"He did say it was a mistake. He was drunk, and he thought that Anna was you. He had no idea how she got into the bedroom."

"I do not care. He must have been glad I wasn't there, and taken her himself."

Before Rudy could answer, the phone rang. Rachel got up and picked up the phone.

She listened for some time and then placed the receiver in the cradle. "That was Martha. She will be here tomorrow."

"All right, I have to go to the office. Please give Martha my regards."

The next day, Martha arrived with Sidney. "Oh Martha, it is so nice to see you. How is Sidney? Right now, he is the only man I would trust," she laughed.

"I am very sorry to hear that you and Fred are getting a divorce."

"Yes, it is true."

"What happened? I was in Europe for the past few weeks. I was shocked when I heard about the upcoming divorce. Nobody could give me any details. I hope it is just a rumor."

"No rumor; it is true. We have tried to keep it quiet because we did not want any scandal to hurt the business. Only a few people know. I would have told you anyway, when I met you."

She looked at Sidney and said, "Let Sidney and Barbara play together. I will tell you everything while we have lunch."

The children played in the garden while Rachel and Martha sat outside at a table, which was already set for lunch. Rachel recounted the whole story. Martha was stunned. "I am sure there is another explanation. It just doesn't seem like Fred to do a thing like that. If Harry were alive, he too would have told you the same thing. He always spoke very highly of Fred."

"Apparently, Harry did not know him that well."

Martha's face flushed. "Where is Fred living now?"

"He is now in the guest house on the property. He agreed to move there and still has some of his things here. He will be going to California soon for a few months to help start two hotels in San Francisco. The divorce papers will be ready for him to sign when he gets back. Since he made me co-owner of his properties, my lawyer, Mr. Sagan, said that he could convince the courts to let me have my share."

"I don't like the whole thing, Rachel. Think about what Aunt Victoria would say. What about the church?"

"Obviously, Aunt Victoria is not very happy with the upcoming divorce. I told her that I would not be living with a man who has no regard for me or his marriage vows. I am getting an annulment from the church on grounds of adultery. Excuse me." Rachel walked inside to her desk, unlocked it, took out two letters, and placed them in front of Martha.

"I received these two anonymous letters about Fred having an affair with Helen. I confronted Fred about this but did not show him the letters.

"What did he say?"

"He denied it. I asked him why anyone would write such nasty letters if the allegations were not true."

"I cannot believe that Fred would do this. What did Helen have to say?"

"She does not know. I have not asked her. She would obviously deny it."

"Yes, that is what she would do." Barbara came in crying with her sleeve torn and birthmark exposed.

"Sidney tried to take away the ball from me. He hit me and tore my dress." Sidney came running after her.

"No, she is lying, that's not the way it happened. She started hitting me first."

Martha got up and slapped Sidney in the face. "That is not the way you treat a young girl. Shame on you!" Sidney began to cry. "Oh, I'm sorry, Sidney," said Martha, and she hugged him.

"Rachel, I think I need to go. Just hearing what Fred has done to you has made me mad at men. I am sorry I cannot stay longer."

"That's all right, Martha."

Martha took Sidney, who was still crying, out of the house. As she was getting into her car with the chauffeur holding the door for her, Fred came and greeted her.

"Fred, how could you do that to Rachel? She's like a sister to me, and Harry had great regard for you," Martha yelled.

"Martha, it was all a misunderstanding."

"I'm sure the affair with Helen too was a misunderstanding!" she said sarcastically.

"Martha, that is not true," Fred said in anger.

"I am leaving now. You better treat Rachel well." Saying that, Martha got into the car, and her chauffeur closed the door. A few seconds later, the car headed out of the compound.

Fred stood fuming at what had just happened. He went into the house and found Rachel trying to pacify Barbara.

"What happened?"

"Why do you care? She is all right."

Barbara tried to break away from Rachel, but Rachel held on to her. She pulled at Rachel's sleeve and tore it. Rachel hit Barbara in the face, and her nose started bleeding. Barbara ran towards Fred, crying.

"Rachel, I'm going to San Francisco today, and I'm taking Barbara with me. She is not safe with you."

"No, you're not."

"Daddy, I want to be with you. Please take me with you."

"She wants to go with me, and I'm taking her. You have been too busy with your other activities to look after her, and she doesn't even know you."

"All right, but when you come back, I'm going to ask the courts to let me keep her. She needs her mother."

"Oh, that's why you hired Helen. I have seen what sort of a mother you are. You hit her and gave her a bloody nose."

"She tore my sleeve."

"You're just a pitiful woman. You have become a monster. Barbara doesn't know you. No wonder she likes Helen more."

"I'm going to fire Helen today."

"All right. I'm going to pack Barbara's things and take her with me to California." After saying this, Fred went upstairs with Barbara. He came down after a while and had Alfred take the suitcases to the car.

"We will be gone for a few months and in that time, I hope, you will reconsider your decision. Think about Barbara."

"I have, and I think she will be better off with me."

Fred opened the door and turned just as he was about to walk out and said, "I fell in love with a different girl on the Lusitania who was warm and kind. That is why I married her. I don't recognize this other woman you have become, and it's painful for all of us to see you like this."

Rachel was shocked. For the first time in several days, he said something that pricked her conscience.

He went out carrying Barbara and slammed the door. Rachel went to the window and watched the car driving out of the compound. She began to cry. This was not how she intended her life to be.

The next morning, Helen entered the drawing room and walked

towards the desk where Fred used to sit. "Good morning, Mrs. Jo…"

"Stop calling me that," snapped Rachel. "You are to call me Ms. Williams."

"I'm sorry."

"Since Barbara has gone away with her father, I no longer require your services. You can pack your things and leave today," said Rachel, without changing her tone.

"But Ms. Williams, I have worked here for three years taking care of Barbara and also doing other housework and have been a good worker. I really need this job."

"I don't need your services any longer; you must leave."

"My family is in dire need of money. My sister died last year, leaving her two children in the care of my parents, and I have to support my three children. Please do not send me away." There were tears streaming down her face.

"Look, Helen, I know you've been a good worker, but I can't trust you. Here, take a look at these letters."

She handed Helen two envelopes. Helen opened them and read the contents. She put the letters down and looked at Rachel in surprise. "These are all lies. I have never ever gone against my conscience and done what is stated in these letters. These are just malicious lies."

"Oh! I suppose that whoever wrote these letters just wrote them for fun. I knew you would deny it."

"Ms. Johnson, I swear that Mr. Johnson never violated his marriage vows with me."

"You know what happened in New Jersey?"

"Yes, Bridget told me when I came back the next day. Mr. Johnson was just an employer and a kind father to Barbara who only spoke to me concerning the welfare of your child. Nothing else, I assure you."

Rachel's face became contorted with rage, and her voice grew louder. "Look, Helen, I don't need your services nor do I care to be bothered about your personal problems. So, please pack your belongings and leave. Here is an envelope with money, and it includes today's pay as well."

Helen took the envelope and began sobbing bitterly.

"I want you out of this house by this afternoon."

"Yes, Ms… Williams," she said and left the room.

After packing her belongings, Helen hugged Marcy and the other staff and left the house. As she neared the gate, she turned towards the house and said under her breath,

'One day, I will make you pay for this injustice, Rachel Johnson.'

Rachel stood at the window watching her leave and saw Helen turn back and say something. She waited until Helen went out of the gate. She moved away from the window and started crying.

A week later, Martha came over to meet Rachel. Rachel told Martha the whole story over dinner.

"How could you let one incident with Barbara make you hate your own daughter?"

"I don't hate her. I just felt that since she preferred to be with Fred, the best thing was to let her go with him. I will fight for custody when they get back. Mr. Sagan is a good lawyer."

"Rachel, it seems that you have let all this wealth go to your head. You want to show that you are a strong independent woman, but you have neglected your duties as a mother and wife."

"Now, whose side are you on? Harry never cheated on you."

"I understand, Rachel, but for the sake of your daughter, you should have forgiven Fred."

"I am sure you would have done the same thing if Harry had cheated on you."

"I don't know what I would have done. Anyway, it is time to go to bed. I will see you in the morning."

The next morning, Martha noticed that Rachel had not yet come for breakfast. She asked Marcy if she had seen Rachel and Marcy replied she had not.

Rachel walked in looking flushed and ill. "Rachel, you look sick. Are you all right?"

"No, I'm not. I woke up feeling sick this morning. It may have been the dinner."

"Couldn't be, we ate the same food. Please have breakfast."

"No, I don't feel well at all." She sat down and placed her head in her hands.

Martha asked Marcy to call Dr. Thompson. Rachel went to her bedroom when Dr. Thompson arrived. He came out after a while looking very pale.

"What is it, Dr. Thompson? Is it bad news?"

"Not exactly. Rachel is pregnant."

"That's wonderful news, Doctor. Why do you look upset?"

"I advised Rachel after she had Barbara that she should not conceive again because she was not likely to survive the childbirth. The accident with the horse caused some damage to the uterus, and she bled a lot during her last delivery."

"Can she bring this baby to term?"

"Yes, she can," replied Dr. Thompson, "but she may die in the process of giving birth."

Martha gasped and held her hand to her mouth. "That is bad news, indeed. Have you told her yet?"

"I have, but she wants to go ahead with the pregnancy. She is resting right now. Let her rest; I will talk to her later."

An hour later, Rachel got up and went to the study. Martha was in there, reading. Martha congratulated Rachel and asked how she was feeling.

"I feel better. Thank you."

Martha hesitated and asked, "Are you going to tell Fred about the baby?"

"No, I'm not."

"Why?" asked Martha, a little shocked by the reply.

"He need not know now. He already has Barbara, and I am not going to let him come back and take this child. I am not going to make my pregnancy public, at least not until I start to show. I have also told Dr. Thompson and the staff not to mention it to anyone until I have done so."

"This pregnancy must have happened so that you two could get back together."

"As far as I am concerned, it happened because we were drunk."

"Dr. Thompson did tell you what could happen if you went ahead and had the baby?"

"Yes, he did, but I am confident that I will get through this. If I could survive that ordeal once, I can survive it again," said Rachel in a condescending tone.

"I never thought that you would behave in this manner, Rachel," said Martha, as she got up.

"You know what happened and how Fred cheated on me. How do you think I should behave? You know what we suffragettes believe in, and you introduced me to them."

"That is one thing that I rue daily. I wish I had never introduced you to them. It was all about the vote and we got that right. I see that you have none of the attributes that you used to have before you were married, and I am disappointed in you."

After saying that, Martha walked out of the room, leaving Rachel stunned at Martha's response. The last thing Fred said to Rachel about becoming a different woman came to her mind.

Almost five months later, when she could no longer hide her pregnancy, Rachel announced that she was pregnant. People who were not aware of the current marital problems asked why she had waited so long to announce her pregnancy and if Fred would be back in time for the delivery. She tactfully answered that, after her last difficult pregnancy, she was not sure if she could carry it to term and that Fred would be back when he finished his work on the West Coast.

As the baby grew within her, she grew more anxious about the birth. Nobody knew about the danger, except Martha. Rachel had no other family except for Aunt Victoria and her daughter's family who lived far away. Lucy was now in England. Someone had to take care of the child in case she did not survive the childbirth. Fred would eventually know about the child, but he needed to be here during the delivery if anything were to happen to her. She knew that Fred was a good father and had more right to the child than anyone else.

Marcy entered the room, placed a letter in front of her, and left. It was from Martha. Martha had heard that Rachel had announced her pregnancy. She urged Rachel to think of the unborn child, swallow her pride, and take Fred back. She needed to do that for the sake of the children and to let things be amicable if anything happened to Rachel. She hoped Rachel would make the right decision.

Rachel picked up the phone and asked the operator for Dr. Thompson's office. That evening, Dr. Thompson came and examined her. When he had finished, he told her that there was a slim chance that she might survive the childbirth, and she may start hemorrhaging if the uterus ruptures.

After Dr. Thompson left, Rachel wrote a letter. She called Robert in and said, "Please ask Alfred to post this immediately."

"Yes, Ms. Williams."

"It's Mrs. Johnson, Robert."

Robert looked at Rachel and smiled. "Yes, Mrs. Johnson."

Two weeks later, in San Francisco California:

Fred had just come home from the studio where he was having his portrait painted.

"Daddy, when can we go back to New York? I miss Mother terribly."

"When she realizes that she misses us, she will let us know when we can go back."

Cecil, the butler, handed over Fred a letter, which he opened and read.

Rachel apologized for the way she behaved towards Fred and for not being a mother to Barbara. She told him about her pregnancy and that she wanted Fred to be there since her chances of surviving the pregnancy were slim. She forgave Fred for all his transgressions and asked him to forgive her. She agreed that she had become another person and vowed that she would go back to her former self.

Fred reread the letter and tears streamed down his face. It was a bittersweet moment. He remembered that night when they were drunk. It was the night before the whole nightmare began. He straight away decided to go back to Rachel.

"Barbara," he shouted, "we are going back home to be with Mother again."

Fred went into his room and brought out the locket that Rachel had given Barbara on her first birthday. It had a picture of Barbara on one side and a picture of Fred and Rachel on the other. Under Barbara's picture were the words 'To Barbara on her first birthday, July 25, 1919.'

Barbara came running. Fred picked her up and put her on his lap. She began playing with his moustache, which he had grown while living in San Francisco. "Now you can wear the locket again. Let your mother see you wearing it when we meet her."

The next day, Fred bought tickets for the train leaving two weeks later and sent Rachel a telegram about their arrival in New York. He then met with a bootlegger to ship wine to his hotel in Manhattan.

Back in New York, Rachel read the telegram and closed her eyes. 'Everything is going to be just fine,' she said to herself. Rachel had no idea that it would not happen for a long time.

Chapter 5

The train departed San Francisco Station on its way to Colorado. "I will send the portrait as soon as it is completed, sir," said Cecil.

"Very good. Thank you for everything. Say bye to Cecil," said Fred, as the train pulled away from the station. Barbara waved at Cecil who waved back.

A few hours later, the train made its way up the Sierra Nevada Mountains. Barbara went towards the window, looked at the mountains, and said, "Daddy, don't they look pretty with all the snow on top?"

"Yes, they do, and I'm sure that your sibling will be as beautiful as those mountains."

That was the last thing Barbara heard Fred say. The next moment, she heard people crying for help, as the carriage started slanting downwards.

"Daddy," she cried, as she saw the water gushing into the carriage. The train had gone over a bridge built of wood and steel in the 1880s over the river. Mild tremors had struck the area a few days earlier, weakening the bridge. The weight of the trains passing since then had further weakened the supporting beams. The swollen river flowing rapidly due to the recent rains and melting snow caused the small cracks in the structure to widen. The strong current dragged Barbara. She felt somebody pulling her out of the water and dragging her to the shore. She then passed out.

Barbara got up moaning and opened her eyes. She saw a man with a blond beard looking at her.

"You're up! Are you all right?"

"Yes."

"What's your name?"

"I... I don't know."

"Who was with you on the train?"

"I don't know. My head hurts," and she held her head.

"You must have bumped your head as the train fell." Barbara looked at his hands and saw broken chains hanging from them.

"I thought chains go around the neck, like the one I have around mine."

"In certain cases yes, not always," he said, amused.

"What's your name?"

"John Monroe. See, I remember my name."

"I'm sorry that I can't remember mine," she said with a sad face.

"It is all right, I will call you Little Girl."

Just then, they heard a gunshot.

"Come on, we have to go. I'll take you with me; you may be useful to me."

He held Barbara's hand, and they walked into the thick woods.

John Monroe was the illegitimate son of a Norwegian immigrant, who did not want to have anything to do with him, since his family was on its way to the United States. After giving birth to John, his mother went to work as a maid. She married the gardener and had five more children. Mr. Monroe adopted John giving him his last name. John, unfortunately, inherited his biological father's height, hair, and bad habits. He was expelled from school at the age of fourteen when he was discovered stealing from the principal's office. He discovered during this robbery that he had a knack for picking locks, and breaking into safes.

He joined a band of robbers and started robbing banks. Being tall and muscular, he was a great asset. At the age of twenty, when trying to rob a bank, he accidentally shot and killed the guard on duty. The police went on a manhunt, and he was caught hiding in a brothel in Los Angeles. He was brought back to San Francisco where he stood trial, and was sentenced to twenty years in prison on charges of manslaughter and armed robbery. He had spent three years in jail and was being transferred to Denver, Colorado, to stand trial for a crime he had committed there. He was chained to the seat, with two police officers, one on either side of him.

John broke free when the carriage he was traveling in broke apart and was swept by the current. He managed to swim towards the riverbank. He saw Barbara holding a piece of wood, screaming. He jumped back into the river and pulled her out. Both the police officers survived the accident. They took out their pistols and went in search of John. One of them fell on a rock and accidentally shot himself in the leg. John and Barbara heard this shot. After walking for several hours, they reached a clearing. It was dark and they were tired. The weather got colder, so John collected some sticks and built a fire.

When Barbara said she was hungry, John went towards a tree and collected a few apples. He gave one to Barbara and ate the rest. After eating, Barbara yawned, indicating that she was sleepy. John made a clearing near the fire for Barbara to sleep. When she was asleep, John took a closer look at the gold chain around her neck. Greed overtook him, and he opened the locket and saw the pictures. He unhooked the clasp and took the chain from her neck. He took the locket out, put it in her pocket, and put the chain into his pocket. 'She will be a liability to me and will slow me down. I must be on my way.'

He heard Barbara moan as he got up. He felt a sense of remorse and this was one of the few times, he felt this way. 'I cannot do this. I cannot leave her here all by herself. She may get sick and die or be killed by some wild animal. I cannot have another death on my conscience.'

He threw some dirt on the flames to kill the fire. John lifted Barbara up, put her over his right shoulder, and went into the woods. He walked for about a mile and came to a log cabin. He went near the window and looked inside. He saw a woman sitting on a chair stitching some clothes and a man smoking his pipe.

'These people look like some nice old folks who will take care of this child. I will leave her outside.' John went to the front door and placed Barbara gently in front of it. He took one last look at her and said, "Saving you is the only good thing I have ever done in my life. May God consider this good act when I meet Him in the next life. I hope you find your family and are happy." He kissed her and disappeared into the woods.

* * * * *

The people inside the cabin were Annette and Pierre, who were eagerly waiting for the day to board the ship that would take them back to France.

"Our last few days in America and then we sail back home to France," said Annette.

"Yes, ma cherie, we have spent over five years here. We are doing the right thing by going back."

They heard a loud cry. "What was that, Pierre?" asked Annette.

"Sounded like a cat."

"It may be the police." She listened again and said, "No, it sounds more like a child crying."

"It must be a wild animal. There is no way a child could be out here." The crying got louder.

"Pierre, please look outside, someone might be in trouble," her voice was getting anxious.

Pierre took his double barrel gun and opened the door. He found Barbara sitting outside, crying. She looked at him and said, "Papa", wrapped her arms around his leg, and cried. He called Annette who came out and picked up the child. She took her inside and tried to comfort her. Pierre closed the door and went near them.

"Mama, Mama."

"Yes dear, what is it?"

"Did you see that big man?"

"No dear, you just had a bad dream. What is your name?"

"I don't know."

"Never mind, now go to sleep."

The child whimpered, closed her eyes, and fell asleep. Annette carried her and put her on the bed. Before covering her, Annette went through her pockets and found the locket.

"Pierre, look what I found." She showed Pierre the locket and he opened it. They both looked at the pictures in the locket.

"Must be her parents," said Annette.

"Yes. I wonder why they abandoned her on our doorstep. They don't look poor."

"Who wouldn't want such a sweet child?"

"It could be that her parents died and who knows…" Annette's eyes widened with excitement. "Pierre, this maybe the child, the priest who visited our village, told us that we would find in America. She is just how he described her. Look at her brown curls and blue eyes!"

"Yes, but she also has her parents."

"They may have died or may not want her. That is why they left her on our doorstep."

"But, why leave a locket in her pocket?"

"She could probably trace her family when she comes of age. She called me 'mama' and that made me bond with her at once. Please let us keep her."

"I don't know what to say, Annette."

"Pierre, when she called you 'papa', did you have a strange feeling passing through you?"

"Yes, I did. It made me feel like I was her father."

"Yes, that's exactly what I felt when she called me 'mama'. Please, Pierre, let us keep her. It looks like she does not remember her real parents. Perhaps it is a sign that we are getting another chance to be parents again. Please Pierre."

Pierre thought for some time. He looked at Annette and saw her eyes pleading with him. He remembered the reason they had come to America in the first place.

"Yes, I see what you mean. We'll keep her and raise her as our own, but how are we going to take her to France?"

"Pierre, we have some extra money Mother Grace gave me. We can buy a passage for her on the ship."

"Yes, we can do that."

"Thank you, Pierre," said Annette, and she hugged him.

"What about this locket?"

"I will keep it with me," said Annette.

"We will go and see Mother Grace tomorrow."

"Yes, we will go together and ask her what to do. Do you know something? The police are perhaps looking for a man and a woman but not a couple with a child. Therefore, she will be helpful to us as well. Let us call her by our dead daughter's name."

The next day, they drove down the mountain. Annette was pleased that the child kept clinging to her as the car drove down the winding road of the mountains.

'Mother Grace,' as she was affectionately known, ran an orphanage that helped destitute women and orphans. Her real name was Grace Halliday. Annette worked as a cook and helped take care of the orphans, and Pierre worked on the vineyard owned by Mother Grace's brother.

Pierre parked the car, got out, and went to meet Mother Grace while Annette stayed in the car with the child. "Mother Grace, we found this abandoned girl on our doorstep last night, and we want to adopt her. Could you please help us?"

Mother Grace looked at him and said, "Why do you want her? You have known her for a short duration of one night only."

"She calls us 'mama' and 'papa.' She is very attached to us, and that is a good enough reason to adopt her."

"Did she have anything that might identify her?"

"No, Mother Grace," he said, without batting an eye. He knew he was lying.

"What have you decided to name her?"

"Annette and I have decided to call her Catherine."

The middle-aged woman shook her head and said, "All right, I will meet this girl."

The two of them walked towards Annette and the child.

"Hello, little girl. Who are your parents?" The girl looked confused and turned towards Pierre and Annette. "What is your name?"

"I don't know."

Mother Grace held out her hands, encouraging the girl to come to her, but she wrapped her arms around Annette's waist and buried her head in Annette's skirt.

"All right, I have seen enough. She seems to have taken to you. I will help you adopt her."

"Thank you, Mother Grace," said Pierre.

"I have no doubt that Annette and you will take care of her and will treat her as your own."

The adoption papers were drawn up quickly - thanks to the influence of Mother Grace - and her ticket to France was booked. The girl's name was officially Catherine Boucher.

A week later, the Bouchers were on their way to France. "We got what we came for. We found the daughter that the priest said we would find," said Annette.

"You are forgetting another important thing," said Pierre.

"What is that?"

"We have, once again, become very close." Annette looked at him and realized that it was true. She fell into Pierre's arms and hugged him as they both watched the Californian coast disappear.

* * * * *

Marcy picked the newspaper from the doorstep and was shocked when she read about the disaster. She was not sure if it was the same train, Fred and Barbara were traveling in. She decided to hide the newspaper.

When Rachel was having her breakfast, she noticed the newspaper missing. "Marcy, where is the paper?"

"It has not yet been delivered."

"That is the second time this month that the paper has not been delivered." Marcy nodded and walked away. An hour later, Rachel rang for Marcy. "Marcy, please tell Alfred that I will be going to the hotel in Manhattan."

"Mrs. Johnson, the doctor advised rest."

"I know that, Marcy. I have some accounts I need to settle before

Mr. Johnson and Barbara get here." At the mention of their names, Marcy let out a small gasp. "Is anything the matter, Marcy?"

"No... I am not feeling well."

"Then, get some rest, after you have told Alfred to get the car ready."

Fifteen minutes later, Rachel was on her way to Manhattan. When she entered the hotel, she saw a man sitting in the lounge reading the New York Times. She saw the headlines: 'Train Disaster in the Sierra Nevada Mountains.' She hurried towards the man and snatched the paper from him. As she read the article, her eyes widened with horror. She collapsed on the floor. Two men gently picked her up and placed her on a couch. A man claiming to be a doctor tended to her. She opened her eyes and whispered, "Take... take me home," and lost consciousness.

She was put inside the car, and the man claiming to be a doctor got in. The car drove to the Johnson Manor. The doctor got out and told Marcy to call the family doctor. The doctor asked Robert and Alfred to help carry Rachel to her room. He revived her, and she woke up crying. Dr. Thompson arrived in the meantime. When Rachel saw Dr. Thompson, she began to cry hysterically. "Dr. Thompson... Fred and Barbara... they were on the train. I know it." He tried to comfort her, but all she could do was cry. Dr. Thompson gave her an injection to calm her down. He then went out and met the doctor.

"What is your name?"

"Maurice Barton. I am a psychiatric intern at Harvard Medical School. I was in the Johnson Hotel when I saw her collapse. I did what I could to help her."

"Thank you, Dr. Barton. You did well. You will definitely be a good doctor someday."

Dr. Barton smiled and said that he had to leave. Alfred drove him to the train station to get back to Manhattan.

In the meantime, Marcy called up Rudy. He came over to the house immediately and spoke to Dr. Thompson. "She's in shock which is not good for her."

"What should we do?" asked Rudy.

"She needs only rest and no excitement at all. Anything shocking could make her go into labor, and she is not ready yet. I hope that the news is not true."

Rachel slept throughout the day and night while Marcy and Rudy kept watch. She woke up the next morning, still shocked. The death of her parents came back to haunt her. It looked like everyone whom she loved was dying.

Marcy entered the bedroom and greeted Rachel. Rachel ignored the greeting and shouted almost hysterically, "Where is today's paper? Has it come?"

"It has not yet come, Mrs. Johnson."

"Do not lie to me. I want to see today's paper." Rachel got out of the bed, ran out of the door past Marcy, and ran down the stairs. When she reached the bottom of the stairs, she let out a loud scream and clutched her stomach.

"The baby... I think the baby is coming."

Marcy put her hand to her mouth and exclaimed, "Oh no!"

Rudy rushed out from one of the rooms and caught hold of Rachel. Marcy called for Alfred. Rudy and Alfred carried Rachel to the car and drove to St. Leo's Hospital run by Dr. Thompson. Rachel was bleeding profusely and groaning in pain.

"I was afraid this would happen," said Dr. Thompson. Rachel was taken to the labor room to be prepared for the delivery. One of the nurses pulled her dress up and spread her legs apart. Dr. Thompson stood with his hands reaching out and shouted, "Push, Rachel, push. The baby is ready to come out."

"Doctor, I am only about seven months."

"That's fine, the baby is coming out. Now, do your part." Rachel took a deep breath and pushed. Only a few gasps escaped from her. "Push harder, Rachel."

"I am trying to," she managed to say.

"Try harder," he commanded her once again. "I'm going to use the forceps".

She took a deep breath and pushed. She was getting weaker by the minute due to the heavy loss of blood. She took another deep breath and pushed as she clutched the bed sheets for support. "Come on, more effort. I can see the head." She took a deep breath, once again, and pushed harder, screaming with pain, as it racked through her body.

Rachel then heard the baby's cry and was relieved. She fell back on the pillow, exhausted.

"Congratulations! It's a boy."

Rachel did not respond. She passed out with exhaustion, and she was bleeding profusely. Dr. Thompson asked the nurse to get Rachel ready for a hysterectomy. The hysterectomy was a success, and Dr. Thompson managed to stop the bleeding. However, Rachel lost a lot of blood and was in a coma for a week, during which, she had to have several blood transfusions.

After Rachel came out of her weeklong coma, and she was strong enough, Dr. Thompson told her that Fred was dead and Barbara was missing.

"No, that can't be," cried Rachel hysterically.

Dr. Thompson sat by her side, held her hand, and said, "Rachel, I know you are upset. Please be strong for your son. He needs you right now."

She cried for a few minutes, then sat up, and wiped away her tears. She tried to sound composed and said, "All right, please give him to me."

Dr. Thompson signaled to the nurse standing at the door, and she entered carrying the baby.

She placed the baby in Rachel's arms. Rachel looked at the baby and smiled.

"He has his father's blue eyes."

"Yes, he has. He will grow up to be as handsome as Fred."

"Where is Rudy?"

"He has gone to California to bring back Fred's body. Since you were in no condition to travel and were in a coma for a week, he volunteered to go and identify the body, and bring it back."

"If not for Rudy, I would be lost, Dr. Thompson. Is there any hope for Barbara?"

"I'm afraid not, Rachel. The rescue teams have combed the entire length of the river for several miles, and there has been no trace of Barbara. Several missing people cannot be found. The river was overflowing due to the recent rains."

Rachel began to cry. "Barbara, I wish you were here to see your brother. I'm not giving up hope that you will be found."

"Yes, she may be found one day, Rachel," said Dr. Thompson, patting her arm.

The baby woke up and began to cry. "He needs you now."

"Thank you, Dr. Thompson." He smiled and left the room along with the nurse. Rachel began nursing the baby.

A few days later, Rudy arrived with the embalmed body of Fred. Rachel was well enough to leave the hospital. All of New York's elite attended the funeral. Before the funeral, Rachel had the casket opened to have a look at Fred's body. Fred looked peaceful, as if asleep. The embalmers had done a good job. Rachel held her son over the coffin so that the baby could see the body.

"Here is your son, Fred. The son you always wanted. Here is Andrew Frederick Johnson." Rachel almost thought the body smiled. She struggled to remain composed as she wiped away her tears and signaled for the casket to be closed. A few days later, the child was baptized at St. Mark's Church. Martha and Rudy were the godparents.

Chapter 6

Normandy, 1899

Pierre was a blacksmith's assistant. He was born in the village of St. Lacroix to a farmer who grew apples and pears, and made cider. Right from an early age, he knew that farming was not for him and decided to join Francois, the blacksmith. Francois taught him how to make horseshoes, fix farm tools, and help fix other farming equipment. Francois was also an avid hunter and taught Pierre to hunt. Occasionally Pierre would help his father in the orchard, pruning trees and picking apples. He would also help make cider, bottle, and sell it. He preferred being a blacksmith but felt that his main duty was to his father and the farm, which he was going to inherit as his older brother died of sunstroke. To put food on the table, he would go to the woods and hunt rabbits or deer. He also learned how to fish in the sea, but hunting was his passion.

It was while returning from one of his hunting trips that he felt hungry and could not wait to get home. He hung the dead rabbits, which he had killed, from his bicycle and started speeding towards home. After he left the woods, while riding on a narrow road on a small hill near the seashore, he saw a girl riding her bicycle coming towards him. He thought he could pass her on the narrow road. As they came closer, he could see that she was struggling to ride the bicycle and got nervous. She veered to the right and started going down the hill towards a huge boulder at the bottom of the hill.

"Jump, jump," he shouted loudly.

The girl panicked and let go of the handles. She tried to jump, but the bicycle started tilting to the left, and she fell to the ground filled with tiny rocks. Pierre ran down the hill and lifted the girl.

"Mademoiselle, Mademoiselle, are you all right?"

"Oui Monsieur."

Pierre helped her get up and she thanked him. Their eyes met, and he noticed that she had the most beautiful eyes he had ever seen. She bent down, picked up her hat, and ran downhill to pick up her bicycle. She examined her bicycle and saw that the front rim had been damaged. She looked at him in anger and yelled, "You have destroyed my bicycle. Look at it, you fool."

"I'm Sorry, Mademoiselle. I was in a hurry to get home."

"Your hurry has caused you to ruin my bicycle," she retorted angrily.

"Sorry, Mademoiselle. I am Francois the blacksmith's assistant, and I will gladly fix the bicycle for you at no cost."

"Good, but how will I get home? I need to be home in a few minutes," she said, trying her best to be rude.

"You take my bicycle and I will take yours. You can come to the shop tomorrow at noon, and I will have fixed it for you."

"Good," she said sarcastically.

Pierre transferred the dead rabbits on to her bicycle, and she rode off on Pierre's bicycle.

"Au revoir," he shouted. She did not respond.

Pierre was surprised that she did not seem interested in him. He was not bad looking. He had brown hair, brown eyes, and a strong body, doing all that farm labor and working at the blacksmith's shop. He had had a few girl friends off and on and knew that women always found him very attractive.

His stomach started growling. He dragged the bicycle as he walked home.

The next day, Pierre woke up early and went to the blacksmith's shop. He worked on the front rim of the bicycle and fixed it before the girl arrived promptly at noon.

"Good afternoon, Mademoiselle," he said with a smile.

"Good afternoon," she said, with no expression on her face. "Is my bicycle ready?"

"Almost, Mademoiselle. Please do sit down," said Pierre, pointing to the wooden chair.

Pierre went back into the workshop and pretended to work on the bicycle. Fifteen minutes later, he came out with the bicycle.

"Here you are, Mademoiselle," he said with a smile.

She got up, looked at the bicycle, and smiled for the first time. "It is wonderful. It looks better than it did before."

"Merci, Mademoiselle. Could you please tell me your name?"

She looked at him and asked, "Is it of any importance to you?"

The question surprised him. Girls usually told him their names without being asked, and even if he did ask, they never replied so sharply. He decided to keep a bold front and said, "Yes, Mademoiselle, it is of great importance to me."

She looked at him shocked and then smiled and said, "You did a good job repairing my bicycle. My name is Annette, but people call me Anne."

Pierre smiled and said, "Anne, my name is Pierre."

"Merci beaucoup, Pierre. I better be going home."

"Au revoir, Anne."

That night, Pierre could not sleep. Anne's face came to his mind every time he closed his eyes. He saw her with her family at church on Sunday. He asked his friend, Francois, about her.

"Yes, she is Annette, the niece of Jean Dupuit."

"She is beautiful," said Pierre.

"Yes, she is. Do you like her, Pierre?"

"Oui."

"Then, you should ask her for a dance at the church fair."

"How long has she been in our village?"

"About two months. I heard that after her father died, her mother, Monica, came to live here along with her four children. Annette is the oldest. They lived in Toulouse."

"Thank you, Francois. I will ask her for a dance at the church fair next Sunday night."

One week later, the church grounds were illuminated. People were selling rosaries and candles to be lit in front of the statues of Christ and the Virgin Mary. There were stalls where people were selling flowers, food, and other items. At the church hall, there was a band of musicians playing, and people were dancing to the music. Pierre was with Francois, and they were walking around. They went into the church hall to watch people dancing. Francois spotted Annette with her sisters. He patted Pierre's back in excitement and said,

"Pierre, look, there is Annette. Now is your chance."

"What if she refuses?"

"Then you ask her again. Be quick, before someone else asks her." He almost pushed Pierre towards Annette. After regaining his balance, Pierre walked towards Annette and said,

"Excusez moi, do you remember me?"

Annette and her sisters looked at him and there was a look of recognition on Annette's face. "Ah, yes, you are the one who fixed my bicycle."

"It was my pleasure, Mademoiselle. Mademoiselle Annette, may I have the pleasure of this dance, please?"

Annette looked startled and looked at her sisters. "I guess so," she managed to mumble. Her sisters giggled.

She stepped towards Pierre, and they walked to the dance floor. They danced quietly to the music. After the musicians stopped playing and while they were getting ready for the next dance, Pierre asked, "How long have you been here?"

"About two months. After my father died, my mother came here to live close to her brother. She brought me, my sisters, and my brother along."

"I am sorry about your father."

"Thank you."

"I know your uncle, Monsieur Jean Dupuit."

"Really? He has been very kind to us ever since we have been here."

"Have you been around the surrounding areas, like the woods and the beach?"

"No. My uncle is too busy with his son and farming, and my mother still mourns for my father. My brother is trying to learn how to be a farmer."

"Would you like me to show you around?"

Her eyes widened with excitement. "Yes, I would like that."

"Meet me tomorrow noon under the big pine tree near my shop, and I will show you around."

"Merci beaucoup, Monsieur Pierre. You are very kind."

The musicians began playing, and they started dancing.

The next day, Pierre took the afternoon off and went to the rendezvous point to meet Annette. He saw her waiting under the tree with a basket. He went towards her riding on his bicycle and greeted her.

"Where would you like to go?"

"I would like to go to the beach. I have never gone into the sea in my life."

"That is one experience everyone should have in their life. I think I will make it happen today."

"Don't you have to go back to work?"

"No, I took sick leave," he said and winked at her. Annette laughed a bit. Pierre put the picnic basket in the basket behind the seat of his bicycle, and they walked towards the beach. When they reached the shore, Annette took a blanket from the basket and spread it on the sand. They sat down and ate the sandwiches Annette had made. After drinking some wine, Pierre said, "Now, I will take you for your first dip in the sea." They got up and walked towards the water.

"This is lovely. The sea is beautiful, and the water is so cool and nice." She bent down, took some water, and splashed it on Pierre. He smiled, took some water, and threw it back on her. They started splashing water on each other. All of a sudden, they were knocked down by a wave, and Pierre fell on top of Annette. The next moment, they found themselves kissing each other. They pulled away, saw the shocked expression on each other's faces, and laughed.

A few months later, Pierre asked Annette to marry him, and she accepted. The only problem was, Annette's mother was horrified because she was still mourning for her dead husband. She ranted and raved that her husband was not yet cold in his grave, and Annette was marrying a stranger in such a short time. Jean Dupuit, her brother, stepped in. He knew Pierre and his family and managed to convince Monica that this was what her husband would have wanted. She finally agreed; Annette and Pierre were married in the local village church.

A few months later, Annette became pregnant. Pierre had now stopped working at the blacksmith's shop and was working with his father at the family orchard. They were living with Pierre's parents.

Nine months later, Annette gave birth to a boy. They named him Louis. She was ecstatic with the birth of her son. He would be the heir to all the farmland that his father's family owned. She wanted to have a girl the next time. After three years, Annette was pregnant once again. The months went by and she was sure that this was going to be a girl. In the eight month of her pregnancy, as she walked down the stairs, she slipped and fell. She landed at the bottom of the stairs on her stomach and started bleeding profusely. The doctor came and tried to deliver the baby. The baby, a girl, was born dead.

The doctor gave Pierre the bad news that Annette would never be able to have any more children. Annette was devastated. Pierre began to notice a change in Annette. She would pine for her dead daughter whom she had decided to name Catherine. She would get into a terrible rage anytime somebody mentioned her. She had this image of her daughter in her mind that she was blue eyed, with brown curls, and a very pretty face.

Pierre and his parents brought up Louis. Annette constantly begged Pierre to make love to her so that she could conceive. Pierre submitted because he loved her. He would do anything for her. Nothing happened, and her inability to conceive would drive her into deep depression. Her periods of depression would last a very long time. Pierre took her to various doctors to get her treated. Nothing worked.

Finally, after years of putting up with Annette, he threatened to institutionalize her. That brought her out of her depression and she slowly began to recover. She never got over the loss of her daughter. By the time she recovered, the war had begun.

On June 28, 1914, Archduke Franz Ferdinand, heir to the Austro-Hungarian throne and his wife, Sophie, were shot and killed by Gavrilo Princip, a Bosnian member of the Black Hand. The situation escalated and resulted in a world war.

France soon joined the war. Pierre and Francois decided to enlist and fight in the army. Francois was married and had three children. Annette begged Pierre not to go. He insisted that his duty lay in defending France. Both Francois and Pierre joined the army and went to the training camp. After training, they were sent to fight in the trenches.

It was during this time that Annette became close to her son. She regretted the years she spent mourning for her dead daughter. Louis was surprised that his mother was showing some interest in him. When he was growing up, she would sometimes ignore him and then show a lot of affection. Her periods of depression were what turned him away from her. He doted on Pierre and his grandparents. Pierre's mother became a surrogate mother to Louis when Annette was still mourning for her daughter. At first, he resisted, but then found it in his heart to forgive her, and they bonded very well. Annette would wake up early and along with the other women of the village, go to church to pray for the safe return of the men. Louis, in the absence of his father, had learned how to manage the farm and make cider. He seemed to have inherited his grandfather's ability to manage the farm and was very good at it.

In late 1915, the French Commander-in-Chief, Joseph Joffre, came up with the idea of a joint French–British attack against the Germans. The first day of battle began on July 1, 1916, north of the Somme River and went on until November 1916. It was during one of these battles that Pierre and Francois happened to be fighting together. At the end of the day, Pierre was shot in the arm and knee, and Francois was dead with a bullet straight to his chest.

Pierre was taken to a military hospital for surgery, and while the doctors were able to remove the bullets, there was damage to his knee. He was discharged from the army, and he went back to the farm.

Annette was relieved that Pierre came home alive rather than in a coffin, like Francois. She could see the pain in the face of Francois' widow, whenever they met. She took care of Pierre, and their love for each other was rekindled. They continued to work on their issues, until an American missionary came to their village.

Fr. James Norton was a Jesuit Priest who had come to France with the Red Cross to take care of the children orphaned during the war. He was staying at St. Lacroix for a few days, when he went to the village church and happened to meet Annette. She told him about how she lost her daughter, and Pierre's miraculous escape in the Somme Battle. He told her that he worked in an orphanage in California before coming to France. The orphanage was located at the foot of the Sierra Nevada Mountains and was run by a woman called Grace Halliday. She was looking for women to help her with the orphans. Her brother, Mark Halliday, had a vineyard close by and wanted someone from France to help him with the farm machinery and help him make wine. Fr. Norton suggested that Annette and Pierre move to California. Annette could work in the orphanage and Pierre at the vineyard.

On her way home, Annette thought about what Fr. Norton had told her. She never did completely get over the death of her daughter, and Pierre always wanted to immigrate to America for a little while and learn how to grow grapes and make wine. He always talked about going to California. He also wanted to get away from the bad memories. This was a good opportunity for them to leave and seek their fortune in America. However, due to the war, they were hesitant to leave France.

A few days later, Annette went back to Fr. Norton and told him her concerns. He said that he had the gift to see the future if he prayed over her. She agreed, and he put his hands on her head and prayed. He said aloud, "I see a young girl with blue eyes and brown curls. She will come to you. You need to go to California to help this girl. She will replace your daughter whom you lost."

"Will she be at the orphanage?"

"No, she will come to you."

Annette was excited. She now felt that she had spiritual confirmation that they were meant to go to America. She hurried home and found Pierre sitting in the garden. She ran to him, excited. "Pierre, Pierre. I met this American Missionary in church by the name of Fr. James Norton. He talked about a woman who has an orphanage in California, and her brother owns a vineyard. We have been waiting for this opportunity. You have always wanted to go to California to learn how to grow grapes and make wine, and I have always felt guilty for giving birth to our dead daughter and destroying the possibility of having more children. The priest had a vision when he prayed over me and saw that we will find a girl who will replace our daughter. Can we go there and begin a new life? Please, say yes."

Pierre looked at her and said, "No."

Her smile vanished; she stared at him and said, "Why did you say no?"

"It is because I'm tired of hearing about our dead daughter. How could you fall for such nonsense?"

Annette began to cry. "Pierre, you don't understand. This is a good chance for us to do what we desire. Louis is old enough and takes good care of the farm."

"I said, no. I do not want to talk about it. Now, leave me alone."

Annette ran into the house crying. Pierre sat thinking. He thought about the day he met Annette. He thought about the happy times they had together and the sad times after that. He thought about everything he could remember. It was true that it was not a happy marriage. It all started because of her miscarriage. He went to war mainly to fight for France and to get away from Annette. The separation made him realize how much he missed his wife and son. He was happy, in a way, that he was injured in the war because he could come back home, but the sad part was that Francois died in the same battle in which he was wounded.

He could not bear to see Francois' wife, Marie, and their three children, because he knew that Francois died trying to save his life. Francois jumped in front of him and took the bullet that would have hit Pierre in the chest. When Annette came with the news and told him how guilty she felt about the miscarriage, it brought some painful and guilt feelings about Francois' sacrifice. He thought about Annette's proposal and realized that the village held many painful memories for both of them. It would be better to leave France and go to America, maybe for a while, or maybe for forever. He always wanted to do this and now, there was a sign from the priest. He wiped the tears rolling down his cheeks and went into the house.

A few days later, Pierre and Annette were on their way to America. After a stormy crossing, and fearing that they would be sunk by German U-boats, they came close to the American coast.

They were relieved when they heard that the Statue of Liberty was spotted. They ran up from their third class cabin, along with the other immigrants, and went onto the deck. Annette started crying as she crossed herself and said to Pierre, "That statue gives me hope. We, the French people, gave it to America as a gift. I know that things will be good for us in this country. I can feel it." Pierre gave her a reassuring hug.

They landed at Ellis Island, and were processed. They were relieved that they were not detained like some of their fellow passengers for having lice in their hair or diseases. They went through grueling physical, mental, and literacy tests to prove that they were fit to enter the new world.

After many days of traveling by land from the East Coast, Pierre and Annette arrived at the orphanage run by Grace Halliday. They had references from Fr. Norton. Grace found them to be friendly and cheerful. They insisted on talking to her in English so that they could become fluent in the language. Grace Halliday read the reference letters for each of them and was satisfied. She took them around the orphanage. Annette and Pierre saw the rooms where children between one and two years of age were being cared for. They were also shown the rooms where the older children, infants, and unwed mothers were being looked after.

"When did you start this orphanage, Miss Halliday?"

"My father used to own the vineyard where Pierre wants to work. My brother now owns it. He wanted me to get married. I said that I would give it a thought. One day in 1888, when I went to San Francisco, I saw this child abandoned on the roadside. I immediately asked the driver to stop the carriage and got out. I took this little girl in my arms, and she stopped crying. It was then that I realized that my destiny lay in taking care of unwanted children. I felt that it was no use getting married and taking care of a house and family when children were being abandoned on the streets and did not have anyone to take care of them. I took the child home and told my father that I did not want to get married but take care of abandoned children and help unwed mothers. My father, of course, was livid. The thought of his dear daughter giving up everything to take care of abandoned children was out of question. He refused to help me start my orphanage. My mother was dying, and she left me a small inheritance, which was not sufficient. It was my brother, Mark, who understood me and helped me start this orphanage. Over the years, I have had a number of volunteers and full time workers. It has, therefore, been a success."

She looked at Annette and smiled. "Annette, I am glad that you have come to work here."

"I am very pleased, Madame Halliday. I like what I have seen and am very happy to be here."

"Good, Annette. You can start work tomorrow and Pierre, my brother will come and take you to the vineyard in the morning. I am sure you will like what he has to show you."

"Thank you, Madame Halliday. I am looking forward to working in the vineyard."

"Why is your orphanage so far away from the city and close to the mountains?" asked Pierre.

"This place is safer for the unwed mothers. When I started the orphanage in the city, the building used to be attacked, and people used to protest outside because it was deemed that these women had fornicated and were sinners. For their protection and everyone's safety,

I decided to move closer to the mountains. I have a small place in the city to keep women for the night and then bring them here because they are safer here."

Grace Halliday showed them the accommodation she had prepared for them. Pierre and Annette slept well that night. They knew at once that they had made the right decision to come to America. This, was a fresh start, from all the pain that they had gone through in France and felt that they would be happy here.

The next morning, after breakfast, they heard the sound of a car. They looked out of the window and saw a middle-aged man coming towards the house. They saw Grace Halliday run and give him a hug. They heard them talk and laugh and saw them come up to the door of the building. Pierre opened the door for Grace and the older man.

"Howdy you two. Did you sleep well?"

"Good morning. Yes, we did," said Pierre.

"Good. Annette and Pierre, this is my brother, Mark Halliday. He owns the vineyard where Pierre is interested in working."

"Pleased to meet you, Mr. Halliday," they said in unison.

Mark Halliday was taller than Pierre, middle aged, and had a big graying moustache. He seemed to have a very benign face and a friendly personality. He shook Pierre's hand and kissed Annette's.

"Pleased to meet you both. Grace has told me all about you. I am very pleased that you have come, Pierre. I have always wanted someone to show me the French way of making wine. I think you also know how to make cider from apples?"

"Yes, I own an apple orchard in Normandy, and I learned how to make wine from my father's cousin in Bordeaux, when I was young. I always wanted to come to California and try my hand at wine making."

"Wonderful!" Halliday exclaimed. "Are you ready to leave and take a tour of my vineyard? We can learn a lot from each other."

"Yes, I am, Mr. Halliday."

They went out of the cottage, and Mark escorted them to the car. Pierre got into the car; Mark kissed Grace and got in. The car started and they headed to the vineyard.

After showing Pierre the vineyard and the wine making process, they went to the house. It was a warm day. Mark had fruits and wine bottles spread out on a table. He invited Pierre to sit down. A maid came and poured the wine for them. After she left, Mark said,

"Pierre, is there anything you would like to ask me?"

"Yes, Monsieur Halliday. When did people start to grow grapes in this beautiful state?"

Mark chuckled a bit, and Pierre looked startled.

"I am sorry, Pierre. I admire your interest in the history of growing grapes in this region. I guess it is because you come from France where growing grapes has more of a history than America. Anyway, to answer your question: In 1769, a priest by the name of Fr. Jumpero Serra from Baja, brought vines and taught the native Indians to gather grapes, prepare the earth, trample the grapes, and place them in suspended cow skins to slowly leak into casks that would be left to ferment. The wine making techniques and the vineyards spread as the mission spread. In 1830, the missions were secularized and that was the end of the vineyards in California, or so it looked that way…" Mark paused, drank from his glass, and continued. "It was good that General Mariano Guadeloupe Vallejo, California's Mexican Governor, arrived in Sonoma and revived the vineyards in 1833. General Vallejo offered George C. Yount land in Napa. At the same time, a fellow countryman of yours, Jean-Louis Vignes, came to Los Angeles from Bordeaux, France, and by 1840 had developed his 100 acre El Aliso Vineyard. From then on, various people came and helped develop the wine making business in California. My father bought this vineyard from a man named John Meyer when he grew too old, and could no longer take care of it."

"Mon Dieu," said Pierre. "I did not know that Napa Valley had such an interesting history."

Mark noticed that Pierre had finished his glass of wine. "Would you like another glass of wine?"

"Yes, I would. Thank you." Mark poured him a glass. "I have some good news for you."

"What is it?" Pierre asked with excitement.

"A few days back, I found that my manager, who was in charge of my vineyard and the winery, was secretly selling grapes to others without my knowledge. I had to fire him. Since you are knowledgeable about growing grapes and wine making, I have decided to put you in charge of my property. I hope you will accept this position."

"Yes, I accept. Merci beaucoup, Monsieur Halliday."

"I am glad that you have accepted my offer. You will have to stay here in the house which my manager occupied."

"Thank you for your generosity, Mr. Halliday. Can my wife stay here with me?"

"She can, if she wants to, but the only problem is that, if she wants to work at the orphanage, she cannot, since it is very far, and Grace would want her to assist her at all times. You ask your wife, and we will see what she says."

Pierre was back at the orphanage a few hours later. He told Annette all that he had seen and asked her about staying with him at the vineyard. Annette thought for a little while and said,

"I want to work here, Pierre, but cannot stand the thought of being away from you. I am undecided on what to do."

"I will ask Monsieur Halliday if we can meet every weekend and if he would let me drive up here."

"That is a wonderful idea, Pierre. From what you have told me, he sounds like a good man."

"Yes, he is. I am sure he will agree."

Mark agreed to Pierre's idea, and the next day, Pierre kissed Annette goodbye, took his bags, and moved into the house at the vineyard. Pierre started working at the vineyard. He was managing the entire operations: from plucking the grapes, to storing them, and converting them into wine. He found that the knowledge he acquired while helping his father and uncle in France, was very useful to him. The workers at the vineyard were very pleasant to work with. Mark was away most of the time trying to find buyers for his wine.

Annette found life at the orphanage very satisfying. She would sometimes accompany the other volunteers to the city and comb the streets to find children abandoned by their parents. They would also take in unwed mothers and find families for those children who were abandoned. She found that she was getting over the loss of her daughter. Every month, there would be people who would come to the orphanage and sometimes adopt children. Grace Halliday was in charge of seeing that the children went to good homes and help in the adoption process. Annette would miss the children who were taken away for adoption, but she would soon get over them when new children came into the orphanage.

Annette and Pierre missed each other very much. Their plans for meeting once a week were not successful. Pierre had a lot of work at the vineyard and winery. Sometimes, Mark would take Pierre to other counties and cities in California. At times, they did not see each other for a whole month. They were both homesick and felt better when they were in each other's company. It was during this time that Mark and Grace Halliday realized that Annette and Pierre were getting very slack in their duties. Mark decided to confront Pierre about this. He called Pierre aside and said, "Pierre, Grace and I have observed lately that Annette and you have not been working like you used to. Is anything wrong?"

"Monsieur Halliday, our plans to meet each other during the weekends do not seem to materialize. We miss each other terribly. My wife and I are also homesick, and the only way we feel better is when we are together."

"Do you have any children?"

"Yes, we have a son. Annette was going to have a girl, but she was stillborn."

"I am sorry about that, Pierre."

"That is one of the reasons we came to America. The last time I spoke to her, she told me that she was getting over the death of our daughter by living in the orphanage. That is why she prefers living there."

"Do you still miss each other?"

"Yes, we do."

"I understand, Pierre. I too was married at one time and when my wife died, I could not live with myself."

"I did not know that," Pierre said in surprise.

"I have a son who lives in Chicago. He never writes or comes to see me."

"Why is that?"

"He blames me for his mother's death. I have a cabin in the mountains, and when we were driving back, the car slid off the road and hit a tree. My wife died instantly, but I managed to survive the accident. Some hunters found us. This happened five years ago. My son loved his mother very much. He blames me for her death, and I have not seen him since the funeral."

"I am very sorry, Monsieur Halliday."

"Pierre, would you and Annette like to use the cabin this weekend?"

"Yes Monsieur. Merci beaucoup," said Pierre.

"I have an old car which I hardly use. You could fix it and use it."

"Yes, I will. I know a lot about engines. I learned to fix engines during the war."

"Good, Pierre. I hope Annette and you like the cabin." That weekend, Pierre and Annette spent time together in the cabin.

Time passed and very soon, it was the end of 1919. At midnight of January 16, 1920, one of America's favorite pastimes was going to end. The Volstead Act enacted the eighteenth Amendment. It banned the importing, exporting, transporting, selling, and manufacturing of intoxicating liquor. All over America, wineries and breweries were very unhappy with this Act. As a result, the crime rate and consumption of illicit alcohol increased, which was not the intention of this Act.

News of this Act at the Halliday Winery was not well received. Mark managed to sell some casks and bottles of wine during Christmas and New Year, but he still had many remaining and was about to start exporting wine to Canada and Europe. The sudden news of the prohibition ruined his plans to make money for the year.

"Oh no!" he said. "This cannot be happening. I have twenty casks of wine to be shipped to England and Sweden next week and many bottles to be delivered to New York and Boston. What am I to do?"

"Can't the government make an exception in your case?" asked

Pierre.

"No, they won't. If the government has made this the law all over America, they will surely not make an exception in my case. I will be ruined since I will not be able to make any more wine or sell it."

"What are the neighboring wineries going to do?"

"They too will have the same problem. This law needs to be repealed." Pierre opened his mouth to speak, but Mark cut him off. "Pierre, please excuse me, I need to be by myself." Pierre was taken aback, but realizing the gravity of the situation, he got up and left.

Two days later, Pierre found the neighboring vintner, Vincenzo Caggiano's car, parked outside the house. He heard that Vincenzo was born in Italy, and he immigrated to America forty years ago at the age of two. A rival mafia Don in Italy had murdered his family. Vincenzo was the sole survivor of that bloody massacre only because he was taken to the market by an elderly aunt. The whole household consisting of five children, including the maids and the gardener, were shot to death. Even the newborn baby was not spared. When they returned home and discovered the carnage, the elderly aunt took Vincenzo into hiding, and managed to obtain a passage to America.

In New York, Lorenzo Ciaggiano, the son of Vincenzo's elderly aunt, took care of them. He ran brothels and liquor stores from New York to Massachusetts. He became the protector of Vincenzo. When Vincenzo was old enough, he was sent to California to start a vineyard with the backing of Lorenzo. Everybody from the East Coast to the West Coast knew about Lorenzo. Therefore, nobody dared to interfere with Vincenzo. It was said that Vincenzo went back to his hometown in Italy and personally killed the Don who had killed his family. He hanged the Don upside down, cut off his tongue, stuck it back into his mouth, and then cut off his hands, before stabbing him to death. In memory of the deed, he cut off a lock of the Don's hair and fed the Don's body to the street dogs.

Vincenzo's vineyard prospered, and he became richer. Everybody in the valley feared him. Pierre heard Vincenzo's story from Mark. Mark had always said that he would never have anything to do with

Vincenzo because of his reputation. Therefore, Pierre was surprised when he saw Vincenzo's car parked outside.

Pierre waited for some time, and the door opened. Mark emerged from the house with another man. The other man was dressed in a clean brown suit with a flower in the lapel. He wore a hat, carried a cane, and had a small moustache. He was almost the same height as Mark. Pierre figured that this must be the notorious Don. He had never seen him before. He saw Mark shake his hand before the Don got into the chauffeur-driven car and drove off.

Pierre saw a broad smile on Mark's face. It was the first time he had seen Halliday smile like that ever since he received news of the prohibition. He walked up to Halliday who was still smiling to himself. Mark saw Pierre walking towards him and said, "Ah Pierre, you are just in time for some good news."

"I'll be delighted to hear some," said Pierre, with no expression on his face.

"Yesterday, I paid a visit to Don Ciaggiano to talk to him about selling the wine I have, and he has agreed to help me sell all of it in return for forty percent of the profits I make in selling my wine."

"Forty Percent? That is a lot, Monsieur Halliday," he said, with his eyes widening and his voice louder than usual.

"I know, but it is better than not having anything at all."

"But... but, that's terrible."

"Why do you say that?"

"He's a Mafia Don who has no conscience and won't think twice about killing anybody. Why do you want to be associated with him?"

Mark's expression changed. He was now stern. "Pierre, you do not understand the consequence if this wine is not sold. I have to do something to survive, or I will be ruined. Don Ciaggiano has been kind enough to help me, and that will be my only association with him."

"But, if anything goes wrong, you will be dragged into it."

"Enough. I will not hear anymore," Halliday said, getting agitated and his voice getting louder. "Tomorrow, you will go and deliver some bottles of wine to him, and you are to comply with everything he tells you to do."

Pierre was startled. He never expected anything like this. "I do not wish to be a part of this."

Halliday replied, "Remember, you came here to make a life for yourself and make Annette happy. If you do not do as I say, Annette and you will have to go back to France."

Pierre was shocked beyond words. The sudden change in Halliday was too difficult to comprehend. A month ago, he had bought the cabin and car from Halliday, and he had no money remaining. He thought about returning home penniless and being the laughing stock of his village. After all, nobody who came to America did badly, and he was not going to be that exception.

"All right, I will do it. Not because you want me to, but because of the current circumstances."

"Good," his voice softened and he tried to smile and said, "Pierre, I too am a victim of these unpleasant circumstances just like you. Please try to understand."

Pierre nodded and walked away without saying a word.

The next day, Pierre got up early and went to the wine cellars. He got the workers to load the crates of wine bottles into the trucks and drove the shipment to the Don's house.

Halliday watched these activities from his window. He was wondering if he was doing the right thing. Once this shipment was gone, he would never again ask the Don for help. This favor was giving him nightmares.

The moment Pierre got down from the truck, men with guns surrounded him. A man came to Pierre and introduced himself as Antonio. He took Pierre to meet the Don. Pierre went into the house and entered a room. The Don was sitting on a chair. Pierre went and introduced himself. "Ah yes, Mr. Halliday has told me about you. He said that you were very efficient and reliable, and he thinks highly of you. I am sure I can think the same of you too."

"Thank you, Don Ciaggiano, I am honored," he said, with not much enthusiasm.

"Join me for breakfast. We will discuss our plans after breakfast."

Pierre followed the Don and sat opposite him. The Don asked

Antonio to tell the cook to prepare more breakfast.

Pierre looked around and saw the portraits on the wall. He saw the portrait of the Don with his wife and six children and next to it was a portrait of an older man.

"Ah, my mentor and protector, Don Lorenzo Ciaggiano! If it were not for him, I would not be here. He helped me come up in life, and I owe him a lot. He is seventy-nine years old and in good health."

Pierre saw a glass box with a lock of hair. His eyes widened, and it did not go unnoticed by the Don.

"Ah! I see you have seen the lock of hair. It is my pride and joy. Makes me think how sweet revenge is and feel satisfied that the souls of my parents and siblings can finally rest in peace. Have you heard what I did to him?"

"Yes... yes, I did. Why do you ask?"

"Most people have heard the story from others, like you may have heard it from someone. It is distorted and many vital facts will be missing. Do you want to hear the story first hand?" he asked, with a smile on his face.

"No... no... that will not be necessary. However, there is one thing I would like to know. Did you have his family killed?"

"No. Do you think I am a monster? The good book says, 'eye for an eye and tooth for a tooth'. That is what I did. He harmed me by killing my family. I killed him for harming me. His family had nothing to do with me, and I left them alone."

Pierre heaved a sigh of relief. He had heard about Mafia Dons killing entire families to avoid revenge later. He found himself respecting Vincenzo a little because he appeared to be unlike the other Mafia Dons.

The maid brought Pierre a plate of bacon and eggs, and a pot of coffee. Pierre remembered the breakfast he used to have at his farm back in Normandy.

After Pierre finished his breakfast, Don Ciaggiano took him to a room, and Pierre found himself standing in front of a map of the United States. "We are here," pointed the Don on the state of California. We will take the wine from my property to the train station on the outskirts of the city. To fool the federal agents, we will put some apples along with the bottles of wine. It will be your job to go and deliver it to the station. My men will accompany you and help you. Once everything is cleared, the train will leave San Francisco for Portland, Oregon. From Portland, the wine bottles will be shipped to Canada. Some of the bottles will go to New York, where my uncle Lorenzo's men will take care of the cargo. Some of it will be sent to England and to other countries in Europe. It is a risky business, smuggling all this wine under the government's nose, but it is what the government has forced us to do."

"I understand, Don Ciaggiano." Pierre knew better than to argue with a dangerous man. Antonio entered the room and said that the trucks were loaded and ready to leave.

"Excuse me, Don Ciaggiano, how are we going to get the cargo, along with the apples, into the trains? Wouldn't the police be suspicious?" asked Pierre.

"Ah, you do not know the power I have here. I am very good friends with Officer Reynolds. I did him a favor and he is indebted to me. He will not bother us. The only people we have to worry about are from the Federal Government. They will be lurking at the stations and seaports, trying to stop the illegal transportation of alcohol. If we play our cards right, we can succeed."

Pierre and Don Ciaggiano walked out together. The Don lit a cigar and took a few puffs. They came out into the open and saw four trucks waiting outside. "Mon Dieu! Those are a lot of wine crates."

"No, Pierre. We have apples packed in separate crates and on top of the wine bottles in each crate. Now, you better get going, as the train will be leaving shortly."

Pierre got into the first truck, started it, and they all drove onto the main road. Pierre looked out of the window and looked back. He could see the Don smoking his cigar and looking at the trucks. He was glad that it would be the last time he would be seeing the Don.

They drove to a small train station north of San Francisco, where trains would come for servicing, and freight trains would load and unload cargo. The truck stopped and Antonio went inside the office. A few minutes later, he came out with two men - one was short and balding and the other tall, looked like a cop. "Pierre, this is Bruno Farrelli, the director of the railway station and Officer Reynolds. They will help us with our cargo." They shook hands and exchanged greetings. "Since this consignment belongs to Don Ciaggiano, I will let it through. He has helped me and my family a number of times, and I am indebted to him," said Officer Reynolds.

"I am sure you are," said Pierre, nonchalantly. Bruno told them to hurry and load the crates into the train. Antonio gave the order. The men began unloading the trucks. Pierre supervised the workers.

As they were about to finish, a man with a coat and hat came towards them. "Agent Taylor from the government. I want to know who owns these crates." The question caught them off guard. Pierre replied, "They belong to Don Ciaggiano."

"All right," he said sternly, "I would like to know what are in the crates."

"They contain apples to be shipped to other parts of the country."

"I would like to inspect one of them."

Pierre motioned the workers to bring the last crate and ordered it to be opened. One of them brought a crowbar and tried to pry the cover open.

"No, I will choose one," said Agent Taylor. He took the crowbar, went into the railway carriage, and opened one of the crates. Pierre and the others held their breath.

"Good. Thank you for being honest. Sorry for disturbing you," said Agent Taylor, and he walked away.

"For a moment I thought we were going to be caught," said Pierre.

"Yes, now quit talking, hurry and shut that crate, and get the last one in," said Antonio.

Pierre, along with one of the men, took a hammer and few nails and got into the railway carriage. He looked at the crate and saw apples in them. Agent Taylor had taken only a few apples from the top and thought that there were apples underneath. Out of curiosity, Pierre removed a few more apples and saw a bottle of wine. He started sweating and then put all the apples back. That was a close call. He had never been so nervous in his life, except on the battlefield. He placed the cover and nailed the crate shut.

Fifteen minutes later, the remaining crates were loaded, and the train left the station. Though it was a bit chilly, Pierre could feel the sweat trickle down his forehead. He was glad that this was all over.

Chapter 7

California, 1922

"I cannot stand this," said Annette.

Pierre looked at her in amazement. "What are you talking about?"

"You smuggling wine. It makes me feel like I am married to a criminal." Two months after he began smuggling wine for Halliday and the Don, Pierre told Annette about his involvement. She was taken aback. She cried and he warned her not to tell Mother Grace.

As he watched the train leave the station, he was sure that Mark would not put him through this ordeal again. He was wrong. Mark got more profits than he had ever imagined, and he decided that collaborating with the Don was going to make him richer than ever. Thanks to Grace Halliday's influence - he obtained permission to grow limited grapes in the vineyard and to sell those grapes to the local churches for making sacramental wine and local markets as table grapes. In a portion of his vineyard, he grew apples and made cider for the market, which he used as a cover for making wine. He knew that by selling wine he would make a huge profit, especially when it was prohibited, and people were willing to pay more than before.

He joined forces with the Don, obtained more grapes from Canada and Mexico, and made wine. Thanks to Officer Reynolds - there were no further incidences of the Feds opening the crates at the station. Informants warned the Don and Halliday about the Feds visiting the vineyard. Mark hid the wine in an underground chamber specifically made for the purpose. The workers knew better than to collaborate with the police.

When Pierre told Annette about his involvement in the smuggling operation, she wanted to go back to France. However, the bad memories were still fresh. Going back was not an option. The Don would get them before they could even get on a ship. They both decided that they would follow orders, but would take the first opportunity to leave.

Annette could take it no longer. They received a letter from Louis telling them that he had found the girl of his dreams and wanted to get married. He wanted his parents to be present at the wedding. Annette knew she now had a good excuse to go back to France. She said to Pierre, "I can see that you are tired of being in this dangerous situation. Tomorrow, please tell Mr. Halliday that we are ready to go back to France, and I will communicate the same to Mother Grace. We will tell them that our son is getting married and that we would like to be there for the wedding.

"But Annette, we have just become U.S. citizens, and you want to go back to France? What about all the bad memories we wanted to leave for good?"

"In France, we will be doing honest work and not leading dangerous lives. I hate telling a lie and also worrying about what will happen to us. We are not being good citizens by doing this. I realized when we took the oath that we should not resort to anything wrong." Pierre agreed with her.

The next day, they drove down the mountain. Pierre dropped Annette at the orphanage and went to the vineyard. As he was driving into the vineyard, he saw a car pass by. A man with brown hair and moustache sat behind. He looked at Pierre through the window and smiled. The car then picked up speed and drove off.

Pierre found Mark sitting on the porch drinking wine. When he saw Pierre, he smiled and said, "Ah Pierre, you are back. Did you have a nice time in the mountains? Sit and have a glass of wine with me."

Pierre sat down and Mark poured him a glass. Pierre did not touch it but leaned forward and said, "Yes, we did. Can I tell you something?"

"Yes, you can."

"Mr. Halliday, it has been a pleasure to work for you. I am ready to go back to France with Annette. We would like to spend our last years with our son on our farm. Our son needs us. He is getting married, and we would like to be there for the wedding."

Mark looked at him for some time. The silence made Pierre uncomfortable. He reached for the glass of wine and began sipping the wine. Halliday always knew that Pierre was uncomfortable with the smuggling operation. Halliday smiled and said,

"Of course, you can leave anytime you want. Before you leave, there is this one last thing I want you to do."

Pierre felt the urge to groan but restrained himself. "Okay," he said, trying to control his disappointment.

"We have a lot of wine to be sent to New York, via Canada. The cargo has to leave by ship tomorrow night. Don Ciaggiano will give you the details. Do this for me, and I will pay you double."

"All right, I will do this for you, and then I will leave for France."

He smiled at Pierre and said, "I spoke to the gentleman whom you must have passed by as you came in. He will be returning to New York in a few weeks for the birth of his second child. He will pay us well for this shipment. I am sure you will not regret it."

Mark was wrong. The next night, Pierre drove the wine from Don Ciaggiano's vineyard. Because of the increase in Police and Federal Agents at the train stations, they decided to ship the cargo to Canada, from San Francisco port.

The trucks reached San Francisco port. Don Ciaggiano had a cargo ship ready. They had already loaded wheat, corn, and apples onto the ship. They started unloading the trucks when, all of a sudden, a beam of light shone on them, and they heard the order to stick their hands in the air.

Four Weeks earlier:

Alberto Gaglio was hurrying home to see his family. They lived in San Francisco, and he got to see them when he was not working. He had two bottles of wine in the bag he was carrying, which he obtained as payment for taking part in the smuggling operations. The clock in the clock tower struck midnight. He wanted to get home before it was too late. He started running and collided with two burly police officers and all three fell to the ground. The bag fell and the bottles broke. Alberto tried to get up and run, but the officers were quicker, and they caught him. They both held onto him while he trashed about. Alberto, at five feet seven inches, stood no chance against the two well built police officers who were over six feet tall. They handcuffed and took him to the police station along with the bag, with the wine dripping from it.

They presented him to Sergeant Tracy. One of the police officers lifted the bag, with the wine still dripping, for the sergeant to see. Alberto refused to talk when he was questioned. He was warned of dire consequences for not cooperating. Alberto still refused to answer. "We will let him have his way," said Tracy with a smile that sent a shiver down Alberto's spine.

Sergeant Tracy was known for his ruthlessness. He had been in the Great War in Europe and was responsible for obtaining more information from POWs than other interrogators. After the war, he came back to San Francisco, his hometown, and resumed his job as a sergeant in the police department. He was harsh with prisoners, especially if they did not cooperate.

The two officers dragged Alberto to a room, stripped him to his underwear, and tied him to a pole. Alberto screamed when the fists hit him in the stomach and the chest. He fainted when he could not take it anymore.

A bucket of water was thrown on Alberto. The cold water woke him up. Tracy stepped in front of Alberto and asked him, "From where did you get the wine?" Alberto refused to answer. The mafia code of silence prevented him from giving any information.

He felt another punch on his stomach. He could stand it no longer and just before passing out said, "From... Don Ciaggiano."

The next morning, Alberto found himself on the bed with his torso bandaged. His body was still sore. He tried to get up, but his body hurt. He finally managed to get up and sit on the bed. He heard a noise and looked up. He saw Sergeant Tracy standing outside his cell with another man. Tracy introduced the man as Agent Frank Taylor. "What do you want?" asked Alberto, with some irritation in his voice as he groaned with pain.

"Federal agents in New York and other cities have suspected Don Ciaggiano of smuggling wine for the last two years. We need your help to stop him," said Agent Taylor.

"I don't know anything about that."

"Yes, you do. Last night before you passed out, you said that you got the bottles of wine from Don Ciaggiano. The labels on the bottles in your bag match with a bottle our agents sent from New York. We knew that they were coming from this area in California. Since you said that you obtained the bottles from the Don, our suspicions were confirmed. You must help us by telling us when the next smuggling operation will take place."

"I will help you under two conditions. First, you take me and my family to safety and second, all my past crimes are forgiven."

Agent Taylor looked at Sergeant Tracy and he nodded. "We will do everything possible to ensure the safety of you and your family. We can also make sure that your association with the Don and your crimes are forgiven. I give you my word," said Agent Taylor.

Alberto sat up and thought. He had wanted to get out of the mafia for a long time and to live like an honest citizen. He was coerced to join the mafia by his relatives when his father died, leaving him to pay off his father's debts and to marry his sister off. He wanted his four children to be proud of him by doing honest work. He had killed people for the sake of the mafia and now he was getting away without being punished. If the Don found out that he gave the police information, it would be the end of him. However, if he was silent, the Don would take care of his family, but that would only encourage his sons to join the mafia. He knew what he had to do. "All right," Alberto said, "I will tell you what you want know."

* * * * *

Agent Taylor and a few Federal Agents were waiting along with the police. Alberto gathered information and passed it on to the police. He identified Officer Reynolds as the Don's informant and Reynold's was arrested. Alberto went home with plain clothed police officers and surprised his family when he told them that they had to move to another part of the country for their safety. They packed whatever they could and three hours later were on their way to a small city in Minnesota.

The Federal Agents and police watched as the crates were being loaded onto the ship. Agent Taylor gave Sergeant Tracy the signal to speak. He placed the loud speaker to his mouth and said,

"You are surrounded. Drop everything and put your hands up in the air. Our guns are aimed at you."

This sudden announcement caught Pierre and the Don's men by surprise. They dropped the crates and some of them put their hands up, trying to shield their eyes from the blinding light. Some stood shocked, still holding onto the crates, and some pointed their guns at the darkness in the direction from where the voice was coming.

Tracy saw the reaction of the men and repeated the order. Few of the men began putting their guns down and put their hands up. Tracy gave the signal for his men to advance, and they moved forward. Suddenly, a shot rang out. The police started firing. The Don's men picked up their guns and fired back. Pierre ran to an empty truck and got into it. He started it and drove away. Bullets whizzed past the truck and some hit the windshield on the passenger side. He managed to get out of the port. He reached the main road and started driving towards the Halliday Vineyard. As the sound of gunfire diminished, Pierre wondered who betrayed them.

He got out from the truck, ran to the house, and banged on the door. A maid greeted him. He ran inside and pounded on Mark's bedroom door. Mark got up from the bed and opened the door.

"We've been discovered by the police," said Pierre, trying to gasp for breath.

"Calm down and tell me what happened." After Pierre had finished, Mark sat down on a chair and put one hand on his head. "So, it's finally over."

"Yes… I cannot be arrested," said Pierre, agitated.

"I know. Since I forced you into this, I'll take the entire blame. I won't let you be punished for something that is entirely my fault."

"What makes you say that?"

"Pierre, men died today because of the Don and my greed. I put you all in this situation and now I must take the blame. Take your car, go to the mountains, and stay in the cabin."

Mark opened his safe and gave a stack of bills to Pierre. He told him to book passage to France at the earliest time possible. Pierre took the money and went to his room. He gathered whatever he could, and loaded his car. He went and hugged Mark. He could see tears in Mark's eyes.

"Thank you. May God be with you."

"You too," said Mark.

Pierre got into his car and drove to the mountains. When he reached there, he went inside the cabin and bolted the door. He had a narrow escape, indeed!

A few days later, when he was sure that the situation had died down, he went to the orphanage. He learned from Annette that Mark and Don Ciaggiano had been arrested. The police followed some of the men to the Don's vineyard. The Don surrendered without a fight. Halliday confessed that it was he, who was in the dock that night and he was the one that drove the truck. Fortunately, for Pierre, Alberto had not mentioned his name but told the police when the crates of wine would be arriving at the dock. They had caught some of the men, and the police were looking for more. It would be just a matter of time before Pierre's name would come up. The Don was sentenced to twenty-five years in prison and Mark Halliday, twenty years.

Grace Halliday had taken the news very badly. She asked Pierre to be honest with her, and he told her everything. She was horrified that her dear brother was a lawbreaker. Grace Halliday agreed that Pierre and Annette should leave the country immediately. It was for the best, since her reputation would be ruined, if she were caught harboring an accomplice of the Don.

Pierre went to San Francisco and bought tickets to return to France. They were to sail in two weeks and decided that it was safer to hide in the cabin in the mountains until then.

Fateful Decisions

One night, they heard a child crying outside their door...

Chapter 8

Long Island, 1928

Rachel was a recluse for about two years after she lost Fred and Barbara as she mourned for them. The first event she attended was Rudy's marriage in 1924. His mother chose a German girl whose family was from Berlin. She was the daughter of a successful baker, and the family had immigrated to America a few years earlier. After that, she started attending social events organized by Fred's friends. She became acquainted with new people and was very popular. Her beauty and charm won over many wealthy men who wanted to marry her or propositioned her. She rejected them saying that she was still faithful to Fred. She and her friends took turns organizing social events every summer, and it was her turn to organize the Independence Day celebration.

The guests started arriving, and one of the first to arrive was Mrs. Henrietta Smith, an elderly woman with a bubbly personality. She looked around after they exchanged greetings and saw the patriotic decorations.

"Oh Rachel, everything is simply marvelous and patriotic," said Mrs. Smith.

"Thank you, Mrs. Smith."

"You must meet my friend's son. He is a widower with two grown up sons. He will be here shortly. I brought him along so that he could meet you. I hope you do not mind. Oh, there he is."

"Walter, Walter," she called out.

A tall, distinguished man in his mid forties with graying hair came towards them.

"Walter, this is Rachel Johnson. She owns the Johnson Hotels." Turning to Rachel, "Rachel, this is Walter Morton. He owns the Morton Hotels in Pennsylvania, and has just opened one in Manhattan." Rachel and Walter shook hands and greeted each other. "Well," said Henrietta, "I will leave you two to get to know each other." She winked at Rachel and went away.

"I met Fred a couple of times. He was a fine man. I hear you opened a hotel recently."

"Yes, in Washington D.C., and we are now planning to open one in Texas."

"Marvelous. I have my hotels in New Jersey, Pennsylvania, and Manhattan."

"Mr. Morton..."

"Please call me Walter."

"All right, Walter, you can call me Rachel." She smiled. She liked Walter. He seemed down to earth like Fred.

"Do your sons help you with the business?"

"Adam is twenty and Alexander is eighteen. After their mother died five years ago, they joined me in the family business. Adam would like to continue, but Alex has told me that he wishes to join politics."

"Well, politics is a fine way to serve the country."

As they were speaking, Rachel saw Rudy with his wife, Erma, a heavyset blond woman, on his arm, walking towards them. Rachel introduced Rudy and his wife, Erma, to Walter. The four of them talked for some time. After the fireworks display, Walter invited Rachel and Andrew to Manhattan the next day for lunch. Rachel agreed.

The next day, Rachel and Andrew arrived at the new house bought by Walter when he moved to Manhattan. The butler escorted them to the living room where they waited for Walter. He appeared a few moments later and greeted them.

"Good afternoon, Rachel. This must be little Andrew." Walter went over to the boy and shook his hand.

"Good afternoon, Mr. Morton."

"Good afternoon, Andrew. You have a handsome son, Rachel."

"Thank you, Walter." Rachel looked around and saw the painting of a blond woman.

"Is that your wife?"

"Yes, that is Louisa."

"She was a beautiful woman."

"Thank you. She was my wife for fourteen years until she died of cancer five years ago."

"I am very sorry, Walter. I know what it is to lose someone." The butler came in and announced that lunch was served. The three of them followed the butler into the dining room. An older woman, with gray hair, sat at the table.

"Rachel, this is my mother, Mrs. Amelia Morton."

"Good afternoon, Mrs. Morton."

The old woman looked at Rachel from head to toe. "Goodness woman, does your dress and hair have to be that short? Walter, what sort of a woman have you brought to dine with us? She looks like a man dressed in women's clothes."

Rachel was taken aback. She tried to speak and all she could say was, "I... I..."

"Calm down, Mother. She is Mrs. Rachel Johnson and that is her son, Andrew. Women now wear their dresses and hair a little shorter than they used to. The war changed everything."

"I do not approve. Women should always be covered from head to toe, just like your dear wife, Louisa. This woman looks like those flapper girls in magazines. No morals at all. Disgusting! When women lose their morals, the world will go bad."

"Mother, stop it. You are making our guests uncomfortable." At that moment, two young men walked into the room. The older was tall and blond-haired, and the younger, a little shorter and had brown hair. Both resembled Walter.

"Good afternoon, Gran and Father. Sorry we're late," said the blond youngster. Walter introduced them to Rachel and Andrew. "Pleased to meet you, Mrs. Johnson and Andrew," they said in unison.

"Pleased to meet you. You are fine young men, just as your father described the two of you."

They sat down, said grace, and began eating. Adam was studying at Yale, and he was on the football team. Alexander was going to Harvard the next semester to study politics. Amelia Morton ate her lunch silently and wished them goodbye when she finished and got up to leave. Rachel noticed her dress was still in the style of the previous decade. She gathered that Mrs. Morton did not like the latest fashions. After lunch, the two young men took Andrew out to play ball. Rachel looked outside the window and saw Andrew playing with the two youngsters.

"You have such fine sons. They are a delight. My son seems to get along with them."

"Yes, they are easy to get along with. They got closer when their mother died and love being around children."

"You have raised them very well."

"Thank you, Rachel. It was not an easy job being a single parent. Mother was a great help until Father passed away, and then she had a stroke four years ago. That made her what she is now."

"I am sure she will come to like me."

"She will."

The next time they met was at Mrs. Henrietta Smith's seventieth birthday party, attended by most of New York's elite. Walter asked Rachel for a dance. After several dances, they had dinner together, then went for a walk in the garden.

"Phew! Doing the Charleston tired me... How is Andrew?"

"He's fine. He enjoyed playing with your sons the other day." Walter tried to say something, but he was cut short by the noise of the fireworks display.

"Walter, aren't they beautiful?"

"Yes, they are, but not as beautiful as you."

"What?" said Rachel in surprise and turned to him.

"Yes, Rachel, I fell in love with you the moment I saw you."

"I... I don't know what to say."

"Don't be embarrassed. You are a lovely woman."

Rachel managed to regain her composure and said firmly, "Walter, I'm not interested in you. I thought we were just friends. I didn't think you had those feelings for me."

Walter was taken aback, and she could see the hurt on his face. "I am sorry, Rachel. I did not mean to embarrass you."

Rachel, now a little calmer said, "Walter, I should be the one who should apologize. I admit that I was shocked, but you did take me completely by surprise."

By now, the fireworks display was over and there was silence, except for the chatting of the guests who were going back inside. "Let's get back before tongues begin to wag. I am a widower and you are a widow; you know how people in our circles love gossip."

"Good idea," said Rachel.

* * * * *

The next day, Marcy came in with a bunch of flowers and placed them on the table. Rachel looked at the flowers and opened the note. Walter apologized for embarrassing her when he said he loved her. He hoped they could meet again and get to know each other better. She crumpled the note and just as she was about to throw it, the phone rang. She placed the note on the table and picked up the phone. Martha at once sensed that Rachel was upset and asked her about it.

"Yesterday, Walter declared his love for me at Mrs. Smith's party. I was shocked, and I told him that I had no other feelings for him and that we were just friends. Today, he has sent me flowers and in a subtle way wants me to reconsider my feelings for him."

"Rachel dear, you should be glad that he is showing some interest in you. He was a devoted husband and is a good father. Let me tell you a secret; I wish I could remarry. I would love for Sidney to have a father."

"My goodness, Martha, I didn't know you felt that way."

"Yes, I do, and would not want you to feel this way later in life. Is Andy fond of Walter?"

"Yes, he is, and his sons were very nice to Andy."

"There you go. I'm sure Walter will be a good father and a good husband. Please don't let go of this opportunity. I hope you will set things right." After thanking Martha, Rachel asked Alfred to get the car ready.

Rachel waited in the living room while the butler went to inform Walter of her arrival. He arrived shortly and greeted her. Rachel returned the greeting, sat upright, drew a deep breath, and said, "I received the flowers and your card. You must realize that it is hard for me to reciprocate your love. I know you still love Louisa, just as I still love Fred. I need to know that you really meant it when you told me that you loved me."

Walter looked at her kindly and sat next to her. He took her hand in his and said,

"Rachel, we have the loss of our spouses that is common between us, and we also yearn to be with someone. My sons said that they liked you and Andy. I will be a good father to Andy. Let me help you realize I truly do love you."

Tears started rolling down her cheeks. She knew that Martha was right and that Walter was an honorable man. He hugged her, and she knew that she was right in going to him.

October 1929

The wedding of Walter and Rachel was scheduled for November 10. Rachel brought out the wedding dress she wore when she married Fred, and her eyes filled with tears. She knew in her heart that Fred would have wanted her to remarry so that Andy could have a father. She started planning for her wedding from the time Walter had proposed to her on his yacht that hot June day. She accepted but was worried that his mother may not accept her.

"What about your mother? She hates me. I knew the way she looked at me when I first met her that she did not like me. She ignored me at your birthday and at the Christmas party.

"Oh, Mother will be fine. Give her some time. She thinks that you are going to take me away from her. She did not mind when my two sisters were married. She did give Louisa a little trouble but gradually came to like her and was fonder of her than of me. It is that stroke that has messed her up."

"She accused me of having an affair with Rudy at the Christmas party. She saw me talking to him a few minutes earlier and came up and said that awful thing to me."

"She did?" Walter said in surprise.

"Yes, and I am afraid that she may cause trouble for me."

"No, she will not! Over my dead body!" Since announcing their engagement and regularly meeting with Amelia Morton, Rachel found that she was starting to believe Amelia was beginning to like her. Andy too was excited that Rachel was getting married. Walter and his sons had taken Andy to the ball games and spent time with him making him feel like part of the family. The future was beginning to look good with the business doing well and the opening of a new hotel in Chicago.

Rachel put the wedding dress down and went outside. It was getting cold. She would have to leave this house and move into Walter's house in Manhattan. Johnson Manor would be closed, but she would have the gardener tend to the garden in the spring, summer, and fall. She looked at the leaves turning to various shades of color and was sad. She loved spring and autumn at the Johnson Manor. She would be in Manhattan next autumn.

She heard the phone ring and ran inside the study. "Rachel, this is Rudy," his voice sounded agitated.

"Yes, what happened?"

"The stock market has suffered a loss of about 12%."

"What are you talking about?" she asked, sounding anxious.

"You know the conversation we had a few days ago about the stock market falling; it just happened today."

"No, it can't be. We were discussing a hypothetical situation."

"It has happened, Rachel. We have lost a lot due to this sudden plunge in the stocks."

She could not believe her ears. The stock market collapse, which she had heard being whispered, was now a reality. "Walter Morton has lost a lot more than we have and is almost ruined."

The news stunned her. She could not believe that yesterday Walter was a wealthy man and now, he was almost wiped out. "Thank you, Rudy," was all she managed to say, and she put the phone back in its cradle. She called for Alfred to get the car ready to take her to Manhattan.

As the car reached the Morton residence, Rachel saw Walter standing outside the door. "Walter," she shouted, as she ran into his arms. "Oh Walter, what are we going to do?"

"Don't worry, Rachel, it will soon be sorted out. This situation will last for a few months and then things will improve." As they walked into the house, he turned to her and said, "Rachel, we can't have the lavish wedding we had planned."

"I understand. We can just have a simple ceremony. I, too, have lost a lot in the crash."

Walter was silent. "Is anything wrong?"

"Just before you arrived, I received news that Albert Cross shot himself because the crash wiped him out completely."

"What?" Rachel was horrified. "Poor Jane... and his four children."

"Yes, he is one of the few who have killed themselves today because of the crash."

Rachel looked at him anxiously. Walter could tell what she was thinking. "Don't worry, Rachel, I am stronger than that. It's just as bad for me, but I will not do that to you or my boys. I brought the business back when my father ran it to the ground due to his gambling habit, and I am sure I can do it again."

"Sorry, I was foolish for thinking that you would do that," she said, feeling ashamed.

He smiled at her and they went into the living room. Maybe, Walter was right; this would soon be over and everything would go back to normal. She silently prayed that it would.

Two days later:

Rachel was thankful that she was not as affected by the crash as the rest of her friends. Walter had invested his money and had borrowed more to invest in more stocks like the others. They had been wiped out; thanks to their over-confidence during the economic boom. Rachel would lose her newly opened hotels in Chicago and Texas, and business would be slow, but she knew that as long as people were traveling, they would need a place to stay. Walter on the other hand, would have to sell his hotels in New York and Pennsylvania. He would be able to keep only the smaller hotels in New Jersey. She promised herself that she would help Walter rebound and not sink. In a few hours, Rudy would be going to Chicago to help with the closure of the hotel. They already had a buyer, and she would use that money to help Walter.

Rachel heard the doorbell ring, and a few minutes later, she heard footsteps come towards the study. "Mrs. Johnson, Detective Howard is here to see you. He says it is very urgent," said Marcy. Rachel went to the living room and found Detective Howard and a police officer waiting for her.

"Good afternoon, Mrs. Johnson," said Detective Howard. "This is Officer Pierce."

"Good afternoon. What brings you here?"

"Mrs. Johnson, when did you last see Mr. Morton?"

"Two days ago. Why do you ask?

"How did he sound?" asked Officer Pierce.

"He sounded fine. He was worried about the losses he had incurred. Now, why do you ask me all these questions?"

"Mrs. Johnson, please sit down. Prepare yourself for some bad news." She sat down without a word and looked very upset. "Mr. Morton killed himself. He threw himself from his office window located in the Manhattan hotel."

She could feel the tears coming down. She could not believe her ears. "He told me that he would not harm himself. He could not have done that. There has to be some mistake."

"I understand, Mrs. Johnson, but he was apparently depressed by his financial loss in the stock market and fell to his death at nine a.m."

"Did he leave a note?" asked Rachel, wiping away the tears.

"Yes, he did," said the detective. "It said, 'I am sorry. I cannot take it any longer.' The paper was still in the typewriter."

Rachel could not control herself any longer. She broke out in tears, sobbing bitterly. Detective Howard and Officer Pierce got up and left the room. They closed the door behind them.

Rachel saw the picture of Walter and her getting married fade away. She felt alone and felt the same sense of loss come back when she lost Fred and Barbara. Marcy and Robert knew that she wanted to be alone at this time. They had been there when Fred brought her home as a bride, when she became a mother, and a widow. They sat by the door and waited until she was ready to come out.

Grief was on the faces of the Morton boys. At the funeral, they conducted themselves with grace and dignity. They had lost their parents, most of their wealth, and they were now left with a senile grandmother and some extended family. During the funeral, many people eulogized Walter, praising him for his intelligence and dedication in bringing the failed business back, and for his charitable work.

At the repast held at the Morton residence, people offered their condolences to Rachel and the Morton brothers. Henrietta Smith came by. Rachel fell into her arms and cried.

"I am very sorry, my child. He was such a wonderful man. This all feels like a bad dream."

Rachel regained her composure and stood erect. "Mrs. Smith, this does seem like a bad dream; first Fred and now Walter. When will this nightmare end?"

"I don't know, my child, but you must be strong for Walter's boys and Andrew."

"Where is Walter's mother?" asked Rachel.

"From what I heard, she is so distraught, that she had to be sedated. She went berserk and started breaking things when she was told of Walter's death."

Andrew was extremely agitated and could not stop crying. Rachel kept him at the house. When she went home, she tried to be brave in front of him. She did not want him to see her grief.

A few days later, Rachel went to the Morton residence to return the engagement ring. As she waited in the living room, she noticed that Walter's portrait was hanging next to his wife's. His sons walked in and hugged Rachel. Rachel opened the box, which she removed from her bag, and showed them the diamond ring Walter had given her for the engagement.

"I am returning this ring to you. It is worth a lot and should fetch a good price."

"No, Rachel, we cannot take it back. It was our father's gift to you. It is the last thing he gave you," said Alexander.

"No, I will not keep it. Before your father died, he told me about the financial status after the crash, and it wasn't good. You two are young, and he would have liked to see you finish your education. Please do as I say for your sake and for the sake of your grandmother."

She placed the ring back into the box and left it on the table next to her. The expression on their faces told her that they were grateful, and no words were needed to express their gratitude.

"How is Andy? We miss him."

"He is fine and obviously distraught, but he will get through."

The door opened all of a sudden, and they all turned around to see Mrs. Morton standing at the door with a cane in her hand and her gray hair uncombed. Her eyes were bloodshot and she shouted, "You murderess!"

She ran towards Rachel swinging her cane. Before anybody could react, she brought the cane down on Rachel's shoulder. The Morton brothers got up and tried to restrain her. She kept on shouting at her saying, "You murderess, you and that Hun killed my Walter."

She collapsed in the arms of her grandsons. Two nurses entered the room and one of them said, "We had no idea that she had left her room."

Adam said, "Never mind, now help us get her to her room."

The two brothers carried the older woman, followed by one of the nurses while the other nurse examined Rachel's shoulder.

The two brothers came into the room a little later. "How are you, Rachel?" asked Adam.

"The pain is getting better."

"Nurse, will she be all right?"

"Yes, she was lucky the cane just brushed against her shoulder."

"Nurse, could you go and help with grandma?"

"Yes, Mr. Morton." She left the room closing the door behind her.

"You have our sincere apology, Rachel," said Alexander.

"Do not worry about it. You cannot be blamed for what happened just now. Why did she attack me? I thought we were getting along after Walter and I got engaged."

"She has never attacked anyone before," said Alexander.

"What did she mean by calling me a murderess and what did she mean by 'that Hun'?"

"We do not know why she called you that. I think she meant your accountant, Rudy."

"She did accuse me of having an affair with Rudy when she saw me talking to him at the Christmas party last year. Why would she even think like that about me?"

"Grandma has always been like this, talking out of the way, ever since she had that stroke after grandpa died. She was always nice to us and to her other grandchildren, but she did say some nasty things to other people. It was very embarrassing when she talked like that. She visited Father just before he…" and Adam's voice trailed off.

"She was at his office on that day?"

"Yes, and she had a breakdown after she heard the news. She kept on repeating, "My Walter was killed." That is why we had the nurses sedate her before the funeral."

"I will go home now. I hope you sell the ring, and if you ever need anything, please do not hesitate to ask me. You two are like my sons too."

"Thank you, Rachel," they said together and hugged her.

On the way home, Rachel was glad that she was not badly injured. She felt sorry for the Morton brothers because they had to look after their grandmother, go to college, and try to salvage the family business.

Three months later, Rachel attended the funeral of Mrs. Amelia Sarah Morton.

Chapter 9

Long Island, 1936

Rachel got over the death of Walter Morton. After the hotel in Chicago, in the next three years, one of the hotels in Los Angeles had to be closed. She decided to concentrate on keeping the remaining hotels open. After Walter died, there had been a few chance meetings with the Morton boys. They were busy finishing their education and managing the hotel business. Rachel noticed that Andrew would read the newspapers and feel sorry for the people who were facing the depression. He would help at the church when they had free soup dinners for the less fortunate. She asked him if he would volunteer his time at the soup kitchen set up by the Jesuit priest, Fr. Arthur O'Malley, in Manhattan. Andrew readily agreed and spent his weekends and summer vacations helping in the soup kitchens.

By 1935, Rudy's marriage to Erma was waning. Erma filed for divorce, and it was granted a few months later. Erma won custody of their two children Sabine and Axel.

Rachel heard about Rudy's divorce when he came over to the house drunk one day. He walked into the study where she was reading and yelled, "She has left me."

"What happened?"

"Erma asked me for a divorce, and her rich father made sure that the judge granted it."

"I am sorry, Rudy. Why did she want a divorce?"

"She declared that she was tired of me and that she could no longer stand being married to me."

"I'm sure she did not mean that," she managed to say.

"Yes, she did, and now she has taken the children away from me. Her father saw to that."

"When did all this happen? You didn't say anything at all."

"It was just too fast. I thought it would never happen and now it has."

"I am very sorry, Rudy."

He came close to her and she could smell the alcohol in his breath. "I love my children and want them back."

"Rudy, you are too close to me."

"I want them back." He bent down and took Rachel into his arms. "I want you, Rachel. I have always wanted you."

He lifted her and kissed her on the lips. She was stunned. She tried to break away from him, but he was stronger than she was. She reached behind herself, grabbed a paperweight, and hit Rudy over the head.

He let go of her and she fell on the couch. He stepped back, sat down on the chair, and started rubbing his head. "Why did you do that?" asked Rudy.

"Rudy, you are drunk. Go home now," she shouted at him.

"I love you, Rachel. I have, ever since I first saw you."

She stood up and yelled, "Now, go home. I want you out of my house." Hearing her shout, Robert, Marcy, and Alfred came into the study. "Robert and Alfred, take Mr. Holzmann out and make sure he goes home."

"Yes, Mrs. Johnson," they said in unison and lifted Rudy up by the arms and took him outside.

Rudy was too stunned to struggle. He was still holding his head where Rachel had hit him.

Rachel was very upset. She actually felt sorry for Rudy rather than anger. She hoped that he would come to work sober the next day.

Much to Rachel's surprise, Rudy did not come to work. There was no sign of him anywhere. She even went to his house. His mother had not seen him ever since he got the news that his divorce had come through. On the third day, he showed up at his mother's house, and his mother sent Rachel a message saying that he was not well. Rachel thought it best that she stay away and let him recover.

Five days later, in a bar in downtown Manhattan, three men were drinking. Alfredo, Sergio, and Hector were three friends who met on the same ship while immigrating to America. They hoped to make it big in America, but sadly, all they found were long lines at the soup kitchens. The depression had set in. They found some work as odd job men at construction sites and cleaning latrines. They were determined to be successful in America, even if they had to sell their souls to the devil. When they had an opportunity to rob or make some money by illegal means, they went in and came out with no remorse. "After all, we too are poor and stealing from the wealthy is only right in these hard times," is what they said to justify their illegal ways.

The first crime they committed was roughing up the owner of a store who owed his creditor, Ralph Baumgartner, money. They found that these criminal activities were more rewarding than the honest jobs, which they kept. They, however, made a vow never to murder anyone unless their identities were discovered. They hid their faces from their victims and only Ralph Baumgartner, who had hired them to rough up the storeowner, knew them. He would contract them to other jobs that he would obtain for them.

On the weekends, they would go to the bars and drink. One evening, in September 1936, they went to the speakeasy as usual and got very drunk. They staggered out of the bar when it closed using the back door, which led into an alley away from the eyes of the police. All of a sudden, out of nowhere, they heard a voice,

"You three, do you work for Mr. Baumgartner?"

"Who are you?" asked Sergio. They looked around and could not determine the origin of the voice.

"I am a friend of Mr. Baumgartner. Now, do you work for him?"

"Yes, we do. What business is it of yours? Show yourself, if you have the guts to do so." The three of them drew their guns.

"Okay, no need for that. You need not feel threatened by me.

Actually, you do, since I have my gun aimed at the three of you, and at any moment, I can drop you three like a ton of bricks. Put your guns away and listen to me."

The three men, seeing that they had no choice, put away their guns.

"Mr. Baumgartner tells me that you have done excellent work for him in the past and made sure that people got the message."

"Yes, we have," said Alfredo.

"Well, now I have something for you to do. I will pay you, maybe, $5,000 each. How does that sound?"

At the mere mention of money, the three of them gasped, and Alfredo said, "That's a lot of money, but what do you want us to do?"

"What I want you to do is very simple; do it and you will get paid. You are to…"

After they were told of the plan, the three of them were not entirely happy. They had never done anything like this before.

"You will never see me but only hear my voice. Now, be off. You will hear from me soon."

The three men left the alley.

* * * * *

In October 1936, on a Saturday, Andrew went to Manhattan as usual to volunteer at Fr. O'Malley's soup kitchen. He left the soup kitchen after his shift and saw that the car was parked on the opposite side of the street. This was unusual because another car was parked on the same side of the street as the soup kitchen where their car was usually parked. Fr. O'Malley came out and stood next to Andrew and they waved at Rachel. Andrew loved the priest but resented having the priest help him cross the street, though he was now fourteen years old.

He saw Rachel standing next to the car and waving back. Two men got out of the car waiting on the street and grabbed Andrew by the arms. Fr. O'Malley tried to react, but one of the men pushed him to the ground. Andrew was pulled into the car and a sack was put over his head. He felt his hands being tied. He tried to struggle, but the more he struggled, the more the ropes cut into his hands.

Rachel watched all this in horror. Before she could raise an alarm, the car sped away. She screamed, shouted Andrew's name, and ran after the car. The car disappeared in the traffic. Rachel collapsed on the road.

She woke up in her bed at the Johnson Manor. She got up, looked around, and began shouting for Andrew. She saw the door open and felt happy.

"Andy, is that you?" she asked excitedly.

When the door opened fully, she realized that it was Marcy and behind her stood Dr. Thompson.

"Is Andy all right? Was I just dreaming?"

Dr. Thompson came and sat by her and said, "Rachel, I'm sorry, but it's true. You didn't dream it. Andrew has been kidnapped."

"Why is this happening to me? Why take him away? He's just a boy."

"We don't know why he was kidnapped. Detective Howard is downstairs. He wants to talk to you."

"Detective Howard? That name sounds familiar."

"Yes. He was the one who informed you about the death of Mr. Morton."

"Oh no! Is he here to tell me that Andy has been killed?" She started panicking.

"No, Mrs. Johnson," said Marcy before Dr. Thompson could answer. "He's here just to question you since you witnessed the kidnapping."

"I'll leave the room and let Marcy help you change," said Dr. Thompson and left the room.

Rachel walked down the stairs a few minutes later. She tried to remain calm as she went to the study where Detective Howard was standing with another man.

"Good evening, Mrs. Johnson. This is Detective Novak from the Manhattan Police Department. He would like to ask you a few questions since the kidnapping took place in his jurisdiction."

"Thank you. It all happened so fast. I was just stunned. I still can't believe it."

"I understand, Mrs. Johnson," said Detective Novak. "Please try to remember any details you can, however insignificant they may be."

Rachel described what she witnessed and mentioned that she saw a third man at the wheel.

"Did you notice the color of the car?"

"Yes, it was a brown Ford, Model A."

"Are you sure?"

"Yes, I am, because my chauffeur said something to that effect when we parked on the opposite side. I am sure he can confirm it for you."

"All right, I will check with him," said Detective Howard.

"How were the men dressed?"

"It was cold and the men were dressed in dark overcoats and had hats on. I could not see their faces because the lower portions of their faces were covered with scarves. It happened too fast, and I was only looking at Andy."

"We have already spoken to Fr. O'Malley," said Detective Novak. "He said that when he was pushed to the ground, the scarf on the man's face partially fell off, and he saw a scar on the lower jaw. Do you know anyone like him?"

"No, I don't."

"Do you know why anyone would want to kidnap Andy? Has anyone threatened you or said something to that effect?"

"No, nobody has said anything. Everyone I know loves Andy, and he has never hurt anyone. He is just a child. Do you think it was random?"

"I don't think so, Mrs. Johnson. The very fact that the car was parked there and they were waiting for him, tells me that it was premeditated."

"Detective, do you think this will be like the Lindberg baby kidnapping?"

"What are you implying?"

"That my son may never come home," said Rachel and began to cry.

"Mrs. Johnson, please don't think that way. As far as we know, your son is still alive. Kidnappers generally do not harm their victims without obtaining something from the family. I have a feeling that you will receive the ransom note either today or tomorrow. Please let us know when you receive it."

"I will, Detective Howard," she said, wiping away the tears.

The detectives questioned Alfred. He confirmed the make of the car. He did not see anything until Rachel screamed and only saw the car drive away. He gave Detective Novak the license number he had noted.

The detectives left the premises and went to investigate. The precinct that Detective Novak belonged to, managed to question some of the people waiting in line there, and they too could not tell them anything more than what Rachel, Alfred, and Fr. O'Malley had told them. Detective Novak had the license plate number investigated. It turned out that no car with that license plate number existed in the New York system. They concluded that the car must have been stolen and a false license plate used. A quick investigation found that a certain Daniel Lloyd, who was visiting New York City from Connecticut, had his car stolen when he went to eat at a deli a few days before the kidnapping. Detective Novak interviewed him, and they were sure that it was his car.

A day later, Rachel informed Detective Howard that the ransom note had been delivered. Detective Howard came over immediately and read the note. It was typed on a slightly crumpled, old piece of paper. It read: 'If you want to see your son again, have $100,000 in bills ready, and come alone to the park close to the Parker Trucking Company building in Manhattan, on Thursday at two p.m. You are to leave the money in a black bag on the park bench under the oak tree and depart. Your son will be returned after the money has been received.

P.S. No police if you want to see your son alive.

Rachel was almost in tears. "How am I going to do this?"

"You will have to," said Detective Howard. "We have to follow the directions given in this note, or we may antagonize the kidnappers."

"Does that mean that you will not be there?"

"We will follow you at a safe distance. Now, please do not tell anyone about this note. Not even your closest friends. We must have absolute secrecy so that we can plan. Today is Sunday and you need to give the kidnappers the money on Thursday. Can you arrange for the money?"

"Yes, I can get the money from the office and the bank."

Thursday could not have come fast enough for Rachel. She got ready the money and the black bag. She felt awful that she was in a heated house while Andrew was probably in a place where there was no heat, proper food, or water. Dr. Thompson advised her to eat well to keep her strength.

The dreaded day arrived, and Rachel was driven to Manhattan. They could see the Parker Trucking Company and the park. The workers were busy working on the trucks. Rachel told Alfred to stop the car and leave. After he drove away, she walked to the park and found a bench under the oak tree. She looked at her watch and saw that it was almost two p.m. She walked to the bench, placed the bag on it, and waited for someone to come. She had decided that she would plead with the kidnappers to return Andrew to her right there.

At a distance in a car, Detectives Novak and Howard watched Rachel's every move.

"What is she doing? She's supposed to leave after placing the bag," said Detective Novak.

Detective Howard looked through his binoculars and saw Rachel standing there, nervously playing with her fingers.

"She needs to leave, or nobody will show up," said Howard.

Rachel could feel the cold even though she was dressed warmly. She looked around and didn't see anyone. As she began to move, she saw a man on a bicycle. She lifted her hand for him to stop, but he went away without acknowledging her. She began to sweat and started moving away from the bench, when she saw a man with a limp, holding a walking stick for support, come closer.

"Surely, this must not be the person," said Detective Novak. "This must be another passerby. Looks like a hobo."

Rachel thought the same and walked further away from the bench, looking around to see who else would come by. The man with the limp came closer; he was looking towards the ground. As she passed by him, she nodded and he nodded back. She took a couple of steps and heard the man say, "Thank you for the money. You will see your son in hell."

She turned around and saw that the man had straightened up and grabbed the bag. She went after him and managed to grab his shoulders. He turned around and hit her on the head with the bag. She shouted out in pain and fell to the ground. The man ran in the opposite direction.

The detectives saw the whole scene and got out of the car along with the two police officers who were hiding in the bushes in front of the car. They ran towards the bench but saw that the man had disappeared, and Rachel was on the ground trying to get up.

"He said that I would see my son in hell." Rachel was hysterical and crying loudly.

"Damn, he got away. They were onto us. They knew that we would be watching and were set up," said Detective Howard.

"What about my son?"

"I don't know. We will have to wait until they contact us again." It was all Detective Howard could say to soothe her and was angry with himself at the same time.

Rachel was now hysterical. She ran outside the park and saw Alfred parked on the opposite side of the street. She ran across the street and narrowly missed being run down by a car. She got into the car and asked Alfred to take her home.

She reached home; the household staff could see that she was visibly shaken. They knew something had happened. She ran into the room, closed the door, sat on the bed, and cried.

The police cars followed Rachel, and the detectives went into the house. They asked Marcy to bring Rachel down, but she refused to see them.

Ever since the kidnapping, the newspapers were keen on reporting the case. Reporters from all over came to the manor to get an interview with Rachel. She refused to see them. The news made front-page headlines, and some papers even compared the kidnapping to the Lindberg baby kidnapping that had taken place a few years earlier. Rachel read the headlines and was devastated. She too was wondering if the outcome of this whole ordeal would result in the death of her now only child. The words of the limping man played repeatedly in her mind.

She kept getting calls from friends but did not want to speak to anyone. She only spoke to Martha and poured out her feelings to her. The only person she did not hear from was Rudy. She assumed that he was still depressed over the divorce and did not want to have to deal with anything more.

Rachel had police protection. It had been two days since the ransom was delivered, and the detectives were concerned that the kidnappers would target her. Only people whom she approved of were allowed to visit her. One evening, a constable came to her and told her that Rudy wanted to see her. She told the constable to allow Rudy to enter. When she saw him, she ran to him and he hugged her.

"I am so sorry, Rachel. I hope they find Andy."

"Thank you, Rudy. How are you doing? I thought you weren't going to come because of the divorce."

"I was upset about the divorce and had to take time off, but I am now reconciled to it. I had to come and see you when I heard about Andy."

"Thank you, Rudy. It means so much to me that you are here. You are, after all, his godfather, and we always thought of you as one of the family."

The door opened and Detectives Howard and Novak walked into the room. "Mrs. Johnson, we have…" began Detective Howard, but he stopped when he saw Rudy.

"Detectives, this is Rudolph Holzmann. He is a family friend and works for me. He can be trusted."

"Pleased to meet your acquaintance, Mr. Holzmann," said Detective Howard.

"Likewise," said Rudy.

"What is it you wanted to tell me? Is there any good news?"

"I'm afraid that we have nothing yet, Mrs. Johnson, but can we speak in private?"

"You can tell me anything you want in front of Mr. Holzmann, Detective Novak. I trust him fully."

"No, this is for your ears only, and I am afraid that is how it should be."

"All right, Detective. Rudy, I'm sorry, but I have to do what they say."

"I understand, Rachel. I hope they find Andrew. I will come again another time. I hope you receive another typed note from the kidnappers saying that they will release Andrew since the ransom has been paid."

"Thank you, Rudy."

Rudy got up, bid the two detectives goodbye, and closed the door behind him.

"What is it you wanted to tell me, Detectives?"

"Nothing," replied Novak. "Mrs. Johnson, have you heard of the group called 'Friends of Germany'?"

"No, I haven't. Does it have to do something with the kidnapping?"

"We will have to see if it does, but tell me, how long have you known Mr. Holzmann?"

"I've known him for the past twenty-one years. He saved me from drowning. We were on the Lusitania together."

"Okay, how long has he worked for you?"

"He had been working for the Johnson Hotel Group before I met my husband. Now, what is all of this about? I think you owe me an explanation."

"All right, Mrs. Johnson. The group, which I asked you about, has been suspected of being involved with subversive activities and supporting the Nazi Government in Germany. We have them under surveillance in New York and, if I'm not mistaken, I did see Mr. Holzmann go to one of those meetings."

"No, no, that's impossible, Detective Novak. Rudy is not into all that."

"I'm afraid I'm right, Mrs. Johnson. The group has now been

renamed the 'German American Bund,' and we are following it closely. We have no definite proof that they are violent or committing crimes, but I think Rudy does know something about the kidnapping."

"What makes you think that?"

"For instance, how did he know that the ransom note was typed? Did you tell him anything before we came in?"

"No, I'm sure anyone can guess that it was typed."

"That maybe so, but I have a hunch that he knows something."

"Detective Novak, Rudy would never harm my son. You are going about this the wrong way. I'm sure that none of the kidnappers was Rudy."

"I am sorry, Mrs. Johnson, but my gut feeling tells me that we need to keep an eye on Rudy. He may have hired those three men. I know it's something wild, but I will have him followed."

Before Rachel could protest any further, the two detectives left.

* * * * *

Andrew woke up alone in a dark room. He had lost track of the days since he had been kidnapped. The room was cold, but he sat next to a wall and kept himself warm. 'There must be a furnace here,' he thought to himself.

He looked at the plate with bread and did not feel like eating it. He drank a little water from a bowl. He wondered how many days they would keep him there. They told him that he would be released after the ransom money was delivered, but that was a while back. He heard footsteps. The door opened, and the three men walked in. He could only see their eyes from the little light that was streaming in through the open door.

"How are you boy?" asked one of them.

"When are you going to let me go? You promised me that I would be free when my mother paid the ransom money."

"You will be free whenever the boss says so," said another of the masked men.

"Where is your boss? Tell him that I want to go home."

"Well, what do we have here? So, now we have a brat who is demanding," said the other masked man. The three of them laughed. They heard the sound of footsteps above them.

"The boss is back. Now we will be paid. We must hurry." The three men ran out of the room and closed the door.

Andrew heard the sound of footsteps wane away. In a way, he was happy that the 'boss' was back. He then heard more footsteps, and the door opened again. "Come on boy, the boss wants to see you."

They left the basement, climbed the stairs, and entered a large room with lots of discarded wooden beams, steel pipes, and empty crates. "Here is the boy, Boss."

"All right, now that you are going to get your money, there is just one last thing for you to do."

"What is it?"

"You are to kill the boy."

The three men gasped. "No, we cannot," said Sergio. "We don't murder anyone unless they have seen our faces and they can identify us later. He is a child and we are not going to kill him."

"If you do not do what I tell you, you will not get your money," said the voice.

"Now, look here, whoever you are, we did not discuss killing anyone. You promised to release him after the ransom was paid. Let him go and give us our money. I got that money and gave it to you. You promised to give us our share."

"I have your share, but you will not get it unless the boy is killed." Andrew looked in the direction of the voice. He thought he found the voice very familiar.

"Do as I say, or there will be consequences."

"Look here, whoever you are, we are not killers. Give us our money, and we can all go," said Hector. Sergio rushed towards the darkness from where the voice was coming and there was a gunshot. The bullet hit Sergio's thigh, and he fell to the ground crying out in pain.

"Are you all right, Sergio?" asked Hector.

"Shut up, you fool. You are giving away our identities," said Alfredo.

"If you don't do as I say, and if you try anything stupid again, the rest of you will meet the same fate," said the voice.

"So, where does that leave us? You make us murderers. This boy is the son of an influential person in New York, and killing him would make us fugitives for the rest of our lives."

"Enough talk," said the voice with irritation. They heard a voice from a loudspeaker. "We have the building surrounded. Come out with your hands up. We want the boy unharmed."

The three men were distracted by the sudden development. Andrew took the opportunity and ran into the darkness.

"Catch the boy," said Alfredo.

"Where did he go?" asked Hector.

"Never mind, you fools, the police have us surrounded. We need to get out of here."

"Wait," said Sergio, "take me with you."

The two men bent down and picked him up. They tried to run towards the door but realized that the police would be on the other side.

"We will have to shoot our way out. Where's the boss?"

"Never mind him. We should never have taken this job in the first place."

Andrew ran into the darkness and hid behind a barrel. He could see the three men clearly. He knew that they would not be able to see him in the darkness. He crawled towards the door and saw someone next to it. The door opened and a ray of light came in. He saw the face distinctly and realized why the voice was familiar.

The door slammed shut; Andrew tried to open it. The men removed their masks and realized that they would have to fight the police if they wanted to leave. They left Sergio on the floor and went to the window to look at the police that had surrounded the building. They broke the window glass and again heard the voice coming from outside say,

"We have surrounded the building. Surrender and come out." A shot rang out; it seemed to have come from outside the building. They knew that their 'boss' had fired the shot. In response to that, the police started firing. The two men took cover and realized that the only way they could get out of this was to fire back and maybe make a run for it when the police force surrounding the building was weakened. They started firing at the police.

On the adjacent building, two snipers from the police force were crouched on top of the building. Both of them had been snipers in the previous war and had been an asset to both the marines and the police force. They cocked their guns and looked through the telescopes. They had their targets in sight. They were waiting for orders to shoot the men inside the building. The man next to them gave them the signal. They took aim and fired.

Sergio saw the heads of both his friends explode and blood and brain matter scattered everywhere.

"Noooooooooooooooooooooooo," was all he could say. Sergio was aware of the sickening silence and all of a sudden heard footsteps as the police came running towards the building. It was pointless for him to fight back.

Detective Novak gave orders for the police to storm the building. The police broke the door and scattered. They entered the main storage area and saw the devastation. The beams and the walls were riddled with bullets. They saw the corpses of the two men on the floor. One of them went towards Sergio. After making sure that he did not have any weapons, the doctor was brought in.

Detectives Howard and Novak went towards Sergio. "Where is the boy?" asked Detective Novak.

"He was here and ran away before the shooting started."

"Which way did he go?"

"I don't know. I was shot earlier by the boss because I tried to rush him when he wanted us to kill the boy."

"Who is this boss of yours? Where is he?"

"I don't know. He never showed us his face."

"Search for the boy," yelled Detective Howard.

The police started searching. Five minutes later, they heard one of them shout, "Here he is."

The police found Andrew hiding behind a metal drum. He was

shivering with fear. The two detectives rushed to the spot and shone their flashlights on Andrew. They could see the fear on his face. Detective Howard bent down and said, "Don't worry, Andrew, you are safe now. We are the police."

Andrew started to move slowly. They could hear him mumbling. "What are you saying?" asked Detective Novak. Again, Andrew started to speak. Detective Novak bent down, and Andrew now spoke a little louder. "Did you catch him?"

"Two of the kidnappers are dead, and one is wounded."

"No, the other man, it was Uncle Rudy. I saw him come down those stairs and leave through this door before the shooting began."

"Do you mean Rudolph Holzmann?"

"Yes, yes, it was him all along."

"Men, go through that door after him. He is blond, medium built and about five feet eleven inches tall."

The men tried to pry open the door and found that it was jammed.

"He has locked it from the other side," said one of the men.

One of them took aim and shot the lock. Wooden splinters flew at the impact of the bullet, and they managed to open the door. They entered the room and found it empty. There was a hole in the wall with bricks lying next to it.

"So, that's how he escaped. He opened the wall and escaped into the alley," said Novak.

The detectives went through the hole into the alley. "He must have parked his car on the opposite side of the street and got away," said Howard.

They could see a large crowd had gathered on the street. The sun was beginning to set. "Now, where would he go?" asked Novak.

"Probably to his house. No, he wouldn't go there," said Howard.

"I think I know where. He must have gone to the Johnson Manor. Quick, we must get there before anything happens to Mrs. Johnson." The two men went around the building to the waiting police cars. They jumped in and ordered the other police cars to follow them.

Rachel was unaware of the developments that had just taken place in Manhattan. She was unable to sleep and took a sleeping pill. She had just gone to bed when she heard the doorbell ring. She got out of bed thinking it was the police, who had come with some news.

Just as she was about to open the door, she heard a scuffle, two shots being fired, and a woman scream. She heard the footsteps come towards the room and stepped back. The door flung open and she saw Rudy. He had a gun in his hand. He came in, shut the door, and locked it.

"What's going on?"

"Be quiet. Everything is lost. Now, all my plans are ruined," said Rudy.

"What are you talking about?"

"I planned things so meticulously, and they are ruined; thanks to those detectives."

She gasped and held her hand to her mouth.

"So, Detective Novak was right. It was you who masterminded the whole kidnapping."

"He is only partly right. I have done more than that. I've made your life a living hell."

"Why are you doing this?"

"This is because you are ungrateful. You should have married me and not Fred." He brought the gun closer to her face. "We could have been happy together. I have made your life miserable ever since you rejected me."

"In what way?"

"You want to know the truth about Walter? He did not kill himself. Do you remember that I had to go to Chicago? I made use of that opportunity to kill Walter. I went to the station and checked in my bags. I then went to the hotel and took the elevator. As I was getting out of the elevator, I passed this older woman who just sniggered at me…"

"Oh my God! That was Walter's mother. No wonder she was rambling that you and I killed Walter. She saw you there."

"She did?" He laughed. It sent shivers down her spine. "Anyway, I went inside his office, and he was surprised to see me. I told him that I was there because you sent me to ask his advice on closing hotels. The poor fool was very helpful. He then got up to offer me a glass of brandy, and it was then that I hit him over the head with a paperweight. He saw me in the mirror as he was pouring the brandy, and before he could move, I knocked him out cold. I put the paperweight in my pocket, carried his limp body towards the window, and threw him down. I also typed his suicide note. It was that easy."

He laughed again, and Rachel covered her face in horror as she pictured Rudy hitting Walter with a paperweight and throwing him out of the window. "I wanted to kill Andrew. I tried to get the three men who kidnapped Andrew to kill him. They refused, so I shot one of them in the leg. I would have finished off all of them, but the police intervened."

"How could you do that Rudy? Andrew loves you very much. You were so good to him."

"I only pretended to care for Andrew. I did that just to get close to you." Rachel gasped in disbelief and could not believe the hate she saw on Rudy's face. "I hated Fred for marrying you. He deserved to die in that accident."

"How could you say that? He was always nice to you and treated you like a brother."

"He may have, but he was the reason you and I are not together. I wanted to get away from this country, but the police thwarted that. I could not enlist in the Great War because of my eyesight, and people sent me nasty letters accusing me of being a Kaiser lover. I will show America what I can do. I will go back to Germany..."

They heard footsteps coming towards the door. "Mrs. Johnson, are you all right?" yelled Detective Howard.

Rachel sat still. She didn't know what to do. She looked up at Rudy. "She is fine," Rudy yelled back.

"Now, Mr. Holzmann, we do not need any more trouble. Please release Mrs. Johnson, and we can take it from there."

"No, she is not going anywhere. She will be with me. We are going to come out now and leave the house. Do not try to stop us."

He pointed the gun at Rachel and said, "Get up, Rachel, we are leaving now."

"Where are you taking me?"

"We are going to get out of here. Then I will decide where to go next. Now, get up," he commanded her.

Rachel felt the sleeping pill take effect but tried to fight it and got up. He held her by the arm and placed the gun to her temple. They moved towards the door and he said, "Open it." She did as she was told.

She saw Detectives Novak and Howard in the corridor along with two police officers with their guns out. "Go down the stairs and keep away from us," Rudy shouted at them.

The men backed away and went down the stairs, keeping their guns aimed at Rudy. When they reached the top of the stairs, Rachel saw Robert on the landing with a bullet wound in his leg and the constable wounded near the door. Marcy was tending to the wounded men, trying to stop the bleeding. "Now, Rachel, let's go down the stairs. We are going to leave this house, and you are never going to come back."

Rachel put her foot on the first step and saw Fred's portrait. It had arrived a few weeks after the accident. It was a painting of Fred with a moustache and was the last item she had of him. She could never leave this place. She belonged in this house.

She put her foot down and turned. As she turned, Rudy's grip on her right arm loosened. She raised her hand and hit Rudy in the face. Rudy staggered behind. Taking this opportunity, Rachel pushed him and ran down the stairs. Rudy recovered and tried to shoot at her. Instead, Novak fired a shot, which hit Rudy on the chest. Marcy screamed and covered her eyes. Rachel turned and saw Rudy hold his chest. The gun dropped on the floor and he fell. He rolled down the steps and landed at her feet. Rudy was still alive, and his lips were moving. Rachel bent down to hear what he was trying to say.

"Rachel... I did this all for you..." and she saw him take his last breath. She was overwhelmed and felt the room spinning. She then collapsed on the floor.

Two weeks later, Rachel was sitting in her study and thinking about the events of the past few weeks. After she fainted, she woke up in her bed and thought it was a bad dream. She saw Dr. Thompson next to her. He told her that she did not dream it and that Rudy was dead. Andrew was going to be back with her. Robert and the constable were in the hospital and were going to be fine.

Two days later, Rachel attended the funeral of Rudy Holzmann. The only other people in attendance were his mother and children. People were surprised that Rachel was going to attend the funeral, but she told them that she owed Rudy for saving her life. After the burial, Rachel met Erma outside the cemetery. Erma refused to go to the graveyard and remained in church. Erma told Rachel that their marriage was doomed when she could not get rid of the weight after the birth of their children. Rudy started avoiding her and hardly came home. She heard from one of her friends that Rudy was in the company of several women who had brown hair and beautiful figures. When she confronted him about it, he slapped her. That went on for many years, and she couldn't take it any longer. She confided in her family, and they helped her obtain a divorce. The only reason she and the children were at the funeral was because she felt that it was the right thing to do. She was, for the most part, glad that he was out of their lives.

In church, Rachel noticed a woman clad in black sitting right at the back. She tried to see who it was but could not see the face as it was covered with a thick black veil. 'Must be one of his ladies,' she thought to herself.

The day was cold and damp with an overcast sky. At the graveyard, Rachel noticed the woman was behind a tombstone. Rachel looked again, but she was gone. Rudy's mother was very apologetic. She wished that she had known what was going on. She was moving to Ohio to be with her sister. Rachel felt sorry for her.

Just as she was ending her thoughts, she heard the doorbell ring. A few minutes later, Marcy announced and brought in Detective Howard. "How are you, Mrs. Johnson?"

"I'm fine. Robert is going to come back to us in a few days."

He placed three books on the table in front of her. "These are

Rudy's diaries. I thought you should read them since they concern you."

"How do they concern me?"

"There were many unexplained incidents in your life for which you had no explanations, and these diaries will enlighten you. He wrote his diaries sporadically."

"Does it talk about Walter and kidnapping of Andy?"

"Yes. We found out that he had bought a ticket to sail on the SS Berlin after he had obtained the ransom money. Thankfully, the ship was delayed by two days, and he could not leave for Germany immediately after the money was delivered. He planned to have Andy killed, then kill the three men, take the money, and leave the next day. He did not want anyone to know that there was a fourth person involved. He executed his plan carefully. Thanks to Detective Novak who recognized him; we managed to foil his plans. He wanted the money to start a new life in Germany and be a part of the new Nazi Government. His only mistake was paying you a visit that night."

Rachel put her hands to her face and shook her head. "I didn't know anything about his involvement with the Bund."

"Neither did his wife or mother. He was very discreet about it. His friend who put him in touch with the three men to kidnap Andrew was also arrested. He is wanted in a number of unsolved crimes in New York."

"Thank you very much, Detective Howard."

"You're welcome. I will give you a week to read these diaries and then I need them back. We are also filing a motion to reclassify Mr. Morton's death as murder. The ransom money was found in Rudy's car, which will be returned to you."

He got up and left.

Rachel started reading the first diary and was horrified. She now knew that the horse incident was no accident. What she had heard was actually a gunshot. Rudy had taken a short cut to the stream and fired a shot in the air. His intention, at first, was to scare the horse away and leave Rachel alone in the woods. He wanted her to feel all alone and hopeless, just like he was feeling. He was shocked when he saw the horse kick her in the abdomen because of which she fell to the ground. When he went closer and saw that she did not move and was bleeding, he panicked and went back to the cottage. He tried to shake off the guilt and remain calm. He was relieved when Simon told him that the horse had come back without Rachel. Only then, did he organize a search party and pretended to be shocked like the rest.

The next incident that made her full of remorse, and she blamed herself, was with the Russian dancer. Rudy knew that Fred got drunk fast and encouraged him to drink. Rachel played into his plan by running away when Fred was whistling at the dancer. Before leaving to search for Rachel, Rudy went backstage and told Anna to go to the hotel where they were staying and seduce Fred. Fred being too drunk did not realize that it was Anna and ended up in bed with her.

Rachel read about how much Rudy loved her and how hurt he was that she rejected his marriage proposal. Rachel was very upset that Rudy was glad Fred was out of the way, even though he hired Rudy and paid a doctor to falsify information about his eyesight so that Rudy did not have to enlist. He did feel sorry for Barbara because she was innocent. When she came to the part of his marriage to Erma, he said that the only woman he would ever love was Rachel and that Erma would never replace her. Rudy was glad that she was pretty, but once she put on weight during her second pregnancy, he was repulsed by her and did not want to have conjugal relations with her again. However, he adored his children.

'So, he did have a heart,' thought Rachel.

She read the gory details of how he murdered Walter. He hoped that by getting Walter out of the way, Rachel would fall in love with him, but he was very disappointed when that did not happen. He stated how he felt at home when he joined the 'Friends of Germany' organization. He felt that America had never been good to him because of his German heritage and that his loyalty was to Germany.

He elucidated the plan to get money from Rachel. He wanted her to feel the pain of not having Andrew, the person she loved most. He, therefore, decided to kidnap Andrew, extort money from her, and then have Andrew killed. After that, he would be free to travel to Germany.

Ever since Erma took the kids away, he felt he had nothing holding him back and that he had to help Germany rebound after being humiliated in the previous war.

After reading all the diaries, Rachel decided that it was time to leave the country. Andy had recovered remarkably from the ordeal. She planned to tour Egypt, Palestine, and Europe. They set sail for the Mediterranean in March, visited those countries, and finally went to England in May. Lucy was now in London with her husband and four children. It had been many years since they had seen each other. They landed in time for the coronation of King George VI. They attended the ball given by the American Ambassador to England in honor of the new King. After spending three months overseas, they returned to New York.

A few weeks later, they attended the funeral of Victoria Harlow in Hartford, Vermont.

Chapter 10

Pierre and Annette were relieved to leave the bad memories of the prohibition behind and looked forward to being back in the comfort of their village and the people they knew. They discovered that Catherine had a flair for languages. By the time they reached France, Catherine had learned French. After they disembarked, they hired a carriage that took them to St. Lacroix.

Their son, Louis, was the first to see them. He ran to welcome them. He hugged them and then saw Catherine.

"Papa, Mama, who is that little girl?"

Pierre said, "She is your sister, Catherine."

"Why do you say she is my sister?"

"We adopted her in California".

They noticed Louis' crestfallen face. Pierre took him aside and said, "Louis, you know how much your mother has always wanted a daughter. Since she could not conceive because of the miscarriage, we decided to adopt her. Please treat her well."

Louis looked at him and said with a smile, "Yes Papa, I will treat her like a sister. I missed you and mama while you were away, and I thought another child in the house would take away the affection I have missed these past few years."

Pierre smiled and said, "Louis, you will always be our son. We found this girl alone in the mountains of California and decide to adopt her. We will give her a good life here and raise her as our own. Look at your mother with her. They seem contended to be together."

Louis looked at them and saw the special bond between Catherine and Annette.

"Papa, what will you tell the villagers? They will want to know and will ask questions."

"I will tell them the same thing I told you, and they will not mind her being here since they know how much your mother wanted a daughter."

Within the hour, most of the villagers had come to the farm. The villagers were awe struck when they saw Catherine. Pierre dealt with the questions in a tactful manner. Catherine's innocence, her pretty face, and the way she spoke French charmed the villagers.

"She may have been born in America, but she was meant to be French," said one of the women when she heard Catherine speak French. The rest laughed. Pierre and Annette were relieved that the villagers accepted Catherine.

Catherine made friends with the children and started playing with them. The next night, there was a celebration in honor of the Bouchers. A few weeks later, everything was back to normal. Pierre came to terms with Francois' death and no longer felt guilty. Louis and Catherine got on well together, and they adored each other. Life was good for the family. Pierre continued his business of making apple cider.

It had been five years and everything had been normal for the family, until the day Catherine's playmates told her that she was not the child of Pierre and Annette. She came home crying.

"Of course, you are. You live with us, we take care of you, and Louis is your brother. So, you are part of our family," they told her.

Catherine told her playmates what Pierre and Annette told her. After that, the children never taunted her again. Catherine went to the local school and was a very bright student. She grew up to be a beautiful woman and was a great help on the farm. She had an independent streak in her and got her way in most cases. When she was eighteen years old, her parents wanted her to marry, but she declared that she was not yet ready for marriage and that Annette herself got married at the age of twenty-four. However, at the beginning of 1938, she started to feel disenchanted with village life and wanted to study.

"Mama and Papa, I want to go to Paris to study," said Catherine.

"Go to Paris to study!" Pierre exclaimed. "No woman from this village has ever done that. Women have always married, stayed on the farm, and had large families. Don't you want that?"

"I do, Papa, but I would also like to see the world. Paris has a lot to offer. I like art and would like to learn more about it. I promise I will come back to the village and I will get married. I am still young, and I need to do things by myself for maybe a few years."

"It may be dangerous for a pretty girl like you," said Annette.

"Mama, I could even get killed working on the farm. If I have to worry about danger, I would not step out of the house. Even the roof could collapse and kill me. So, what is the point in worrying?"

Her parents thought about it and realized that she was right. They gave her their blessings to go to Paris.

Catherine sent her application and was accepted by the Paris Ateliers. She was excited to be going to Paris and dreamed of the kind of life she would have there and the adventures that awaited her.

She left for Paris in late summer of 1938. She was twenty years old and looked forward to her new life. While in Paris, she stayed with her cousin, Marie, who was Annette's niece. She then shifted to a boarding house close to the school.

Madame Emile, a widowed older woman, ran the boarding house Catherine lived in. Her children were living on their own. To earn an income, she rented out her rooms only to women. Her rules were; no men in the rooms, and no loud noises.

The girl next to Catherine's room was Collette, a pretty girl with short brown hair and always wore a beret. Catherine and Collette discovered that they were classmates, and they became best friends. While Catherine was studious, Collette was the outgoing type. She had a boyfriend named, Armand.

Armand was a native Parisian. He was the fifth of eight children. At an early age, he got into trouble with the law and spent a part of his youth in jail. After he got out of jail, he worked in restaurants as a waiter and then as a cook. He met Collette when she came to the restaurant to apply for a job. He hired her as his assistant, and they fell in love. He discovered her talent for art and encouraged her to go to art school. Collette had always wanted to go to a university, but her father discouraged her. He told her to find work in a restaurant to hone her cooking skills and provide money to help raise her six siblings and for his drinking habit. She, being disgusted with her father's drinking, was happy to get out of the house and be on her own. When Armand suggested that she join art school, she asked, "How do I go to school on a cook's salary?"

"I have lots of money saved up. Being in jail and being poor have taught me that people do crazy things for lack of money. That is why I promised myself that I would never squander my money, but save it."

"You think I am worthy enough for you to spend all your hard earned money on me?"

"If you become a famous artist and become my wife, I think it's a good investment."

Collette sent her art samples along with the application and was accepted by the art school. She worked at the restaurant on weekends to pay for her board and lodging and went to art school on weekdays.

Collette introduced Catherine to Armand and the three of them became good friends. Soon, it was New Year's Eve 1939, and at the New Year's Eve party, Catherine was introduced to Armand's friend, Roland.

Roland was in his early twenties, six feet tall with red hair. The youngest of three brothers brought up on a farm, he was in the French Foreign Legion for a few years. After stints in Algeria, Tunisia, and Indo China, he returned to France and was discharged. He had known Armand through a mutual friend and was now in Paris working as a truck driver for the restaurant and as a mechanic. It was love at first sight for Catherine and Roland. She was impressed with his tough physique and he, with her blatant honesty and charm.

War clouds were looming over Europe in the fall of 1939. On September 1, 1939, as Europe slept, Hitler's armies marched into Poland. On September 3, 1939, the world was buzzing with the news that England and France, who had treaties with Poland, declared war on Germany.

The Parisians took the news with mixed feelings. Some felt that the Polish people should take care of their own problems with Germany, and the others felt that England and France should honor their treaty with Poland.

To Catherine and Collette the news was very disturbing. They were worried that Armand and Roland would be called up to fight in the war and that the Germans would attack France at any moment. They talked about the possibility of war when the four of them were sitting in a café, and Armand suggested that the girls learn how to shoot. They found it amusing, but he was serious and said that all French women need to be like St. Joan of Arc.

The next day, the four of them went to the garden behind the house where Armand lived and practiced shooting a few cans. Soon, the girls were getting good at shooting with a pistol.

In November of that year, Catherine woke up to Madame Emile shouting. She could hear two voices; one was Madame Emile's unmistakably high-pitched voice, and the other belonged to Collette. She jumped out of bed and went out of the room. She stood on the landing and saw Madame Emile shouting and Collette crying.

"What's happening?"

The two women looked up at her.

"Collette has not been a good girl. She has done something terrible. I never expected that from her."

"What did she do?"

"I cannot bring myself to say it."

"I am going to have a baby, Catherine," said Collette. Catherine was stunned.

"How... how... do you know?"

"I caught her throwing up in the bathroom and sent for the doctor. The doctor examined her and told me that she was pregnant. I had to make the doctor swear that he would never tell anyone. I don't want people thinking that I'm running a house for girls with no morals."

"Madame Emile, I know you're upset, but we must now think of Collette. We must help her."

"Oh no, mon Dieu, no help from me. I am not going to have her staying here. She will have to find a place of her own."

"How could you be so cruel Madame Emile? Her father may not take her."

"Oh no, please do not tell him. He will kill me," said Collette, and she began crying.

"That is your problem, Collette. You should have thought of the consequences before you got yourself in this situation."

"Madame Emile, let me see what I can do. It's clear that you want no part of this, and I respect your wishes, but I can't let her be out on the street."

"She is not staying here a minute longer. I have already told her to pack her things and leave."

"All right, I will help her pack and make arrangements for her to stay somewhere else."

"Do as you wish," said Madame Emile, and she walked away into the kitchen.

Collette and Catherine went upstairs to Collette's room. They saw the two other girls standing at their doors and looking, but then realized that they didn't want to get involved.

Catherine suggested that Collette tell Armand about the pregnancy. Collette was worried he may leave her. Catherine assured her that he would never do that.

They finished packing and brought out two suitcases. They went downstairs and waited for Madame Emile to come out of the kitchen. She came out and gave Collette a brown paper bag with a warm baguette and some apples.

"I can't let you leave hungry. It would not be right. I hope you find a place to stay. Give me your key and you may go." Collette gave her room key to Madame Emile and thanked her. Catherine and Collette picked up a suitcase each and left the house. They walked to the restaurant where Armand worked and asked one of the workers to tell Armand to come out and meet them. Presently, he came out with a dirty white cooking apron around his waist. When he saw them, he smiled, but his face become more serious when he saw the suitcases.

"What's wrong?"

"Collette is in trouble. She can't stay at Madame Emile's boarding house any longer."

"Why did that old witch throw Collette out?" Armand now looked furious.

"I'm pregnant, Armand." He looked at her in surprise. "What did you say?"

"I'm carrying your child. That's why Madame Emile threw me out of the boarding house."

He sat down next to Collette and she began to cry. Armand didn't know what to do, and was just staring at her. "Mon Dieu, what have we done? The one time we went to bed together, this had to happen."

"There is no point worrying about that. We must worry about what to do now," said Catherine.

"I don't know. The only thing I can do now is to marry Collette."

"Don't you love me, Armand?"

"Yes, I do, Collette, but I did not want us to get married like this." Armand drew a deep breath and smiled at Collette. "Well, even though it is unexpected, I am glad that this pregnancy happened. I now have a very good reason to make you my wife, which was what I was intending to do all along."

Armand put his arm around Collette. She looked at Catherine and smiled. Catherine was right; Armand did not abandon her.

"Before that, she needs a place to stay. Then, the two of you can go to the magistrate, get married, and live together," said Catherine.

"Yes, and it will take around a week to get a marriage license. What about living with her family?"

"Oh no, papa will kill me. He will say that I have shamed the family by getting pregnant out of wedlock."

"She can stay here at the restaurant in one of the rooms. I'll speak to the manager."

Armand got up went inside. He came out after a while and said that he had arranged for Collette to stay in one of the rooms and that he would pay for it. The next day, he applied for a marriage license.

A week later, Collette and Armand were married in front of the city magistrate. Catherine stood as Colette's maid of honor and Roland, as Armand's best man. Collette's mother and siblings attended the wedding, but her father refused to come, as he was very upset. Her mother told her that he was more upset that money was not going to come to fund his drinking habit. Collette wore a simple white dress suit. After the ceremony, they had dinner at the restaurant where Armand worked, and Collette moved into Armand's apartment.

As the year 1940 began, Hitler's war machine was marching towards France. In early May, when Collette was getting dressed to go to the market, she felt labor pains, and called the neighbor to help. The elderly neighbor, who was fond of her, took her to her room and called the midwife. Someone ran to the restaurant to tell Armand that his wife was in labor. He dropped everything and ran home.

When he entered, he could hear Collette scream. The midwife and two older women were with her, and one of them shooed him out of the room. He tried to argue, but the older women won. Shortly after, he heard a cry. The door opened, and one of the older women came running out and rushed past him. Before he could ask her anything, she was gone. She came up a few minutes later with a pot of hot water.

"Excusez-moi. What's going on?"

"She is having another baby," she said and went into the room.

A few minutes later, he heard another baby cry. He could feel the excitement rush through him. The door opened and the two older women came out, each holding a white bundle.

"Armand, meet your sons," said one of the women. He looked into the faces of the babies and smiled.

"How is Collette?"

"She is fine and is resting." He went into the room and saw Collette with her eyes closed. The midwife looked at him and said, "Congratulations, Armand. Be very quiet, she is tired. Don't stay long."

"Merci beaucoup, Madame Clara."

The midwife left taking the remaining water, soiled rags, and empty basins. Collette opened her eyes and smiled.

"How do you feel?"

"Tired," said Collette.

"You know we just had twin boys."

"Yes, I know. I never thought that we would be blessed with two babies." She closed her eyes and fell asleep. Armand sat by her side holding her hand and watched her sleep.

The next day, they woke up to the news that the British were evacuating their troops from the shores of Dunkirk.

On June 14, 1940, the German Army marched into Paris. The residents of Paris stopped whatever they were doing and came out to watch the spectacle. They saw German soldiers marching on their streets, with proper decorum, in their pristine German uniforms. Some of the women admired the soldiers and even declared that they looked handsome in their uniforms, with stern faces and rugged looks. Some Parisians began crying at the loss of their beloved city to the invading German forces.

Armand was at the restaurant when he heard the news that the Germans were marching into Paris. Collette was in her bedroom and rushed to the window to see what was going on. Catherine was at the park when someone came and told people around her that the Germans were marching into Paris. Roland was at the garage fixing a car. Each of them felt sadness that their capital city was now under Nazi occupation.

On June 22, the Armistice with the Germans was signed dividing France into Vichy France and German occupied France. Very soon, the Jews in Paris had to wear yellow stars on their clothes. Catherine found herself displeased with the situation. She did not want to return to the village even after repeated attempts by her parents asking her to come back where they thought it would be safer. She decided to stay on in Paris and be where Roland was. Ever since the school closed at the outbreak of war the previous year, she had worked at the restaurant where Armand was working. The restaurant was very popular before the occupation and was now frequented by the Nazis. Armand found it humiliating to be cooking for the Nazis but had to comply.

The twins were named, Dion and Denis. They were baptized at the local church. Catherine and Roland were the godparents. After the baptism, Armand purchased a house he had been eyeing close to the apartment where he lived, and Collette loved it. She could now grow vegetables and hang her own washing in the small yard.

At the end of September, all the Jews in the occupied zone had to register with the police. This made Armand and Roland angry since they had Jewish friends. Armand saw a Jewish couple forced out of the restaurant. A few days later, he witnessed a Jewish family being evicted from their apartment. Armand decided that he would not stay quiet while people were being victimized.

A few days later, a few men came to the house of Collette and Armand. Collette was ordered by Armand to go to the bedroom and stay there. She was not to ask questions. Collette took the twins and stayed in the room until the men left. She waited until Armand came into the room and he said nothing.

"What is happening?"

"I can't tell you, Collette."

"I think I deserve to know."

"It is for the safety of you and our boys."

"Why won't you tell me?"

"I just told you why."

In May 1941, Catherine and Roland were in the park with their godsons. Since it was getting warmer, Collette agreed that the twins could be taken out in their baby carriage. Collette and Armand stayed back home since this was their chance to spend time together without the twins.

Catherine and Roland sat on a bench in the park. They secretly scoffed at the French women walking with German soldiers. They could not understand how these women could lower themselves and mingle with the enemy. It started getting dark, and they decided to get back home. They reached the corner and were just about to go into the street where Collette and Armand lived, when a truck passed by and almost knocked them over. They saw the truck, filled with German soldiers, stop in front of the house and the soldiers get out. They went in and dragged Collette and Armand out of the house. They could see

Collette crying and Armand trying to free himself. Roland tried to go and help them, but Catherine pulled him back. Their friends were forced into the truck and driven away. Catherine and Roland were speechless. They could not believe what had happened.

Two days later, two bodies were discovered floating on the Seine River. They were identified as the bodies of Collette and Armand. The local priest who baptized the twins claimed the bodies, and their families were notified. The bodies bore the marks of torture. Both of them had been executed and had multiple gunshot wounds. Collette's family wanted to keep the twins. Catherine had kept them with her ever since their parents were taken away. She was heartbroken when they had to go but knew that giving them to Collette's parents was in the best interest of the boys.

Catherine noticed that Roland was very depressed. He and Armand were like brothers. She could not understand why Collette and Armand were executed. When she visited Roland, she decided to ask him. Roland refused to tell her, but she insisted. Roland knew that she was right. Catherine and Collette were like sisters, and Catherine had every right to know. He asked her to keep what he told her confidential, and she agreed.

He told her that Armand, he, and a group of men were trying to help Jews and French patriots escape Paris to safety. Many German Jews who had escaped to France told them that after they registered, the Gestapo came and arrested them. Armand and his group successfully managed to get two families out after they registered. Only Armand knew who were in their group because if anyone was caught, they would not be able to identify the others.

"Did you know who else was involved?"

"I knew a few men who were involved, but Armand knew everyone. He was the ringleader."

"Did Collette know?"

"At first, she didn't. Collette was always very curious, and she could not contain her curiosity. She somehow found out what was going on. She wanted to be in from the moment she found out. She even hid a Jewish family in their house for a few days. This is all just a nightmare."

"Poor Collette..." said Catherine and began to cry. She then composed herself and wiped away her tears. She suggested that they continue what Armand and Collette had started and not let this setback deter them.

Roland was against the idea because it was dangerous, but she convinced him saying that if they were in a similar situation, they would have wanted someone to help them.

Roland looked up at her. He knew that Catherine always spoke her mind and was very firm. That was what he found attractive about her. She seemed to be willing to help and was very committed about it.

"All right, Catherine, we will continue our work. I will have to get together the people I know who were a part of the group and see if they, too, would like to continue."

Catherine smiled. She sat next to him, kissed him on his cheek, and said, "I'm sure Collette and Armand would be very proud of us."

A few days later, Catherine found herself in an abandoned stable with six other men. Roland introduced the men to Catherine. "Catherine, these are Andre, Gaston, Julian, Tomas, Vincent, and Olivier. Mes amis, this is Catherine, the love of my life."

The six men stared at her and one of them whistled. "Enchante, mademoiselle. Roland, she is exquisite," said Tomas.

Catherine could feel herself turning red with embarrassment.

"Now, stop that. She will probably leave if she thinks we are all womanizers," said Julian. The men laughed.

"Okay. Let us now get back to business," said Roland. "The reason I think we should know each other is that, if any of us is caught, we will be able to help one another and also warn the others in time. There are still some people hiding, and we have to get them out in the next two days. We can never tell when the Nazis will take the remaining Jews."

"We need a place for them to stay until they can escape," said Gaston.

"Before our friends were apprehended, two families were kept in the basement of their house. We cannot use that house any longer since the Nazis will watch it. We have to find someone who will let us use their house. I know a farmer in Normandy who lives close to the sea. He will keep people in a hidden room in his barn for a few days, until a boat can be arranged to take them to England. If that does not work out, then they will be taken to the Swiss border."

Andre offered to keep them in his house. He was separated from his wife, and the children were with her in Leon. Roland thanked him and said, "Okay. We need to act fast. Here is what we will do..."

Chapter 11

Yale, 1940

It had been almost four years since Andrew was kidnapped. He grew up to be a tall man with brown hair and piercing blue eyes like his mother. Ever since he was kidnapped, he had the fear of being harmed and, therefore, spent his time building his body. He was on his high school football team and did well enough to get into Yale. Before he left the house, he told his mother that he wanted to go to Yale by himself by bus.

"To seem like a normal kid and not like a spoiled rich kid, Mother," he told Rachel.

Rachel was disappointed, as she was looking forward to the day when she could drop him at college.

"Why, are you ashamed of your mother?"

"No, Mother, you're simply wonderful. It is just that I don't want anyone to know that I am the heir to the Johnson Hotels. I want people to like me for what I am and not for my inheritance or for who they think I am - a spoiled, rich kid, which I am not."

Rachel looked at him with pride. Her son had grown into a humble man like Fred.

"I understand, Andy. You are a fine young man, and I need not worry about you."

Rachel offered to drive him to Manhattan to catch the bus to Yale. Andrew agreed on one condition: that she would not cry and embarrass him, she would wear old clothes, and Alfred would park the car far away from the bus depot. She agreed, laughing.

They waited with the other students bound for Yale at the bus depot. They could see other students and their families tearfully bidding each other goodbye. The bus arrived, and the students got into the bus. Before boarding the bus, Rachel said to him, "Goodbye, Andrew. Please write regularly. Your father and sister would have been so proud of you." Her eyes filled with tears, and she could feel the tears beginning to fall.

"Now, Mother, you promised, no tears." She laughed and hugged Andrew.

Andrew deposited his two suitcases in the trunk of the bus. He got into the bus and the door closed. Rachel and the others watched as the bus went down the road, disappearing from view.

Andrew sat next to the window and watched the city pass by. He was excited about being away from home and on his own. He would be studying economics and meeting new people from all walks of life.

The person next to him nudged him. He turned, and the boy held out his hand and introduced himself as Patrick Sanders. Andrew did likewise, and they shook hands. Patrick was going to study geology at Yale.

The bus reached Yale and they got off. After collecting their suitcases, they went to the dormitories to be registered and got the keys to their rooms. Patrick and Andrew discovered that they were going to be roommates. They went to their room and unpacked. The whole experience was new to all of them, and Andrew enjoyed every minute of it.

A week into the semester, Patrick invited Andrew to a party. "It will be like no other party you have attended," Patrick told him. The party was in a house off campus owned by Emma Lowe. Patrick introduced Andrew to Emma. He found her very attractive and started talking to her. He also drank alcohol for the first time.

"Isn't it against university regulations?" asked Andrew.

"This is an off-campus house, so my rules say we can have alcohol," replied Emma. The people standing around laughed.

After the party, Andrew helped Patrick to the dorm and had to get one of the students to sneak them in because it was locked for the curfew.

* * * * *

They went to the same house again two weeks later, and this time there were fewer people. Emma also had something else other than alcohol. She had made cigarettes with marijuana in them. As soon as Andrew smoked one, he could feel the room spinning, and he passed out. When he woke up, he found the rest of the people had also passed out. He tried to get up, but his head was spinning. He had to go for football practice. He held the edge of the table and stood up with great difficulty. He slowly made his way to the washroom and splashed water on his face; that helped him feel better.

He came out of the washroom and found everyone still asleep. He left the house and stopped for a few minutes to take deep breaths. When he felt better, he jogged towards the campus. On reaching the dorm, he changed into his football clothes and ran towards the football field where Coach Lowell was waiting.

"Where have you been?" growled Coach Lowell angrily at Andrew.

"Sorry, coach, I overslept."

"All right, you have never been late for practice. You need to be here on time. Fifteen minutes late is inexcusable."

"I apologize once again, coach. It will never happen again."

Coach Lowell smiled, patted Andrew on the back, and said, "All right, don't be late again. Now, get in there."

Andrew was relieved he got away so easily. He joined his teammates who were warming up. After showering, Andrew got back to the dorm to find Patrick there. "What the heck happened?" Andrew asked. "I just smoked one of those cigarettes, and I was out for the night like you."

"Oh! Those were just joints. Emma has a good stock of them."

"I am never going to try them again. I was almost booted out of the team by Coach Lowell."

Patrick put one hand on his shoulder and said, "Andrew, you need to relax and enjoy yourself. Life is too short to miss out on fun."

"Nevertheless, I'm never going to smoke them again." Andrew kept his promise and never again smoked at Emma's place. The rest of the semester flew by. Soon, it was the end of the semester, and he was home for Christmas.

Rachel was happy to see him and observed that he had grown and matured during the few months he was away from home. They spent Christmas with Martha and Sidney. Sidney was glad to see Andrew. He had always considered Andrew as a younger brother. Sidney had graduated from Harvard Business School and had joined the family business.

He asked Andrew about his first semester and Andrew told him that it was a great experience and that his roommate, Patrick, introduced him to many people.

"Do you mean Patrick Sanders?"

"Yes, how do you know him?"

"I don't know him, but his older brother, Jonathan, was my classmate in Harvard and also in high school. He got into Harvard because his childless, rich uncle paid Harvard a lot of money. Jonathan was up to no good. He was into many things that college students shouldn't be doing. I hope Patrick is not like that."

"Oh no, he's not. He's a good friend. I would be lost without him." Andrew knew that he was lying to Sidney. He did not want Sidney telling Rachel about his friendship with Patrick, as she would be very upset.

"Oh good! I'm glad that he is not following in Jonathan's footsteps," said Sidney, relieved.

Andrew was back for the spring semester in 1941. Patrick and Andrew were roommates once again. They had many discussions about the war in Europe. They all agreed that America should keep out of it and let the Europeans solve their own problems. One day, Andrew saw a flyer on the bulletin board that the U.S. Navy would be coming to the campus. His curiosity got the better of him, and he decided to go and see what it was about.

Andrew sat in the auditorium and saw many other students there. Most of them were senior to him, and he was one of the few freshmen. The recruiter was introduced and he began speaking. He spoke about the dangers in the world, due to the war in Europe and how the United States could get involved. He also encouraged students to consider a career in the navy to serve their country. The U.S. Navy needed fresh young blood to keep the country safe.

Andrew was fascinated. He loved swimming and the ocean, but serving in the navy was not what he thought about until now. He overheard some students next to him talk about how the U.S. should never get involved with the war in Europe. Yet, some others pointed out that it was the same case in the previous war, but eventually the U.S. got involved with the European war in 1917.

After the lecture, some of the students walked out of the auditorium saying that it was a waste of their time coming for it. Some students congregated around the recruiter, and they were asking questions. Andrew didn't leave but looked at the pamphlets on the table and picked a few. When he looked up, he saw the recruiter standing in front of him.

"Can I help you? You seem interested in joining the navy."

"Not really. I was just looking through the information in these pamphlets. I don't understand why you're here. The U.S. will never get involved with the war in Europe, and we don't need to build a strong defense. If we don't interfere with other countries, we won't be attacked."

"That is what people will have you assume. Believe me, there are a number of countries that would like to see the United States involved in the war in Europe for various reasons. It takes one incident to trigger the mood of the people towards America going to war. You never know when that will happen. It is always good to have a strong defense force available when that time comes."

"I'm not sure if I agree, but I'm still a freshman and not that acquainted with the political arena."

"Doesn't matter. We have many young men like you who are clueless about what is going on in the world or about what they want to do in life. They join us and they are glad they did. You also get to see the world," said the recruiter, smiling at Andrew.

Andrew laughed and said, "I will finish college and then decide."

"Judging by your build, I'd say you are a football player, am I right?"

"Yes, I am."

He put his hand on Andrews shoulder and said, "Strong shoulders! We need strong men like you."

"Yes, but I will let you know when I am interested."

The recruiter took out a card from his pocket and gave it to Andrew. "Here, take my card, and give me a call whenever you feel like joining. Even if it is three years later, you can call this number and someone will answer."

"Thank you, sir." He took the card and put it in his pocket. They shook hands and Andrew left the auditorium.

A few weeks later, Andrew was invited to Emma's house for her birthday party. Patrick and Andrew went together. The house was spic and span. Andrew did not recognize many people, as some were older. When he inquired, he was told that they were Emma's relatives. 'No wonder the house is so clean,' he thought to himself.

He noticed a woman looking at him in a peculiar way. She came up to him and said, "You look very familiar. Have we met before?"

"No, I don't think so."

"Where are you from?"

"Long Island."

"Hmm, I used to live in Long Island when I worked as a nanny. That was a long time ago. I left in the early 20s."

"What's your name?"

"Helen MacDonald and what is yours?"

"Andrew."

"Emma is my niece - my older sister's daughter. She was the youngest of three children she had before she died of the Spanish Flu in 1918. I raised her and my children together."

"She is very popular."

"Yes, everyone knows her in this area. She had a tough life and is determined to stand on her own two feet."

Andrew smiled and said to himself, 'If only you know what she is popular for!'

"What is your last name?"

"Johnson."

"Strange! Johnson was the last name of the family for whom I used to work. Are you related to Rachel and Frederick Johnson?"

Andrew didn't like the question. As far as possible, he did not want anyone to know where he was from."

"Yes… they are my parents."

Her face turned red. She held her hands to her mouth and said, "Oh my God… It's you. You look like your mother. No wonder I found you looking familiar."

She turned around and walked away. Andrew was perplexed. He followed Helen and went into the room she had just entered.

"What is wrong?"

"Your mother is a horrible woman."

"What prompts you to say that?"

"It is because of her that your father and sister are dead."

"I don't understand."

"Your father was caught in bed with this woman, and your mother was very harsh towards them. She was harsh even to your sister, and that is why they went to California. They died in the train accident while they were returning."

"I know that they died in an accident, but my mother is not responsible for that."

"She is. She is also responsible for the troubles I had to encounter after she dismissed me. She even had the gall to accuse me of having an affair with your father. In reality, she was having an affair with that German."

"You mean Uncle Rudy?"

"Yes. I read in the papers that he kidnapped you." She laughed, and Andrew felt very cold and confused at that laugh.

"How do you know that my mother was having an affair with

Uncle Rudy?"

"I happened to be passing by, and I heard your parents arguing. I couldn't resist listening. It seems that he also proposed to your mother, and your mother married your father for the sake of money." She snickered at Andrew.

"Rudy was the vilest man ever. Your mother, I could see, was very close to him, and that is why your father ended up with some other woman when we went to New Jersey. I was your sister's nanny, and she was one of the loveliest children I ever took care of. Your mother is the reason you grew up fatherless, and you do not know your sister." Andrew could not believe his ears. He felt like he had been punched in the face. "After she accused me of having an affair with your father and showed me letters, which she and that German collaborated upon, she dismissed me without a reference, and that is why I could no longer work as a nanny. She destroyed my family and me. We had to struggle to earn a living. My poor sickly father had to work and died of a heart attack on the job. We hardly had anything to eat. Your mother is a very wicked woman. She has many deaths on her hands."

"She is not that kind of a person. You're just trying to spoil her name." Andy's voice was now getting louder with rage.

"If you don't believe me, you ask her and she will confirm what I have told you. I can see that she has hidden many things from you. She has made herself to be a saint and a virtuous wife who was widowed at a young age. If I could see her now, I would spit on her."

"Here, you do not talk like that about my mother."

"Or, you will do what? I challenge you to confront her with all that I have told you, and you will see that I am right. She caused a lot of suffering and untold misery to a lot of people."

Andrew had had enough and left the room. He went to the closet, took his jacket, and left the party without saying goodbye to anyone. He stepped out into the spring air and took a deep breath. He could not believe that his own mother, whom he loved so much, was an evil woman and that she was responsible for the deaths of his father and sister and for the sad situation Emma's aunt and her family were in. He ran back to the dorm. His head ached and he went to bed.

A few days later, Patrick invited Andrew to Emma's house even though it was a school night. Emma was having a party to celebrate her friend's birthday, and Emma wanted Andrew to be there, as she wanted to apologize to Andrew for her aunt's behavior. Andrew had nothing else to do and decided to go along.

It was the usual party at Emma's place; drinking and smoking pot. Andrew was coerced by Emma to have a few drinks and smoke a few joints. Once he had a few, he started to feel sick. Emma put him in the center of the room, and the others surrounded him.

"Here lies the son of that woman who made my family suffer." The people in the room started to jeer and laugh at him. Someone threw a glass of beer in his face, and the rest laughed.

Andrew felt his head spin. He could hear what they were saying but could not say anything in his defense. He tried to get up but fell back on the floor. He could see people laughing at him. He looked at Patrick and saw that he was with his arm around Emma. They were both encouraging people to make fun of him.

"Are you really your father's son?" asked one of them.

He was enraged at this and shouted, "Shut up."

The whole room was silent. They began to laugh at him. He pulled himself up and pushed through the crowd. He went out and walked towards the dorm.

Andrew felt alone. His so-called friends were no longer his friends. He was tired of staying on in college. He needed a change. He put his hand into his pocket and felt something. He pulled it out; it was the card, the recruiting officer had given him. He went to a phone booth and picked up the receiver.

"Hello, operator. Could you please connect me to the Navy Recruiting Office in New Haven?"

A few seconds later, a familiar voice came over the phone. "Officer Darren Holmes speaking."

"Good evening, Officer Holmes. I am sorry for calling this late. This is Andrew Johnson. I hope you remember me."

"Yes, I do," he said, excitedly, "and, how are you?"

"I'm fine. I am calling about joining the navy. When can I do that?"

"How old are you?"

"I am eighteen and will be nineteen shortly."

"Very well, you can enlist since you are of age."

"Very good, sir. Can I come tomorrow morning?"

"Of course you can, and I look forward to seeing you. Be here at eleven a.m. sharp."

"I will, sir." Andrew went to his room and wrote a letter to Rachel. He packed his suitcases, lay down on the bed, and fell asleep.

Andrew woke up when the alarm rang and found that Patrick was not yet back. He got up, shaved, dressed, and took his baggage. He took one last look at the room and left. As he was about to leave the dormitory, he ran into Patrick. There were other students walking around the corridor trying to get ready for class.

"Well, Andy, we did have fun at your expense last night."

"You tricked me, Patrick, and that was very rotten of you."

"Come on, Emma wanted you there to give you a piece of her mind. She wanted to get rid of all the anger she had in her when her aunt told her what your mother did to her family."

Andrew was now seething with rage. "Don't you dare talk about my mother like that."

"Oh come on, Andy boy, now you know what she is. By the way, where are you going with your suitcases?"

Andrew put the suitcases down and said, "This is for what you put me through," and he punched Patrick in the face.

Patrick fell on the ground, stunned. He tried to get up and felt his broken jaw. The other students started making fun of Patrick.

"Now you know what it is to be made a laughing stock. As to where I'm going, it's none of your business. I'm going far away from you, Emma, and this whole damn place."

He picked up his suitcases and left. Andrew could still hear the students making fun of Patrick, and others cheering Andy as he walked out of the building, holding his head high and with a smile on his face.

Johnson Manor – Two days later

Marcy looked at the envelope and saw that it was from Andrew. 'High time he wrote,' she said to herself and smiled. She handed over the letter to Rachel, who opened it at once and read it.

As she read the letter, she felt the color drain away from her face. She put the letter down and started crying. Andrew had come to know the real reason Fred and Barbara had gone to California. She had tried very hard to keep it from him. She had even told the household staff never to tell Andrew anything regarding what had happened, and they swore that she could trust their loyalty.

He also wrote that he knew about Rudy's love for her and about the marriage proposal. How could Andrew have known all that? Only Rudy, Aunt Victoria, Fred, and she knew about it, and the three of them were dead.

She telephoned Martha and told her about the letter. Martha was stunned. "That is not the Andy I know. Something must have happened to him."

"I wonder who could have told him details of events that took place before he was born. Can we get the navy to discharge him based on his age?"

"I'm afraid not, Rachel. He is almost nineteen years old and is well within his rights to join without permission from you."

"I was afraid of that."

"I'm sorry, Rachel. He may come around one of these days, and then you will know what happened."

"I do not care about why he did it. I just want him back home. He said he never wants to see me again" Rachel began to cry and placed the receiver in the cradle.

Pearl Harbor, October 1941

Andrew had arrived at Pearl Harbor three months earlier. After he enlisted in New Haven, he went to San Diego for boot camp. He underwent his physicals, standing with other men in their underwear. He was grateful that he was in good health. At six foot one and one hundred and eighty pounds, he knew that he had a good chance of getting through the tough physical challenge of the boot camp.

The camp lasted for ten weeks. He learned to shoot, defend himself, give first aid, personal hygiene in times of war, firefighting, and to pack a sea bag. Because he knew how to swim, he was far ahead of other recruits during swimming lessons. He knew that joining the navy was a good choice. He occasionally thought of Rachel and the past but tried to put those thoughts away. He wanted to be independent and to have nothing to do with the wealth that he was used to.

After boot camp, he was sent to Pearl Harbor. He noticed that there was tension in the air. When asked, he was told that they were wary of the Japanese attacking the West Coast. Many people laughed at the thought of a Japanese attack. It would be sheer madness on the part of Japan to attack a large country like the United States.

He made a number of friends at the camp. His best friends were, Brandon Malone, Phillip Cassidy, and Irving Wizen. They, too, left home, as they wanted some adventure, and the navy was the only way that they could see the world. The four of them were thick as thieves, and Andrew now realized what it was to belong to a group, where he could trust people, after his bad experience at Yale.

The four of them were assigned to the USS Arizona. They got up early morning to scrub the decks, practice drills, and naval maneuvers. On the weekends, they would go into the city to the Pearl City Tavern and Monkey Bar and smoke Camel cigarettes. Andrew had never smoked before in his life. Brandon told him that, "Girls love a sailor who smokes." In this case, it proved to be true.

It was on one of these weekends that four pretty girls came by their table when they were having dinner. "Hello there, handsome fellas. I am Maryanne. This is Sally, Evelyn, and Hazel. Can we join you?"

"Sure," said Phillip.

Irving got up, grabbed four chairs from a neighboring table, and placed them on the opposite side of the table. The girls sat down. The men introduced themselves. "Let me tell you what we do," said Maryanne. "I work here as a bar maid and sometimes take photographs of people. Tonight is my night off. Sally works as a nurse at the hospital. Evelyn and Hazel both work in the mess hall at the hospital."

"Where are you from?" asked Irving.

"Evelyn is from Schneider; Hazel from Boise, Indiana; I am from Philadelphia; and Sally is from Fargo, North Dakota."

"Irving is from Michigan; Phillip from Houston, Texas; Andrew from New York; and I am from Madison, Wisconsin," said Brandon.

Hazel looked at Andrew and said, "Where in New York?" Andrew looked uncomfortable and said, "From Long Island."

"Are you one of those rich folks from Long Island?" asked Maryanne with a laugh.

"No, not me," he said, without batting an eye.

"All of us joined the navy because we wanted to see the world. I'm hoping to see the Far East and Europe. It also gives us a chance to experience something different from the lives we were used to back home," said Brandon.

"Well, that was the same reason we all came here. I wanted to get away from Philadelphia. It is too cold in the winter. I saw a picture of Hawaii and knew this is where I wanted to be. I met Sally while trying to find a place to stay, and we met Hazel and Evelyn at the beach. We have been here for almost a year and love this place," said Maryanne.

"We do, too. I would like to make a toast. To these four lovely ladies and no more wars," said Irving.

"Amen. Let us drink to that," said Evelyn.

They all raised their glasses and took a sip. After that, they all met every weekend.

It was during these outings that Andrew took an interest in Hazel. He wanted to tell her about his feelings for her but was afraid to do so. Once, Hazel saw Andrew looking at her; she smiled, and he reciprocated. When they were going home one evening, Hazel winked at Andrew, and he knew that she shared his feelings. He smiled at her and nodded. The following week, Hazel sat next to Andrew, and they began talking. As she left, she shook his hand and pressed a note into his palm. He put the note into his pocket. When he was alone, he opened the note and found that it was her telephone number and address. It said to call her on Sunday after one p.m.

On Sunday, he managed to get to a telephone booth and dialed her number. A woman picked up the telephone. Andrew introduced himself and asked for Hazel. Hazel told him that she noticed he liked her but was rather shy. She, therefore, decided to take the intiative. She suggested that they meet on Monday at seven p.m., at the Monkey Bar for dinner.

After disconnecting, Andrew felt a series of shocks going through his body. He now had his first date.

He reached the Monkey Bar at seven o'clock. and waited. It was seven-fifteen, and Hazel had still not shown up. Just as he was about to leave, he heard a voice behind him call his name. He turned around and saw Hazel in a red dress, wearing a hat. She looked beautiful.

They went in and got a table, ordered, and started talking. "You seem very different and a lot more polished than your friends," said Hazel.

"In what way?"

"It's just that you're not very loud and have delightful table manners unlike the other men I see around here."

"I guess I was raised right?"

"Oh, we were all raised right."

They both laughed. Hazel told Andrew about her life in Boise. Andrew told her that his parents worked in the hotel industry. It was as close to the truth he could get.

As they finished dinner, the band started playing. They walked to the dance floor where other couples were dancing. They danced to the music for a while, until Andrew looked at the clock and told Hazel that he had to be up for drill early in the morning. They got their belongings from their table, and Andrew hurriedly went to the counter and paid the bill.

Andrew offered to walk Hazel home. When they reached her apartment, Andrew asked if he could kiss her goodnight. She nodded in the affirmative. Andrew bent down and kissed her cheek. She said goodnight and went into the building.

Andrew was ecstatic. As he walked back to the ship, he kept whistling and jumping as if he were walking on air. He almost collided with two sailors who yelled at him, asking him if he was blind. Andrew didn't care. He at last knew that he had met someone special.

The months rolled by and soon, it was the end of November. For Thanksgiving, they went to Evelyn and Hazel's apartment. They cooked the food and the men were grateful for the home cooked meal. At dinner, Irving and Evelyn announced their engagement. Everyone was taken by surprise, especially Hazel, since Evelyn was her roommate. Nobody knew that they were dating, so there was indeed a reason to celebrate. They decided that they would have a small engagement party at their favorite hangout, Pearl City Tavern, on December 6.

As Christmas approached, the talk of everyone spending Christmas with their families made Andrew think of the last Christmas with Rachel, Martha, and Sidney. He missed everyone. He missed Rachel most of all. Even though she kept things from him, he still loved her. He decided he would write to her.

During his free time, Andrew wrote to Rachel. He told her that he was stationed at Pearl Harbor in the battleship Arizona and that he was the happiest he had ever been in his entire life. He now dated a girl who cared about him and he wished Rachel could meet her. In many ways, Hazel reminded him of Rachel; the way she threw her head back and laughed and the way she looked at him. He was thinking of asking her to marry him but maybe, a bit later. He ended the letter saying that she should be happy for him and not worry. He put a Christmas card with a Hawaiian theme inside and sealed the envelope.

The next morning, Andrew went to the post office. The gray haired man collecting the mail was surprised to see Andrew. "Johnson, you have never mailed a letter since you've been here. What's so special about today? Sending a letter to your girl back home?"

"No, Mr. Stuart," he laughed, "I'm sending my mother a letter and card for Christmas."

"Well, you should be writing to her every month, if not every week.

Make sure you do that."

"I promise, Mr. Stuart."

Mr. Stuart stamped the envelope and put it in a box to be sent out. December 6, was a beautiful Saturday. They met at the Pearl City Tavern along with a few other friends. A small area was set aside outside where they held their private party and when it got a bit windy, as the night progressed, they went inside. Andrew saw one of the women with a camera taking the picture of three sailors. Andrew drew Brandon aside and suggested taking a picture of their group. Brandon raised his voice and said, "Fellas, let us take a picture of the eight of us for posterity. Who knows what the future holds for us, but this picture and the memories of our youth, will remind us of the good times we have had, as we grow older."

The rest agreed, and they sat together for the picture. Irving, a bit drunk, nevertheless, posed for the picture. Maryanne had her camera with her and had been taking pictures the whole night. She gave her camera to one of the sailors and he took their picture. She promised to give them a copy each as a memento.

After the party, Andrew and Hazel walked towards Hazel's apartment hand in hand. When they got inside, Hazel offered him a drink. Andrew thought for a moment and said, "Sure, why not, if it makes you feel like a good hostess!"

She chuckled and poured him a drink. He took a sip and said, "Hmm, Pineapple, it tastes great."

"Well, this is where they grow pineapples."

"You know, I've been thinking, Hazel."

"About what?"

"About us! I would like us to get married. We have known each other for around four months, and I feel that you are the one for me."

"Andrew, we are only nineteen. This is the first time that you've even dated. Marriage is not something one gets into without giving it a serious thought. It's a life time commitment."

"I know, and I want to spend the rest of my life with you, Hazel. We are made for each other, and I love you."

"Andrew, I love you too, but marriage is not something that I'm ready for right now."

"You know, I could be shipped out if ever there is a war."

"That will never happen, Andrew. War is not something that happens overnight, especially in the United States, where we are far away from the conflict in Europe and Asia."

"Can we still date each other?"

"Sure, we can, Andrew, but marriage is not something I want to get into right now."

"I understand, Hazel," he said, with a tinge of disappointment in his voice.

Evelyn entered the apartment at that moment. "Look at the time, Hazel, I have to get back. I have to go for mass in the morning and be back on board the ship for mess duty," said Andrew.

"Irving and the others have already left. They dropped me off and drove to their ship," said Evelyn.

"I better go after them," said Andrew. As he got up to leave, Hazel stopped him.

"You can spend the night here."

"What will people say?" asked Andrew.

"Andrew, it is past midnight, and there is no way I am going to let you walk out of that door all by yourself. It can be dangerous. Many people will be going back drunk. I have heard of drunken sailors picking fights with each other this late. You can sleep on the couch."

"I'll get you a pillow and blanket," said Evelyn.

Andrew thanked Evelyn, placed the pillow on the couch, and lay down. Hazel covered Andrew with the blanket.

"I'm getting a preview of what it will be like being married to you," said Andrew.

Hazel laughed. "You can be sure that I'll make a good wife."

"I will wake you up in the morning, and we can go to mass together." She kissed him on the forehead, turned off the light, and left the room. Andrew closed his eyes and drifted off to sleep.

He felt Hazel waking him up. The couch was very comfortable, and he didn't want to get up.

"Come on, we will be late."

Andrew got up and went to the washroom. He washed his face and got ready. He then walked to church with Hazel and Evelyn. After church, he dropped them off at their apartment and walked back to the ship. He ran towards the dock and wondered how he could get to the ship. He spotted a small motor launch about to leave for the ship.

"Hey there, are you heading for the USS Arizona?"

"No, but I can take you there. Jump in."

He jumped into the boat and looked at his watch. It was a few minutes before eight o'clock. He was relieved that he would be on time to report for duty at the mess hall for cleanup.

The boat reached the ship, and Andrew thanked the boatman. Andrew climbed onto the deck and saw Irving come out with a group of sailors.

"Hey there, Andy, where were you last night?"

"Well, Evelyn and Hazel would not let me leave the apartment since it was late. They didn't want me to get into a fight with some drunken sailors."

"So, you were at Hazel's apartment last night!" said Irving with a sly smile.

"It is not what you think, Irv. I guess you need to get your mind out of the gutters," said Andrew and laughed. They heard the sound of planes coming toward them. They turned and saw many planes in the sky. It looked like a big flock of birds.

"Hmm… I didn't know the air corp was having a training session this early, and on a Sunday, too," said Andrew.

"Beats me, Andy. They never tell us anything. I guess our superiors know all about it."

From a ship far away, they could hear the sound of a brass band playing "The Star Spangled Banner" and the sound of Hawaiian music from the radio of one of the crew scrubbing the deck. They all stopped what they were doing and looked at the planes coming toward them. It was a beautiful sight with the sun and clouds in the background.

"I can't see the American flag on the planes," said one of the sailors.

"There is something on the side of the planes, but it sure does not look like the American flag," said another.

They saw the planes coming closer and dropping huge cylinders.

"What are those?" asked one of the sailors.

The explosion answered his question. They were all stunned. No one had warned them of an air raid. They saw the first set of planes pass by and could see the pilots smiling at them. The pilots seemed amused at their shocked faces. They then saw the roundels on the planes.

"It's those Japanese that we were worried about."

"It is an air raid. Get the ammunition."

"The ammunition is locked up below," shouted one of the sailors.

"Well, get them out. We need them now."

Irving ran with the other crewmembers towards the inside of the ship. He stopped and looked back and saw Andrew staring at the planes. Andrew stood transfixed. Irving ran back and shook him trying to get his attention.

"Andrew, snap out of it! Come with me."

Andrew was shaken out of his trance and followed Irving below deck. They could see men scrambling about from the mess hall and their bunkers, half-dressed, trying to put on their clothes. They heard an explosion and felt the ship shudder. They felt the heat and smelled burning flesh.

"The ammunition must have exploded. We need to get out of here and into the water," shouted Andrew.

"Yes, let's head up."

The men scrambled to the ladder that would take them onto the deck. They could feel the heat throughout the ship. The ladder too was starting to get hot. They finally managed to get out into the open and could see that the front of the ship was on fire. Some of the sailors were trying to put out the flames with a hose but to no avail.

They could hear the siren to abandon ship. Men tried to get out of the burning ship as they felt more bombs hit. The ship started to list dangerously. Andrew and Irving were separated by the mob of men trying to get out. Andrew saw some men on fire and went to help. He removed his shirt and tried to douse the flames when a plane came by and sprayed bullets. The men around him dropped like flies, and he felt a sharp pain in his leg. He realized that he had been shot. He fell and started screaming in pain. He felt someone pick him up and drag him. He looked up and saw Irving trying to push him towards the water. He could see his fellow sailors jumping overboard. Another explosion rocked the ship, and the ship began to list more. The crew, who were standing, lost their balance and fell on the deck. Andrew could feel himself sliding on the deck. He hit the railing and fell into the water. He saw Irving fall into the water and try to swim. Andrew could feel intense pain as the salt water touched his wound.

A plane swooped by and opened fire. The bullets hit the men, and the water around them turned crimson. Andrew was hit in the right arm. He tried to stay afloat with the other arm. Without warning, the water started turning black, and the surviving men realized that the ship's oil was leaking into the ocean. The burning debris falling from the ship set the oil on fire.

Andrew looked around and all he could see was fire. 'No way out,' he thought to himself, 'this is the end.' As he started to slip down into the water, he felt himself being lifted out and placed into a boat. He could see other men lying in the boat next to him covered with oil and some with horrible burns on their bodies. Some had lost limbs and were bleeding profusely. The last thing he remembered before he lost consciousness was the USS Arizona burning, men crying out in pain to be rescued, the sounds of planes flying, gunfire, and explosions. The whole place smelled of blood, oil, and death. What began as a beautiful day in a tropical paradise was now a living nightmare.

'This must be what hell is like,' murmured Andrew as he closed his eyes.

Chapter 12

Rachel woke up early and got dressed for mass. She always attended mass at St. Jude's Chapel where Father O'Malley, transferred from Manhattan, said mass at seven-thirty a.m., every Sunday. She reached the chapel and went to the pew reserved for her. She genuflected and crossed herself. She adjusted the hat and veil on her head, knelt down, and prayed. The altar boy rang the bell, and the cantor started singing a hymn. Father O'Malley walked to the altar and began mass. The sermon was about the love of a mother for her children just as the Holy Mother loved Jesus and his disciples.

She knelt before the priest, received the communion wafer, went back to her pew, and started praying for Andrew. "Dear Lord, please keep Andrew safe from all harm and danger, and let me hear from him."

After mass, Alfred drove her home. As she entered the manor, she thought of Andrew and started sweating even though it was cold. 'How strange!' she thought to herself.

Rachel had breakfast and then read the newspaper. She felt a headache coming on, and needed to rest. She told the staff that she would get up at one p.m. Her dreams were filled with visions of Andrew, Barbara, and Fred. She could see the train plunging into the ravine and was unable to do anything about it. She saw Rudy with a gun trying to kill Andrew. She woke up sweating and was glad that it was just a dream. The alarm started ringing.

After lunch, she turned on the radio and tuned into NBC to listen to the Sammy Kaye Sunday Serenade. As the program ended, there was a news flash that Pearl Harbor had been bombed. It then went back to its regular program. Rachel was horrified. 'So, war finally comes to America,' she said to herself. She listened to the news the whole day, and felt sorry for the families of the men who died in the attack. She went to sleep early.

The next day, she got up and went for mass. Fr. O'Malley urged the congregation to pray for the victims. After the service, she met Fr. O'Malley at the entrance. "It is a pity about what the Japanese did yesterday."

"Yes, it is Father. I, however, feel a bit worried about Andrew."

"Have you heard from him?"

"No, Father. He was very angry with me and you know why. He blames me for everything."

"Do not worry, my child. He cannot stay angry with you for all time to come. My instincts tell me that you will hear from him soon, probably today. You never know. Have faith, my child."

"Thank you, Father. Please keep us in your prayers."

Rachel went home and found that the post had come early. She went through the mail and stopped dead in her tracks. She looked at the envelope again. She looked at the stamp and the mark on the stamp. It said, "Pearl Harbor, Hawaii". She tore the envelope open, took out the Christmas card, and read the first few words. She did not complete reading it. She knew why she was having those dreams. Andrew was at Pearl Harbor. She started crying and the staff was baffled. "What is wrong, Mrs. Johnson?" asked Marcy.

"It's Andrew. He has finally written. He's at Pearl Harbor."

Marcy and Robert did not know what to say.

"We... we hope he is safe."

"I hope so. I have to get there. I need to know if he's all right." She was now hysterical.

"Don't worry, Mrs. Johnson. We'll help you," said Marcy, as she signaled to Robert.

Robert called Alfred and asked him to fetch Dr. Thompson. Marcy helped Rachel to her room, so she could lie down. Dr. Thompson arrived at the house and gave her an injection to calm her down.

"Doctor, do you know people in the navy?"

"Yes, I do, Rachel. Would you like me to find out about Andrew?"

"Yes, please, Doctor. I am very worried about him. I have been having nightmares about Andrew since yesterday, and... I did not know why and..."

"Shhh. Don't try to speak. Please rest. You've had a bad shock."

She closed her eyes and drifted off to sleep. Dr. Thompson left her side and went downstairs. He took a book from his medical bag, lifted the telephone receiver, and dialed a number.

It was getting dark and the wind was blowing. Rachel woke up and thought it was all a bad dream. She got up and went downstairs. She saw Dr. Thompson sitting on the sofa reading the newspaper. He looked up at her and said,

"Feeling better, Rachel?"

"Yes, Doctor. What have you found out?"

"I called my friend who lives in San Diego, and he told me that they are bringing in people from Pearl Harbor to the hospital there. The one on the island had some damage, but the fires are under control. They are still trying to find survivors and keep an account of the survivors and the dead. Nobody knows for sure what is happening there."

"Did the USS Arizona get bombed?"

"Yes, it did, and many did not make it."

"Oh no, Andrew was on that ship."

"Rachel, listen to me," his voice was stern, "it is pointless worrying about him now. Let's hope for the best."

"You're right, Doctor," said Rachel.

He smiled at her and said, "Come, have some tea."

She obeyed the doctor and sat down. Doctor Thompson poured her a cup of tea, and she sipped it slowly.

Two days later, Dr. Thompson arrived at the manor.

"Any news?" asked Rachel.

"Yes, Andrew is alive. He is hurt, but he will pull through. He is still at Pearl Harbor Naval Hospital and has just had surgery to remove the bullets from his knee and arm."

Rachel hugged Dr. Thompson and started crying. "Thank you, Dr. Thompson. The last two days have been hell for me. I am relieved that he's alive. When can I bring him back?"

"I don't know, Rachel. I don't think that they will let him out that easily. He'll have to be discharged first."

"I hope they give him an honorable discharge. The poor boy has suffered a lot."

The next day, Rachel was on her way to Hawaii. She flew to San Diego via Chicago.

Rachel landed in San Diego, apprehensive of what lay ahead of her. She was not sure if Andrew would be happy to see her. She had lost so much and did not want to lose her only living child.

Dr. Thompson arranged everything for her. Rachel took the clipper to Pearl Harbor. A young man in naval uniform welcomed her. He drove her to one of the hotels still functioning after the attack. On the way to the hotel, she could see the devastation caused by the Japanese attack. She could feel the pain mothers around America were going through. She had one comforting thought; she knew for sure that Andrew was alive and would get well.

The car stopped in front of a small hotel. She could see there was some damage and a few bullet holes on the walls. The owners had already cleared the debris and started to patch some of the holes. She went into her room, and the porter, a young Japanese boy around seventeen, placed her suitcases on the floor.

"Wait a minute," she yelled, as he started walking towards the door. He stopped and turned. She could see that he was shivering. She reached into her purse and pulled out two dollars. "This is for you."

He took the money and thanked her. He turned to go and she asked, "Has it been hard for you and your family after the attacks?"

"Ye… yes, Mrs. Johnson. We are now viewed as the enemy."

"I don't think you are. What is your name?"

"Sam Tanaka."

"Well, Sam, thank you for your help." He smiled, nodded, and walked out of the room. He thanked her as he closed the door. Rachel could see that he was glad she was very nice to him. She went to the window and opened it. She could feel the warm tropical breeze enter the room. It was the first time she had experienced the tropics. She could see the coconut palms and the beautiful view of the ocean. Hawaii was really the paradise everyone made it out to be.

She wore a green dress with a hat and a pearl necklace. She wanted to look nice for Andrew. She didn't want him to see the anguish she had been through for the past few days.

The car sent by the naval department arrived at three p.m. She had received special permission to enter the hospital where the wounded were being treated. She could see the devastation as the car came closer to the naval yard. The sight of cranes and people trying to break into the ship's steel hull to retrieve the bodies of those trapped inside, was too much to bear. The car went inside the hospital compound and stopped in front of the building. From what she could see, the hospital was not that badly damaged.

A nurse was waiting for her; Rachel followed the nurse into the hospital. She was shocked to see young men, who were in their prime, bandaged and some badly burned. Some were crying out in pain as the nurses changed their bandages. She was taken into a room filled with wounded men. The nurse took her past a row of bandaged men and stopped in front of Andrew's bed. His right leg and arms were bandaged, and he was asleep.

"How is he nurse?"

"He's fine. Unfortunately, the bullet damaged a portion of his knee, and he will never be able to walk normally. He probably will have to be discharged from the navy. His right arm was burned slightly, and there was no damage by the bullet. He had minor cuts and bruises on his face, and is very fortunate. Some of the men here were badly burned and others were so badly wounded, that their limbs had to be amputated."

Rachel thanked the nurse as she left. She drew up a chair and sat next to Andrew's bed. She looked at Andrew's face and saw that he was calm. The news that the navy may not take him back sent a wave of relief through her. Andrew could come home with her and recover there. She was not sure how he would react to the news; maybe, he already knew.

Rachel heard him moan. He was coming to. Andrew opened his eyes and saw his mother sitting in front of him.

"Mother, is that you? Am I dreaming?"

"No, you are not dreaming, Andy." She smiled as tears filled her eyes.

"It's nice to see you again, Mother."

She held his hand as tears rolled down her cheeks. She was glad that he accepted her. She had worried for nothing.

"Andy, I don't know if you know, but the nurse told me that your knee has been damaged badly and that the navy may not take you back."

"Yes, I know that, Mother. I'm waiting for news about my friends. I can't leave without knowing if they are safe or not. They're like the brothers I never had. No word has come to me about them. I also have to know about Evelyn and the other girls."

"I'm sure they're fine. Have you asked the nurse?"

"Yes, I did, but they don't know anything. At least, they claim not to."

"Let me find out for you. What are their names?"

Rachel left the room and went to the desk where the nurse was sitting. "Excuse me, nurse, where would I find information about people who have died or are wounded?"

"We keep records of the people who were brought here in our Record Room. However, they are classified and cannot be seen by unauthorized persons."

"I understand, but would you like to make some quick money?"

"What are you implying?"

"You are a single attractive woman, and you would like to have nice things to stay attractive, wouldn't you?" She looked at the nametag and said, "Nurse Genevieve, I can help you get some of those nice things. I will give you fifty dollars. I want you to do me a favor."

At the mention of money, Genevieve sat up and said, "What is it you want me to do?"

Rachel gave her the names and asked her to find out information on them. She gave the nurse ten dollars and promised to give the balance when she gave her the details.

Rachel went back to the room, sat by Andrew, and smiled. "I have taken care of it."

Two hours later, Nurse Genevieve called Rachel aside and gave her the list. It had a telephone number of one of Andrew's friends. She also informed Rachel of Irving's death.

Rachel took the information, thanked Nurse Genevieve, and gave her the balance of forty dollars.

Nurse Genevieve thanked Rachel and left. Rachel was very upset with the information. How would she tell Andrew that Irving was dead? She decided to call the telephone number the nurse gave her. She went to the public phone booth and dialed the number.

Later in the day, Nurse Genevieve stood at the door and beckoned Rachel to come. She told Rachel that Phillip and Brandon would like to speak to her. Rachel asked the nurse to send them in.

A few minutes later, Rachel saw two strapping young men, dressed in naval uniforms, come towards her. They introduced themselves to her. Phillip told Rachel that he was in the hospital to be treated for a concussion and shrapnel wound. Brandon, however, escaped without a scratch. They enquired about Andrew, and Rachel told them about his injuries. She also explained that the navy would discharge Andrew because of the injury to his leg.

"May we see him? They would not let us see him earlier since we were not family," said Brandon.

"Yes, you may. He will be delighted to see you."

They went into the room and stood in front of Andrew's bed. He opened his eyes and looked at the three of them. He smiled and they could see the joy in his face.

"Brandon, Phillip, is that really you? I must be dreaming."

"No kid, it's us. We were worried about you," said Phillip.

"I'm glad to see you two."

"We too. Your mother told us that you are going to be fine."

"Sort of, although the navy will not take me back. How is Irving?

Why isn't he here?" The two men were crestfallen. They did not speak. "Well, where is he? Is he all right? He saved my life. If he hadn't pushed me into the water, I wouldn't be here. I owe him my life."

Brandon spoke nervously. "Andrew, Irving passed away two days ago."

Andrew's face darkened. "What happened?"

"He was shot in the abdomen and also badly burned. The doctors tried everything they could, but he had lost a lot of blood, and his wounds were infected. They shipped his body to his family yesterday."

"How are the girls? Are they safe? Oh my God, Hazel, is she fine?"

They looked at each other uncomfortably. "Maryanne and Sally are fine, but Evelyn didn't make it, and we have no news about Hazel. She is missing," said Phillip.

"What do you mean by Hazel is missing? It can't be. We were going to get married someday."

The two men looked at Rachel who was sitting next to Andy. She looked at them with a blank stare. "It's just that she's missing. There are many people listed as missing and then they turn up."

"What happened to Evelyn?" Andy shot back in anger.

"Her body was found in a warehouse that was bombed. Evelyn and some people in there were killed."

"Did Irving know that Evelyn was killed?"

"No, he didn't. He was sedated because of the pain and was delirious. Nobody could tell him anything, and we were not allowed to see him for fear of infection," said Brandon.

Andrew asked them to leave. He had enough bad news for one day. Brandon and Phillip went out of the room and Rachel followed. "He didn't mean to be rude. He's in shock because of the bad news."

"We understand, Mrs. Johnson. He needs time to let this bad news sink in. What will happen to him?"

"I will take him back to New York after he is discharged."

"We would like to say goodbye before he leaves, Mrs. Johnson. We will be leaving for training shortly and then sent overseas to fight the enemy. We'll have to show them we will not be quiet, but will crush them," said Phillip.

"War is horrible. I was on the Lusitania when it was torpedoed, and that is where I met Andrew's father. I know you have a duty to protect this country, and I will pray for your safety."

"Thank you, Mrs. Johnson," they said in unison. They hugged Rachel and left. She was glad that Andrew was not going with them. She went back into the room and found Andrew asleep and tears drying on his face.

Two weeks later, Andrew was well enough to stand on his feet and go home. He received his discharge papers and was officially out of the navy. Before they left the island, Andrew insisted on going for a last tour of the harbor. The taxi took them there, and they could see that the salvage operations and the rebuilding were already underway. At Andrew's request, Rachel had tried to find out what happened to Hazel. She was still reported as missing/presumed dead. While in hospital, Maryanne and Sally visited Andrew. They were training to become nurses to help in war zones. They were upset over the death of Evelyn and the loss of Hazel.

The flight back to San Diego was very quiet. Andrew was in pain, and had taken medication to make him sleep. By the time he stepped onto the plane to Chicago and New York, he had sunk into depression. He hardly spoke. The plane landed in New York; Martha and Sidney were at the airport to greet them. Andrew smiled when he saw Martha and Sidney and hugged them, as they welcomed him home.

"We've missed you, and are glad you're all right," said Martha, as she hugged him and wiped away the tears from her eyes.

"Thank you. It is so nice to see you both again."

Alfred came and collected the bags. He shook Andrew's hand and Andrew reciprocated. Sidney put his hand on Andrew's right shoulder while walking towards the cars.

"How is he?" Martha asked Rachel.

"He will recover from his wounds, but I'm afraid he is sinking into depression. The girl he loved is missing. Nobody has seen or heard from her, and the authorities fear that she may be dead. Her roommate was found dead in a bombed warehouse."

"Oh no, that's terrible. Poor Andy! I hate to see him like this."

"Martha, I fear that he will harm himself if he is depressed."

"Oh, no, he will not do that. He has you to monitor him, and I'm sure the household staff will also keep a close watch on him. Dr. Thompson could get him to meet a psychiatrist."

"I will ask Dr. Thompson about it."

The next day was New Year's Eve, and Martha had invited them to her house for the celebration. Andrew had spent the whole day sleeping. He was not too keen on going to the party, but he agreed to go very reluctantly. Rachel helped him to get dressed because of his leg wound. He looked all right, except for the few wounds healing on his face. He still seemed very rigid and uptight. Rachel believed he would, perhaps, cheer up if he went to the party. Sidney knew how to make people laugh. He was the life of the party, and he would try to make Andrew happy.

Alfred drove them to Manhattan, and Andrew did not speak the whole journey. Rachel tried to talk to him, but he hardly responded.

Martha welcomed them and took them inside the living room. Five other people were seated there. They stood up as Rachel and Andrew entered. "Rachel and Andrew, these are the Murphys. This is Joe Murphy, Janet his wife, Mary their daughter, Tom their older son, and Steven their second son. Sidney is dating Mary."

They all exchanged greetings. Rachel and Andrew sat on the same sofa. Sidney entered the room and greeted them. He went and sat next to Mary Murphy.

Mary Murphy was an attractive brunette with curly hair. Her brothers sat opposite her. Tom was around twenty-two years old, and Steven was around eighteen. Both of them had red hair like their mother.

The conversation between those gathered went well. Andrew seemed to be a bit hesitant at first but then started joining in the conversation as Sidney asked him his opinion on various topics being discussed. Rachel had telephoned Martha earlier to tell her not to bring up the topic of the war or Andrew's service. That tactic seemed to work. They, instead, focused on Harvard and the football teams since the two Murphy brothers were attending Harvard. They were interrupted intermittently by the maid and the butler who brought delicious hors d'oeuvres and drinks.

Soon, it was close to midnight. Everyone gathered in front of the grandfather clock. Ten seconds before midnight, they joined hands and started counting backwards. As the clock struck midnight, they shouted, "Happy New Year," threw confetti, and blew on their bugles distributed earlier by Martha. Rachel was glad to see that Andrew was now back to his old self. They sang "Auld Lang Syne" and wished each other well. From the windows, they could see and hear the fireworks bursting in the sky, as the revelers lit fireworks. Tom turned on the radio, which upset Andrew.

"Due to the events at Pearl Harbor and the subsequent entry of the United States into the war, the whole of New York has been under a 'dim out' to conserve electricity."

Martha turned off the radio, but the damage was done. The mere mention of Pearl Harbor brought pain and horror to Andrew's face. Rachel watched Andrew go from happiness to regression into a childlike state, as he started crying and shouting out Hazel's name. The Murphys looked at him in shock.

"Who's Hazel?" asked Steven.

"Quiet Steve," said Mary.

Rachel and Sidney went to Andrew and put their arms around him trying to comfort him. Sidney led Andrew out of the room and into the hallway. Rachel followed, and from the look on Sidney's face, she knew that it was best to take him home. Alfred was summoned and he brought the car while Martha and Sidney helped him in. Rachel collected his coat and joined him. The car sped back towards Long Island. Rachel could see that Andrew had stopped crying and went back into his state of depression.

The next day, Martha called Rachel and told her that she had warned everyone not to mention the war and she apologized on Tom's behalf. "I'm sure Tom didn't mean any harm, but he should have asked before turning on the radio. Oh, Martha, what's the point? What is done is done, and now Andrew is back to where I hoped he would never go. Dr. Thompson came by and gave him a sedative, and he is sleeping."

"Maybe, that is the best thing for him now. Has Dr. Thompson scheduled an appointment with a psychiatrist for Andy?"

"Yes, he got the best psychiatrist available."

"Sidney has decided to join the army."

"Oh no! What did you say?"

"I told him that I did not like the idea. He said that his country needs him. Since he is an able-bodied man, he should be helping the U.S. and her allies win the war and not sitting in his office in Manhattan while men younger than him have joined. All I can do is pray that he comes back safely."

"That is all anyone can do, Martha."

Two days later, Andrew was well enough to meet with the psychiatrist, but he was moody and withdrawn. Dr. Thompson had managed to get his friend, Dr. Cleary, to take Andrew's case.

When Andrew was getting dressed for his doctor's appointment, he heard the car backfire. Rachel and Marcy heard Andrew yell. They rushed to his room and found him under the bed, cowering in fear. He was shouting, "It's the Japs, they're attacking again. Oh God, I'm going to be killed. My friends are dying around me. Hazel, Hazel..." Rachel had to go under the bed and force him to come out. She held him in her arms, and he cried like a baby.

"It's nothing, Andy. No need to be afraid, you're safe at home. Nobody is going to hurt you or your friends."

He stopped crying, and she helped him to the washroom to wash his face. Rachel let Marcy help Andrew dress while she went downstairs and out of the house.

"What happened?" she shouted.

"The car backfired, Mrs. Johnson."

"Make sure that doesn't happen again. Andrew is scared, thanks to you."

Alfred looked at her in disbelief. Rachel had never shouted at him like that. Rachel went into the house to find that Andrew was ready, and Robert was helping him down the stairs.

Andrew did not speak a word during the entire journey to Dr. Cleary's office. A few minutes later, the nurse led them into the doctor's office. Dr. Gerard Cleary was in his forties with a graying moustache. He was looking out of the window and turned as they walked in. He smiled, walked up to them, and held out his hand.

"Welcome. I am Dr. Cleary. You must be Mrs. Johnson and Andrew."

"Yes, we are. Thank you so much for seeing us," said Rachel, as she shook his hand.

"Dr. Thompson has told me about your case. I will have to have only Andrew in the room because I will have to examine him and talk to him alone."

"Yes, Dr. Cleary, I understand," said Rachel, and she turned to go.

"Thank you, Mrs. Johnson. I will get back to you as soon as I have spoken to Andrew." Rachel left the room and closed the door behind her. She sat down and waited, hoping that the door would open soon.

Andrew's face looked drained and tired. Dr. Cleary looked at Andrew and said,

"Well, Andrew, please lie down on that couch and relax. I will sit next to you on this chair, and we can start our session."

An hour later, the door opened, and Dr. Cleary came out. "How is he, Doctor?"

"I'm afraid he is suffering from depression caused by the ordeal he went through during the attack. The attack took place at a time when he was very happy and in love with this girl, Hazel. However, due to the sudden loss of Hazel and his best friend, compounded with the shock of being attacked and thrust into a battle unexpectedly, he is suffering from shock and also from the fact that he survived and his friends and fellow sailors did not."

"Can he be cured, Doctor?"

"Yes, he can, but I'm afraid it will take a very long time. I saw it with the soldiers from the previous war. They, too, were badly affected by the war and from being exposed to various poisonous gases. They were treated for shell shock and took a very long time to recover. They lapsed into depression and hallucinations very often. In Andrew's case, he may have hit his head on the ship's deck when he fell, or the force from the explosions may have affected his brain. Only proper rest and medication will help him. He will also have to come in for counseling sessions. That will be my chance to evaluate his progress.

"Is that all that can be done?"

"Yes, that is all we can do. I have seen many men from the last war go through that, but they got back to normal life after being treated by a psychiatrist."

Rachel felt tired and sat down. She blamed herself for the situation Andrew was in since he had told her what Helen said at Emma's party, and felt that she was a bad mother.

"Mrs. Johnson," said Dr. Cleary.

She suddenly came back to reality. "Whaaa...?"

"I understand you must feel terrible, but you need to be in good spirits in front of your son. Only that will get him through this. Now, let us go inside. He's just resting." She stood up, straightened her dress and hat, and followed Dr. Cleary into his office.

Chapter 13

It was April 15, 1942. Rachel always felt mournful on this date. On this date, thirty years ago, her parents met their watery grave on the Titanic. She remembered begging her parents not to go to Europe, fearful that they would never return and her father laughing it off, assuring her that they would come back. She loved them but resented them for not listening to her.

Over the years, she looked at their picture from time-to-time for a few seconds and put it away, as she felt the resentment come back. 'I must get over that,' she said to herself.

She took the picture out and placed it on her desk.

* * * * *

Robert showed a woman into the drawing room. Her name was Gulia Faustino Cleary. She wanted to thank Rachel for helping to get her out of prison, and brought canoli as a gift. She hoped Rachel would like it. Gulia grew up on a farm in Northern Italy. She attributed her strength in her old age to all the hard farm labor. After she immigrated to America with her six children, she worked hard to send them to school. That is why they were all successful, including her two American born children.

She took pride in their achievements and hoped that her now growing family of grandchildren would make use of the opportunities America had given them to become successful. When her husband died, she wanted to continue working and not be idle in her house in

Brooklyn.

Cooking was her passion. She learned new dishes and amazed everyone at how delicious they turned out at the first attempt. It was through her cooking that she managed to woo her husband. He was an Irish doctor who came to her village to look after the sick. He had saved her brother from dying and in gratitude, her mother invited him for dinner. Gulia cooked the dinner. When Dr. Kevin Cleary tasted the food, he was smitten not only with her cooking but with her beauty as well. Obviously, her family did not like the match, so they eloped, and got married. Their first three children were born in the village. Even after producing three children, her family would not accept them, so they decided to move to Ireland. In County Galway, they had three more children. Some looked like her and some like Dr. Cleary. He named the boys and she named the girls. The inhabitants there did not take too kindly to them either. Dr. Cleary decided to immigrate to America, and he went ahead. Two years later, he sent for his family. They were relieved to leave Ireland and start afresh in America.

Living in Brooklyn did not go well. The Irish children ridiculed her children, who looked Italian, with names like WOP, dago, and guinea; and the Italian children ridiculed her children, who looked Irish, calling them Paddy and Mick. Gulia and her husband tried very hard to prevent their children from having fights. "From the frying pan into the fire," her husband would always say when one of the sons came home after a fight. It seemed that America too did not spare her children, either.

After her husband died, Gulia withdrew some of her savings, and opened a restaurant along with her friend Guissipina. It did well.

Gulia was not pleased when America went to war with Italy. She was still a citizen of Italy. After some soul searching, she decided to support the United States even though she was called a fascist and there was graffiti on her restaurant windows calling her names.

"We have lived here for most of our lives, and it is only right that we support our adopted homeland," declared Gulia. To show her loyalty, she hung an American flag outside the restaurant.

Her patriotism was questioned when, one day, a car stopped in front of the restaurant, and four men got out. They entered the restaurant and went to where the two women were seated. "We are looking for Gulia Cleary."

"Buonasera. I am she. Who is asking?" said Gulia.

"We have orders to search this place for contraband."

"Why?"

"You've been suspected of being an enemy alien and espionage against the United States."

"I am not a spy. I support this country. Can't you see the flag outside? One of my sons is in the U.S. Army and is fighting the enemy in Europe."

The man gave the three men permission to search the place. They went into the office and kitchen. Everyone, including their employees and customers, could hear desks being opened and searched.

"We found it." The man came out with a camera and radio. "Mrs. Cleary, you will have to come with us."

Guissipina started crying. Gulia looked at her and said, "I am innocent. No need to cry." She complied and went with the men.

* * * * *

That evening, Rachel received a phone call from Dr. Thompson. He told her the mother of Dr. Cleary, Andrew's psychiatrist, was arrested on suspicion of espionage, and told her what the Feds had found. Dr. Cleary suspected that some jealous competitors must have tipped the government.

"So, she is guilty?"

"No, that is the point. Those items were bought before the war. She was arrested because she is not a U.S. citizen."

"How can I help?"

"Do you know someone who can get her out? Like a congressman or a senator?"

"Yes, Senator Morton. I haven't kept in touch with him, but I will contact him and ask him to look into it."

Alexander Morton, after graduating from Harvard, joined politics and was now the Republican Senator for New York. Rachel called his Washington, D.C., office and got his secretary who said that he would call her the next day.

The next day, the phone rang, and Rachel picked it up. "This is Senator Morton's office calling. Putting you through."

"Hello..."

"Is this Alex?"

"Yes, it is, Mrs. Johnson. It is nice to hear your voice. What can I do for you?"

"Nice to hear yours, too. I have a favor to ask."

"Anything. Because of your generosity in giving back the engagement ring my father gave you, I am now a senator. I owe you one."

Rachel smiled. She then told him about the nature of her call. "I can try. We are at war with Italy, and it will be hard. How is Andrew doing? I heard from Adam that he was badly injured."

"Thankfully, he came back alive. He is suffering from shell shock. Dr. Gerard Cleary is trying his best. He too is upset at the whole situation."

"I can see how this affects Andrew. Helping them will be indirectly helping Andrew. I will see what I can do."

"Thank you, Alex." Alexander was right. This incident did affect Andrew.

* * * * *

Gulia was released in October 1942. With her ordeal now over, she decided to thank Rachel for helping her. While waiting for Rachel, Gulia's attention was drawn to a picture of a man and a woman. She picked up the picture and began to cry. Rachel heard her weeping and came into the study. She was surprised to see Gulia holding a picture frame and crying.

"What happened, Mrs. Cleary?"

"Who are these people, Mrs. Johnson?"

"My parents. How do you know them?"

Gulia looked at her and said, "They saved my sons."

Rachel looked at her puzzled. "Where did you meet them?"

"It was on the Titanic that your mother gave up her seat so that my two sons could join us in the lifeboat."

Rachel was taken aback. Here was someone who had seen her parents, moments before they died.

April 14, 1912

Gulia was awakened by Sean, her oldest son. He had felt the ship shake. She assured him that a ship shakes while sailing and told him to go back to sleep. He drew her attention to the water seeping through the door. Gulia got up and put her feet down. She felt the cold water around her ankles.

"Blessed Mother, protect us," she whispered, as she crossed herself.

"We need to go to the deck. Come Sean, help me gather your siblings."

She dressed her children warmly, and they left their cabins. They met a steward on the way helping a wounded stoker.

"Scusami Pietro, what is happening?"

"Senora Cleary, put on the life jackets, and go to the deck. This stoker tells me that the ship is flooding, and it is bad. The captain will speak to us on the deck."

She went back into the cabin, and put lifejackets on the children and herself. She then ushered her children out of the third class area. They climbed the stairs and came onto the deck.

On the deck, they could feel the cold air, and they shivered. They saw some of the lifeboats being lowered, half-empty. She saw Guissipina, whom she befriended on the voyage, with her three children.

"Guissipina, we must get to a lifeboat."

Guissipina looked around her and said, "The officer said to wait here."

"We can wait in the boat. Come, let us get into this boat."

They went close to the boat and saw a woman from the second class arguing with her husband.

"Paige, stay in the boat. I will come after you on the next one."

"No, Gregory, I want to stay with you. We'll go in the same boat," said Paige.

Gulia told Guissipina to go ahead and take her seat, as she got in and sat down. Her two older sons, Sean and Gerard, helped their siblings get in. When they tried to get in, an officer held out his hand and said, "Stop! How old are you?"

"Seventeen and fifteen," said Sean and Gerard.

"Too old. These lifeboats are for women and children." Gulia, after living in Ireland, knew enough English to understand what was going on.

"No, officer, please let my children come with me. They are still young."

"No, they cannot. They are men."

Gulia began weeping, as she got up and pleaded with the officer to let her sons into the lifeboat. The sisters too began to cry.

The officer gave the command for the boat to be lowered. "Wait," said Paige.

She got up and got off the boat. Her husband said, "Paige, what are you doing?"

"Madam, you cannot do that."

"I just did. Now, let these two boys into the lifeboat."

"You are a lady, and the place should be yours."

"Yes, I know I am a lady. This mother cannot think of leaving her children behind. I too am a mother of a girl whom I love very much, and I know what it is to be separated from one's child." Paige then turned to the two boys and said, "Get in there you two, your mother needs you."

"There is place only for one," said the officer.

"True, but the younger brother can sit on the older brother's lap. That way, they can all be together." The two boys got in and sat down. Paige then took the fur shawl she was wearing and gave it to Gulia. "The poor boy is shivering; keep him warm."

Gulia extended her hand and so did Paige. With tears streaming from her eyes, she shook Paige's hand and said, "Mille Grazie, a thousand thanks for saving my two boys."

Paige put her arm around Gregory's shoulder and said, "We will be on the next boat. See you soon. Enjoy the boat ride," and winked at Gulia. The officer gave the command for the boat to be lowered.

* * * * *

"We never saw them again. We saw the ship sink into the ocean and take all those who did not manage to get into a lifeboat. It was because of your mother that my family was saved. She was a wonderful woman."

Rachel was in tears. She looked at the picture of her parents with pride. They did the right thing by saving Gulia's sons. "Do you still have that shawl?"

"Yes, I am wearing it now." She opened her coat and showed Rachel the shawl. Rachel held it to her face and cried. For years, she resented them for dying but now, she felt no resentment at all.

"How are your two sons?"

"Sean is an engineer and Gerard is your son's doctor. They have helped many people, and they are proud fathers as well. Gerard married Guissipina's daughter."

Rachel stopped crying. She gave the shawl back to Gulia and thanked her for telling the story. Her parents made the right decision, which was now benefitting Andrew.

Gulia picked up the box and said, "Thank you for helping me. Please accept this box of cannoli." Rachel thanked Gulia and said, "I, too, was in a shipwreck. That's how I ended up in this house. Would you like to hear my story while we have a cup of tea and eat the cannoli?"

"I will be delighted to."

Chapter 14

Sidney was always a precocious boy. He was almost two when his father died during the Spanish flu epidemic and scarcely remembered him. He looked a lot like his father and was told that he behaved like him as well. With reddish blond hair and broad shoulders, he was almost his doppelganger. He inherited Martha's intelligence.

Sidney hardly saw his father's older sisters and their families and always felt lonely. He treasured Martha's friendship with Rachel. He remembered the incident when he tore Barbara's sleeve accidentally and she started crying. He felt sorry for her. A few months later, when he heard that she was missing in the train crash, he wept for days. When Andrew was born, he felt that he had someone to replace Barbara. He bonded with Andrew and knew what it was to be an older brother. He had always wished that his parents had more children and would ask Martha to give it a thought. Martha would always smile and say, "God willing, it will happen."

When Andrew was kidnapped, Sidney was at Harvard. He went to the nearest church and prayed that Andrew's life would be spared. He was the first one to help Andrew come to terms with his ordeal by taking him to ball games, and helping him realize the world was a better place, and to trust people again.

Sidney was glad Andrew had joined the navy. The navy would toughen Andrew as he had led a sheltered life. All that changed when he heard that Andrew was badly injured at Pearl Harbor. When he saw Andrew break down at the New Year's Eve party, he wanted revenge. He felt he had to do his part to help America and her allies win the war. His business partners would take care of the business, and his mother could help him in absentia, as she had done when he was growing up.

Sidney went to the closest recruitment office, and joined the long line of men. Once inside, he was told to strip to his underwear and stand next to the men waiting to be examined. The doctor held his stethoscope to Sidney's chest and asked him to breathe in and out.

"That's a good pair of lungs, son. You will be a good candidate for the army."

Sidney got his eyes checked. The optometrist had him read the eye chart – he passed the test with flying colors. He was classified as 1A, which meant that he was fit for military duty.

Sidney was assigned to Camp Claiborne, Louisiana. He visited Mary before he left. She was in tears, just like his mother. She begged him not to go, but he said that it was his duty to serve his country. She was worried about being alone and that he would not return. He told her what he told Martha when she voiced the same concern. "God willing, I will be back."

At the end of February, he arrived at Camp Claiborne. He was taken aback at the warm humid weather, far different from freezing New York. His tough physique from playing sports in college helped him with the rigorous training.

Sidney was transferred to Fort Bragg, North Carolina, in October, to be trained as a paratrooper with the 82nd Airborne Division. He learned to leap from an aircraft and open his parachute. He wondered what his mother and Mary would say if they saw him leap out of an aircraft. He passed with flying colors and desperately wanted to see some action.

A few months later, he got his wish. As part of the 505th Parachute Infantry Regiment, he was deployed to North Africa. He was to sail with his division from New York Port in April 1943. He was disappointed that he was not going to the Pacific. He wanted to fight the Japanese for what they did to Andrew. He took comfort in the thought that defeating Germany meant a blow to Japan.

Before he left, he visited his mother and Mary. It was more than a year since he had seen them. He assured them that he would try to be safe. Martha gave him a medal of St. Christopher to protect and keep him safe.

When he disembarked at Casablanca, the first thing that struck him was the intense heat and dirt. He had never seen or experienced the desert before. He had seen the movie 'Casablanca' and had a very romantic idea of the place. However, it was far from that. Since joining the army, he had experiences with different climes, and this was the worst he had ever experienced.

He was on his way to Oujda, a city in the desert. The temperatures were unbelievable. Sidney and his comrades had to keep drinking water all the time. Finally, they reached the camp. There was no escaping the heat. Sidney made friends with two soldiers, Brian and Colin.

"We will have to train in these conditions," said Colin Whitefield.

"I never thought that any place on earth could get this hot," said Sidney

"I'm from Phoenix, Arizona, and the temperature in the desert is very hot like this. However, it cools down at night, so there is some relief."

"Good to hear that, Colin. There are boys like me who have never experienced such heat. This could be bad for our morale."

"They will get used to it. There can be no luxuries in war," said Brian.

Sidney was right. Due to lack of luxuries and the stifling heat, swarms of locusts and flies, the morale of some of the men had started to wane. Sidney tried to remain focused by reading letters from home. Martha had written that Andrew seemed to be doing better. His counseling sessions with his psychiatrist were working. He was taking courses in college. Mary had written that she missed him and hoped that he would return soon. Her two brothers too were now in the armed forces. Tom joined the marines and Steven the navy. He re-read these letters, as they comforted and reminded him of the reason he had joined the army.

He was ready to see some action. In June, General Ridgeway

ordered the division to their staging area Kairouon, Tunisia, to prepare for operation Husky. They were to invade Sicily.

July 9 was approaching, and they had begun preparations to invade Sicily. Sidney began to feel the effects of going to war. He might never make it out alive. He decided to say his rosary and make his confession to the army chaplain. He wrote two letters: one to his mother and another to Mary saying that he loved them and asked them to pray for his safe return. He gave the letters to the postal worker and went for training. When he went to bed that night, he felt a surge of pride sweep through him. He was proud that he was doing this for his country, family, and Andrew.

The whole battalion got up early on July 9, 1943. They boarded the aircrafts and at seven-thirty p.m., the first C-47 aircraft carrying the 505th, along with the 3rd Battalion and the 504th, took off for their destination, Sicily. As they flew over Malta, a severe headwind broke up the formation of the aircrafts. "Looks like we're going to miss our drop zone and will have to make our way there," shouted the group leader over the drone of the engines.

They got ready to jump from the aircraft. The door opened and one by one, the men started jumping out, opening their parachutes. Sidney felt the parachute jerk as it opened. He could see Sicily below him with hills and trees. He landed on the ground and as protocol dictated, he folded his parachute and stashed it under some rocks. The men got together and started walking to their original destination. On the way, they could see the Sicilian peasants looking at them. "I hope they know that we are here to help them," said Brian.

Colin looked at a group of girls and said, "Ciao Bella." The girls laughed. A man with a pitchfork stepped next to the girls.

"Be careful. These men are very protective of their womenfolk," said Sidney.

"Right," said Colin, a bit sheepishly.

"Must be a long march ahead," said Brian.

"Maybe a day's march, but we need to watch out for those pillboxes, which is where the Germans will be lying in wait for us with machine guns. They need to be disarmed or destroyed."

"What do they look like?" asked one of the men.

"They are made of stones and concrete and look like square boxes. The openings are just big enough for a gun to pass through from which the Germans can fire at their target. It is difficult to shoot at them because they are well protected by the stones."

"They would be difficult to spot."

"Yes, unless they shoot at us and then we would know."

A shot rang out at that moment. "Must be from those pillboxes," said Colin, as the men took cover behind huge boulders.

"There, I see it on top of that hill. I can see a machine gun sticking out of that opening. I can also see two helmets."

"We need to stop them before they kill us."

"It's difficult to stop them unless one of us runs there and disarms them."

More shots were fired and bullets flew around them. The commanding officer ordered Brian to run and disarm the pillbox. They would cover him. Brian ran towards the pillbox while trying to fire at the same time. Bullets flew around him.

"He's down," shouted Colin. Brian was on the ground but seemed to be alive. Sidney volunteered to go and asked to be covered. He ran uphill towards the pillbox. Bullets flew all around him, and he hoped that they would not hit him. He saw Brian on the ground and could see the blood oozing from his leg. He passed by Brian and stood behind a boulder. He motioned to his comrades to fire directly at the target. Some of the bullets found their target, and he could see the German soldiers recoil to avoid the bullets and the debris.

This was his moment. He pulled out a grenade and ran towards the opening. He took the pin out, tossed the grenade into the opening, and ran for cover. He felt the intense heat from the explosion. He was face down on the ground. He turned and looked at the target. All he could see was smoke, black and thick, billowing out from the damaged structure. He lay there for a few minutes and got his gun ready. He stood up and walked slowly towards the opening. The smoke was now clearing. He peeped in and saw the three dead soldiers. Sidney turned and motioned to his comrades that it was all clear. A few minutes later, they were viewing his handiwork.

They entered the pillbox and found cache of weapons, not damaged by the explosion, canned food, and clothes. The commanding officer ordered them to take what was needed, like food and weapons. They went out and found the medic treating Brian's wounded leg.

"Just a flesh wound, sir. The bullet grazed his leg, but he can still continue." The officer commended Brian for his bravery. He then turned to Sidney and told him he would see that his bravery was recognized. In a few minutes, they all started marching towards their destination.

By August 17, the whole of Sicily was under allied occupation. Sidney was wounded in the arm by shrapnel from an exploding grenade in the final battle. He was taken back to the military base for treatment. He was awarded the Purple Heart. A few days later, he was told that he was going to be sent to England. When he queried, his superiors told him that everything would be revealed once he got there.

When Sidney landed in England, he was told to wait for details of his new mission. He was surprised that he was chosen for this secret mission. He would rather stay with his troops and fight. His superiors assured him that his services were required for the secret mission that would help the allies win the war. His unit's commanding officer had recommended him because he showed bravery, courage, and a good sense of judgment when he disarmed the pillbox, saving the lives of his fellow soldiers. Sidney was taken to the military hospital, and he was given a physical. He passed it with flying colors. He was taken to a room in the military barracks to get some rest before his training began.

"You will sleep here," said the young soldier pointing to the bed.

"What is your name?" asked Sidney.

"Spencer Moore," he said, with a slight cockney accent.

"I'm Sidney Hardy from New York."

"Pleased to meet you, sir. Have a good rest, and we'll see you in the morning, all refreshed," said Spencer, without any emotion on his face.

"Yes, I presume," replied Sidney, a bit taken aback at his brusqueness. Spencer turned around and walked out.

"That is a traditional British welcome for you with a stiff upper lip." Sidney turned to see who had said that and saw Colin and Brian at the other end.

"Where did you two come from?"

"We were at the other end resting like they want us to do. We came to England two days ago on leave. We thought we would be back to join the division but instead, they have asked us to stay for their 'Special Mission'," said Colin.

"I wonder why they want us here. I thought we were the only ones they sent over," said Brian.

"That is what I was told, too. We'll know tomorrow when they brief us," said Sidney.

"Yes. Now, let's go to the mess hall and get some food."

"English cuisine is certainly not what someone looks forward to," said Colin.

"Yes, but I can tell you, they do know how to make a good steak and kidney pie," said Brian.

They went out of the barracks and went to the building with the sign 'Mess Hall' above the door. They opened the door and went inside. "Hey, look everyone, it is the Yanks. Come on in lads," someone shouted.

"The Yanks are coming, the Yanks are coming..." someone started singing.

Spencer came towards them and smiled. "I'm glad you came to join us for dinner. Sidney, I see that you have met Colin and Brian. You must be thrilled to have two Americans here. Join the queue, and I hope you enjoy the food."

They joined the queue and waited their turn. The servers eyed them as if they were criminals and served them. They took their plates and sat at an empty table. They began eating and saw the other men looking at them. "Has this happened before?" asked Sidney.

"This is the first time we are eating here. We got here a few hours before you did."

"The Yanks are here to help us," shouted one of them.

"They are here to help us win the war. They didn't want to join the war until they got bombed by the Japs," shouted another. The whole mess hall booed them.

"We did what we had to at that time," said Brian calmly.

"Yes, and it was only when you were attacked that you showed interest in joining us."

"America didn't want to be involved in another European conflict," said Sidney, as he put a spoonful of food into his mouth.

"Well, why did you, if you did not want to be involved with another European conflict?"

"It's the same reason you are here; to defend your country and empire. Maybe you should leave the colonies and stop asking the native people to help you. They should rise and drive you British out like we Americans did," said Colin.

The man was stunned. "Blimey, like you Yanks do not have an empire. Isn't the Philippines part of your American Empire?"

"Okay, there is no need for an argument here," said a voice from the door. Everyone turned to see who it was. They saw a tall man, dressed in an army uniform, standing at the doorway. Everyone stood up and saluted him. "Is that the way to treat our guests? They have come to help us with our mission. Do not forget they are on our side and that they are fighting our enemies. So, treat them with respect. Is that understood?"

"Yes, sir," said the men.

The man walked up to the three Americans and said, "I hope your stay has been comfortable so far, except for the spot of trouble now."

"It has been great so far," said Colin.

"I am Officer Howell. I am in command of these men, and I will be guiding you on your next assignment. Get some sleep, and I will see you three in the morning." He turned around and went out of the door. The men started eating and nobody bothered the three Americans thereafter.

After dinner, they went to their room to sleep. They woke up when Spencer banged on the door. Colin opened the door. "Now, go to the showers before they get filled up," said Spencer.

The three of them grabbed their kits and went to the building that had the sign 'Showers' at the entrance. After their showers and a shave, they went to the barracks, dressed in their uniforms, and headed for breakfast. During their meal, they noticed that the British soldiers were being nice to them. The three of them looked at each other and shrugged their shoulders.

Spencer came in and asked them to follow him. It had begun to drizzle a bit.

"The car is waiting for you. Officer Howell will meet you and brief you about the assignment at your destination."

They got into the car and Spencer sat behind the wheel. They left the army compound and drove through the countryside. It started raining heavily. "Fine weather you Brits have here, eh?" said Sidney.

"This is typical English weather for you," said Brian with a chuckle.

"Where are you lads from?"

"I am from New York City, Colin is from Arizona, and Brian is from Tennessee. Where are you from?"

"From London, sir," he said, nonchalantly.

"What made you join up?"

"I lost my twelve-year-old brother in an air raid on December 29, 1940. The air raid shelter took a direct hit from one of the bombs that the Luftwaffe dropped. My parents, older brother, and two sisters survived. I also lost my friend who was a firefighter. He died during the fire storm that brought down some of the buildings." The three men were stunned. "No need to be silent. These things happen during wartime. I had to make a decision. Who would die? My loved ones or the Nazis? I chose to join the army and fight for what they did to my family, friends, and also my beautiful city."

The rain stopped and the sun came out. "It's beautiful when the sun comes out after it rains. Look at the valley," said Spencer. The three men were awe struck at the beautiful English countryside. They heard a loud bang, and Spencer struggled to stop the car. They got out and saw that the front tire had blown off.

"Blimey, I have to get you to your destination and this had to happen."

"Do you have a tire jack?"

"No, I forgot to put one in the boot. Damn!" replied Spencer and kicked the car.

"Boot?" asked Colin, confused.

"I guess he means the trunk," said Sidney with a chuckle.

"Someone is coming," said Brian.

"Oye, there, could you please help us with our car. We seem to have blown a tire."

The man drove the car towards them and stopped. "Yes, what can I do for you?"

"We need to replace the tire. Do you have a tire jack?" asked Spencer.

"Yes, I do… wait a minute, are you Yanks?"

"Yes, the three of us are, and he…" Brian said, pointing to Spencer, "is from here."

"Well, you Yanks can stay here. I'm not helping."

The four of them were taken aback.

"Why?"

"Because, you Yanks, have come into my property just because the RAF Airfield is next to it. They don't listen to me or the neighboring farmers and we have had endless trouble. The noise from the aircrafts is scaring all the farm animals, and you Yanks, along with the RAF pilots, are coming into the pasture and pushing the cows. Cow tipping is what they call it."

"Look, I am sorry about that, but we are here to help you win the war. We are on your side. We are not in the Air Force or the RAF. We are in the army," said Colin.

"You Yanks can go back to America. We don't need your help. We acquired a vast empire without your help and by God, we will defeat Hitler." He started to drive off when Spencer went towards him and said, "Wait, we will pay you. We have the money. We need to get to our destination. You will be helping England if you do."

"I want to have nothing to do with those damn Yanks."

"How about if I pay you for your help or buy the jack from you?

How much do you want?"

"Ten Pounds."

"Ten Pounds for a car jack?" said Spencer in surprise.

"Yes. Take it or leave it."

Spencer put his hands into his pockets and brought out some money. He counted it and said, "Here's ten pounds."

"Sold! You can have it."

The man got out, opened the trunk, and gave the car jack to Spencer. Spencer handed him the money. He smiled and drove away.

"I felt like punching his lights out for all those insults," said Brian.

"He doesn't have a good opinion of us; thanks to those American pilots he was talking about," said Sidney.

"Come on boys, give me a hand, will ya," said Spencer.

Half an hour later, they were on their way. They drove for some time and came to a gate. They showed their identification badges and were allowed to go through.

"Welcome to Bletchley Park," said Spencer.

The three of them got out and looked at the building. Spencer motioned them to enter from where the guards were stationed. They entered after showing their identification badges. They saw many civilians walking around inside. They could hear the sound of typewriters and women talking. "Look at these women," said Sidney.

"Don't let these women fool you; they are very intelligent, recruited by the British Government, to help us win the war."

"Really?" said Brian in surprise.

"Yes, you will meet some of the women and also see the Enigma machines."

"Enigma?"

"You will see."

They entered a room and saw Officer Howell and three women seated around a large conference table. They had machines that looked like typewriters in front of them.

"You are thirty minutes late," growled Officer Howell.

"Sorry, sir, we had problems with the car on the way," said Spencer.

"Okay. Now take a seat, and we'll get on with the meeting."

Spencer saluted and left the room. The three men sat down and the meeting commenced. "You three have come with very high recommendations from your officers to help us with this secret mission. We are going to try to attack the Germans on the beaches of Normandy and liberate France. Our allies have agreed to help drive the Germans out of France."

"It is our honor to be chosen, Officer Howell," said Sidney.

"Good. We want information about the area that we plan to attack. You will parachute into France and obtain information about the area. We have contacts with the French Resistance there. We have decoded several coded messages that the Nazis use to communicate. These Enigma machines have proved very useful in decoding the messages and finding out their next move. We have to thank these young ladies here for all their hard work." The three women smiled at them and the men smiled back. "These ladies here and outside, also know to keep a secret. Nobody who is associated with them knows that they work here. Oh, excuse my manners; meet Maria, Marjorie, and Audrey."

After he introduced the men, he continued, "Your job is to obtain information about various German units and also the surveyed area of Normandy from the Germans and bring it back to England."

"Sounds like a good plan," said Sidney.

"Good. You three are knowledgeable in French and German. These ladies will show you how to decode messages using the Enigma machine and will also tell you what we have learned so far from the Germans and the French Resistance." They stood up and Officer Howell left the room.

They sat down, and the three women showed them how to use the machine.

"How do you manage to keep this a secret?" asked Brian.

"We signed the Officials Secrets Act, and they told us we would be shot if we revealed anything about our work," said Marjorie with a laugh. "Neither our families nor the workers at the café where we take our lunch break, have ever asked us anything about our work. My cousin once asked, and I told her that I do office work here. We were picked from all over England after being interviewed, based on our skills. Maria worked as a German school teacher; Marjorie and I have good maths skills."

"Wow, I never knew that the British were so advanced with their code breaking."

"Yes, we are. We even broke codes that helped the allies win the war in North Africa," said Maria.

"How long have you three been here?" asked Brian.

"I have been here for three years. Marjorie and Audrey came here in 1941. Now, we cannot tell you more. We have to keep our counsel as advised by Marjorie," replied Maria, sounding stern, but they could tell that she was also trying not to smile.

The next few hours were spent learning to use the Enigma machine and about the Normandy area. They were shown information gathered by spies in France concerning the mission, and the German messages decoded by the Enigma machine. At the end of it, the three men were exhausted.

"How do you ladies keep up with all this?"

"We're used to it. We use our mental powers more than you men use on the battlefield. Our weapons are mathematics and our intelligence, whereas yours are bullets and bombs," said Audrey.

"Let's go and have dinner. I'm starving," said Brian.

"All right, but you men need to change your uniforms since you can't let the villagers know the real reason you're here. You can dress up in plain clothes and walk with us. No one will suspect a thing," said Maria.

"We left our bags in the car."

"I am sure Spencer has placed them in your rooms at this pub close to Bletchley Park. He is very efficient, you know!"

The door opened and Spencer walked in. "Speak of the devil," shouted Colin. The rest laughed.

"It's time to show you to your rooms. I have placed your belongings there."

"We will meet you at the pub," said Audrey.

The three men followed Spencer, and they entered from the back door so that the customers would not see them. The three men changed into civilian clothes in their rooms and went down for a pint of beer.

At the pub, they saw only Marjorie and Audrey. When Sidney enquired about Maria, Audrey told him that Maria was married with two small children. Her husband did not know about her work. She told him that she worked as a charwoman at Bletchley Park. Someone began playing the piano, and the customers started singing "Knees up Mother Brown". Audrey and Marjorie joined in and the three men clapped along.

The night went on, and they had many drinks. Colin and Brian got very close to the two women. Some women tried to get close to Sidney. He talked to them but distanced himself from their advances. He felt that, since he was engaged to Mary, he was bound to her.

Far away in New York, Mary sat down and wrote a letter. She addressed it to Sidney and with tears in her eyes, gave it to the maid to post. 'It's the right thing to do,' she said to herself.

Back in Britain, the three men met George and Charles, the two chosen from the British Army who would teach them all that they needed to know. They were in touch with the French Resistance, and they would accompany the three Americans to France on their mission.

As the days went by, the date for their mission drew closer. The leaves started changing colors. The final day of their training was over. They were all set to parachute into France the next day. As part of their final farewell, they decided to meet at the pub for drinks. When Sidney was about to go downstairs, a uniformed man knocked on his door.

"Letter for Sidney Hardy." Sidney opened the door.

"We had to get it redirected from your former station in Africa. Sorry for the delay."

The man left. Sidney saw that it was from Mary. He opened it with great excitement and read it. His face fell. He crumpled the letter, and it fell on the floor.

Sidney went downstairs and tried not to show his disappointment. The rest had already ordered drinks. He drank until he could not stand. The others carried him to his room and placed him on the bed. He slept soundly and woke up with a bad headache. He looked at his watch and realized that it was late evening. He was going to be late for his mission.

He got up and felt his head spinning. Sidney reached for the pitcher and drank water. He opened the window, and the cool air revived him. He felt better and began dressing. He picked the crumpled letter from the floor and threw it in the trashcan. He ran down the stairs and went to the back of the pub. Brian and Colin were already there. "There you are. You were asleep for most of the day. We were just thinking of coming up and getting you," said Brian.

Spencer stopped the car next to them. They got in and the car sped towards the airfield. No one spoke; they were contemplating on their mission. Sidney could not get over the contents of Mary's letter.

The car drove into an airfield where an aircraft stood with its engines already running. Another car was next to the aircraft, and they saw a man standing next to it. "Good luck, lads. Come back safely. God Bless!" said Spencer.

They got out of the car and walked towards the man. It was Officer Howell. "Make me proud, men. The whole outcome of this war depends on the five of you. Come back safely." They shook his hand and thanked him. George and Charles were already inside. They got in and Brian closed the door. The aircraft began taxing down the crudely built runway and was airborne. The sun was beginning to set, as they flew over England.

It was already dark when they flew over Normandy. "Get ready to jump out," shouted the pilot. The five men got up and put on their gear. George opened the door. They could feel the cold air rushing in.

"See you on French soil," said George and parachuted out, followed by Charles.

"It is a good thing we said goodbye to Marjorie and Audrey. It looks like this will be one heck of a mission. See you below," said Colin. He went to the door and jumped out. Brian jumped next, followed by Sidney.

As Sidney descended, he could feel tears rolling down his face. If only he had married Mary before he left for Africa, she would not have volunteered to become a nurse and met Larry, a soldier wounded in the Pacific. Larry proposed to her and she accepted. She wrote that she could not wait for Sidney any longer and wished him well. These last words stung him more than anything else. He yanked the cord and felt his body jerk when his parachute opened. He began to hear bullets fly around him while he descended towards the earth.

Chapter 15

New York, June 1943

Andrew was still seeing Dr. Cleary and studying at Columbia University. He continued to have nightmares about the bombing and, at times, cried for Hazel in his sleep. He seemed to be coming to terms with her supposed death. Dr. Cleary warned Rachel that the road to recovery would be long.

Andrew could now walk without a cane. He wished he were in the navy, fighting the enemy, like his surviving friends.

Rachel went to fundraising events to support the war effort. She visited local houses whose sons were brought back wounded or dead. Whenever Rachel visited a dead soldier's family, she was relieved that Andrew was still alive. She was, however, fearful for Sidney. Martha was being strong about him being in the army, but Rachel could tell that Martha was very worried.

One afternoon, the doorbell rang. Marcy came into the bedroom with a puzzled look on her face and told her that a doctor wanted to see her. Rachel asked Marcy to show him into the drawing room. She changed and went to join him and found a man looking out of the window. "Good evening, Doctor…"

He turned and said, "Good evening, Mrs. Johnson. My name is Doctor Maurice Barton." He shook her hand. She motioned him to sit down, and Marcy came in with tea and cake.

"What brings you here, Doctor?"

He took a sip of his tea and said, "I have come to ask for your help.

We have soldiers that suffer from depression and have suicidal tendencies because of what they have seen or experienced on the battlefield."

"I understand, but are there many soldiers like that?"

"Yes, there are many. These are young boys, mainly eighteen and above, who think war is glamorous, but they are in for a rude shock when they actually see the reality."

"Are you a psychiatrist?"

"Yes, I am. I work at St. Lawrence Hospital."

"How can I help?"

"We need funding, Mrs. Johnson. It is a new branch of study that was recognized during the Great War with soldiers who were gassed in the trenches. The same problems are being noticed with soldiers in this war. I understand that you donate money to organizations that help families of wounded and dead soldiers. It would be helpful, if you could donate money to help soldiers that need psychological and psychiatric treatment.

"I certainly will. My son was wounded in Pearl Harbor, and that is the reason I give money to organizations that help wounded soldiers. Will five hundred dollars be good?"

"That is a generous sum, Mrs. Johnson."

Rachel wrote out a check and handed it to him. "You look familiar. Have we met?"

Dr. Barton smiled. "I was a medical student when I helped you twenty years ago. It was when you were pregnant and fainted in the hotel lobby. I came to your aid and brought you back home."

"Yes, now I remember. I never got to thank you. I was pregnant with Andrew."

He smiled and said, "No need to. You have thanked me by giving me this check. Dr. Cleary told me that Andrew is his patient."

"Yes, and he is slowly improving. Lately, he has been very upset because he's not doing anything for the war effort."

"He could probably volunteer at the hospital. That will be his contribution to the war effort."

"That's a good idea. I will speak to him about it."

"Thank you. I will be in touch."

Dr. Barton smiled and left. Andrew entered the room at that moment. "Who was that?"

"He's Dr. Barton, a colleague of Dr. Cleary."

"What did he want?" Andrew asked in anger.

"He wanted donations for soldiers affected by the war," Rachel replied calmly.

"Well, all you ever do is give money to people. What are we? The Salvation Army?"

"Andrew dear, we need to help people who are affected by this war. It would be nice if you could help the wounded soldiers at the hospital."

"You know, the only thing I want to do is go back into battle. My navy buddies are out there fighting and dying for their country, and I am in this big house doing nothing."

"You are not wasting your life. You're going to college and learning the hotel business. I know it's hard with your leg, but you survived for a reason."

"I wish I had died."

Rachel had gone down this road many times before, and she always managed to calm him down. She hated these situations, but Dr. Cleary had advised her not to show any emotions but talk to him calmly.

"Andrew, maybe you should volunteer to help wounded soldiers. It will help you. You can now walk without a cane, and your leg is getting stronger. I can contact Dr. Barton to help you get situated. Please do try."

"No," he shouted and left the room, slamming the door after him.

There was nothing more that she could do. She had dinner alone. Marcy took dinner to Andrew's bedroom, but he hardly touched it. He only drank the glass of milk. Rachel went to bed and prayed that maybe the next day would be better.

Rachel woke up and felt something was wrong. She had this feeling almost two years ago when Andrew was injured. She got out of bed, ran to his room, and knocked on the door. There was no response. She turned the doorknob and opened the door. Andrew was lying in bed. She went and shook him. She called out his name and still no response. He was breathing faintly. She kicked something and heard a bottle roll on the floor. She bent down and saw that it was a bottle of sleeping pills, 'Nembutal'. He had been prescribed the pills many months earlier for sleep. He had taken them from the medicine cabinet in her bathroom. She yelled out to Marcy to call Alfred and Robert.

Robert and Alfred helped put Andrew in the car and drove him to the hospital. Dr. Thompson and two nurses were waiting with a gurney. They took Andrew inside straight away and started pumping his stomach.

After some time, Dr. Thompson came out to give Rachel news regarding Andrew's condition. "He is asleep now, Rachel," said Dr. Thompson, wiping his forehead.

"Is he going to be all right?"

"He is, but he needs to rest. He will be kept under observation for a few hours."

Rachel heaved a sigh of relief. "I cannot imagine what you are going through," said Dr. Thompson.

"Once you have lost a daughter, a husband, a fiancée, and almost lost a son for the third time, you don't even feel it. I am just grateful that he is fine; nothing else matters now. All I care for is that he recovers." Dr. Thompson put his hand on her shoulder and squeezed it.

"Do you think he meant to kill himself?"

"I don't know, Rachel. He may have taken an overdose unintentionally. These things can happen sometimes. It is a good thing that he had a glass of milk before he took the pills, or it could have been much worse."

"Thank you, Doctor Thompson."

She sat outside for an hour, praying for his recovery, and went in when the nurse told her she could. She found him asleep and could see there was some color in his face. She sat by his bedside and fell asleep. The next thing she knew was that Andrew was calling her softly.

"Oh Andrew, are you doing well?"

"Yes," he managed to smile. "I'm just tired of doing nothing for the war effort."

"Killing yourself is not a way to contribute to the war effort," she said, sounding stern and wagging her finger at him.

He started laughing. Rachel was stunned. She hadn't seen him laugh like this in a long time. She smiled and said, "Helping soldiers or war refugees is also contributing to the war effort. Maybe, that's what you can do. Not everyone is called to fight. There is no shame in helping people."

"I feel that I'll be ashamed meeting wounded soldiers who saw action."

"You did see action, Andy. It's just that you were wounded during the initial attack. I am sure you will meet many soldiers who were wounded badly when they first saw action and never fired a shot.

"I think, I'll try that, Mother."

"I'm sure you'll find it fulfilling. You are all I have, so don't do this again."

"I promise I won't, Mother."

Dr. Cleary entered the room smiling. "I could not help overhearing what you were talking about. I am so glad that you have decided to help the wounded soldiers. This can be a form of therapy for you."

"Yes, I will give it a try."

"I remember, in one of our sessions you said that you used to help Fr. O'Malley in the soup kitchen as a teenager. Did it help you feel better that you helped people who were in need?"

"Yes, it did."

"You will be doing the same here. Dr. Barton needs an assistant, and since you saw action and got wounded, you are a perfect candidate."

"Thank you, Doctor. I'm sorry for failing you."

"All is forgiven. You did give your mother and me a scare. Do not do this again."

When he recovered, Andrew met Dr. Barton who was pleased to see him. He suggested that Andrew start working at St. Lawrence Hospital where wounded soldiers from the Pacific were being treated.

"I warn you that it is not going to be pleasant working there. Many of them have internal wounds, by which I mean of the mind, because of the horrors they have seen, and some have lost limbs and their close friends."

"I'm sure I can help. I have been in that situation and can empathize with them."

"Good, Andrew. You can work with the patients after a few days of training. Can you start right away?"

"Yes, Doctor."

"Oh, we need to be careful of the hospital director, Dr. Fagan. He is a curmudgeon. Try and stay out of his way."

* * * * *

Andrew spent the next few days training and accompanied Dr. Barton on his rounds, interacting with some wounded soldiers. He was reminded of Pearl Harbor and the memories of being in the hospital there. He got upset every time he thought about it but decided that he would not let it influence him.

Some of the wounded soldiers scoffed at him. When they realized that he was not a doctor, they asked him why he was not fighting and would call him a coward. They stopped jeering him when he told them his story.

Andrew could not get Hazel out of his mind. Since more than a year had passed, and there was no trace of her, he too started giving up hope of her being found. Some of the nurses tried to get close to him, but he could not bring himself to be involved with anyone else. It was as if Hazel had a hold on him. Whenever he went out with one of the nurses, after a date or two, he would tell them that they were not compatible. He tried to concentrate on his work and studies. He even volunteered at the refugee center but felt he was needed in the hospital, helping wounded soldiers.

One interesting case was that of William Brewster. He had been sent home from the Pacific with serious wounds and was mentally disturbed. William was taken prisoner in the Philippines and witnessed many atrocities by the Japanese in the internment camps. For not cooperating, he was beaten, starved, and put in solitary confinement. He contracted malaria and was taken to what the Japanese called a 'hospital'. He and another American GI escaped at night by cutting the barbed wires. They floated out to sea on an abandoned boat. A week later, they were found by an American naval ship and were brought to America. Because of recurring nightmares, he would threaten to kill himself and the others around.

"I must talk to him. He may be able to tell me things."

"I would be careful if I were you. He may be dangerous. I volunteered during the last war in France. There was a case of a soldier suffering from shell shock. He stabbed a soldier, took his handgun, and killed himself."

Dr. Barton relented at Andrew's insistence. Andrew went into William's room. William Brewster trembled and stuttered when he spoke. "The soldiers plunged bayonets into women and children. How could they do that to innocent women and children? I could do nothing to help them. I can't get those images out of my mind."

"What made you join the army?" asked Andrew.

"I wanted to see the world. I was eighteen when I enlisted in the army in… in 1940. A year later, America joined the war."

"You were very lucky to escape."

"Yes, thanks to Sherman. I was weak from malaria, and he helped me escape." He held his hands to his face and started crying.

"Give it some time. Time is the greatest healer."

"I know, but it is taking so long. Those memories keep coming back."

"You are in shock. You have been through a lot since you were interned and rescued."

William was silent and refused to speak. He lay down, turned to his side away from Andrew, and closed his eyes. Andrew got up and walked away. His training had taught him that William needed some time to heal.

A few days later, William decided to talk. "Tell me about your life on the farm," said Dr. Barton.

"It was a good life. My family consisted of three brothers, four sisters, and me. We all helped dad with the farm. We would plant corn, fertilize the fields, and milk the cows."

"Why did you want to leave that good life and join the army?"

"Because, it never fulfilled me. I always wondered what it would be to be in another part of the world by leaving the farm and having an adventure. We used to get the National Geographic Magazine. It had pictures of flowers and fruits nobody in my area had seen. I just wanted to experience more.

"Did you like the army?"

"I liked it and the people I met. I learned a lot."

"Did you like the Philippines?"

"Yes, I did. The tropical weather was just marvelous. I got to see the flowers and eat the fruits I used to see in those magazines."

"Now, I'm going to get to the part when the Japanese invaded," said Dr. Barton.

"Why do we have to go there?" William asked in anger.

"We need to understand what happened to you."

"It was terrible. I couldn't believe it when I heard the bombs and gunfire. I saw people being shot down and blown to bits by the aircrafts. It was like a bad dream."

"Then what happened?"

"The Japanese soldiers came and started hounding everyone. They targeted both the Americans and the Europeans, but they were more brutal to the natives. An American showed his passport to this mean looking Japanese commander and asked to be allowed to contact the American Embassy..." William was now getting very upset.

"What happened?"

"He just laughed, drew his sword, made the man kneel before him, and beg for his forgiveness. He then asked him to bow his head and when he did, he chopped off his head. It was horrible. I have never seen anyone being killed like that." He began to cry. "The commander, then spat on his body. He cut off a piece of the man's shirt, wiped his sword clean, and put it back into the sheath."

"Tell me about the march."

"The soldiers came after us with their bayonets pointing at us and forced us to march into the jungle. The Japanese shot and killed many people. There was no food. We had to drink the rainwater or water from the roadside ditches. People trying to escape, were gunned down and bayoneted if they did not die immediately. This woman and her child, who were malnourished and could not walk, were shot and kicked into a ditch." He was now wailing like a baby. "We reached the camp. There was no proper food; just steamed rice, disease, and death."

"I think that is enough for today, Mr. Brewster. You have said enough," said Dr. Barton.

Andrew helped William lie down and covered him. William was still crying.

"Doc.," said Andrew, "do we have to make him relive these painful memories?"

"It is better that he tells someone than keep them bottled up inside."

"It's tearing him apart."

"I didn't say it would be easy. Speaking to someone who will listen will help him overcome his fears. Keeping things bottled up is what is making him a nervous wreck."

Andrew knew that the doctor was right. He too withdrew into that silent phase when he was depressed.

The afternoon was uneventful, until they heard one of the nurses scream. Andrew and Dr. Barton ran in her direction.

"He has gone crazy."

"Who?" asked Dr. Barton.

"William Brewster. He started shouting about the Japanese coming to kill him. He then jumped out of his bed, grabbed a pair of scissors, and is threatening to kill those who come towards him. He's in the women's ward," replied the terrified nurse.

They went into the ward and saw that he was at the end of the ward, waving the scissors at the terrified women patients.

"Don't worry, I have come to protect you from the Japs," he said to one of the women, as she tried to cover her face.

He saw Dr. Barton and Andrew along with other orderlies. "Don't come any closer. I have to protect myself from the soldiers." He ran into the next room, which was empty. They followed him. "Stay away from me. Do not come closer," he shouted.

"Calm down, William. We are here to help you. Nobody wants to harm you."

"No, you are all liars. Some of the doctors there used to say that to the prisoners in the camp and they all died." He looked at Andrew. "Andrew, I must get these nightmares out of my mind because I can't sleep at all." He was getting closer to the window. "Stay away from me. I will be leaving now."

William then stepped onto the ledge. Dr. Barton went towards the window. Andrew pulled him back and said, "Let me talk to him. He recognized me. I think he trusts me."

Andrew peeped outside and saw William on the ledge. William was crying and getting ready to jump.

Down below, the traffic had stopped, and a crowd had gathered. He could hear people say, "*Is he going to jump? What is he doing there? Who is that? What's the matter with him?*"

"William, look at me," said Andrew. William looked at him. "Good. Now, come back inside. It is no use doing what you want to do."

"What do you think I want to do?"

"Honestly, I think you want to jump."

"I feel it's best to end it all. I am weak. I cannot sleep. I let people die."

"You are not weak. You wanted an adventure and were brave enough to leave your comfortable life and go out into the world."

He smiled. "I know, but I feel guilty that I stood there like a coward and did nothing to protect those people."

"You couldn't have done anything. You would have been killed if you had. You are not to blame."

"I didn't stay back to protect them. I escaped when I had the chance."

"You did, and that took a lot of courage. You risked your life for freedom, even though you knew that you could have been killed. You saw other escapees being killed, right?"

"Yes, they were brought back, beaten, forced to dig their own graves, and shot."

"You escaped, knowing what would happen, and that took a lot of courage."

Dr. Fagan came into the room and said, "Who is that talking to the patient? Bring him back. Let me talk to him."

Dr. Barton held his arm and said, "Dr. Fagan, I know you are my boss, but that boy is doing a damn good job and is succeeding."

William heard the commotion and got agitated.

"What is happening?"

"Nothing. There are just some people wanting to help you. That's all," said Andrew tactfully.

"I just want it to end. I see them in my dreams; all those soldiers, those victims."

"Listen, you are not a coward. You survived a death march, a death camp, and risked your life to free yourself. Now you want to end it by jumping from a building?"

"It's not what I want, but I am just sick."

"You will get better. Dr. Barton will make sure that you do. Now, give me those scissors and then give me your hand."

"Will you be there for me, Andrew?"

"Yes, I will. I give you my word. Now, give me those scissors." William handed Andrew the pair of scissors. He then extended his hand and Andrew slowly pulled him off the ledge. He led him to his room, walking past the doctors, nurses, and orderlies, and helped him lie down. They could hear the cheering and clapping from outside.

* * * * *

The incident made headlines in the newspapers. Reporters interviewed Andrew and took pictures of him. They even had a picture of him talking to William standing on the ledge.

Rachel read about the incident in the papers and was proud of Andrew. "See, you saved William's life. If you hadn't been there, he would have ended his life," she said at breakfast.

"It was nothing, Mother. He too had the same guilt feeling that he could not do anything to help. It was awful to see him shut himself up like that and feel guilty."

"That's how I felt when you were in that situation. Remember, you were not only hard on yourself, but it was also hard on those who loved and cared for you."

"I know what you mean, Mother."

"Dr. Barton called and told me that William is responding to treatment and taking his medication."

"Good. He is a good doctor, and his patients like him. One of the nurses told me that he stopped Dr. Fagan from interfering when I was talking to William. I am sure if Dr. Fagan had stepped on that ledge, William would have jumped."

Reporters hounded Andrew and he tried to dodge them. He reached home one day and slammed the door shut. "Damn reporters," he shouted, "they are such vultures."

"You're now famous, darling. It is what they do. Imagine being famous for life and having to dodge these reporters," said Rachel, laughing.

"If I ever see one again, I will knock his lights out." The doorbell rang and Andrew was irritated. "It must be one of them. Let me go out and give him a piece of my mind."

Before Rachel could stop him, he ran to the door, opened it, and yelled, "Now, look here, if you do not leave, I will…" The next moment, he stopped shouting, and he was hugging the woman in front of him.

Rachel and Robert were startled at the change in his tone and went to the door. They saw the scene and were baffled.

Andrew turned around and said, "Mother… this is Hazel."

* * * * *

Hazel was bored with Boise, Indiana. She had one older sister, Erin, whom she adored. She was also her father's favorite. Her boredom began when her father died of pneumonia. She remembered him going out into a snowstorm to get some milk from the neighbor and did not heed his wife's advice to cover his head. Shortly after that, he developed a cold that turned into pneumonia. Two days later, Clarence Sheridan was dead. Hazel was devastated. She wept bitterly at his funeral and could not bear to see his coffin close. Now that he was dead, she had to give up plans of going to college. Her mother sank into depression.

One day, she came across a magazine that advertised jobs in Hawaii and had pictures of the exotic place. Her older sister was married with two kids, and her mother, Molly, was slowly recovering from depression. She begged and pleaded with her mother to let her go, but she was firm.

"I just buried my husband, and now my daughter wants to leave me all alone," Molly said, almost crying.

Erin and her husband, Barney, put in a good word on Hazel's behalf. They reminded Molly that Hazel was an adult and could take care of herself. Molly agreed reluctantly and seven months to the day after her father died, Hazel sent her application to work at the hospital at Pearl Harbor, and she was accepted. She met Evelyn on the bus to San Diego, and they became good friends. Evelyn, like Hazel, was looking for an adventure. When they reached Hawaii, they knew that they had made the right decision. "Tropical paradise, handsome sailors, and lots of sunshine; what more can a girl from the Midwest want?" said Evelyn, with a wink. Hazel laughed and nodded in agreement, as they walked the streets and explored Oahu for the first time.

When the bombing began, Hazel and Evelyn left their apartment and ran to the warehouse for safety with other people. They heard what sounded like a whistle and then a loud explosion over their heads. Hazel woke up after the dust had cleared. She could not remember anything. She saw people running, aircrafts flying, shooting, and dropping bombs. She dusted the dirt off and started walking. She bumped into something and realized that it was a dead body. 'I must get away from here,' she said to herself. She heard another bomb fall and saw a crowd of people running. 'Let me follow them,' she said to herself and started running along with them. They were heading towards a small launch.

"Get in there. The launch will take us to another island. Looks like the Japs are going to bomb the whole island to bits," said a man next to her. Hazel got in. The launch started and went out to sea. She could see the debacle unfolding on the island and was relieved that she was on the launch, escaping from the disaster.

The launch docked at the island. Hazel got out with the passengers. Everybody went their separate ways and she was all alone. She felt dizzy and asked for directions to go to the hospital. She walked in the direction she was directed to go. A man came towards her and said, "You seem lost."

"I want to go to the hospital."

"I can take you. Come this way and get into my car." She followed the man and got in. The car drove through the crowd and went into a road that headed away from the harbor.

"What's a pretty girl like you doing here?"

"I got out of this launch, and a woman gave me directions to the hospital."

"Oh well, I'm glad I found you. Now, how about we getting to know each other?"

"What are you insinuating?" asked Hazel, with some fear in her voice. He took one hand off the steering wheel and placed it on her thigh.

"Take your hand off me."

"Come now, you need to pay to get to the hospital, and you giving me what I want is all I need."

She pushed his hand and hit him on the head. The car went off the road and into a ditch. Hazel opened the door and ran away. The man ran after her and got closer. He grabbed her and tried to push her down on the road. Hazel slapped him; he was stunned. He jumped on her and they fell. Hazel found him too strong and tried to move. She reached out with her left hand and grabbed a tree branch. She hit him on the head. He fell to the side. She got up and tried to run. He grabbed her leg. Hazel kicked him and ran away.

She saw a gate, ran towards it, and opened it. She saw a woman outside the house and she yelled, "Save me. There's this man chasing me, and he tried to attack me."

The middle-aged woman looked at her and said, "Come in, dear. We will protect you."

She ran into the arms of the woman, and they both went inside. Hazel was shaking with fear.

"There, there… you are safe now. What is your name?"

"I cannot remember my name."

"Oh dear, that is a shame."

An older man came out and was surprised to see a disheveled woman sitting with his wife.

"Who is she, Amy?"

"She cannot remember her name. She says that a man tried to assault her."

"The whole place has gone crazy. I just heard on the news that Pearl Harbor was bombed by the Japanese."

"Oh no, we must leave the island and go to the mainland. Who knows what will happen. I would feel a lot safer on the mainland, John."

"Yes, you're right. I'm sure that America will be joining the war against Japan, and these islands, being far away from the mainland, may be attacked again. What about her?"

"We'll take her with us. She too is not safe here. We will try and find her family there."

The next day, Hazel left with the older couple. She was silent throughout the journey. The older couple took her to the hospital when they arrived in San Diego and met Dr. Robards. Amy told the doctor how this woman showed up at her gate, claiming that a man attacked her.

Dr. Robards perceived that she was in shock due to the attack and suggested that she be treated at the hospital. Amy kissed Hazel goodbye, but she did not respond. She sat silently in a catatonic state.

One day, she opened her eyes and saw a nurse. "Where am I?"

"You are in the hospital in San Diego. I am Nurse Jessie."

"What year is this?"

"1943."

"What?"

"Yes, you came here after the attack on Pearl Harbor. Nobody knows who you are. We named you Ms. Jones, after the couple who brought you here."

"My name is not Jones. I just remember that I was at Pearl Harbor." The nurse looked confused and said, "Let me call the doctor."

A man with a white coat came towards Hazel, followed by doctors and nurses.

"I am Dr. Robards. What is your name?"

"Hazel. How come I am in San Diego?"

"Mrs. Amy Jones who brought you here said that a man attacked you and that you could not remember your name. You were covered in dust and had a few bruises. Your clothes were also torn a bit, and Mr. and Mrs. Jones took you in. They decided to come to the mainland due to the Pearl Harbor attack. They brought you here, and you have been here ever since."

"Did I say anything?"

"You have not said anything since you stepped inside this hospital. We have tried to find out who you are, with no success."

"My friends, my family... Did anyone come looking for me?"

"Nobody has come here. We never connected you to the events at Pearl Harbor. You were found on the island of Molokai. Most dead civilians were accounted for. Those who were never found were presumed either to have drowned or been blown to bits." She closed her eyes and could now see the bombs falling. The last thing she remembered was running into a warehouse for safety and then the whistling sound of a bomb falling. She could not remember anything before or after that.

"Do you remember anything else besides the bombs falling?"

"No, nothing at all. I just remember my name is Hazel, and I am from Boise, Indiana. My father is dead. I have a mother, and a sister named, Erin. There is nothing else I can remember." She now seemed frustrated.

The doctor smiled at her kindly and said, "That's all right. You have made great progress, and I think we can track your family." As the doctor turned to leave, Hazel asked, "Doctor... What happened to Mr. and Mrs. Jones?"

"They went back to Molokai because they were told it was safe to return. They have been paying for your treatment and will be happy to know that you have made progress."

A few days later, Hazel's mother and sister came to the hospital. She was elated to see them. It was a tearful reunion. "We thought you were dead. We didn't know what had happened to you," said Erin.

"I do not remember many things. My memory is so selective."

"We're just glad you're alive. We will take you back to Boise with us, and you will be fine," said Molly.

Dr. Robards came in and said, "Well, Hazel, I'm sure you're thrilled to be with your family again."

"I am worried that I can't remember much, Doctor. I have a feeling that there is a key factor missing in those memories."

"Your mind has blocked out certain portions of your life before and after you were attacked. Things may happen, which will trigger those memories to return. It may be a name or someone saying something. The human mind is very tricky."

"I hope it happens, Doctor. Will she need to see a psychiatrist when she is in Boise?" asked Erin.

"Yes. Dr. Dean, a psychiatrist in Boise, was a classmate of mine. I will let him know that you are my patient and that you should see him."

"We are very grateful, Doctor. Please also thank that wonderful couple for taking care of my daughter."

"Mr. and Mrs. Jones are happy that you will be going home soon, and they wish you well."

"Thank you, Dr. Robards. I will write and thank them personally."

Hazel went back to Boise and lived with her mother. Her weekly visits to Dr. Dean were fruitless, as she could not remember anything of importance. Visits to childhood haunts with friends were of no avail. Sometimes, some of the memories seemed familiar, but she could not remember the details.

Hazel discovered that she had a knack for cooking. She would cook a few dishes for Sunday lunch at Erin's house. One Sunday, she found her mother reading the newspaper and was absorbed in the story. "What is so interesting, Ma?"

"A soldier in New York tried to kill himself at the hospital, and another man stopped him from jumping from the building."

"Oh Mother! Stop reading these stories. The papers are always full of stories about the war, the dead, and the wounded." Molly urged her to read the story, but Hazel said that she had to finish roasting the vegetables for Erin.

They went over to Erin's house, and they all sat at the table for lunch along with Erin's three children. Erin kept her fourth child in the crib and went outside to call her husband. Barney, Erin's husband, came to the table. He worked at the local post office. He wanted to join the army but was rejected since he was suffering from asthma. He was injured recently when the mailbags fell on his foot.

"How is the foot, Barney?" asked Hazel.

"It's getting better. I look forward to going back to work."

"The doctors said the cast can come off on Tuesday. He can go back to work on Thursday," said Erin.

"Speaking of doctors, did you read about what happened in New York?" asked Barney.

"Yes, I told Hazel to read the story, but she does not want to."

"You will like this, Hazel, trust me. Let me tell it," said Barney. Before Hazel could protest, Barney began narrating the story. "This soldier named William Brewster was suffering from depression. He decided to jump from the hospital window onto the street below. An orderly named Andrew Johnson coaxed him..."

"Wait a minute, what did you say?" asked Hazel, with some excitement in her voice.

"I said he wanted to jump from the window..."

"No, the name of the orderly."

"Andrew Johnson."

"Yes, that's it! Does the paper have a picture?"

"What is it Hazel? Does that name sound familiar?" asked Molly.

"Yes." Hazel got up, ran to the table, and picked up the newspaper. She looked at the picture and fainted.

She woke up after sometime and saw her family starring at her. "Are you all right? What happened?" asked Erin.

"That man in the newspaper... he is from Pearl Harbor. We were dating, and he wanted to marry me." They looked at each other. "I'm not crazy. I remember now. I worked at the hospital mess hall with Evelyn. She was my roommate..."

"I think we better call Dr. Dean," said Barney. Dr. Dean arrived shortly, went into the room, and checked Hazel. He came out and said, "In all my years as a psychiatrist, I have never seen anything like this. But, I do know that she has regained her memory."

"How can you tell, Doctor?"

"She answered all my questions in detail. I think, it would be best, if she contacted the hospital at Pearl Harbor. She used to know a Dr. Chesterfield who worked at the hospital where her friends, Evelyn and Sally, worked. I asked her to contact him tomorrow and speak to him."

"Thank you, for coming on a Sunday, Doctor."

"It was no trouble, Molly. I hope Hazel is right, or she will be very upset."

The next day, Hazel picked up the receiver and asked the operator to connect her to Dr. Chesterfield in Pearl Harbor, Hawaii.

"Hazel, is that really you? We thought you were dead. What happened? It is like a voice from beyond the grave."

She let out a slight laugh. "It's a long story. I'm trying to piece together everything from the time I lost my memory. Do you remember my friends, Maryanne and Sally?"

"Yes, they shipped out to the Pacific with the navy; so have Brandon and Phillip. They left a few days after the president declared war on Japan."

"What about Irving and Evelyn?"

"I'm sorry, Hazel, but neither of them made it. Evelyn died when a bomb hit the warehouse in which she was hiding. Irving was mortally wounded when the USS Arizona was bombed. He died two days later in the hospital."

Hazel was upset at the news. She tried to remain calm. "What about Andrew Johnson?"

"He survived but was badly wounded. He went back to Long Island after being discharged from the navy. I see that he is the one who stopped that man from jumping from the building."

Hazel was relieved that she had her confirmation. She told Dr. Chesterfield her story. "There may have been some miscommunication. The civilians took care of their own records, and the navy took care of theirs. Now that you have a lead, you need to follow it. Please let me know what you find."

"Thank you, Dr. Chesterfield, I will. I must go."

"Go where?"

"To New York."

Chapter 16

Normandy, October 1943

Sidney landed safely. As protocol dictated, he rolled his parachute immediately. He had to find the others before the German soldiers came looking for them. If they were caught, the whole mission would be in jeopardy.

He hid his parachute behind some bushes and went in search of his comrades. He could see torchlights in the distance coming towards him and heard the dogs barking. He looked for the French Resistance fighters who were supposed to meet them, but there was no one around. Suddenly, he heard someone calling him.

"Psst, psst." He couldn't see anyone. "Over here, in the trees." Sidney looked up and saw a pair of legs. The darkness and branches covered the view of the rest of the body.

He went closer and could see the face under the dim moonlit night. "Colin!"

"Yes, it's me. Get me down." Sidney pulled out a knife from his boot and climbed up the tree. He reached the branch and began cutting the parachute.

"We need to get the whole thing down and hide it from the Germans," said Sidney.

"Cut me down and then I can pull on it." Sidney cut the ropes and Colin fell to the ground.

"Okay, untangle the parachute from the top, and I will pull it from the bottom." Colin jumped and caught the strings of the parachute and tried to yank it down. Sidney tried to untangle the parachute from the top. The tree shook; the branch broke and fell on Colin. Sidney nearly lost his balance. He steadied himself and climbed down. He went towards Colin who was under the parachute. Sidney removed the parachute and helped Colin out. They rolled it, went further into the woods, and hid the parachute.

"Where is everybody?"

"I don't know. We need to get out of here. I can see that the Germans are getting closer."

"Men, this way…" It was the voice of a woman, with a French accent, coming from the bushes. The two men looked at each other puzzled.

"Who's that?"

"I was sent to meet you. I have your three friends." Her voice was stern. "You better come quickly, or the Germans will get you." They looked at each other and went towards the voice. The woman stood up and smiled at them. "Welcome to France. I am Catherine. Come this way, quickly. It looks like it's going to rain in a few minutes."

They looked up at the sky and saw the clouds moving in. They followed her without any argument. They both believed she could be trusted under the circumstances. She ran farther into the woods, and they followed her. They could feel the raindrops coming down heavily. After what seemed like an eternity, she led them to a barn, and opened the door.

"Who is that?" shouted a voice in French from inside the barn.

"It's me, Catherine, with the two Americans."

They went into the dark barn. Charles switched on his cigarette lighter and there was light. They saw Brian and the other two British soldiers with another French man.

"Ah, you have arrived safely. You two gave us a fright when you went missing. It's good the Germans didn't find you. The whole mission would have been up in smoke," said George.

"The wind blew us away from our intended landing area," said Colin.

"It happens, Monsieur. Bienvenue, I am Louis." He stood up and walked towards them. The men shook hands.

"Thanks to Catherine, we are safe."

"Ah yes, my sister is very dedicated to our cause. Since the Germans are looking for you, the five of you will have to wait here until it is safe. The soldiers will be searching the houses in the villages, and when they find no one, they will leave." The lighter went out. The whole place was pitch-dark.

"Sorry, I have to conserve the lighter for later," said Charles.

"Do we have the radio and the Enigma machine?"

"Yes, we do. However, we need to check for any damages in the morning as I dropped them when I was running towards the barn," said Charles.

"How did you meet Louis?" asked Brian.

Before anyone else could answer, Louis said, "Catherine and I saw the two of you being blown off course, and we think the Germans also saw you descend. We could not take you to my barn in the village because it will be searched. Therefore, I told Catherine to find you two and get you here. Nobody will find you here, not even the Germans."

"What if they don't leave the place? We need to get the documents back to England at the earliest. The whole mission they are planning for next year depends on us," said George.

"It is my hope, that when they find no one and no trace of you, they will leave. They will think that you got away somehow. Have you hidden your parachutes well?"

"Yes, we hid them in the woods. Catherine saw us hide them."

"Yes, I did. We must burn them when we have the chance and get rid of all traces," said Catherine.

"We will leave now. The rain seems to be stopping. I'm sure that the rain must have thrown the Germans off," said Louis.

The men thanked Catherine and Louis. As they were walking out Louis said, "There is a bag with tinned food behind the hay stack. Do not light candles or make a fire. It is too risky. We will be back tomorrow with more food."

They left the place, and the five men went behind the haystack. They found the bag and opened the tins with the knives they had with them. There were also some candles and matchsticks.

"Umm, I would never have guessed that ham and beans would taste so delicious," said Colin.

"When one is hungry, anything tastes good," said Sidney.

"Yes, and due to the full moon, we do not need to light candles."

They finished dinner and got ready for bed. They slept on the hay, and fortunately, the autumn chill had not set in, and the air was warm. They got up early morning and waited for Catherine. They heard footsteps, and they all put their hands on their holsters to get their guns out.

Catherine entered with a basket hanging from her right arm. "Good morning, I hope you slept well. I brought you breakfast. I'm sure this will be better than the tinned food you were forced to eat last night."

Catherine took out a blanket and spread it on the dirt floor, strewn with hay. She pulled out two small jars of jam and bread and put five small plates on the blanket. She took out sausage from the basket and placed them on the plates. Catherine laughed when she saw them gobble the food. She took out five small glasses and poured them some wine. The men drank the wine and admitted that it was the best wine they have ever had.

"When do we leave?" asked Sidney.

"Tonight. The Germans searched the houses last night and did not find anyone. One of our people heard them say that maybe the paratroopers have gone southwards. So, they are checking all the vehicles that leave this area."

Catherine collected the plates, took them outside, and cleaned them. She left the basket of food and told them that there was enough food for the rest of the day.

As she walked away, Sidney ran to her and said, "Catherine, I know this sounds very strange, but have we met before?" She stared laughing. "Monsieur Sidney, you must be drunk from the wine. How could we have met? You are from America and I am from France."

"I know, but you seem very familiar. You maybe resembling someone I know. It's just that I have a strange feeling that we have met and... maybe, I am drunk."

She smiled at him and said, "I was born in America. My parents brought me to France when I was four years old. We were in California."

"Okay. I am from New York and have never been to California. My apologies, Mademoiselle."

She laughed at him and walked away. Sidney felt embarrassed and walked back into the barn. The other men were checking the Enigma machine for damage. Sidney could still not shake off the feeling that he had met Catherine before.

That evening, Louis came back and told them that it was safe to go into the village.

"I've brought you clothes and work tools. You will have to wear these farm clothes so that nobody recognizes you. If anyone meets us on the road, you let me do the talking."

They undressed and wore the clothes Louis had brought them. The sun was setting as they walked back towards the village. The men had pickaxes and shovels over their shoulders. They passed by many villagers, but nobody suspected a thing.

On the way, Sidney asked Louis about Catherine. "Yes, she was born in America. My parents went to work in California. I stayed here taking care of the farm."

"Is she married?"

Louis looked a bit sad and said, "No, sadly, she is not, Monsieur. She had a man and he died a few months ago.

"What happened?"

"It was in the outskirts of Paris..."

April 1943

Catherine and Roland suspected that there was an informant among them. The last time they tried to smuggle a couple out of France they were almost caught. Roland also suspected that the same unknown informant had betrayed Collette and Armand. Catherine tried convincing Roland to stop, but he was adamant about helping people escape and also helping the French Resistance in Vichy France.

Ever since Armand and Collette were killed, Roland was determined to continue their work. In a way, Catherine regretted pushing him into it.

A few days later, Roland and five Resistance men were waiting with a truck. They brought out the family who had been hiding in a specially constructed room under a warehouse, for transportation. The family consisted of a couple and three children. They escaped persecution in Germany, but now they had to get out of France. The plan was to take them by truck to the Portuguese border and smuggle them into Portugal.

The truck contained crates of empty bottles, which Roland was transporting for a wine company. He transported bottles once a month, and when he could, he took some of the refugees to the closest place, from where they could get out of France. The last time he was almost caught, but to his good luck, while the truck was being searched at one of the checkpoints, a noise in the woods distracted the soldiers, and he was allowed to go. His German was only basic, but he remembered one of the German soldiers telling another soldier that they were informed that a truck would be carrying Jews trying to escape. Tomas and Gaston were in the truck, and they were ready to start shooting if the people were discovered. Thankfully, that did not happen. The truck passed through the checkpoint after orders were given to check out the noise in the woods.

The Rosen family got into the truck. There was a hollow portion in the truck that could be covered so well, that nobody would suspect that it existed. The family was put in there and just before the board was put in place, Roland said, "It will be very uncomfortable, but you will have to bear with it until we reach the border, or stop on the way. Is that understood?"

"Yes," said Mr. Rosen; his wife and children nodded. They covered the hollow portion and started loading the crates of empty bottles. As they were loading, a light beam shone on them.

"This is the Gestapo. You have been surrounded, and if you do not comply, you will be shot." The men put their hands up. Julian tried to run away but was gunned down. The men were ordered to take the crates out and they complied. A soldier went in and knocked on the wooden board. "Come out, you have been surrounded. We will shoot."

"They cannot get out. We have to remove the board for them," said Roland.

"All right, get the board out." Roland and Gaston got in and removed the board. The five people in there trembled with fear. They knew it was either instant death or to the concentration camps. The family came out with their hands up. They stood next to the five men. "All right, take the family away and execute the men," the voice behind the light said.

Mrs. Rosen and her daughter started to cry, as the soldiers pointed the guns at them and ordered them to move. As they walked away, they knew that the next trip was to the concentration camp.

The five men were led towards the wall, and the remaining soldiers lined up in front of them. The men crossed themselves and started praying. As the soldiers took aim, a man appeared and stood next to them. He was dressed in civilian clothes. He smiled at the men about to be executed. Initially, the five condemned men found it hard to see, and when their eyes got used to the darkness, they realized who had betrayed them.

"You, Nazi pig, you betrayed us," shouted Gaston.

Roland tried to run towards the man with clenched fists. "Why, you son of…"

Those were the last words he uttered. The next moment, the guns expelled their bullets, and the men fell to the ground. Roland's last thought was of Catherine.

Catherine, on her way to work, decided to take a detour to make sure that everything went smoothly. As she got closer to the warehouse, she saw a crowd and an ambulance there. She feared the worst and went towards the crowd.

"What happened?"

"Nobody knows. The residents heard gunfire at night, but nobody dared go out because of the curfew. The bodies of these five men were found this morning. Looks like the Nazis killed them for something they did," replied a man.

Catherine felt sick. She saw the five stretchers with sheets on the bodies and recognized Roland's boots. She resisted the urge to run there and hug him. Her eyes filled with tears. "Are you all right?" asked a woman.

That snapped her back into reality. "Yes, I am."

"You look red in the face. Did you know those men?"

"No... no, I am just upset to see them. That is all." Catherine saw the bodies being loaded into the van and the van door close.

"All of you leave. Nothing to see here," shouted the gendarmerie.

The crowd started dispersing. Catherine tried to steady herself and walk away. She stopped and said to herself, 'Mon Dieu, I need to get the list. If that falls into the hands of the Gestapo, everyone will be caught.'

She started running into another street where Roland lived. She went into the house and saw that it was intact. She went upstairs into the bedroom. This was where Roland and she had made plans on how to smuggle people out of France; this was where he proposed to her a few weeks earlier; and this was where he kissed her for the last time, the previous night. She felt tears streaming down her cheeks. She went towards the desk and reached behind it. She pushed the small lever behind, and a small section of the desk opened. She reached in and pulled out two sheets of paper. As she folded them, she heard a voice behind her. "Thank you, Catherine. I knew you would know where to find that list."

She turned around with a surprised look and saw who it was. "Tomas, what are you doing here? Roland and the men are dead. I saw them. It was just horrible and..." She noticed that he was grinning.

"I know. I was there."

"What do you mean you were there? How did you escape?"

"I didn't need to escape. I was the one who led the Gestapo to them."

Catherine could not believe her ears. "But, why... why would you do something like that?"

"Because, Roland and the rest of them treated me like a nobody. I was made to follow orders and did what I was told to do in the hope that they would respect me. Did I get any respect or any part in the planning? No. They all thought that they were the intelligent ones and only they could plan the escape routes."

"Tomas, everyone had to do their part. They all trusted you. We had to save the lives of all those innocent people."

"Oh, what do I care about those people who are meant to be in the concentration camps, anyway? I have always dreamed of being important. That never happened with Armand and Roland around."

"Armand and Collette…" She gasped. "That was you too?"

"Yes, that was me. Armand did not appreciate my work, either, and gave me only tasks to do. He, like the rest, treated me like dirt. Therefore, I called up the Gestapo anonymously and told them about Armand and Collette. After Armand was gone, I thought that Roland would let me be the one to make the important decisions since I was a lot closer to Armand, but Roland came in and just took over. He never bothered to acknowledge my achievements. Now the Nazis will acknowledge them. I have promised them the list of other agents, and I will be rewarded."

He looked at her, and she could see his eyes feasting on her body. "First, I will have my way with you. I have always desired you, and now is my chance. After that, I will personally turn you over to the Gestapo."

Catherine looked at his corpulent body and felt sick. She always had misgivings about Tomas and did not like him. She tolerated Tomas for the sake of the Resistance.

"No, Tomas, you don't know what you're saying. Roland trusted you and so did Armand, Collette, and the others."

"Shut up and come over here," he roared. He came closer, caught her by the wrist, and pulled her towards him. He kissed her, and she tried to break away. She felt a knife being pressed to her belly.

"If you don't do as I ask, you will be sorry. Now, get on the bed." He threw her on the bed and went towards her, as she tried to move away. He caught her leg, and the knife fell on the floor. She wriggled her foot out and kicked Tomas on his corpulent stomach. He fell backwards on the desk.

She bent and picked up the knife. "I'll use this if you try anything," said Catherine.

He stood up and laughed. He came at her and tried to grab the knife. She moved her hand and the knife cut him on his arm. It started bleeding.

"You bitch, you will pay for this." He lunged at her again, and she thrust the knife forward. It stabbed him in his stomach. He yelled in pain and tried to regain control of the knife. She pulled the knife out and stabbed him in the chest. Tomas fell dead on the floor.

Catherine was sweating. She had blood on her hands. She felt dizzy at the sight of blood. She held onto the desk and walked towards the washroom. She washed off the blood and felt better.

She came into the bedroom and saw the dead body. Very soon, the Gestapo would arrive, and she needed to get out. She saw the list on the floor. She picked up the pages, folded them, and put them inside her blouse. She went to the table, took the picture of Armand and her, and put it in her bag. She took one last look at the room and left.

Catherine took the back alley so nobody would see her. She saw a car and knew that it was Tomas'. The key was still in the ignition. She got in and drove home. She packed her things, put them in the car, and drove out of Paris. The Nazis would eventually find Tomas' body and start searching for her. The only place she could now go was to Normandy.

"Where is the list?" asked Sidney.

"It is with me. It is good she brought it here because my name is on it. That list had the names and addresses of the Resistance members who helped the Jews and other dissidents escape the Nazis," said Louis.

"How did you help them escape?"

"The people were smuggled from Paris in a truck. When they came here, we would arrange for a boat to cross the English Channel. They would be received by one of our people on the English coast."

The group had reached the farm, and they went into the house.

Annette, Pierre, and Catherine welcomed them. "The sun is setting, so we will have dinner now. We will show our guests from America and England what true French hospitality is," said Pierre.

Annette had prepared a nice meal, and the famished soldiers ate and drank to their hearts' content. It had been a long time since they had eaten such a big meal.

"Sleep well. Tomorrow, we will plan for the success of your mission. The commandant keeps the documents in a safe. The woman who cleans the office is one of us, and she knows where the safe is. She will be here tomorrow," said Catherine. The men were shown where to sleep, and they promptly got ready for bed.

The farm animals woke them up in the morning. For Brian and Colin, who were farm boys, it was a pleasant sound to wake up to. They got ready for breakfast and went to the dining room. Breakfast had already been prepared. They saw the food and Sidney said,

"Looking at the quantity of food here, nobody would say that there is a war going on."

"In Paris, you definitely can tell there is a war. There is a lot of food to eat only on a farm; thanks to the livestock," said Catherine, amused.

They had breakfast and got ready for their meeting with the janitor. Catherine brought her in, and she sat down in front of the men in a seductive pose. Blanche was an attractive brunette who had the attention of all the men when she walked into the room. She had on bright red lipstick that enhanced her beauty. "Bonjour, I am Blanche. I work for the commandant in the village. Catherine tells me that you need help getting certain information to the allies."

"Yes," said Sidney. "We need to know where the commandant keeps the reports of his troops in this region and also their activity: the number of units stationed here, weather reports, maps of the region, location of weapons along the beach, and also the type of weapons."

"He keeps some of them in his safe and the maps in his cupboard upstairs. He is very thorough and does not miss a thing. You cannot take them as he checks some of them every day."

"We have miniature cameras with us. We can take pictures of some of the documents."

"Okay, that will be possible," said Blanche.

"How do we get in?"

"It would be possible only at night. There is only one guard guarding the door to the building. They know that no one will try to enter the office because, if they are caught, they will be executed at once."

"How will we distract the guard?"

"You leave that to me. This guard, whose name is Hermann, fancies me and always tries to gain my attention. So far, I have not responded to his advances, but for the sake of defeating the enemy, I will make it worth his time."

The men looked at each other and smiled.

"I am sure France will thank you for helping the allies win this war," said George.

"How do we get there?"

"You can use the car Catherine brought from Paris," said Louis.

They all looked at Catherine. She looked at them and said, "Sure, I don't care about that car. It brings back bad memories. It still has the Paris license plate and nothing to tie it to St. Lacroix."

"That would give us a good cover," said George. "They would try to track the car and think that the thieves came from Paris."

"Nice way of thinking, George," said Sidney.

"When do you think is the best time to carry out this mission?" asked Charles.

"On Friday night. That is when the German soldiers are in their barracks. There are patrols on the streets, but we will have to try to avoid them. As you know, they will start shooting if they see anyone on the streets."

"How do we get back to England?" asked Charles.

"We have a motor boat ready for you at the jetty. You must be quiet and not turn on the motor until you are far away. The Nazis have pillboxes on the beach, and they will start firing the moment they hear any sound. I will show you where I will keep the boat. It will have a map and will also be stocked with food and water," said Louis.

"All right, here is what we will do…" said Sidney

On Friday night, the five men got into the car and drove towards the office. Blanche told her supervisor that she was sick and that she would come in late and stay late. The previous day, she told Hermann that she would stay late so that they could talk. It was getting dark and was almost eight o'clock - time for the curfew. The villagers hurried to get home. The car drove past the office and went to the next street. They saw Hermann guarding the building. The five men got out and waited for Blanche's signal.

Presently, they saw Blanche come out and call the guard. The guard entered and shut the door. They waited for a few minutes and then went close to the building. It was dark. No one would be around, except the patrols. According to Blanche, they patrolled the streets every half hour. They entered through the back door that Blanche had unlocked earlier.

The building was empty and quiet. Blanche had written the instructions to help them find their way inside the building. Brian stayed near the door as a lookout. They went down the hall and found the staircase. They saw a light on in one of the rooms and could hear Blanche and Hermann talking and kissing. They climbed the wooden staircase and made it to the top. Charles stood outside the door to keep watch. The other three men went into the main office room and found the safe. George, a master safe cracker, went to the safe and started turning the knob. Finally, after a tense five minutes, the door opened. Using torchlight, they found the documents they wanted. They spread them out on the table and looked at them.

"These are a lot. We will not have enough time to take pictures of all these documents," said Colin.

"You're right. We'll just have to take them with us," said George.

"No, we can't. Blanche said that the commandant checks these papers every day, and she maybe blamed if they are lost. We cannot let her go to prison or be shot," said Sidney.

"You're right. We need to find a room. What about the one upstairs? There are maps there, as well. Blanche said the room doesn't have windows facing the street, only the alley. Since it's after curfew, nobody will be in the alley."

"Okay, let us go there."

The three men hurried out of the room and went up the stairs along with Charles.

They reached the room and went in. They turned on the light and saw two tables. "Perfect. Let us work on the documents here while Charles can get the maps from the cupboard," said George.

Charles brought the maps and spread them on the table; Sidney and George took pictures with their cameras. They finished in thirty minutes and put the maps in the cupboard. They went downstairs, put the documents in the safe, and closed the safe. They then went to the first floor, went through the hall towards the back of the building, and closed the door. "Did you get everything?" asked Brian.

"Yes, we did. We need to leave now and be in England by morning. There's some very important information that the allies must see," said George.

The others agreed, and they walked towards the car. They could not risk starting the car, so they decided to push it until they got out of the street. Charles got behind the wheel while the four of them pushed it. They manoeuvred the car until they were out of the street.

All of a sudden, they heard a loud voice behind them. "Halt, halt!"

They turned around and found a German soldier running towards them.

"What do we do?" asked Brian.

"Don't panic. Let him come to us, and we will see what he wants." The soldier came towards them with his machine gun.

"What are you doing here? Don't you know it is curfew time?"

"We do. We are just getting home," said Colin.

"Where are your papers?" They looked at him. "Where are your papers?" he now demanded angrily.

"We don't have them with us."

"You will have to come with me. You've broken the law."

George rushed towards him and punched him in his face; the soldier fell. He tried to get up, but George kicked him again. "Get in the car," he yelled.

The men tried to get in. The soldier shot at them, and the bullets bounced off the car.

Charles started the car and drove away.

"To the jetty, Charles. The shots would have alerted the rest of the patrol," said Brian.

Colin looked out of the rear windshield and said, "There's a Jeep filled with soldiers following us."

"Faster, Charles, faster," shouted Sidney. The car sped along the road with the Jeep following them. They reached the jetty and got out. They found the motor boat that Louis had shown them earlier and jumped in. Sidney started the motor, and Charles began cutting the rope. They heard the Jeep stop and shots fired. The bullets flew over them and some hit the boat. The rope gave way and the boat sped forward. They headed towards the open sea with bullets whizzing past them. A few minutes later, they were out of range, and they stood up.

"That was a close call. I'm glad we made it in one piece," said Colin, laughing.

"Yes," said Sidney.

Charles felt something wet on his shirt and touched it. In the moonlight, he could see the dark color and felt the pain shooting through his body.

"I've been shot," he said. The others froze, and their smiles, one by one, turned to frowns.

"Where is the medicine kit?"

"It should be in the cabinet," said Colin. He opened the cabinet and found a box with a Red Cross symbol on it. He opened it and saw that it contained medicines and bandages.

They removed Charles' shirt and saw the full extent of the injury. The bullet had entered from the back on the left and exited through the front. He was losing a lot of blood.

They managed to clean the wound but could not stop the bleeding. "The wound has to be bandaged. It will help stop the bleeding," said Colin.

They put a piece of cotton at the entry and exit areas of the wound and then wrapped the bandage around his body.

He was getting weak, and they decided to let him rest. They gave him some whisky, which was in the cabinet. He managed to sip a little and fell asleep.

"Damn, just one bullet, and he had to be there at the wrong place at the wrong time," said Sidney.

"If that German soldier hadn't caught us, we would have been able to drive quietly and none of this would have happened. Some tough luck," said George.

"Now, now... sometimes things happen which are not under our control," said Brian.

They looked at him and George said, "You're right. It is just that he is badly wounded, and I'm not sure if he will survive."

"Now, don't say that. We'll probably reach the English coast soon, and he can get medical help," said Colin.

The engine sputtered and started smoking. The boat slowed down and stopped. "Oh no. What happened?"

Brian looked at the engine and said, "The tank may be low on fuel."

Brian opened the top and peered in. "No, it's full. There must be something wrong with the engine." The engine was too hot to handle.

"We will have to wait for a while until it cools down. The tide seems strong. It is taking us towards the English coast," said George.

"How do you know?" asked Brian.

"I was a fisherman with my father, and I know all about tides," said George.

They sat down and decided to eat some of the food that Louis had kept for them. Charles was still asleep. "He was always a very quiet man. Charles never spoke much."

"Yes, he never said much. Do you know anything about him, George?"

"I do. He's from one of the local fishing villages close to mine. The reason he joined the army was because his family was frowned upon for not taking part in the Dunkirk Operations."

"Did you participate?" asked Brian

"Yes, and so did my father and almost everyone I knew."

"Why didn't Charles' family take part?"

"They were poor, and his father was worried that the boat may be damaged or sunk. Some boats were sunk at Dunkirk and some fishermen were killed. I narrowly escaped being gunned down by a German aircraft. My boat was badly damaged, yet we managed to get back to England. After that, it couldn't be used for fishing. After the Dunkirk Operations, everybody shunned Charles' family. They called them cowards and Nazi sympathizers. Nobody would buy their catch at the local market, so they had to travel all the way to other villages or to London to sell their catch."

"Tell me, when you lost your boat... is that when you decided to become a... you know, a safe cracker?" asked Brian. The rest of the men looked at Brian, but they knew he was one for being straightforward.

"Not then. I had to find work in London. The pay was not enough to get a new fishing boat. I always knew that I had the gift for cracking safes. I tried it once at the pub where I was working, and when nobody found me out, I did it again and was caught the fourth time and sent to jail. When the Germans started bombing London, they needed men to join the army, so I decided to join the army and serve my country."

"Is that when Charles decided to join the army too?"

"Yes, he did, so that his family would not be shunned. He told his pregnant wife that he wanted his children to be proud of him and also wanted to restore his family's pride."

"I would have done the same thing if I were in his place," said Sidney.

"I guess the engine has cooled down. Let me check," said Colin. He checked the engine and saw that the wires had burned out.

"I think we pushed the engine to work beyond its capacity, and it has broken down."

A wave of sadness descended on them. They hoped that the boat would reach England soon.

They sat drifting for hours while Charles bled slowly. The sun began to rise, and they saw the white cliffs of Dover. It was a beautiful sight. They heard a moan as Charles woke up. "Hey there mate, we will soon be in England, and you will be all right," said George.

"I don't think so. I'm getting weaker. I wish I could see my unborn child, Cynthia, and my daughter. What will they do without me?"

"Don't say that, Charles. If anything happens to you, the government will take care of your family. Besides, they also have your family and Cynthia's," said George, with tears in his eyes.

"I'm dying, but I am glad that I am dying for my beloved country. I have taken away the shame my family had to face for not participating at Dunkirk. Lift me up and let me see England for the last time."

George and Colin propped him up so that he could see the cliffs. "It's a beautiful sight. I'm glad that it is the last thing I'll be seeing." He turned his head towards George.

"Please sing "There will always be an England" by Vera Lynn. I hope we win the war, and England will never be invaded by our enemies again."

Charles began singing, and George joined in. Charles closed his eyes for the last time.

The next day, the four men were in front of Officer Howell. "Well done, gentlemen. The pictures you took were developed by the laboratory, and we can now determine the weak and strong points in the German defences in Normandy. The information will be given to the allied commanders to guide them in planning the invasion."

"Thank you, Officer Howell," said George.

"Private George Sawyer, you have served your country well. You will be honored with the 'Distinguished Service Honor' at a special ceremony. General Eisenhower has recommended that the three American soldiers be awarded the 'Distinguished Service Medal' by the American ambassador, next week. Nothing will be said about this mission, except that you will be awarded for gallantry shown in the line of duty in North Africa and Sicily."

"Thank you, sir. May I ask a question?"

"Yes Sidney."

"Could Charles Crabtree receive a medal for his service to his nation? He died getting us to safety, and it is only fitting that he be honored for his efforts."

"Yes, he certainly will. It will be given to his widow."

"Thank you, sir. May we request permission to attend the funeral of Charles Crabtree, sir?"

"Yes, and I will be in attendance too."

Two days later, the four men were at the village church where Charles' casket was laid out with the British flag. His pregnant widow dressed in black with their daughter, the family, and most of the villagers were present at the funeral. After the service, Officer Howell spoke about the gratitude England owed to such a brave man. He then presented Crabtree's widow a small box containing the medal, which she accepted with her thanks. He then offered his condolences to Charles' parents and siblings.

After the burial, Officer Howell left. The four men attended the repast at the parish hall. They expressed their condolences to the widow and parents. Cynthia opened the box and saw the medal. Her face beamed with pride. His parents were jubilant.

"He has taken away the stain from our family. This medal, though it will not bring him back, will always keep his memory and sacrifice alive," said Cynthia.

"I'm sure you're proud of what he did," said Sidney.

"Yes, we are. I feel I am going to have a boy. I will name him after Charles. He will not be forgotten."

A few days later, at the American Embassy in London, the American ambassador presented the three Americans with the 'Distinguished Service Medal' for their mission. After the ceremony, a cocktail party was held in their honor attended by the embassy staff.

While Sidney was sipping his cocktail, a voice from behind him said, "Excuse me, aren't you Martha Hardy's son?"

He turned around and saw an attractive middle-aged woman, dressed in a pink dress, wearing a hat with flowers on it.

"Yes, how did you know?"

"I'm Lucy... Rachel Johnson's cousin. When they introduced you and said that you were from New York City, I had to know if I was right."

"Yes, I remember now. You married Paul Hatfield, the diplomat, and you've been living abroad, attached to the U.S. embassies."

"Yes, we have lived in France, England, the Philippines, Belgium, and at the start of the war, we returned to England. My oldest son is in the army. My two daughters are married to RAF pilots, and they are living in London. My youngest son goes to school here. It has been a long time since I saw Rachel and Andrew. I hope he has recovered from that dreadful attack at Pearl Harbor."

"He has, in a way. But, he still needs a lot of emotional help."

"I am glad she didn't lose him. Poor Rachel lost her husband and daughter. Life would have been so cruel, if Andy had…"

"Yes, I know what you mean."

"It was nice meeting you, Sidney. I hope to be back in the U.S. after this war is over."

"Pleasure is all mine, Mrs. Hatfield."

Sidney watched as Lucy walked away and all of a sudden thought of something. 'No, it cannot be.' He put the thought aside and joined Brian and Colin.

Chapter 17

New York, April 1944

It was Easter Monday. Martha and Rachel were shopping in Manhattan. Andrew and Hazel had been married for a few months. Rachel remembered the joy on Andrew's face when Hazel showed up at the door. Hazel told them her story about how she regained her memory after reading the newspaper.

Rachel liked Hazel. She was everything Andrew said she was. After two weeks, Andrew asked Hazel to marry him, and she accepted. The wedding took place in October. It was a beautiful wedding. Some of New York's high society was not impressed with the bride. They complained to Rachel saying that Hazel was not from the same class as them and she probably is a gold digger who will swindle Andrew of his wealth. Rachel's reply to those criticisms was, "I am happy with Andrew's decision, and I believe he has made a very good choice."

Hazel looked resplendent in her white dress, and Andrew looked handsome in his suit. More than anything else, Rachel was very happy to see Andrew smile. That was what she missed most when he was depressed. The best man was William Brewster. He had started recovering, and Andrew and he had become good friends.

Martha was at the wedding. Rachel could tell that she was worried about Sidney. Sidney had contacted her sporadically but not in the recent past. Martha was glad that Sidney and Mary had broken off. "She was too stuffy for me," Martha declared.

Rachel's Christmas gift was the good news that Hazel was

pregnant. Rachel was ecstatic. She never thought she would see the day when she would be told that she would be a grandmother. She almost lost Andrew three times, and Barbara was dead. She was happy that the Johnson family would continue.

Martha was the one Rachel would call and confide in. In recent months, they had become closer. When Andrew was depressed, she didn't have the time to go out or to meet Martha as she needed to be there for Andrew. Now that things were all in place, she and Martha were back to being best friends.

They were walking down 5th Avenue in Manhattan, when Gulia Cleary came to them. After exchanging greetings, Rachel told Gulia about Hazel's pregnancy and that she wanted to get Hazel a gift for Easter. Gulia suggested that she go to a Russian shop down the road and buy Hazel a Fabergé egg.

They went down Fifth Avenue and saw the shop. It was easy to spot. It had Cyrillic script at the top and a wooden carving of a Fabergé egg. They went in and a blond girl came to attend on them. "Good afternoon, ladies. May I help you?"

"Yes, I would like to buy a Fabergé egg for my daughter-in-law. She's pregnant with my first grandchild."

"I think you will like the one I have in mind," said the girl. She led them through a small aisle and showed her a Fabergé egg decorated with blue stones and pearls on the side."

"That is very beautiful. How much does it cost?" asked Rachel.

"One hundred dollars, ma'am."

"I think Hazel will like it."

"I'll pack it and take it to the front desk." She opened the cabinet and took out the Fabergé egg. She then disappeared into a room hidden by a curtain. She came out a few minutes later and said, "My mother wants to talk to you."

"Really?" said Rachel in surprise. "Do I know her?"

"Yes, she says that you know her. You can step this way and go through the curtain."

Rachel walked through the curtain into a dimly lit room. She could see an altar with Russian orthodox religious icons and lighted candles.

She saw the figure of a woman in the shadows.

"Yes, Mrs. Johnson, my prayers have been answered. You have finally come. We meet again after twenty-two years."

Rachel could detect a foreign accent. "Who are you? Please show yourself."

A woman came out from the shadows. Her head was covered, and Rachel could see the face. "Do you remember me?"

"No, I don't. Who are you?"

"Do you remember the speakeasy you went to in the early 20s?"

"Yes, and you must be..." her eyes became wider. "You are that dancer, Anna, 'The Star of Russia'."

"Yes, I am."

Rachel could now feel the anger welling up inside her. She could not believe that the once beautiful Anna was now a haggard woman who looked old beyond her years. "What do you want from me?"

"I'm hoping I can get your forgiveness."

Rachel was stunned at the strange request. "You slept with my husband and now you want forgiveness?" she retorted sharply.

"It was not intentional. Rudy Holzmann ordered me to do it. I asked no questions. I was in this country as a refugee from Russia and all alone. He used to come to the speakeasy on the weekends and that's how I got to know him.

"I know that."

"He told you?"

"No, I read his diary. I know he was a wicked man."

"I read that he was killed when he tried to take you hostage."

"Yes."

"We were both used by a very cunning man, Mrs. Johnson. I know because of what I did, your marriage was ruined."

"You did more than that. Because of what you and Rudy did, I hated my husband. Because of that, he went to California with my daughter, and they died in that horrible train accident in the mountains."

Anna closed her eyes and sighed. "I am very sorry. If I had known my actions would cause the death of two people you loved, I would not have done what I did. That is why I need your forgiveness now more than ever. Every day, I pray to God to forgive me for my sins.

"No, no, you shall never get my forgiveness." Rachel turned to leave the room.

"Please, I have cancer. I don't have long to live, and I need your forgiveness."

"You can rot in hell for all I care." Rachel ran out of the room with tears in her eyes.

Martha looked at her in surprise and said, "What happened?" She followed Rachel who was running out of the store.

"What about the gift for Hazel?"

"I don't want it. I want to get out of here." Rachel went into the street and stood next to a lamppost. Martha ran towards her and asked, "Are you all right? What happened in there?" Rachel tried to compose herself and told Martha what happened. Martha was amazed.

"The nerve of that woman! She wants your forgiveness after what she did to you?"

"I know. I could not believe that I would meet her again after twenty-two years. She does not deserve my forgiveness at all. Not after what followed."

"I don't blame you, Rachel. Forget her. We'll go home now. Let's buy Hazel's gift some other time."

"No, let's go to Tiffany's and buy her a bracelet. I liked one of those diamond bracelets I saw when I went there last week."

They went home after buying the bracelet. When she saw Hazel and Andrew at dinner, the events of that day were forgotten. She presented the bracelet to Hazel who liked it. Rachel went to bed happy that night.

Unfortunately, she could not sleep. The scenes of Fred and Anna in bed together and the train falling down the bridge appeared in her dream. She saw Anna, dressed like a Russian peasant woman, imploring Rachel to forgive her. She woke up covered in sweat. She tried to sleep but could not.

Over the next few nights, she had the same recurring dream. She could no longer get a restful night's sleep. She had to tell someone about these dreams. She did not want to burden Andrew and Hazel with this problem. She called Martha and confided in her. Martha suggested that Rachel talk to Fr. O'Malley for guidance. Rachel did not like the idea, but Martha insisted.

Rachel called the church and made an appointment to see Fr. O'Malley the following evening. She arrived at the church and saw him in the garden. They greeted each other, and he invited her to come into his office. They went into the office and sat down. "Now, tell me, what troubles you?"

"Father, I haven't been sleeping very well. It's because of this recurring dream I have been having for the past ten days."

"Is there a story behind this dream?"

She said softly, "Yes, Father, there is."

"Go ahead and tell me everything, my child."

She began by telling him the events from twenty-two years ago. She told him what she read in Rudy's diary and the unexpected meeting she had with Anna at the store. She was crying by the time she finished telling him everything.

"And, why is it you cannot forgive this woman?"

"She ruined my life and my family. I lost my husband and daughter because of her."

"I understand your anger, my child, but you should not let it rule you."

"Why? I have every right to be angry with her."

"Yes, you do, and I understand your reasons. You also have an obligation to forgive her."

"I am not obliged to forgive her. She does not deserve it."

"Are we not deserving of God's forgiveness?"

"Yes, we are, but I have not done anything as bad as her."

"Rachel, it is your pride that refuses to let you do the right thing."

"What are you implying?" she asked, annoyed.

"I see you want to keep your pride. You will not lose it by forgiving her. Maybe, things will be better if you do forgive her."

"Things are good. I do not know what else can happen."

He smiled at her and said, "You never know. Try and see."

She thanked the priest and left. As she rode in the car, she thought about what Fr. O'Malley had told her. She reached home and had dinner with the family. She went to bed and slept soundly that night.

The next day, the doorbell rang and Robert announced, "A Ms. Olga Volovosky is here to see you, Mrs. Johnson."

"I don't know her. Tell her to leave."

Robert left and returned saying, "She insists on meeting you. She will not leave until then."

"All right, show her in," replied Rachel in exasperation.

A few minutes later, the butler let in a young woman wearing a black dress and a hat. Rachel recognized her instantly. "Oh, you're the girl from that Russian shop."

"Yes, Mrs. Johnson."

"If you're here to plead on your mother's behalf, I am not interested."

"Please listen to me. If after I tell you what I have to say, you still don't want anything to do with us, I will respect your wishes."

"All right, have a seat, and tell me what's on your mind."

Olga sat down and took a deep breath. "Thank you. I just found out why Mama was upset. She is desperate for your forgiveness."

"She told me that."

"She has had a hard life. She was part of the Russian aristocracy and had to leave Russia when the Bolsheviks murdered her family. She then came to America and had to start life again. The only thing she could do was sing and dance."

"I know all that."

"Yes, but what you do not know is that Rudy Holzmann was the one that made her life miserable. She was made to do his bidding."

"What do you mean by his bidding?"

"I mean, be his…" she looked away in embarrassment.

Rachel's mouth dropped in surprise. The spectre of Rudy Holzmann was still haunting her even after all these years.

"Rudy would come to the speakeasy on the weekends. The owner, Joshua Frankel, introduced them, and he told Rudy about my mother's actual identity. Rudy started blackmailing her that he would tell the immigration services she was a Bolshevik spy and get her deported. Since she was all alone, she did as she was told."

"Was Frankel involved in making my husband drunk?"

"Yes, he was. Rudy told him that your husband acted that way when he had too much to drink. He made sure that his glass was full."

Rachel wanted her to stop. Her head was spinning. She took a deep breath and listened as Olga continued. "She was told exactly what to do. Rudy knew that you would run away when you saw Mr. Johnson behaving in that manner. Women normally do that, don't they?" Rachel nodded. She always thought of herself as an independent woman, but she did show weakness at some point.

"Rudy gave my mother the number of your hotel room and told her to dress like you and wait. He arranged for Mr. Johnson to go to the hotel and then went after you. He also sent those anonymous letters informing you that your husband was having an affair with the nanny."

It all made sense to Rachel why Fred and Helen denied any knowledge when she confronted them about the letters. "My mother continued working at the speakeasy. Once your husband and daughter died in that horrible train accident in California, Rudy stopped coming to the speakeasy."

"What happened to your mother after that?"

"In 1923, the speakeasy was raided, and Frankel was arrested along with his workers and some customers. My mother managed to run out during the raid and ran into the arms of a man. He grabbed her and told her to stop struggling. She looked up and saw that it was one of the customers. They ran and hid in an alley. His name was Ivan Volovosky. He owned a store selling Russian paintings and artifacts. He asked my mother to marry him and she did. She figured that this was her only chance to get out of the hell she was in. I was born in 1924. Life was good until my father died in 1933. He was in debt, and the local Russian mafia, whom we all feared, sent his goons to destroy the shop. It was the height of depression, and he did not have the money to pay. The goons beat him and set fire to the store. My mother heard about what was happening from the neighbors. She ran into the store and got him out, but it was too late. He died of smoke inhalation, and she was burned a bit on the face and hands. We lost everything that night."

Olga shed no tears, but was very stoic. Rachel marvelled at her courage. "After the fire, my mother decided that she would do the same business my father did. She worked as a maid for the Mafia boss to pay off my father's debt. After he died, with the money she had saved, we moved to New York City, and started the store which you came to."

"We moved after Rudy died. Because of what he did to her, she was scared to move to New York before that. When she read in the papers that Rudy was killed, she was not surprised. Rudy had always told my mother that you belonged to him since he was the one who saved you when the Lusitania sank. To make sure that Rudy was dead and buried, my mother attended his funeral dressed in black with her face covered. She saw you. She hid behind one of the graves with a large tombstone so that nobody would see her. She was surprised to see you and wondered why you were there."

Rachel smiled. "The only reason I attended the funeral was because he saved my life when the Lusitania sank." Rachel was glad that she gave Olga a chance to speak. Everything was clear now. No matter what happened, the main person responsible for everyone's suffering was Rudy. She knew Olga was telling the truth as only Rachel knew these details.

"Olga, you can tell your mother that I will not only forgive her but will make sure that she gets the best treatment." Rachel could see the stress drain away from the girl's face, and her eyes were tearing up.

"Thank you, Mrs. Johnson. My mother will be pleased with your kind offer."

Olga got up and grabbed Rachel's hand. Giving it a gentle squeeze, Olga wished her goodbye. As she ran out, she bumped into a man who was coming in.

"Hello there. You seem to be in a hurry."

"Yes, I am," she said and ran away.

William Brewster entered the room. "Who was that girl?"

"She is the daughter of an acquaintance. She works at a Russian store, off Fifth Avenue in Manhattan. Welcome back, William. Has the army let you stay after your treatment?"

"Yes. The army psychiatrist examined me after I visited my family in Iowa and found that I was not fit for active duty. The doctor examined me and said that the torture had weakened some of the bones, especially in the right arm. The army needs me in New York. Is Andrew around?"

"No, he is at the hospital. He and Hazel will be back for dinner. I'm glad you're back."

* * * * *

It was July. Hazel was in the eight month of her pregnancy. The doctor said that she was carrying twins. Less than a year ago, she had lost a key part of her past, and now she was married and about to give birth. She missed Boise and her family, but she knew that she was happier here. She got up and walked towards the stairs. She suddenly felt a sharp pain. 'The babies must be kicking,' she thought. She again felt a sharp pain go through her body. She yelled for Marcy as she held onto the banister. In the next few minutes, she was in the car on her way to hospital.

"The babies are not due for another few weeks," said Rachel.

"The babies have no set schedule. They will come out when they are ready," said Dr. Thompson.

"Andrew will be here. I have sent for him." Rachel was also preoccupied because she was waiting for news from the detective she had hired a few weeks earlier.

A few weeks earlier...

Rachel had gone to the hospital to see Anna. Anna was delighted and thanked Rachel for forgiving her.

"Olga told me everything, and I know they are true because only you and I could have known certain details. You have a very brave daughter."

"Yes, she is. Thank you. I don't know what I would have done without her. She is all I have."

The nurse came in and announced that visiting hours were over. As she walked out of the hospital, a thought occurred to her, 'Why not eat lunch with Andrew?' It was a long time since she and Andrew had lunch together. She went to the information desk and asked to meet Andrew.

As she waited, she heard two nurses talking about a patient on his deathbed in Room 81. He kept mumbling that his only good deed was saving a girl from drowning many years ago in a train accident in California. He wondered if that would save his soul since he had led a sinful life.

Rachel was in disbelief. Could this man have saved Barbara? Barbara's body was never found and maybe, that was a sign that she was alive. Rachel had to know. She got up and walked toward Room 81.

John Monroe was terminally ill and in a semi-conscious state. When he was released from jail, he realized he had breathing problems. His vices of smoking and drinking had caught up with him, and he was going to die. His mother was dead and only his half-sister, Eliza, who lived in New York, tolerated him. He called upon her for help. Eliza put him in the hospital for treatment.

Rachel found the room and entered it. She saw a frail man on the bed with graying hair that was once blond. She walked towards the bed. The man stirred when he felt Rachel's presence in the room. John had developed the trait to sense when people got close, especially when he was on the run.

"Who is there?" he managed to ask.

"It's me, Rachel."

"Who... are you?"

"I want to ask you something." She heard him groan. "I heard that you once saved the life of a young girl in California."

"Yes, I did. When I die, I hope, God will have mercy on my soul for that one good deed. I can still remember the screams of the passengers when the train went down, as the bridge broke apart." On further questioning from Rachel, John told her how he saved the life of a young girl from the river. He described their journey into the woods and coming upon a cabin inhabited by an older couple. He then told her about taking the chain and placing the locket in the girl's pocket before leaving the girl outside the cabin door.

"Where did you go after that?"

"I sold the chain and went back to my life of crime, until I was recaptured in Texas. Oh, I have led such a terrible life and alienated my whole family. I have only my sister, Eliza. I got what I deserved."

"What's your name?"

"John Monroe."

"Mr. Monroe, thank you for telling me this." She held his hand and squeezed it. "I am sure God will be merciful to you." He fell asleep and Rachel left the room.

She had lunch with Andrew but didn't say anything to him. After she returned home, she called a private detective agency. Detective Shaw told her that he would go to California and find out if the story was true. A week later, Rachel called the hospital and found out that John Monroe had died. She attended his funeral and was glad to see his sister and a few family members in attendance. She got the idea of covering her face from Anna. Rachel placed a wreath of flowers next to his coffin with the words 'Thank you' on the card.

She was waiting for Andrew to show up when she spotted Detective Shaw. She had asked him to meet her at the hospital. He was a tall man with brown hair and olive complexion. He reminded Rachel of Humphrey Bogart.

He sat next to Rachel and told her what he found out when he went to California. He located the cabin in the mountain owned by Mark Halliday. It was abandoned and in ruins. After Mark's arrest and incarceration, his son sold the vineyard and moved back to Chicago.

Mark died in prison. A prison guard killed Don Ciaggiano while trying to escape. Mother Grace had died a few years before. Her orphanage no longer functioned. A former orphanage worker told him that a French couple adopted a girl a few days after the train accident. She was not certain if it was Barbara when he showed her Barbara's picture.

He checked the departure records for the ship and found out that the French couple were Pierre and Annette from Normandy and their daughter's name was Catherine.

"So, there is no proof that their daughter is Barbara?"

"I'm afraid not. It could be that the man who told you this may have been just rambling and hallucinating. I am sorry that he misled you."

Rachel looked sad. "I was so sure it was Barbara. At least now I know it is not true."

"I am sorry, Mrs. Johnson. You're going to be a grandmother now, and that can give you some peace and happiness."

Rachel thanked Detective Shaw and he got up and left. Andrew came running and sat next to Rachel. He was almost out of breath. Dr. Thompson came out and said, "Congratulations. You have twins: a boy and a girl."

Rachel started crying and hugged Andrew. This was a bittersweet moment for her. A few moments ago, she had bad news about Barbara but had double the joy now.

A few days later, Alfred drove the new family to Johnson Manor. Rachel opened the door. "Welcome. Have you decided on the names?" asked Rachel.

"Yes. The boy will be named Irving Fredrick Clarence Johnson and the girl, Evelyn Barbara Johnson. Frederick and Clarence, after our fathers and Barbara, after the sister I never knew. Irving and Evelyn were our best friends in Hawaii who died during the bombing.

The doorbell rang and Robert came and announced, "Mr. Brewster and his fiancée are here."

They looked at each other bewildered.

They entered, and Rachel was surprised to see Olga holding William's hand. "Olga? William? When did this happen?" asked Rachel.

"You know her, Mother?" asked Andrew.

"Yes, I do. She is the daughter of an acquaintance."

"I know it is a surprise, Mrs. Johnson," said William. "When you told me who she was and where she worked, I went there and asked her out on a date. She refused. I impressed her mother by speaking to her in Russian. Her mother then convinced her to go out with me."

"You speak Russian?"

"A little. I learned a few words and phrases from Russian soldiers in the Philippines. I knew it would be useful someday, and it has." The rest laughed.

"Oh! I am so glad for the two of you. I hope you are not rushing into things," said Hazel.

William looked at Olga. "It... it is because of her mother." Olga nodded her head as if giving him permission to speak. "She would like to see Olga married."

Olga explained that Anna was not responding to treatment and had not long to live. The rest sympathized with her. Olga took a deep breath, smiled, and said, "We are here to see the twins. Can we see them?"

"Yes, they are asleep in the nursery. Follow me," said Hazel.

Chapter 18

Normandy, June 1944

After being honored at the American Embassy in London, Sidney, Brian, and Colin went back to their unit. They met with intelligence officers to brief them about information they obtained in Normandy.

They met George and Spencer during a training session with their unit. They were glad to see each other. Sidney asked George about Charles' family. George told them that the wife named their son after Charles. Charles' father had displayed the medal for all to see and was proud that the family name was restored.

Spencer said he would like to introduce them to someone he knew. They walked towards a tall man with brown hair who was backing them. Spencer said, "Payne, meet my American friends." Payne turned around and the three Americans and Payne looked at each other with a surprised look.

"You! You were the one heckling us at the mess hall when we first ate there," said Brian.

"Do you know each other?" asked George, confused.

"Yes. He was rude to us and told us that America joined the war only after we were attacked."

"Well, you got that right, Yanks, but let's let bygones be bygones. We are on the same side now," said Payne with a smile. They all agreed and shook hands. Before training began, General Eisenhower spoke to them. Sidney, impressed by the speech, told his friends that if Eisenhower ran for president he would definitely vote for him.

General Patton spoke next. As a surprise, Prime Minister Winston Churchill made an appearance. The soldiers cheered the aging Prime Minister. After his speech, they went back to training, reinvigorated by the speeches.

The invasion originally planned for June 5, was postponed to June 6 due to bad weather. Sidney and his friends got into the same aircraft. They were going to be dropped around Vierville to support the Utah Beach landings.

On the British side, Spencer, George, and Payne were in the First Special Service Brigade. They were assigned to Sword Beach, so they got into the amphibian boats and headed that way.

Meanwhile, the plane with Sidney, Brian and Colin was almost over the coast of Normandy. The 101st Airborne Division was flying together in formation along with the 82nd division. It was dark and foggy. The planes were forced to break formation due to the anti-aircraft fire. They were now close to the French coast, and they were briefed that some of them would miss their landing spots. They would have to find their units when they landed.

Sidney called his friends to the front of the aircraft while the other soldiers sat and talked or prayed with rosaries in their hands.

"Fellas, we had a similar experience last year when we were on the mission, and we made it out. We may or may not come back from this one. Only time will tell. Let us do one thing before we jump. Let us pray together," said Sidney.

"What prayer shall we say?" asked Colin.

"I am Catholic. Brian and Colin, you are Methodist and Presbyterian. I think it is safest to say 'The Lord's Prayer'."

"Good idea," said Colin. They said the prayer, hugged, and wished each other good luck.

"Time to go. Good luck and God Bless," said a loud booming voice.

The door opened, and the soldiers started jumping out of the aircraft. For the three men, this brought back memories of their previous mission in Normandy. "Hopefully, I don't get stuck in the trees again," said Colin, just before he stepped out of the aircraft.

Hours later, the amphibians, with the British Infantry Division embarked, were close to the coast. Dawn was breaking and the seas were getting rough.

"Steady there, lads. Good luck, and may God be with you on this day," yelled the commander over the howling winds.

From one of the amphibians they heard the faint sound of a bagpipe being played. The doors opened, and the soldiers stepped out. They were met with a volley of bullets from the Germans in the pillboxes. Some of the men fell into the water, turning it blood red.

"This is it," said the commander.

They all rushed forward and started firing in the direction of the bullets. Bombs fell all around them, and they could see their men falling. One man had his legs blown off. He was holding the stumps of his legs and crying out in pain. George thought of Charles and went towards him shouting for a medic but none came. George tried to drag him but realized that the man was dead. He then ran, with bullets flying around him, and dove for cover.

Payne dove behind a mound of sand and looked to see if he could shoot at the pillbox that was shooting at them. He looked for a split second and bent down just in time, as bullets hit the top of the sand mound, sending sand flying everywhere.

The pillbox needed to be destroyed. Nobody volunteered for fear of being killed. George finally volunteered. He crawled from his hiding place, lifted himself with one hand, and threw a grenade with the other. He crouched down and covered his ears. There was a loud explosion with dust and sand flying everywhere. Some of the men peeped out of their hiding places. They could see the two German men trying to get the sand out of their eyes. One succeeded and was about to shoot. George took another grenade and threw it. It landed next to the opening of the pillbox and exploded. The men cheered.

Spencer looked at George in astonishment. "I was the top bowler in my school cricket team," said George and winked at Spencer. The soldiers came out of their hiding places and charged forward.

The Germans shot at the soldiers who had parachuted in, killing and wounding some in mid-air. The main task of those who survived the landing was to regroup with their unit. They had difficulty identifying their target locations in the dark. Sidney, Brian, and Colin finally made it to their location. They were told that gliders with reinforcements were arriving soon.

The gliders arrived and some landed safely, but some crashed and caught fire. Soldiers were trying to get out; some of the men ran and helped them out of the gliders.

"We need to move ahead," the officer shouted.

"What about the injured?" asked Colin.

"This is a war zone, son; not a Red Cross hospital. We are here to fight and not be nurses. Come on," came the curt reply from the officer. The soldiers started moving forward towards their target.

After thirty-three days of fighting, the 82nd Airborne Division was relieved in Normandy. Sidney and Colin visited Brian who was in the makeshift hospital. He was shot in the left arm. The village doctor extracted the bullet and bandaged his arm. "With this heat and flies, I hope you don't get an infection," said Sidney.

"The army medic injected me with this new medicine called penicillin. He told me it should prevent infection. I've never heard of it."

"Hmm, I guess they discovered it in time to save you, Brian."

"Too bad you missed the party outside. One of those French women came to me when the Jeep stopped and kissed me," said Colin.

"Is that supposed to make me jealous, Colin?"

"Yes, I knew it would."

"We all know who Sidney is thinking of," said Brian

"Who?" asked Sidney.

"Catherine."

"Lay off, you two." He got up and walked away.

As he stood near the window and looked at the streets, he wondered if Catherine and her family were safe. He thought of visiting her when things quietened down. She was always on his mind, ever since they left Normandy the previous year. He decided to go and see her.

He walked up to his friends and asked them if they would like to come with him. They both said they would.

After they obtained permission for two days leave, with Brian's arm in a sling, they drove in a Jeep towards St. Lacroix, and arrived that evening.

Catherine saw a Jeep come towards the farmhouse. She knew who it was. She still loved Roland, but she also had feelings for Sidney. She went outside and waited. The Jeep stopped in front of her.

"Mama, Papa, it is those three Americans. They are here."

"Hey there, Catherine. Have you been expecting us?" asked Colin.

"No, but it is a pleasant surprise." Pierre and Annette came out and were delighted to see the three Americans. They all went inside the house.

"I see all of you are fine, except for Brian."

"Yes, he is our wounded hero. He will be all right," said Sidney.

"You five did me a favor with the car."

"What happened?" asked Colin.

"They found the car abandoned at the pier when you escaped, and from the license number, they found that it was stolen from a murdered Frenchman in Paris..." she looked at the three men.

"We know the story. Louis told us about your involvement with the Resistance and your escape from Paris," said Sidney.

"They determined that the five of you were part of the Resistance and it was the Resistance that murdered the traitorous Frenchman. So, they have closed the case."

"You must be relieved," said Sidney.

"Yes. That's how we knew that everyone got out safely."

"Not everyone," said Colin and proceeded to tell them about Charles' death.

"Mon Dieu," said Annette, as she crossed herself.

There was silence and Sidney asked, "What happened during the invasion?"

"We had some excitement here. One of the Americans parachuted and fell through the roof of the barn. We hid him in the hayloft. The Germans came but could not find him. We uncovered him and let him go. Papa has just finished fixing the roof."

"The invasion was a success because of you. You saved us and arranged for the getaway," said Sidney.

"Come and eat. Dinner is served," said Annette.

They spent the night there. In the morning, Sidney was yearning to tell Catherine how he felt about her. He wondered if she would ever leave France and come to New York. She seemed so contented living in this rustic French village.

They went to Louis' house and met him. He was happy to see them again. He too had helped some of the allied soldiers during the invasion. It seemed like everyone had a story to tell.

In the evening, Catherine took them to an English pub founded by an Englishman. After he was wounded in the Battle of the Somme, he married a French nurse and stayed on in France. They entered the pub. It was filled with many French, American, and British soldiers. They sat down and saw a familiar face come towards them. It was Blanche. She was glad to see them. They ordered beer, and sausage with mashed potatoes.

"How did you end up working here?" asked Sidney.

"The allies came and the Germans went away. So, I had to get a new job." They all laughed. Blanche went away and returned shortly with their order.

"After the Germans left, the American and British forces ransacked and burned the building."

"What happened to your boyfriend, Hermann?" asked Colin.

"He ran away when the allies came. I'm glad that I don't have to look at that pig anymore. Ever since that night, I had to be careful and avoid him."

"What you did was very brave," said Sidney.

She smiled and said, "Merci. Bon Appetite!"

They began eating and a few minutes later Catherine said, "I see Blanche outside. Let me ask her something quickly." She got up and left.

It was now twilight, and the breeze was blowing from the sea. Two French and two American soldiers, who were drunk, came out of the pub and went towards the two women.

"We overheard you say to those American soldiers that you worked with the Germans here," said the French soldier. Blanche looked at him and ignored him. "Answer him, you stupid traitor," shouted the American soldier.

"I am not answerable to you."

"Yes, you are. We know what to do to those who collaborated with the enemy. You do not deserve to live in France. You are a common whore for the enemy."

"Stop it, stop it," shouted Catherine. "You got it all wrong. She helped..."

"Shut up. You defend her, and you are the daughter of Pierre? Your father will be ashamed of you trying to defend a traitor. We need to teach you women a lesson."

The four men rushed forward and caught them. Catherine had heard rumors of rapes committed by allied soldiers and French men on French women, who they suspected of being Nazi collaborators.

One of the American soldiers held her while the other soldier tried to pull off her blouse. The other two Frenchmen were doing the same to Blanche. They screamed, but they knew that due to the noise in the pub, nobody would hear them. Even if they did, they would have thought that it was the wind.

The two women struggled as their clothes were being torn. They saw the faces of Sidney, Brian, and Colin in the dim light. The three of them pulled the four men away and hit them. The men were too drunk to fight back. One of the men fell against the window and broke it. The door opened, and the people inside the pub came out and saw the scene.

"I will kill you," said Sidney, as he punched the soldier who was pulling on Catherine's clothes. The other customers came and stopped the fight.

"What is going on?" asked someone with an English accent.

"Alvin, these men attacked us," replied Blanche, crying.

"It is a good thing we heard the noise and came out," said Brian.

The heavyset Englishman came forward and held one of the French soldiers. "Get out, the four of you. If I ever see you again, I will shoot you myself. I still have my gun which I used in the trenches, and I promise I will kill you."

"These women are Nazi collaborators. You should be ashamed of hiring one," said the French soldier.

"Is that true?" Alvin asked, looking at Blanche.

"No Alvin, it is not true. I only worked for them, cleaning their offices. I was always true to France. I swear it."

"Blanche speaks the truth. She helped us escape the last time we were here. These men should be begging her forgiveness," said Sidney.

"It is true. We cannot give you the details, but these women are not Nazi collaborators," said Colin.

"I believe you, and I know that no offspring of Pierre and Annette would betray France." Alvin looked at the four men and said, "Now, get out of here before I shoot you."

The four men got up staggering and tried to wipe the blood from their bruised faces. Two women from the crowd took Blanche and Catherine in. The rest followed. Sidney removed his jacket and as he handed it to Catherine, he noticed the birthmark on her shoulder. He felt he had seen it before. Alvin brought the women water to drink.

"I want to go home," said Blanche.

"We will take you," said Colin.

"I'm scared to go out. What if the men come back, and what if the others think that I was a Nazi collaborator?"

"No one will. If anyone does anything, they will be answerable to me," said Alvin.

They got up and left the pub. Sidney tried to pay Alvin, but he did not accept the money.

"You saved the honor of two French women, and that is enough for me."

They got into the Jeep and drove off. They dropped Blanche at her house. Her parents were upset at what happened to her. They went back to the farm; Pierre and Annette were also very upset. They thanked the three Americans for saving Catherine.

Catherine went to take a shower while Annette served the men dinner. Sidney was thinking about the birthmark on Catherine's right shoulder all the while. He went to bed, and it suddenly dawned on him where he had seen it. He then remembered what he had thought at the American Embassy in London.

'It just cannot be. She is dead.'

He had to know. He got up and sat on the bed but decided that it would not be a good idea to ask Catherine since she was already traumatized. Sidney heard a knock on the door and shouted, "Enter." The door opened and Catherine walked in.

"I want to thank you for your jacket and saving us from that horrible indignity."

"It was nothing. We're glad we heard you scream, and got there in time."

He looked at her bruised face.

"Catherine, can I ask you something?"

"Sure," said Catherine as she came and sat next to Sidney on the bed.

"That mark, on your right shoulder, shaped like a horseshoe… is that a birthmark?"

"Yes, it is."

"I used to know a girl in Long Island, New York. She had the same type of birthmark in the same place."

"Strange. What happened to this girl?"

"She died in a train accident along with her father in California."

"How sad! How old was she?"

"She was around four years old." He looked at her, saw no reaction, and then decided to proceed. "You said that you were born in America. Is that true?"

"Yes. I don't remember anything about that place. I just remember a lot of water, a tall blond man, and my parents."

"When did you come back to France?"

"In 1922. I was four years old. I remember coming on the ship. Louis was a bit aloof when he first met me, but then we got closer. He is almost eighteen years older than me."

"Do the names Rachel and Fred Johnson mean anything to you?"

She looked at him and shook her head. "What about Barbara

Johnson?"

"No. Why are you asking me these questions?"

"Catherine, I think you may be Barbara, the girl who supposedly died in the train accident."

She looked at him shocked and was now getting hysterical. "Why would you say that? That is very cruel of you to say such a thing."

She tried to get up, but Sidney grabbed her arm. "Catherine, I would never be cruel to you; I love you. I have a feeling that you are Barbara."

"How can you be so sure?"

"I remember playing with Barbara and for some reason, I accidentally tore the sleeve of her dress. I saw that birthmark, and it was the same as yours. I then remember her running to her mother complaining and..."

"Then what happened?"

He was silent. "What did her mother do?"

"My mother slapped me, and we went home. Her mother, from what I learned later, slapped Barbara giving her a bloody nose when she had a fight with her husband, and he took Barbara to California."

"My mother, Annette, is a wonderful woman. She would never do that to me."

Sidney let go of her arm. Catherine got up and walked towards the door, then turned and said, "You said that you love me. I do have feelings for you and hoped that you would come back, but now I am just confused." She had tears in her eyes and ran out, slamming the door behind her. Sidney wished he had not said anything to Catherine. He turned off the light and closed his eyes, but he did not sleep a wink that night.

He got up the next morning and got ready. He went down for breakfast and saw Pierre and Annette at the table. "Good morning. We hope you slept well," said Pierre.

"Actually, no."

"Would you like some coffee?"

"Yes, please. We leave today and coffee would be welcome. We are being redeployed to England tomorrow."

Pierre got up to get the coffee. "Can I ask you something?"

"Sure," replied Pierre.

"About your life in America. Did you live in California?"

"Yes."

He then drew a deep breath.

"Why did you come back?"

Pierre and Annette looked at each other. It was a long time since anyone had asked them that question. When they came back years ago, their family members and friends asked them the same question, and they always said that they came back for the sake of Louis and the farm. They told Sidney the same thing. "When was Catherine born?"

"She was born in 1918."

"When is her birthday?"

"On June 2nd."

"I am going to ask you something that you may not like. Is Catherine your real daughter?"

Annette dropped the glass of water she was carrying.

"Oh, I made a mess."

"Why do you ask that?" asked Pierre.

"I think she is Barbara Johnson from Long Island, New York, and she is a survivor of the train wreck that took place in California in 1922."

Sidney noticed the shocked expressions on their faces. He hated doing this, but he knew that he was right.

"Her birthday, June 2nd, is one day after the train accident and that was the day you found her. Am I right? The real Barbara Johnson was born on July 25, 1918."

They heard the door open and Catherine walked in. She too looked like she had not slept a wink.

"Now, why are you questioning my parents?" she sounded angry.

Sidney stared at her. "Catherine, we knew that a day would come when we would have to tell you the truth," said Pierre.

Catherine got emotional. "Oh no, it is not true. I am your daughter. You even assured me that I was your daughter when I told you that the children at school said that I was not"

"Yes, you are, but not by blood, Catherine. We have to explain."

Sidney got up to leave. "No, please stay. You must hear what we have to say," said Annette.

He sat down and Catherine sat next to him. Half an hour later, Catherine was in tears and Sidney was angry. "How could you do that to her? She has a younger brother born after she was supposedly dead. Her mother was very upset about losing her daughter and husband. So, the only reason you two came back was because Pierre was involved in criminal activities."

"That was not the way it was. I was forced into it," said Pierre.

"I have a younger brother?" asked Catherine.

"Yes, his name is Andrew."

Annette could not speak. She was in tears.

"We did not know who she was. She bonded with us, and since the priest told Annette that her daughter would be found in California, she did not want to give her away. We kept your locket all these years," said Pierre.

"Which locket?" asked Catherine.

"The one which has the pictures of you and your parents in it."

Annette went into her room and brought the locket. She opened the locket, and Sidney saw the picture of Rachel, Fred, and Catherine as a child.

"I was right."

Catherine looked up and saw the pictures. She looked at Sidney and said, "Please do not hate them," was all she managed to say and started crying again.

"I will not spend another minute in this house," said Sidney. Colin and Brian walked in.

"Sorry, we overslept, we…" said Brian

"Never mind, we are leaving," said Sidney.

"What about breakfast?" asked Colin.

Sidney turned and looked at Colin in anger. They had never seen Sidney like this. They followed Sidney to their rooms, brought their bags out, and loaded them into the Jeep. Brian and Colin went in and thanked Pierre and Annette while Sidney stayed outside.

Catherine stood at the door. Sidney looked at her and said, "I will be back for you." He then got into the Jeep and drove off.

On the way, Brian and Colin forced the story out of Sidney. They were shocked at the truth. They each tried to justify what had happened, but Sidney was not interested. He was thinking how he would tell Rachel and Andrew that Barbara was alive.

When they reached their unit, they were told to pack and get ready for their trip back to England.

Chapter 19

London, 1945

Sidney landed in London on May 6, 1945. The German Army had surrendered two days earlier. His unit had just redeemed the Wöbbelin concentration camp. The whole of Berlin was under the occupation of the Soviet Army.

Sidney was to fly to London to deliver a report on the Wöbbelin concentration camp to the American commanders in London. He packed a few things and went to the Berlin airport with few other soldiers bound for London, each given a specific task. He produced his special pass to the Soviet guard and was waived through. The airport was in shambles. The bombing of Berlin had left the city in ruins. As the aircraft took off, he could still see the smoldering ruins of the city.

'So, this is the result of war,' he said to himself and closed his eyes. Sidney was now tired of war. It seemed like a good idea fighting for his country. Ever since the Normandy invasion, it was one battle after another. He could see Catherine in his dreams. Would she forgive him for storming out of the house? She was ready to forgive Pierre and Annette for bringing her to France and maybe, she would forgive him too. Now that Germany had surrendered, he could go back to Catherine and see if she would accept him.

He opened his eyes and saw the clouds pass by. The sky looked so peaceful. 'Wish peace would come soon,' he said to himself and closed his eyes again. He pictured the scene where Colin was shot in the Battle of the Bulge. It was a fierce battle. Death was everywhere. Colin tried to move forward to disarm the German soldiers that were firing at them but was gunned down. The snow around him turned blood red. Sidney rushed forward and found him still alive. He dragged Colin to safety and was lucky not to be shot. A medic came and tried to stabilize him. After the battle, the medic took him to the field hospital. He was sent to France and then to London to recover.

Brian, too, was wounded in Belgium, but not seriously, and he was also recovering in London. Sidney almost lost his two best friends. He did not think he would have survived the war if one of them were dead.

He opened his eyes and, finding the plane descending, was relieved to be back in London, far from war-torn Berlin.

Sidney went to the U.S. Army Headquarters and submitted the report. He left the building and walked on the streets of London. He wanted to go to the hospital to see Brian and Colin. Colin was now better. After having five bullets in him, he was on the mend. He went to King Edward VII Hospital and was told to wait. A middle-aged nurse showed him to the ward for American soldiers, and gestured toward two beds. "Here they are."

She looked at the two covered men and said, "Look, who is here to see you!"

Slowly, the sheets came off, and they could see the heads of the two men. "Nurse Ramsay, we will not take our medicine unless a pretty nurse gives it to us," said Colin.

"You two may have upset your girlfriends. So, next time, be careful and see who it is before you say something cheeky," said Nurse Ramsay.

The sheets came off and they sat up. "Oh, it is you, Sidney. We thought that Marjorie and Audrey were here," said Brian.

"Well, next time, you may not be so lucky," said Nurse Ramsay laughing and walked away.

"You are still giving the nurses a hard time!" said Sidney.

"Yes. She doesn't mind us at all. She even got our beds together."

Sidney told them why he was in London. Brian and Colin thanked Sidney for saving them and told him the good news that Marjorie and

Audrey had agreed to marry them. A jubilant Sidney congratulated them.

"What about you, Sidney? Any news of Catherine?"

"No. I'm going back to Berlin tomorrow and will try to see her when I get leave. I hope she's not angry with me. I did act like a jerk the last time we were there."

"Yes, you did, but we don't blame you. You had every right to be angry."

"I guess what's done is done. Pierre and Annette did do a good job raising her."

"Yes, they did, and she is a swell girl, Sidney. You must go back and see if she still loves you."

"I will." He got up and said, "I will be back before my plane leaves for Berlin tomorrow evening. Behave yourselves fellas." He grinned at them.

As he was walking out, Nurse Ramsey was coming towards him. "Take care of my boys, Nurse."

"I will. You can be sure of that."

Sidney left the hospital, went to a little restaurant, and had dinner. He was happy to be eating food different from what he got on the battlefield. Even though he had heard how bad English food was, this meal tasted great. He then went back to his hotel to sleep.

The moment he closed his eyes, he saw Catherine in his dream. His mother and Rachel appeared in the dream, pleading with him to come back to America. He could not leave Catherine in France.

He woke up and tried to sleep again but could not. He had to leave on the evening flight, so he got up to pack. He went down, had breakfast, and could feel the excitement.

"What is going on?" he asked the waitress.

"The war... the war... It's over."

He could not believe his ears. Finally, it was all over. He had heard rumors that it would be over soon, but it was not official and so, he ignored those rumors.

He ate his breakfast and gulped down the coffee.

He went out of the hotel and was amazed at the people on the street. People from all walks of life were joining the party. He noticed American soldiers, nurses, and English soldiers joining the conga line with the civilians. People on the lampposts were waving the Union Jack. Young lovers were kissing each other. He went with the crowd towards Trafalgar Square, Westminster, Piccadilly Circus, and the Palace. People shouted that they wanted to see the Royal Family. He waited outside the palace gates. People all around him were shouting, "We want the King." The doors opened and out came the King, Queen, and their daughters. The crowd roared with cheers. Prime Minister Churchill stepped out on the balcony and started waving and flashing the victory sign. The crowd went wild with excitement. Women held their babies up for them to see the Prime Minister. Planes were flying with their trails clearly visible. The people on the balcony went inside, and the crowd started dispersing. Sidney was caught up in the frenzy.

Many women came up to Sidney and danced with him. Some kissed him and thanked him for fighting. He suddenly remembered that he had promised Brian and Colin he would see them before he left. While he was walking, a crowd came by and the only way he could get through the crowd was to join the conga line.

"Would you mind letting my sister through. I do not want to lose her," said the girl in front of him. Sidney could not see her face because her hair was dishevelled.

"Certainly!" he said. The young girl came and stood in front of him. Both the sisters had long brown hair. They danced until they came towards the end of the street and had to turn back. They waited until the crowd in front dispersed. Sidney decided to break away. He removed his hand from the girl's back. She turned and said,

"Oh, you are leaving us?"

They turned and looked at him. "Yes. You look familiar. I think I saw you earlier... My God, it's you two..." He was tongue-tied.

"Oh, please do not give us away. Our parents would not allow us and so, we had to slip out of the Palace. Giving us away would spoil the fun," said Princess Elizabeth.

"I will not. I promise."

"Thank you for letting me join in," said Princess Margaret. "Are you married?"

"No, but I am thinking of asking someone."

"Whoever she is, she is very lucky," said Princess Elizabeth.

"Thank you. I must be off now." He broke away from the line and moved to the side.

He was speechless and could not believe his eyes. His friends would never believe him.

He hailed a taxi and went to the hospital. He could see that they had been celebrating in the hospital as well. Nurse Ramsay greeted him as he entered the ward. "They are waiting for you."

"Yes. I almost forgot with all the fun I have been having."

He walked to their beds and found them talking and laughing. "Fellas, you will never guess who I bumped into."

He told them about the fun he had and meeting the two Princesses. He stopped, as Brian and Colin both looked at each other and burst out laughing.

"I think Sidney had too much to drink," said Colin.

"Sure, he has. Princesses dancing on the street, and our very own Sidney got to do the conga with them."

"It's true. I'm not joking. They sneaked out of the Palace," said Sidney, disappointed that they did not believe him.

"Yes, and the fact that they asked you if you were married, doesn't make your story plausible. Royals are brought up not to ask such questions."

Nurse Ramsay happened to passed by. She looked at them and said, "Well, what's all the fun about?"

Brian told her what Sidney told them, and she too laughed and said, "My goodness, I have never heard of such a thing. The Royal Princesses doing the conga with commoners? I bet, Queen Victoria must be rolling in her grave."

"Well, believe if you want to. When the truth comes out eventually, I will have the last laugh," said Sidney, annoyed

Nurse Ramsay continued laughing as she walked away.

"Sorry old friend," said Colin. "We laughed at your expense. We had a celebration here too. The staff let us shout and act crazy for a few minutes. We also watched the celebrations on the street from the windows."

"I will be going back to Berlin tonight. I came to say goodbye."

"We have been ordered to go back to Berlin two weeks from now. We have to help with the occupation of Berlin."

"Well, good, we will be together again." Sidney looked at his watch and said, "I better leave. With these crowds on the street, I may not make it to the airport in time to catch the flight."

"Thank you for coming to see us," said Brian. "You are truly a good friend."

"Leaving already?" asked Nurse Ramsay, as Sidney was about to leave the ward.

"Yes, I have to fly back to Berlin." Sidney went and hugged her.

"What was that for?"

"For taking care of my best friends."

"Ooh, aren't you sweet!"

"Thanks," he said and grinned at her.

"Goodbye, Sidney. I do not know if we will meet again, but I will always remember you. Thanks for the laugh, and in Berlin, be careful and try not to dance with Eva Braun."

"I won't," he smiled at her and left.

* * * * *

The aircraft landed in Berlin. He was back to this devastated city. An army Jeep drove Sidney to the temporary headquarters of the U.S. Army.

"Nice work, Sergeant Hardy. I am glad that you were in London for the victory celebrations. Wish I could have been there."

Officer Davis then looked serious and said, "Now, we have a problem on our hands."

"The Nazis still want to continue the war?"

"No, it is not them but the Russians. They have begun targeting German civilians in retaliation for what the German Army did in Russia. There have been reports of rape, murder, and unlawful imprisonment of Germans in uniforms."

"I thought the Russians were our allies."

"They are, but they are thirsty for revenge. They were the first to enter the city and find Hitler's bunker, so they think they own the city. We cannot let them continue committing atrocities. Everything will have to be handled diplomatically."

"Understood, sir."

"All right, I have also briefed the other soldiers about what I just told you. We have to help feed the starving civilian population. Many of them are homeless. We are now the peace keepers and the humanitarians."

As Sidney left, he was relieved that it was not as bad as he had thought. He felt that after the Russians had cooled off, they would stop committing atrocities. From what he saw in the concentration camp and stories he heard of the German atrocities in Russia, he determined that it was fitting that the Russians gave the Germans a taste of their own medicine. He chided himself for thinking that way.

A few days later, Sidney was waiting at the Berlin Airport. Finally, the two passengers he was waiting for emerged from the plane. "Good to see you all patched up and well again," said Sidney.

"Good to see you too," said Brian. "By the way, Nurse Ramsay sends you her love. She seems to be smitten by you." Sidney grinned.

They got into the Jeep and drove through the bombed city. They saw Berliners walking the streets in tattered clothes, and women collecting water from the streets to wash clothes and for drinking.

Colin could not believe that this was the same Berlin, whose beautiful pictures he had seen in the February 1937 issue of the National Geographic.

Sidney told them about the Germans starving and the atrocities perpetrated by the Russians, especially raping German women of all ages. Brian and Colin were shocked.

On reaching the U.S. Army Headquarters, the two men unpacked. After lunch, they headed out to patrol the area.

After the division of Germany and Berlin by the four allied powers, the 82nd Airborne Infantry Division relocated to the American sector. At the orientation, they were told that the first rule was, no fraternizing with the civilian population, and they each received an emergency prophylactic kit and three condoms.

"I bet, Saint Sidney will prevent us from having our fun with the lonesome German women," they teased.

"You two are engaged to be married," Sidney reminded Colin and Brian.

The accommodation was in a bad state. They were housed in apartments that were vacant and cleaned of furniture and fixtures when the Russians took over the city. The 504th Airborne Division had managed to get some furniture, but just a table and three chairs were not going to do for these men.

The unit was divided into teams. Some were sent to bury the dead and commandeer the locals to clean the rubble, some had to cut down trees in the nearby forest to provide fuel for the winter, and some were assigned guard duty. Sidney, Brian, Colin, and John Lazenby, one of the replacements the unit received in France, were assigned guard duty.

One day, John told them that a soldier named Kerry was showing off a watch and other valuables. Kerry would not reveal where he obtained them, but always invited soldiers to come along. This piqued the curiosity of Sidney and his friends, and they told John that they would like to come along.

The next day, John introduced Sidney, Brian, and Colin to Kerry and the other men in the first Jeep.

"You will like what I have to show you," said Kerry. Sidney took an instant dislike to Kerry. He seemed vulgar and uncouth. Keeping his comments to himself, Sidney got into the second Jeep with the others. They followed the first Jeep and very soon drove along a row of houses where some of Berlin's elite lived during the war.

"All right, we stop in front of this one," said Kerry. They all got off. Kerry went to the top of the stairs and knocked on the door. A woman opened the door, and Kerry stormed into the house. The rest of the men followed, screaming wildly.

Sidney followed in shocked silence. He went inside the house and saw the men stealing the valuables. He saw the weeping woman on the floor and picked her up.

"Mein mutter..." shouted the son and he and his siblings came running towards her.

"Oh no! The clock has been in the family for many generations. Please don't take it," pleaded the woman in accented English.

"Shut up, bitch," shouted Kerry. The men continued looting. "No, not my jewels. Those were a gift from my husband."

"Where is your husband?" asked Sidney.

"He died in the Dresden bombings."

Kerry came and held a gun to her head. "Look, bitch, shut up. You Germans did the same thing when you took over other countries. It's only fair that we do the same to you. Now, shut up, or you and your kids will face the barrel of my gun."

The next moment, the gun flew from his hand as Sidney kicked him in the face. Kerry fell to the floor, and the other soldiers came towards them.

"What's going on Sid?" asked Colin, as they all looked at Kerry nursing his bruised jaw.

"I want this to stop. This is wrong."

"What about the victims in other countries? This hausfrau has no right to protest."

"She is also a victim. Her husband was killed in the war, and she's taking care of her children single-handedly."

"We need the stuff, Sid," said Colin.

"Yes, we do, but we can buy it from her."

"Yeah, what are we going to give her?" asked one of the men.

"We have cans of food in the Jeep which we consume on patrol duty. We can give her some cans in exchange for whatever she does not need."

Sidney looked at the woman and she smiled while trying to dry her tears. "Hausfrau, what would you like? I am sure you need food for your children."

"Danke schoen. I would like some cans of meat and beans. I can give you those chairs and that table upstairs."

"Yes, and we will give you eight cans of food for that; two for each of you."

She smiled. Sidney looked at the soldiers sternly and said, "Give everything back. Sorry, I will not let my fellow soldiers steal."

"Oh yeah, and what are you going to do about it?" asked Kerry, still on the floor.

Sidney picked up Kerry's gun and pointed it at the soldiers. "I think you know what I will do. Besides, I will report this to our supervisor. You know it will lead to a dishonorable discharge."

The men started giving everything back. One of the men helped Kerry to his feet, and he walked out glaring at Sidney. The men went to the Jeeps, brought eight cans of food, and gave them to the woman.

Sidney commanded the men to take the table and chairs. The four men scattered around, picked up the chairs, and loaded them in the Jeep. Two men went upstairs and brought the table down. It was an old table, but it would do.

Sidney looked at the woman and smiled. "What is your name?"

"Frau Gretel Mueller."

"Sorry for the trouble, Frau Mueller. Thank you for the furniture and Auf Wiedersehen."

He walked out of the house and went down the stairs. He got into the waiting Jeep, and they drove back to their apartments.

"Come on, Sid, we needed the stuff. That's why we did it," said Brian.

"I was shocked that you would do something like that," Sidney said in anger.

"They convinced us that it was all right since the Germans did that to the people they overran," said Colin.

"I was raised better than that, and I'm sure you were too. We are here to help these people, not terrorize them. They, too, have suffered," said Sidney.

"We're sorry, Sid. We have never seen you this angry. What has gotten into you?" asked Brian.

"You know what? I just could not bear to see the look of pain on that lady's face, and her children were terrified."

"We're sorry. We won't do that again."

"All right, I will forgive you this time. But, please keep your heads on your shoulders."

"Thanks, Sid. We promise we will," said Colin.

Chapter 20

Berlin, 1945

The war in Europe was officially over. There were rumors that the whole division was going to be transported to the Pacific to fight the Japanese who were still continuing the war. In August, they received sudden news that the Japanese had agreed to surrender.

The weeks dragged on, and Sidney was beginning to like Berlin. The Berliners were grateful to the Americans. He could not believe that a few months earlier they were fighting each other. The rules about fraternizing with the Germans were strictly enforced. Sidney tried to be nice to them but always had to maintain a diplomatic ambiance in order not to appear too friendly.

By now, he had forgiven his friends for the incident. They were back to their old selves. John too was now included in their off duty social activities. John was smitten with a German nightclub singer named, Helga. They tried to dissuade him from continuing the relationship with her. "You cannot marry her and take her to the U.S., so you need to forget her. Go back home and find someone from Texas," suggested Sidney.

"Well, you're one to talk, Sidney. I heard that you want to marry a French girl."

Sidney glared at Brian and Colin.

"They talk too much. What they forgot to mention is that she was born in the United States. She was with the French Resistance and that makes her an ally. Brian and Colin are engaged to two English girls.

The whole point is that we will have no problem taking our women to the U.S. It is you and Helga who will have the problem."

"Does she have any family?" asked Colin.

"They were all killed in the bombings."

"See, she will use any means to get out of Germany and get an American passport."

John assured them that Helga was not that kind of a person and invited them to the nightclub to meet her. The three men accepted the invitation reluctantly.

The nightclub was in the American sector and close to the Russian and British sectors. The owner had fixed the club when the occupation had begun. He hired women, who had no other means of support, as singers and waitresses. The club was filled with American, Russian, British, and French soldiers and smoke filled the air from the profuse smoking of cigarettes.

"So, this is where your girlfriend works!" said Colin in a rather sarcastic tone.

"Yes, you will see her in a few minutes when she comes onstage to perform."

The men ordered drinks. They saw the soldiers ogle at the waitresses and pinch some of their behinds. The waitresses did not mind the attention.

Colin pointed Kerry out to the others. Kerry was standing next to a wall, which had a crack above his head. Sidney and Kerry looked at each other at the same time, and their eyes met. Sidney could see the hatred in Kerry's eyes. Sidney smiled and looked the other way.

The four men drank their beer, and the nightclub owner came onstage accompanied by the sound of a drum.

The crowd started whistling and yelling. The music began, and the girls came onstage from behind a curtain and danced.

John pointed out Helga, a blond girl, third from the right. The other three men looked and Colin remarked that she was very attractive. The women danced to a song sung by Helga in German, French, and English. When the song ended, they exited the stage.

"She is not only pretty, but a talented singer and dancer too," said

Sidney.

"Thank you," said John. "Now you can see why I want to marry her." Shortly after that, Helga came out dressed in regular clothes looking very attractive. As she moved through the crowd, the men cheered. She came towards their table and sat down.

John introduced Helga to the others. As they drank their beers, Helga told them about her childhood and that her mother encouraged her to sing and dance. It seemed that her story was like every other German they met: wonderful life until the war began.

"I have to go home and get up early for work in the morning. I work as a cook in a house a few streets away. It was nice meeting all of you. Auf Wiedersehen and Gute Nacht."

John got up and went with her. He came back a few minutes later.

"Well, fellas, how do you like her?"

"Just as you described her. I can see why you like her so much."

"Good. I knew you would like her."

Sidney looked at his watch and said, "We'd better get going. We have to be up for duty first thing in the morning."

John hailed the waitress. They paid the bill and left. As they crossed the street, they heard a whimper from the alley.

"Sounds like a cat."

"Let's go. We can't be bothered about a cat," said Colin, impatiently.

"No, listen, it sounds human and it is coming from that alley," said John, as he ran towards it.

The other three followed reluctantly. They found two women on the ground. They went closer and saw that it was Helga and her friend. They had been robbed and beaten.

The other woman opened her eyes and said, "Russen, Russen."

"Does she mean Russian?" asked Brian.

"Yes," replied John and knelt near Helga to see if she was hurt.

"She's breathing. We have to get them to a hospital," said Sidney.

Two men picked each of the women and carried them to their Jeep. They went closer and noticed that the Jeep was tilting in an awkward way. When their eyes got used to the darkness, they noticed that the tires had been slashed.

"What do we do?" asked John.

"We are close to Frau Mueller's house. We can take the women there," said Sidney.

"Isn't that the house we…" said Colin with some embarrassment and then stopped himself.

"Yes, it is, but we have no other choice," said Sidney.

"Yes, we do. We can go to the nightclub and ask for help," said Brian.

"Who do we ask for help? If word gets around that the Russians did this, they will start to deny it and then blame the Americans for setting them up."

"You're right," said Brian. "Let's go to Frau Mueller's house and ask her to help us."

The men carried the women through the deserted streets of the bombed out city. They reached the house after fifteen minutes. The house was in darkness that was typical for this time of the night because of the curfew. Sidney went up the stairs and knocked on the door.

He knocked again and then heard the sound of footsteps. He saw someone peering through the glass window and the door opened partially.

"Please, I have nothing more to give," said a pleading voice.

"No, no, Frau Mueller, it's me, Sidney Hardy, the soldier who saved you last time."

He heard a sigh of relief and the door opened fully. Frau Mueller turned on the light, stepped out in her nightgown, and smiled.

"Yes, how can I help you?"

Sidney explained the situation to her. She told them to bring the women in and place them on the couches. The men carried the two women into the house. They tried to avoid Frau Mueller's gaze, but she smiled at them as they entered, and greeted them. They were forced to reply.

"Please be quiet, my children are sleeping."

The men put the women on the two couches. Frau Mueller went towards them and looked at them.

"Are you a doctor or a nurse?" asked John.

"I used to be a nurse before I got married." She examined the two women and stood up. "Both have slight concussion due to the beating. They should be fine. I will bring some bandages and medicine for their wounds."

They heard Helga moan. John went and sat beside her. He held her hand and looked at her face as she woke up.

"Are you all right?"

"Yes, John," she managed to say.

"What happened? Your friend said that it was the Russian soldiers."

"Yes. When we came out of the club, three Russian soldiers came towards us. It looked like they were waiting for us. Bettina and I tried to run, but they came after us and caught us. They slapped our faces, forced us into that alley, and pointed a gun at us. They took our watches and jewellery and then told us to leave. As we were passing by them, I saw one of them hit Bettina on the head with the gun, and I think they did the same to me."

"I am going to kill those Russians," said John in anger.

"Calm down, John. Doing that is not going to help. We can't risk this incident starting trouble," said Colin, a bit stern.

"I remember one name being mentioned - Dombrowsky, and I heard someone say 'spasibo.' He didn't sound Russian."

"What is spasibo?"

"It means, 'Thank you' in Russian," replied Frau Mueller.

The men turned back and looked at her. "I went to Russia with my husband before the war."

"We must report this incident to our superiors the first thing in the morning. We have got to go now," said Brian.

"What about Helga and Bettina?" asked John.

"They can stay here. They are in no condition to go anywhere. With good rest, they will be all right. Now, you gentlemen have to leave, and let me finish cleaning their wounds."

The men looked at each other and started walking towards the door. Brian asked if they could borrow her car and she obliged by giving them the keys. She told Sidney to return the car in the morning.

They went to the garage, got into the car, and drove to their apartment.

In the morning, they reported about the incident and slashed tires to their superiors. Officer Davis questioned their relationship with these women. Sidney told Officer Davis that they only had good intentions to help these women in their time of need. He also told him that a German woman, who happened to be a nurse, was willing to treat the wounded women. Officer Davis was impressed with their discretion, since relations with the Russians were deteriorating.

"Phew! That was close. You very tactfully avoided mentioning my relationship with Helga. If not, my goose would have been cooked. Thank you, Sidney." said John, after they were dismissed.

"You're welcome, John. We have to return the car to Frau Mueller. We'll take three tires and fix the Jeep," said Sidney.

* * * * *

The car and Jeep stopped in front of the house, and Sidney got out and knocked on the door. Frau Mueller greeted them in German. "Guten Tag. Wie geht es dir?"

Sidney had learned German in high school, so he responded, "Wunderbar, Frau Mueller."

"Your German is getting better, Sergeant Hardy. You have come to return the car keys to me?"

"Yes," and he handed them back to her.

He inquired about the two women, and she said they were fine, and had left earlier. She invited him in, and before he could object, she opened the door wide, and he went in. She closed the door behind her and followed him.

Her three children seated at the table got up, greeted Sidney, and handed him a card.

"My daughter, Elke, and sons, Henrik and Helmut, have made a card to thank you for saving us."

Sidney thanked them. "Now, I have something for you. Is your mother still alive, or do you have a wife or someone you want to marry?"

"I do have someone I want to marry."

"What is her name?"

"Catherine."

She took a box from the table and gave it to Sidney. He opened it and in it was a ring with a ruby and diamonds around it.

"It's beautiful," was all he managed to say.

"Danke. I made this ring for myself when I got married. Give it to Catherine"

"I will. Thank you for your kindness."

Sidney saw a portrait of a man with blond hair and moustache on the opposite side of the room, dressed in a surgical coat, sitting on a table with a background of books. "Is that your husband?"

"Yes, that is Rochus, my husband. He was a doctor."

He looked at his watch and said that he had to leave. He thanked them for the gifts and left.

"What happened?" asked Brian, as Sidney got into the Jeep.

"She is a wonderful lady. I know what I'm going to give Catherine when I meet her."

* * * * *

A few days later, John came in excited. "Kerry has some more new stuff which he's showing off."

"Never mind that man. He's nothing but a common thief," said Sidney in disgust. "What is this Kerry's last name?"

"I don't know. Why?" asked John.

"It is just that he does not look Irish. He looks more eastern European."

"Come to think of it, yes, he does. Let me find out."

John came back a few minutes later and said, "I asked one of his friends and Kerry's real name is Kirill Dombrowsky. You were right. His family is from Eastern Europe."

"Wait a minute... that name Dombrowsky... I've heard it somewhere," said Brian.

"Yes, that is what Helga said she heard before she was hit on the head with a gun," said Colin.

"That swine is the one who mugged Helga and her friend," said John.

"Helga said that he spoke Russian, so it can't be him. What about the other two men who were Russian?" asked Colin.

"Remember, he was standing and talking to two Russian soldiers in the nightclub," said Sidney.

"I never noticed. I just saw him staring back at us," said Colin.

"It has to be him. Who else would slash the tires of our Jeep? There were other Jeeps around and none of their tires were slashed. Why only ours?" said Brian.

"Exactly, it has to be Kerry. His name matched the name Helga overheard, and his real name is Russian," said Sidney.

John wanted to confront him, but the others dissuaded him, and said they would tell their superior of their suspicions.

"What will that achieve?" asked John, sounding annoyed.

"Kerry will be brought forward and made to admit about collaborating with the Russians, stealing valuables from the German civilians, and also slashing our tires. Our superiors are well aware that the Russians have been stealing from the civilians in their sector."

"Kerry will say that we were also stealing when we went to Frau Mueller's house," said Colin.

"No, he will not. The slashing of the tires and the attack on the women will be given more importance. Besides, I am sure, the superiors are aware of American soldiers stealing," said Sidney.

"You're right. Let us stick to what Sidney suggested," said Colin.

The next day, Officer Davis summoned Kerry. When questioned, Kerry admitted that he had slashed the tires, but he did not give the reason. The men knew that it was to get back at Sidney for hitting him and stopping him from stealing. He also admitted to the beating of Helga and Bettina and confessed that he was the one who instigated the robbery. He said that he sympathized with the Russians since his parents were from Russia, and he wanted to get back at the Germans.

The military police took Kerry to prison. He was to be dishonorably discharged and sent back to America.

"You were right, Sidney. He never breathed a word about the incident at Frau Mueller's house," said Colin, when they were alone.

"Thank you, fellas. Kerry got what he deserved," said John.

New York, August 1945

Anna was very weak and aware that she had only a few days to live. She got up and slowly walked to the window and peeked outside when she heard people celebrating. She saw people crowding the streets, cheering. She smiled as she watched the crowd get bigger with each passing minute. 'So, the war is finally over,' she said to herself.

She remembered when she saw another crowd gather like that. They had guns, swords, and bludgeons. They were angry and calling for blood and revenge. Russia 1917 was a year Anna preferred to forget, but this last memory of her youth in Russia always haunted her.

A few days earlier, when the doctors told her that she was not responding to the treatment, she called a heavily pregnant Olga aside. She gave Olga a key and told her to go to the Bank of New York, open the safety deposit box, and bring the contents to her.

Olga went to the bank and was back several hours later looking very upset.

"What is it?"

"It is what is in here. I cannot believe that we had them all along."

Anna took the box from her and opened it. In it was a necklace, a pair of earrings, a sapphire ring, and a ring with the Romanov Crest in diamonds. There were a few pictures: one of Anna with her husband, one with an unknown man, one with her parents and brothers, and one of the Russian Royal Family.

Anna held the necklace and said, "This was a gift from Czarina Catherine the Great to my ancestor for her wedding. It has been in the family for many generations." She held the ring with the crest and said, "This was given to me by Grand Duchess Marie Romanov. We were playmates for some time."

Olga was now in tears. "I don't care who they are from. You could have sold them and saved father's store."

"Is that what troubles you? Your father was a very honest and upright man. He was the only one who treated me well ever since I came to this country. He found these jewels in my possession, and I told him what they were. He realized in his own kind way that, if I had sold them, I would not have had to work in that speakeasy. I had promised my mother that it would always remain in the family."

"Selling these jewels would have saved his store, and he would not have died in that fire."

"I offered to do just that, but he was adamant that I keep my promise to my mother. Your father was a great and kind soul."

Olga stopped crying and tried to smile.

"Ever since this necklace has been in the family, every mother has presented it to her first-born daughter before her marriage. I received this a few days before I was to be married."

"I did not know that you were supposed to marry someone else."

"I was to marry this Count, but he was killed in the revolution. A few days later, the peasants surrounded my father's home and stormed it. When my mother saw the imminent danger, she forced me to dress like a peasant girl. She gave me these jewels in a small bag. My older two brothers were killed in the war, and my younger two brothers wanted to stay and defend our home. My mother wanted me to live, so she had Sergei, the groom, to take me to safety through the tunnel. My last memory was hearing my parents cry out when they were being killed. I wanted to die with them, but Sergei did not let me. We came out into the woods and walked to Hamburg. We were almost caught twice by the Bolshevik guards patrolling the area. We trusted no one. Once we reached Hamburg, we took a ship to America. At Ellis Island, I hid the jewels in my underwear so that the immigration authorities would not confiscate them."

She held the photo of the unknown man and showed it to Olga. "Sergei and I had to pose as husband and wife, or they would never have let me in. After we passed through, we settled in New Jersey. Some of the Russian immigrants were not welcoming when they came to know who I was. Sergei had a drinking problem and gambled away the money we had. One day, he was found frozen to death. People speculated that he was drunk and had passed out in the cold. Frankel hired me to work at the club because Sergei worked there."

"...and then you met that awful fiend, Rudy Holzmann. I bet he is rotting in hell."

"I have something else to tell you. Vladimir Laganovich did not die a natural death. I cooked him poisonous mushrooms. My father told me about them when we went mushroom picking in the woods."

"But, you worked for him for three years."

"I did it to gain his trust. Once he trusted me to cook his meals, I knew I had him. I did it for your father. I married your father because he gave me security. I did not love him at that point in time; love came gradually, and I had to avenge his death. He, after all, gave me you. Laganovich was an evil man. Once he threatened to harm you, I knew I had to act."

"Oh Mama, I wish you did not tell me all this."

"You must know everything. Maybe, God is punishing me for killing Laganovich. I am ready to go to your father, and I only hope God will let me."

Olga hugged her mother. "He will."

Andrew and Hazel heard the news of the Japanese surrender on the radio. When they told Rachel, she was ecstatic. Finally, Sidney can come home. The household staff was also celebrating. They had sons or nephews in the armed forces who would be returning.

She tried telephoning Martha, but the lines were jammed.

"I cannot get through; I must go and see her."

"We will come with you. The wireless says that Times Square is filling up with people celebrating," said Andrew.

Alfred drove them to Manhattan. On the way, Alfred mentioned that he was glad his son in the marines was returning.

People were coming out of their houses waving the American flag. The roads were clogged with people.

"I hope we can make it through this crowd," said Hazel.

"Leave it to me. I'm sure that my thirty years of driving will be of use now."

Alfred skillfully maneuvered through the thickening crowd and arrived at Martha's home.

"Atta boy, Alfred, you got us through like you said," said Andrew and patted Alfred's shoulder.

Martha's butler greeted them at the door and they went inside. "Rachel, Andrew, and Hazel, what a pleasant surprise!" said Martha.

"The war has ended. Remember, I was with you when the last war ended," said Rachel.

"Yes, I do remember. Now, Sidney can come back home."

"Six years of war! It has to stop sometime," said Hazel.

"We can go to Times Square and watch the celebrations," said Andrew.

"You can come with us, Martha."

Alfred drove towards Times Square, but it was impossible to get there. Andrew suggested they get out and walk, so the four of them got out while Alfred parked the car. They began walking, and it was getting impossible.

"You two go ahead. Martha and I will stay here," said Rachel. Andrew nodded, grabbed Hazel's hand, and walked into the crowd.

"Do you remember the celebration after the end of the last war?" asked Martha.

"Yes, I remember it very well. I'm sure, half the people here were not born then," said Rachel. She thought of Fred and Barbara and got misty eyed.

The noise was continuous. People cheering, colored paper falling from the buildings, and flags being waved by people.

Hazel pulled Andrew's arm, pointed out, and said, "Look, isn't that Brandon and Phillip?"

"Yes, it is, and the girls are with them."

They pushed through the crowd and reached the four people. "Maryanne and Sally, is that really you?"

The four of them were surprised when they saw Andrew and Hazel together.

"Hazel, you're alive!" shouted Maryanne.

"Yes, I am."

"We thought you were dead."

The two women got down from the stone structure they were standing on and hugged Hazel.

Andrew went to the two men and hugged them. Brandon and Phillip told Andrew that they were recovering in San Diego after being injured in the Pacific. Before joining their unit, they decided to visit Maryanne and Sally, who were in New York, after their rotation with the Army Nurse Corps. They were glad not to be going back to the Pacific.

"Would you like to come home and meet our twins? We named them after Irving and Evelyn," said Hazel.

"Twins! We would love to see them," said Sally.

While they were leaving, they saw a sailor kissing a nurse being photographed.

"Probably trying his luck," said Phillip and the rest laughed. They reached the car, and Andrew introduced his friends to Rachel and Martha. Rachel was glad to see Brandon and Phillip. They got into the car and headed to Long Island.

Berlin, November 1945

The division took part in the victory parade to celebrate the end of the war. At the end of November, they received word that the whole division would be sent to America and not be disbanded. Everyone was elated with the good news, except for John who was worried about having to leave Helga behind. They tried to comfort him by telling him that since the war was over, they would lift the ban, but John was still upset.

Before Sidney left Berlin, he visited Frau Mueller. She was happy for him but sorry to see him go. He hugged the children and gave them chocolates. As he was leaving, he could sense that Frau Mueller was crying.

The whole division moved to Camp Chicago in Laon, France, by train. They practiced for the victory parade to be held in New York, after they returned. When Sidney heard they would have to take the train to Le Havre, to be ferried to England, he knew he had to act. He obtained permission from his superior and took a Jeep.

"I will meet you at Le Havre," he told his friends.

He drove all day to St. Lacroix, and was finally at the farm; he felt the trepidation in his heart. He got out, walked to the door, and knocked. He wondered if Catherine would still want him.

305

Catherine opened the door. Their eyes met. She jumped into his arms and kissed him. As he kissed her, he knew that he had worried for nothing. He took out the ring and said, "Catherine, will you marry me?"

"Yes, I will, Sidney. I have been dreaming of this moment." He placed the ring on her finger.

Pierre and Annette came out. Sidney knew what he had to do. He went over to them, apologized for his behaviour, and told them that Catherine had agreed to marry him.

"Whatever Catherine wants; we will not stand in her way. She needs to be back with her family, and we must let her go," said Annette.

Catherine went and hugged them. They were all crying.

Sidney drove Catherine around the village to say goodbye to Louis and his family; Blanche, now married to Alvin's son; and other friends and relatives. After eating one last meal at Annette's insistence, they left St. Lacroix.

When they reached La Havre, Colin and Brian came to Sidney and said, "Look who else is bringing his bride along!" He turned and saw John and Helga walking towards him. John explained that Helga was born in France to a French mother and German father. Therefore, the rules did not apply anymore since she was French by birth.

Sidney congratulated John and said, "You crafty devil, you did figure out how to bypass the rule."

* * * * *

Sidney got in touch with Spencer and George when he arrived in England. They were wounded and could not go back to active service. When the war ended, they were discharged from the army and went back to civilian life. Catherine, Sidney, Brian, and Colin met Spencer and George in a pub in London.

"It's nice to see you, Catherine. I remember you were very helpful to our mission. How is everybody in St Lacroix?" asked Spencer.

"They are relieved that the Germans have left. My parents, family, and friends are obviously sad that I had to leave suddenly, but they are all going about their lives."

"What happened to Payne?" asked Sidney.

"He was injured when a German soldier threw a grenade. He survived the attack and managed to shoot the soldier who threw the grenade but died shortly after. If not for him, we would not be here today. He saved the lives of eight men," replied George.

"I will never forget his cheerful personality. He did put us off when we first met but was very nice thereafter."

"That was Payne. He could intimidate you one moment and make you feel comfortable the next. He was a marvelous person - one in a million!"

"How is Charles Crabtree's wife doing?" asked Brian.

"She is fine. I saw them a few days ago. The son is almost two and looks like Charles. The villagers have pooled money for her needs, and she lives comfortably."

"Sidney, I have a favor to ask of you," said Spencer.

"Sure, anything for you, Spencer."

"The British economy is not doing well and, I fear, we will be under recession for a long time. I am planning to immigrate to America with my wife. Can you help me?"

"Of course, I will. I know the person at the American Embassy who can get you and your wife visas to immigrate. I am meeting him tomorrow. I will surely tell him about you."

"Thank you, Sidney."

"What do you plan to do when you come to America?" asked Brian. "Do you have any relatives?"

"I have an uncle who immigrated to New Jersey in 1913. We have kept in touch for many years. As for work, I do not know what to do."

"Do not worry about work, Spencer. I can hire you until you find something else."

"What about you, George? Don't you want to come to America?" asked Colin with a wide grin.

"Who will take care of the fishing business if I leave? No, I am happy here in jolly old England."

"I am sure England would not be the same without you, George," said Colin. The rest of the group laughed.

The next day, Catherine and Sidney were at Lucy's house in London. Sidney rang the doorbell and Lucy came out and hugged him.

"Welcome back, Sidney. I'm so glad you made it back unscathed." She looked at Catherine and said, "Who is this, Sidney? She is very pretty."

"This is Catherine, and she is from a small village called St. Lacroix, on the Normandy coast. I think you had better sit down because you are not going to believe what I have to tell you."

"Let us go inside and sit on the couches in the living room. I will arrange for tea to be brought," said Mrs. Hatfield.

They went into the living room and sat down. It was a large living room and had paintings hanging from the walls - mostly of American scenery, one of Thomas Jefferson, and another of George Washington. There was a grand piano, and a few photographs of the family displayed.

"We have lived in this house for almost ten years. I am sorry to be leaving all this behind. We will be back in America shortly," said Lucy.

"Is Mr. Hatfield leaving the State Department?"

"No, he is being transferred to Washington D.C., in late January next year."

"How are the children? Are they all right?"

Paul came back into the room and sat down beside Lucy.

"Yes, they all came back safely. They will all be moving back to the United States with us." Lucy eyed them curiously and said, "What is it you wanted to tell me?"

"I do not know where to begin, but let me tell you everything," said Sidney.

They were flabbergasted when they heard the whole story.

"I am speechless. I do not know what to say," said Lucy.

"Me too."

"What do you want to be called?" asked Lucy.

"You can call me either Barbara or Catherine." It was the first time Catherine spoke.

"I met you as a little girl and was abroad after I was married, but I know Rachel was devastated when Fred and Barbara went missing. I was there for Fred's funeral, and it was an awful time."

"I know it must be a shock to you, Aunt Lucy," said Catherine.

"Aunt Lucy?" She sounded surprised, then smiled, and said, "Oh, now I know why you are calling me aunt," and she looked at Sidney.

"Are you sure that Catherine is Barbara?"

"Yes, I am sure. She has the birth mark shaped like a horseshoe and also the locket with a picture of her and her parents."

"Do you remember anything about your childhood in America?" Lucy asked Catherine.

"No. I only remember lots of water and a tall man with blond hair holding my hand, and then I see the people I have called 'mama' and 'papa' for years."

"Now, how do we tell Rachel?" asked Paul.

"I was hoping that you would, Mrs. Hatfield," said Sidney.

"Me?" Lucy said in surprise.

"Yes you. You are close to Mrs. Johnson, and you have heard the story and met Catherine."

"All right, I will do it. I will send a telegram. But, before I do anything, I want to see the locket and the birthmark."

Catherine handed the locket to Lucy, lifted her sleeve, and showed her the birthmark. Lucy opened the locket, saw the pictures, and read the inscription. She got up and went towards Catherine. "You know, you look so much like your father. Welcome home, Catherine." She hugged Catherine and began to cry.

Sidney was pleased at what unfolded in front of him. He was very worried about how it would turn out but was now relieved and happy. He then turned to Paul and said, "We need to get her a U.S. passport. The old one has expired, and we need a new one."

"Sure."

"There is one other thing. I have a friend named, Spencer Cooper, who is English. He would like to immigrate to America. Can you help him?"

"The 1924 Immigration Act has strict quotas. Because of the war, there were not many applicants, but now that the war is over, there will be a surge of applicants, so he needs to apply without any delay. Does he have any relatives in America? What will he do for work?"

"He has an uncle who immigrated to America many years ago. For work, I can employ him."

"Good, then he will not become a public charge and should be all set to go to America."

"Thank you, Mr. Hatfield. I am happy for Spencer. He helped us with our mission, and he deserves to become an American citizen."

New York, December 1945

Martha telephoned and told Rachel that Sidney was coming back in early January on the Queen Mary along with his future wife. Martha was glad that St. Francis, Sidney's confirmation saint, answered her prayers and he had survived the war unscathed.

Rachel put the receiver down. She wondered who Sidney's bride was and if she would like her.

Robert came in and placed two telegrams in front of her. After Robert left, she opened them.

The first one said that Lucy was returning to America with her family in late January. They would be in New York for four months and then move to Washington D.C.

'Finally, Lucy is coming home too,' said Rachel to herself.

Her mind went back to the times when they were children. How she missed those carefree days. She opened the second telegram and read it. She let out a small scream. It read,

'Barbara is alive and will be arriving on the Queen Mary early January. She will explain everything when she gets to America.'

Her pulse raced. Rachel wondered if the telegram was really from Lucy. She knew that Lucy would not play a mean trick on her. What should she do? She took a few deep breaths and felt calm. She decided not to tell anyone. Only time would tell if it was all true.

Chapter 21

England, December 26, 1945

Brian and Colin were on their way to church to be married. They were unhappy about getting married in England. They wanted to be married back home, with their families in attendance, in the spring. Sidney explained to them that Audrey and Marjorie's families would like to see them married as well. Entry for them into the United States would be easier if they came as wives of American citizens.

They reached the church and saw that their guests were already there. Officer Howell was present and so were Nurse Ramsay and Maria.

The minister came and said, "It is almost time..." He turned and looked at Brian and Colin and said in a stern voice, "Grooms, please take your places. We will begin."

A few minutes later, Marjorie and Audrey were standing next to Brian and Colin. Half an hour later, they were celebrating in the parish hall.

On December 29, 1945, RMS Queen Mary left England with the 82nd Airborne Division bound for New York.

"Looks like you're going to America after all," said John to Helga and kissed her.

"The war was good to us," said Colin. "All of us are going back with brides. Good things do come out of evil."

Sidney chuckled, "Yes, that's true. It never crossed my mind."

"It doesn't look like we're the only war brides on board. There are others as well, and one of them, a Red Cross worker, has babies - triplets, I believe," said Marjorie.

"Well, we can think of babies in the future," said Colin. "Right now, I want to settle down with my English Rose."

"Oh, that's the last of England. The next stop is America," said Catherine in excitement.

They all stood silently and watched the English coast disappearing.

January 3, 1946

"The Statue of Liberty! Come up and look," shouted one of the soldiers. They all ran up to the deck. As the ship approached New York harbor, the statue came into view. Some of the soldiers became emotional and started to cry.

"Oh! How I have missed that lady. I thought I would never see her again," said one of the soldiers.

"She is the most beautiful lady I have ever seen, and she is here to welcome us back," said another.

"So true!" said Sidney, and he too felt tears streaming down his cheeks.

"I am finally home," said Catherine. "I can feel that everything is going to be all right."

Sidney held her hand and squeezed it.

* * * * *

Rachel urged Alfred to hurry through the traffic as they drove towards the harbor.

"I am excited to see Sidney after all these years. I wonder who his bride is. I hope she is nice," said Andrew.

"I am sure she is," said Rachel, trying not to sound anxious.

Rachel had not told anyone about the telegram from Lucy regarding Barbara. She wondered how she would recognize Barbara.

"You will like Sidney, Hazel. He was like a brother to me," said Andrew.

"I look forward to meeting him. Is Mrs. Hardy coming?"

"Yes, she is on her way. She may have already reached the harbor by now. Oh, this traffic!" said Rachel, with exasperation.

"Relax, Mother. Anyone would think that you are Sidney's mother. We will get there in time to see him." Rachel tried to force a smile but could not. If they only knew why she was desperate to get to the harbor!

"The traffic seems to be thinning out, Mrs. Johnson. I think I can make it," said Alfred.

"Good. I am counting on you, Alfred."

Alfred whizzed past the cars and entered the harbor. They could see crowds of people rushing towards the pier.

"Don't worry, I will get you there before the ship does," said Alfred. Alfred drove to the parking lot and parked the car. Rachel got out and started running.

"Mother, wait for us. What are you hurrying for?" asked Andrew.

She did not respond but ran towards the pier until she found Martha. Andrew and Hazel tried to find Rachel. They scanned the vast crowd. Andrew finally spotted her and said, "I see Mrs. Hardy and mother. This way, Hazel."

People on the ships saw the swelling crowds and heard the cheering from the pier. The ships went towards the pier and dropped anchor. The cold wind was howling but nobody seemed to care.

They went down the gangplank and heard someone shout out Sidney's name.

"Oh look, it is Mother, Mrs. Johnson, and Andrew with a girl."

They went down, and a tearful Martha hugged Sidney. From the corner of his eye, he saw Brian, Colin, and John run to meet their families.

"Let me look at you," said Martha. "You're still the same but are looking much more handsome."

"Oh Mother! You always say that." Andrew and Rachel hugged and welcomed him.

Rachel looked at Catherine. "This must be your bride. She is pretty. Well, introduce us!"

"Everyone, this is Catherine, but her real name is Barbara."

"Oh Barbara!" said Rachel, putting her hand to her mouth.

"Yes, Mrs. Johnson, this is Barbara, the daughter you thought was dead," said Sidney.

Rachel hugged Catherine. The others looked bewildered.

"Andrew, this is Barbara, your sister, who you thought was dead. The French couple renamed her Catherine. I know it is unbelievable, but I will explain later. She has the birthmark and the locket." Sidney held out the locket. Rachel took it, read the inscription, and looked at the pictures.

Rachel looked at Catherine. "Lucy sent me a telegram about you, but I didn't tell anyone. I waited until now to be sure."

"Mother... I..."

"Oh Barbara! To hear you say that makes me so happy," said Rachel, caressing Catherine's face.

Andrew stepped forward. "I am Andrew, your younger brother. This is my wife, Hazel." Andrew and Hazel hugged Catherine.

"We better leave. There are more soldiers coming, and the crowd is getting thicker," said Martha.

Sidney kissed Catherine and said, "I will let you go with your mother. I will see you soon."

She smiled and said, "Yes, darling."

Rachel took Catherine by the hand, and Andrew carried her suitcases.

"I hope you brought us some French wine, Sis."

"Andrew," said Rachel, sounding stern.

"Don't worry, Mother. Andrew and I have a lot to catch up on. He may as well start by teasing me like brothers do."

Rachel smiled. Her happiness was now complete.

* * * * *

The troops gathered on the cold January morning to march in the parade. Spectators were carrying American flags. "Don't they all look handsome?" said Catherine to Hazel.

"They sure do."

Catherine was reminded of the Germans marching into Paris. Roland, Collette, Armand, and the others were all gone. She was here, back with her family. She remembered the twin sons of Armand and Collette. They were being taken care of by Collette's family. She felt the tears welling up in her eyes but wiped them away before they rolled down her cheeks.

The parade began, and the 82nd Division started marching. There were ribbons and ticker tapes falling all around. The day was cold but nobody cared. They were all there to watch their heroes march in the parade.

Rachel was glad that Andrew, Hazel, and Catherine got along. She wanted to call Catherine, Barbara, but Catherine said she preferred to be called Catherine. The house staff was glad to see her. They were all shocked when she introduced herself. The household staff and Alfred wept when they met her, for they remembered her as a child and when she left, never to return until now.

Catherine told Rachel that she remembered nothing of her childhood before the accident, except a big blond man in the woods and water. Rachel knew that what John Monroe told her was true. Rachel was excited that Catherine was marrying Sidney. They made a handsome couple. As Rachel passed by Fred's portrait, she thought she saw a smile on Fred's face.

"Yes, she is home, Fred," she said to the painting.

* * * * *

Rachel was at New York harbour at the end of January. She had not seen Lucy since she and Andrew had returned from their trip to England after Andrew was kidnapped. She recognized Lucy when she saw her descending the gangplank with her family.

When they were alone, Rachel told Lucy about meeting Catherine. "I thought it was a joke until I met her. I did not know that Sidney was going to bring her."

"Sidney and I discussed what should be written in the telegram. We were not sure how else to put it," said Lucy.

"Lucy, I am so happy, the happiest I've been in years, having everyone together."

* * * * *

Olga Brewster chose her dress for the wedding and placed it on the bed. She looked at the picture of Anna holding the baby. It was the last picture of Anna. Olga went into labor in August, around the time the Japanese surrendered. She was concerned about Anna. The cancer had weakened and reduced Anna to a skeleton. Her last wish was to see her grandchild.

At the end of a two-day labor, the baby was born - A beautiful girl with blond hair, just like her mother. The baby was underweight and kept in an incubator.

A few days later, the baby had gained some weight. Olga took her daughter and a nurse to meet Anna. As she opened the door, Anna sat up and said, "Let me see my granddaughter. I would like to hold her."

The nurse placed the baby in Anna's arms. Anna looked at the baby for a while.

"She is very beautiful. She has your hair and reminds me of my mother. What have you named her?"

"Lana, after your second name, Svetlana."

"Svetlana was also my mother's name. The name suits her."

"Mother, William will be here in a moment with a camera to take a picture."

"Okay, I will wear my wig and put on some lipstick."

She handed the baby to the nurse, then got up and walked to the dressing table where she put on a wig and lipstick.

"I hope I look beautiful for the picture."

The door opened and William walked in.

"Ahh... my favorite son-in-law!"

William laughed. "You mean your only son-in-law? Are you happy now?"

"Very happy. Now that I have seen my granddaughter, I am on top of the world."

William asked Nurse Drake to take the picture and handed her the camera. He stood next to Olga. Anna was holding the baby.

"Wait, I don't want the picture with me in bed. Let me sit on the chair by the table. I want the framed picture of Olga's father in this photograph."

Anna sat on the chair; William and Olga stood by her side. Nurse Drake took the picture.

Before they left, she insisted that she kiss them. "Goodnight, everyone. Please tell Mrs. Johnson that I have thanked her for her kindness, and please tell Svetlana about me."

"Goodnight, Mother. We will see you in the morning."

The next morning, Nurse Drake discovered Anna's lifeless body with her eyes closed and a smile on her face.

* * * * *

The day of the wedding was a beautiful March day. Catherine wore the wedding dress Rachel had stitched for her.

"You look beautiful," said Rachel. There were tears in her eyes. "I wish your father could have seen you."

"I know, Mother! The last two months have been surreal. I cannot believe I am home."

"You belong here, Barbara. This is where you were born and you have come back."

She hugged Catherine. "Thank you, Mother."

"I will leave you to yourself. Come out when you are ready."

Catherine watched Rachel leave and closed the door. It was hard for her to call Rachel 'Mother.' Annette, Pierre, Louis, and his family arrived for the wedding. Catherine was very happy but felt homesick. She expected trouble between Rachel, Pierre, and Annette, but they got along well. She thought about Roland a lot. She still had his picture and felt guilty about marrying Sidney.

She walked out of the room and saw Annette standing at the landing.

"Mama, I am delighted to see you."

Annette saw the pain in Catherine's face. She put her hands on Catherine's cheeks and said, "You have made me very happy and proud. Today is your wedding day. Be happy."

"Yes, Mama, but I am so lost," she said, almost tearing up.

"I know what you are feeling but think about your purpose in life now. Come, we must go."

Catherine followed her and they walked out of the room.

* * * * *

Pierre stood next to the staircase. He looked up and saw Fred's portrait. He remembered driving into the Halliday Vineyard and a man with a moustache looking at him and smiling as his car passed by. He realized that it was the same man in the portrait.

"Thank you for your daughter. She made Annette and me happy," he said to the portrait.

* * * * *

Sidney was about to leave for church when his butler came in with three telegrams on a tray. Sidney took the telegrams and opened them. The first two were from Nurse Ramsay and Gretel Mueller. They sent their wishes. The third was from Spencer Cooper. He had obtained American visas for him and his pregnant wife, and he was due to arrive in New York in April. George too had sent his wishes.

He put the telegrams in his pocket and said to himself, 'They may not be here physically, but these wonderful people will be with me in spirit.'

He saw Martha standing at the door. She smiled at him. He walked towards her, and she caressed his face with her hand.

"You look so handsome, just like your father. He too wore his military uniform for our wedding. He would have been proud that you served your country."

"Yes, Mother. I wish Father were here."

"Yes, he is. Look at his portrait and our wedding picture."

They both looked at the portrait of Thomas Hardy, and below the portrait was the wedding picture of Martha and Thomas Hardy.

"Come, it is almost time to go to church," said Martha.

Sidney gave one last look at his father's portrait. He turned and walked with Martha towards the waiting car.

Catherine got out of the car and walked to the entrance of St. Mark's church. It was the same church in Long Island, where Fred and Rachel were married almost three decades earlier. Through her veil, she saw Pierre standing at the door ready to walk her down the aisle.

As she walked down the aisle, her memory kept flooding back to her life in France. She felt overwhelmed with her new life in America. When Rachel had a party for her, friends and relatives came to her and asked her if she remembered them. She had to say she did not. At times, they did not understand her French accent. Did she make a mistake in coming to America? As she kept walking, she saw Audrey, Marjorie, and Helga, all in early stages of pregnancy. Accompanying them were Louis and his family, Annette, and she spotted Ruth. She had met Ruth the day before.

The day before...

Rachel took Catherine to her hairdresser in Manhattan. Irma, the manager of the salon, put Ruth in charge of coiffuring Catherine's hair. Ruth recognized Catherine, but Catherine did not know who she was.

Ruth explained that she was the daughter of Elsa and Isaac Rosen. Ruth, along with her parents and brothers, was arrested and deported to Auschwitz. Ruth remembered the gunshots and knew that the Gestapo executed Roland and his fellow resistance fighters.

Catherine then recalled meeting her earlier and told her that

Tomas had betrayed them. She made Tomas pay for his betrayal. Ruth told Catherine that her parents had died in Auschwitz. After being liberated, she and her brothers were brought to America by a refugee organization. Her brothers attended school while she worked at the salon and went to night school. She promised Catherine that she would make her look beautiful for her wedding.

Catherine looked in the mirror and saw that Ruth had done a great job. Catherine spoke to Irma and invited Ruth and her two brothers for the wedding.

Ruth and her brothers smiled at Catherine. She felt a wave of peace pass through her. She now knew what Annette meant about her purpose in life. She was meant to be in France to rescue people. She looked at Sidney. He stood there, tall and handsome, next to Brian and Colin who were his best men. Louis' two daughters stood there as her maid of honor and bridesmaid. She knew that Sidney loved her. Roland would have approved of him. Now that her task in France was over, she was ready to be Sidney's wife in America. She smiled behind her veil and stood next to Sidney ready to make this lasting commitment.

Fr. O'Malley made the sign of the cross and began the nuptial ceremony.

* * * * *

Sidney and Catherine entered the big hall in Johnson Manor. People cheered the newly married couple.

"The hall looks beautiful. You did a good job of planning everything, Rachel," said Martha and hugged Rachel.

"So, finally, my son marries your daughter. We are now family."

"Oh Martha, you were always like my family. You were the only one I could go to whenever I needed advice and help. I am so glad that this marriage took place."

"Me, too, Rachel. Now we will be sharing grandchildren and will be seeing more of each other."

"I'd like that, Martha."

Maryanne opened the envelope and took out the picture. "I remember this picture. It was taken at the Monkey Bar at Pearl Harbor on the day of Irving and Evelyn's engagement party," said Brandon.

"Yes, and it was taken with my camera. In the chaos, I forgot about the camera, but I found it with my belongings before I was shipped out to the Pacific. I had the pictures developed, and this was the last picture. I always kept the picture with me to remind me of happier times before Pearl Harbor."

"You know, Hazel and Andrew have named their twins after Irving and Evelyn. I think that was a nice gesture," said Phillip.

Brandon smiled and suggested to Maryanne that they recreate the picture again. Andrew and Hazel could bring the twins for the picture since they are named after Irving and Evelyn. It would be a reminder of new beginnings in post war America.

The others agreed, and Maryanne went in search of Andrew and Hazel and found them dancing to "Sing Sing Sing". She told them about the idea to recreate the picture, and all agreed it was a great idea.

They all sat in front of the potted palms to remind them of Hawaii, and Andrew asked Adam Morton to take the picture.

"Everyone smile," said Adam.

"Quick, take the picture, the twins are smiling," said Sally, as she noticed the twins smiling. The camera flashed.

Rachel saw the picture being taken. She turned and saw Sidney and Catherine talking to their guests. Rachel had invited everyone she knew. She was reminded of her own wedding day. For a long time, she had not been sure if she had done the right thing in marrying Fred but now, she was glad she did. Her singular decision to marry Fred brought about these events.

'Thank you, Aunt Victoria,' she said, as she remembered her wise aunt advising her on whom she should marry.

"They do make a handsome couple, don't they?"

She turned back and exclaimed, "Fr. O'Malley! I am so glad to see you. The ceremony was wonderful. Yes, they do make a handsome couple."

"The French couple did a wonderful job raising Catherine. I spoke to them earlier, and they told me how brave she was and the people she rescued."

"Ever since Catherine came home, I have been asking myself why she had to be in France. After meeting Annette, Pierre, those Jewish children, and hearing Sidney's story of how they met, I got an answer to my question. That has given me some peace. The most important thing is that she is back home."

"We all have our purpose in life. I have been wondering what you think of all that has happened," said Fr. O'Malley.

"You know, Father, I was just thinking the same thing. The decisions I have made have all culminated in this moment. If not for marrying Fred and the events that followed, none of this would have happened. I only feel bad about Walter, but Rudy is solely responsible for that."

"Yes, it was your decision that made it all possible, just like your decision to forgive Anna."

"When Olga told me what really happened, I had no choice but to do as you told me."

"Because of that, she found William, and Anna had her life prolonged. She also got to see her granddaughter."

"Yes, and they have a beautiful daughter. Talking of babies, Hazel just told me the good news. I would like you to baptize the child when it's born."

"Congratulations. I am afraid I cannot, Rachel. They will have to come to Rome for that. I have been given an assignment to teach at the Pontifical University for a year and will, therefore, be leaving for Rome tomorrow."

"That is wonderful news, Father."

The band started playing "Moonlight Serenade". Detective Howard came towards Rachel and said, "May I have the pleasure of this dance, please?"

Rachel looked at Fr. O'Malley and he nodded.

Detective Howard took Rachel's hand, and they walked towards the dance floor.

View other Black Rose Writing titles at www.blackrosewriting.com/books and

use promo code **PRINT** to receive a **20% discount** when purchasing.

BLACK🌹ROSE
writing™

CPSIA information can be obtained
at www.ICGtesting.com
Printed in the USA
LVHW111618120121
676308LV00003B/227